DANCING WITH SPIRITS

By

Carol Arnall

Published by Davies, Staffordshire, England.

Copyright © 2009 C A Arnall
ISBN 978-0-9561564-0-2

ACKNOWLEDGEMENTS

Thanks to everyone who has encouraged me with the writing of Dancing with Spirits.

Thanks go to Hazel my best friend, for suggestions and help with checking the script.

Thank you Lyn a good friend, for encouragement when I lost heart along the way.

To Nick Duffy of the West Midland Ghost Society. I so appreciate your input Nick and the laughs over the years! Thanks for starring in the book.

Professor Carl Chinn for advice, much appreciated, Carl you are a real 'Brummie Treasure.' Also many thanks for allowing me to use your name in the novel.

Joe Swynnerton for wonderful research on Stafford Castle, what a star.

My good friend Colin Gooch for Tamworth Castle and Birmingham. Thanks Col. a true friend.

Dedicated to my son Paul.........
Love you forever

DANCING WITH SPIRITS

The story begins thousands of years ago on the outskirts of Rugeley, in the heart of Cannock Chase.

It tells the story of a young girl whose love, Deimuiss, has disappeared without trace and her desperation to find him. Her search leads her to finding herself in the 21st Century where she begins a new life.

Eventually Elvaennia will have to make the decision whether to return to her old life or continue to live life in the 21st Century. She discovers something that may well destroy her family back at the settlement; and realises that yet again tough decisions will have to be made regarding her life.

Will the challenges of her new life take over the old Elvaennia, making her disregard her promise to love Deimuiss for all time and beyond? Will she forget the old ways and values or decide to pursue this new life?

Deimuiss also finds himself torn between his new life and the old. New challenges await him in the 21st Century but will his past, and love of Elvaennia, beckon him back?

Chapter 1

It was cold – a dank clinging cold that seemed to be inside the very marrow of my bones. My feet slipped on the wet muddy ground and I pulled my deerskin cloak closer, but even that brought no comfort. I was so unbelievably cold and wet. Normally, the soft supple skin would enfold me within its warmth and comfort; pictures would form in my mind of the generations of deer that had gone before my time on this earth. Today, the herds were but a distant memory as the weather closed in on me, Grandmamma and my 11-year-old sister, Trieainia. 'Oh for the warmth of a fire,' I thought, slipping and sliding on the muddy, sandy ground. I drew nearer to my Grandmamma for warmth and reassurance. The mist continued to swirl around; creating strange shapes, transforming the winter trees into mystical, ghostly forms, making me think of weird creatures waiting to pounce on us. The tree branches, outstretched like big cat claws, loomed towards us and they seemed to be calling and drawing us nearer and nearer through the ghostly mist that hung and hovered, drifting through the tree branches. I shuddered and my imagination took flight, thinking of the world they inhabited once their time on Earth was spent. The trees that died in winter, I knew, were taken to the gods of the winter forests to stand forever in a cold dark world of evil black bats and animals that fiercely guarded their own territories. How, I wondered, could they live forever in that bleak cold desolate land, covered in black icicles, never again to feel the warmth of the sun on their boughs or the kiss of a butterfly in the spring? Always to stand guard over a despairing landscape of frozen black ground and ice packed pools and lakes, never to hear the babbling of a summer's silver waterfall as it gurgles and babbles into the stream. Instead, they stand frozen forever in a black eternity.

I shook the Winter of Despair from my mind, thinking how strange it was that the weather had changed so suddenly. It had been quite bright and spring-like when the three of us had happily left the settlement to walk to the six Standing Stones of the Mystics. I had invited Trieainia and Grandmamma to accompany me to The Stones as I was going to ask the most powerful of The Stones, Myllou, if I would ever see my betrothed again. Deimuiss set out on a lone hunting trip some 18 months ago and to my horror and utter despair, he has never returned. I remember the day he left; it is seared on my soul forever.

I knew he was going hunting that morning. I had kissed him farewell and watched as he mounted his beautiful black stallion and headed off in the direction of the six Standing Stones. From there, he would head towards the distant forest where he knew the wild boar, bison and herds of reindeer roamed freely. It is a popular hunting territory for the men of our tribe. Watching him ride away as the sun rose high in the sky, man and horse as one, I could see the golden aura that always surrounds Deimuiss. He is such a special person; a wonderful healer, always generous with his time, he will help anyone. I am so proud of him and his wonderful gift. In fact, very few of the Calegi Tribe have the special gifts now. At one time, the whole tribe possessed the gift of healing and the ability to predict the future. Over the years, many of the tribe members have abused these gifts, and, as the law stands, the powers are taken away from the person who has misused them forever if they are abused. The skills are passed on to succeeding generations if they are used for the benefit of humanity. When Deimuiss had not returned by the late afternoon of that fatal day, all the tribesmen from the settlement had gone out in groups searching for him but to no avail. He had gone. Disappeared. No sign of him has ever been found.

Since his disappearance, I have prayed to the gods of Lost Souls to return Deimuiss to me. I have asked The Standing Stones of the Mystics several times, if he will ever return. Today was to be the last time. When I have asked them before, they have replied either yes or no. It is as if they know far more than they are telling me. The only message I received was 'All will become clear in the future, Elvaennia.' Try as I might, they will not tell me anything more.

I had also asked the Elders of the tribe but they had said virtually the same. I was very disappointed, and, on leaving their home, I ruminated on what they had said; or rather what they had not said but had hinted at. Grandmamma has said similar things to me a few times recently and no way could I get her to tell me what she meant. This was why, after agonising over Deimuiss for the last year and a half, I have decided to visit the Mystical Standing Stones for the last time. In the past, I have asked them questions relating to other issues, and immediately received a sign as to the outcome of my problem, whereas now, whenever I ask about Deimuiss, the reply seems to be hidden, wrapped up in a parcel of words that I do not understand. Grandmamma (who I love dearly) agreed to come with me along with Trieainia this time. When I mentioned the purpose of my visit to her, a small frown had flitted across her face, but she immediately agreed to my delight. Grandmamma gives me confidence, we have always been close.

My heart was filled with happiness as we stepped out that bright shining morning. We all waved a cheery goodbye to my mother and two of my younger brothers. I was very surprised that Vionny, my wolf dog, turned away from coming with us. This was extremely unusual but I decided the dog had her own reasons for not coming. Perhaps she was jealous of my companions. I left her with Mamma knowing she would be safe in her keeping.

Despite a wintry chill still lingering, the sun was shining brightly, enfolding everywhere in a promise of new life. I could sense spring was near. All around us, there was vivid sparkling light. I could hear the songbirds singing in the newly leafed trees and wild flowers and herbs were pushing their way through Mother Earth ready and eager to burst forth to greet the world. I was so looking forward to our visit to The Stones and hoped against hope that the outcome would be positive. Grandmamma told me not to be too hopeful that I would receive a message this time and warned me against being too confident, otherwise, the taste of disappointment would linger long. I knew she was being kind, as she did not want me to carry the heartbreak of Deimuiss's disappearance for the rest of my days. Grandmamma knows how much I love him.

Deimuiss has always been around. He lives in the house next door to us at the settlement and our houses are linked by an underground passageway; so even when the weather is inclement, we can visit each other without getting soaked by the rain or snow. Many of the houses are linked in this manner. It also enables a quick escape in case of fire (thatched roofs are treacherous) or attacks from our enemies.

Grandmamma had then gone on to say much the same as the Mystical Standing Stones and the Elders, 'Heed your destiny Elvaennia. You know you are different.' She was of course referring to my gift of 'seeing and hearing'. I was surprised at her mentioning my 'gift' because, when I was younger, if I ever mentioned anything that I had 'seen or heard that was not of our world,' my family would not discuss it with me. I thought perhaps they were afraid; but it seemed as if what I had 'seen' was linked to my destiny and that all would be revealed to me in the fullness of time. All very frustrating, as I have so many questions I would like to ask about the many 'visions' I have had over the years.

The first 'vision' occurred when I was about nine years of age. It happened while I was playing pass-the-ball with Deimuiss and some other children from the settlement; it was a warm sunny day, a gentle breeze was blowing the scent of wild flowers and grasses around, pink and white fluffy lace edged clouds floated gently across a beautiful blue sky. The sound of our laughter carried on the summer breezes like a beautiful song. I remember feeling particularly happy that day; not for any specific reason, simply happy to be alive and fizzing with a strange energy. One girl (Ifreeidia) remarked in passing that she could see different colours of the rainbow changing around me as I constantly leapt about. I remember throwing the ball, that I had made the previous day, by filling a piece of material with soft spring leaves and grass then tying the four corners together. Knotting the ends together, I imagined the fun we were going to have the following day; and we had, until I looked up at the sky and suddenly everything went misty. My head felt muzzy and I felt myself being pulled into a void that slowly filled with scenes of a countryside that I did not recognise. When I scanned the area, I saw a huge mound of earth, on top of which was an enormous wooden fortress. I was amazed at the sight of it, as I had never seen anything like it before. There were stairs winding their way around the building from the bottom to the top. People were ascending and descending the stairway; they were dressed in very different clothing from the type we wear. Surrounding the mound were many houses and animals, and what seemed to be a market. I could hear the traders shouting out their wares. An inner voice told me it was a place I would know in my future as Tamworth Castle.

I blinked hard trying to 'see more' when, as suddenly as I had 'seen' the images, they disappeared. Opening my eyes, all I could see was a circle of surprised young faces. Ifreeidia asked gently, 'Are you all right Elvaennia? You fell down and seemed to have fallen asleep.' She suddenly giggled at her words. This in turn set the others off, myself included, and they all ended up on the ground beside me rolling about with laughter at the very idea of someone falling asleep in the morning.

I could tell they were relieved that I was not hurt.

I was grateful that they accepted her words on what had happened, because I did not want to explain what I had 'seen' to them. I felt I had to 'keep' the images until I went to bed. Then, perhaps, I could understand what had happened. That was the first of many 'visions' I was to have, and I could find no explanation for them whatsoever. Eventually, I just accepted that I 'saw' beyond our time and I kept the happenings in my memory. As I grew older, I began to dream more often; strange dreams that at times were terrifying and unreal. I would see people dressed in strange garments, and buildings so tall I feared they would topple over and kill the citizens that walked beneath them; objects that moved at great speed along wide trackways, and huge birds that flew in the skies making frightening noises. I shook my head to clear the strange pictures from my mind. I needed to concentrate all my thoughts on the days ahead.

Following the track that led to the Mystical Standing Stones, Trieainia sang happily to herself while Grandmamma and I chatted about the different happenings at the settlement. As we drew near the Hill of the Spirits, the weather suddenly changed. The Hill of the Spirits is where we go to release the spirits of the people who have gone to the longest sleep, so they may return to the lands of our ancestors in the time that never ends. (The Mystics visit the Hill of Souls in a separate ceremony of their own after someone has died. No one is allowed to watch this final mysterious ceremony for the dead. The Hill of Souls is the preserve of the Mystics and lies some distance from the settlement.) The Hill of the Spirits suddenly became shrouded in a strange swirling mist. We watched as it twisted, swirled faster, and faster. We began to feel fearful, as by now, the sun had disappeared completely and a strong wind had begun to gust, blowing last year's autumn leaves into strange shapes that floated on the air. Suddenly, the leaves surrounded the three of us and we felt trapped, claustrophobic, as if we were enclosed by a ring of something indestructible and held in thrall by evil. Trieainia screamed, 'Elvaennia, Grandmamma, whatever's happening? Why are the leaves encircling us? I am so afraid.' Her young voice was shaking with fear. My heart went out to her and I prayed to the gods of the Winds of Time to release us from this wickedness.

It was an unearthly experience. I knew that malevolence held us in its grip. Glancing quickly at Grandmamma, I saw she was making the sign to ward off evil: steepling her fingers together and holding her arms up high in the air, she chanted words in a language I did not understand. The leaves disappeared. The force field was broken as if by magic. We all heaved a great sigh of relief, hoping against hope that we were now safe. I hugged and thanked Grandmamma for helping us to escape the wickedness. Seeing Trieainia so pale and wan, I wrapped my arms around her, trying to take the fear from her.

'Come; let us continue our walk to The Stones.' I hoped my voice sounded more confident than I felt and I began to hum a popular tune that we had heard at last week's music evening. Trieainia glanced across at me, smiling, humming along to the song. The day seemed to brighten. We strode out more confidently, once again taking a joy in the morning. I pointed out a herd of red deer racing towards the safety of the dark forest. A hunting party had obviously disturbed them. I frowned, hoping the hunters were not from our tribe; this time of year, we are forbidden to hunt the deer - it is the close season as the does are carrying the young, and hunting cannot start again until the fawns are weaned. The forest looked dark and mysterious from this distance and I prayed the herd would find shelter from their pursuers. I thought back to the time when we were younger and Deimuiss and I would race with the deer along the forest tracks; it was a wonderful exhilarating experience; we felt at one with these majestic ancient creatures who had inhabited the world before us. I wondered again, what could possibly have happened to my betrothed.

As we approached the six huge Standing Stones of the Mystics, the temperature dropped and the eerie mist began swirling around us again. The Stones took on mystical shapes. They towered majestically towards the skies. It seemed as if they too were watching us through the mist; for the first time ever, they looked frightening. We were breathing in the bitter rancid smell of the mist. I was glad that Grandmamma and Trieainia had brought their cloaks with them, but I was concerned for their well-being. The mist and cold were becoming unbearable and I knew we would soon have to seek shelter. I was not too worried for myself. Despite being tiny, I am very strong, whereas my Grandmamma is not as young as she once was, and Trieainia was now visibly shivering and looking extremely frightened.

'Elvaennia,' she asked clinging to me, 'What is happening sister? Everywhere looks so strange. I am scared.'

'All will be fine - just a blip in the weather.'

I patted her reassuringly and hoped I was right; I vowed I would not let her or Grandmamma see how afraid I was beginning to feel. My priority was to ensure they were safe and no harm would befall them. I would never forgive myself if anything bad should happen to either of them.

Passing the trees that stood guard along the track, I caught a glimpse of the six ancient Standing Stones through the mist. They seemed to glow with an incandescent yellow-greenish light. As I watched, the colour changed to red. 'Red', I murmured, quite horrified. Red represented danger to our tribe of the Calegi people. I became concerned as the light began moving eerily in and around the giant craggy stones. They seemed to be taking on a life of their own; at times the mist changed to a faint orange glow, and then reverted quickly back to the yellow, greenish light. Strobes of strange lights began streaking from the sky through the mist. I took a deep breath, as did Grandmamma. 'Try not to worry about the lights, granddaughter,' she murmured. I nodded and, slipping my arm from my cloak, I put it around her tiny frame, squeezing her tightly, wondering how a normal day could have turned so strange within such a short time.

I now knew why my wolf dog had refused to come with me - why hadn't I heeded her? I, who could read signs of what was to come, had been blinded by my desperate need to find Deimuiss. I had shut out everything else. What a fool I was to miss her warning!

The Standing Stones hold me in awe. Knowing their supernatural powers, I have a deep respect for them, as do all our tribe. The Stones represent each Mystic from the settlement. The Mystics are as timeless as The Stones. Nobody knows there age or from where they came. Ask anyone, and they will shrug, and say that The Stones, like their Masters, have always been here. There is a powerful link between The Stones and the Mystics. Each Stone has the name of their Master and has incredible control and influence. Woe betide anyone who does not heed their advice. The largest of The Stones represents the oldest and most influential of the six Mystics. The oldest Mystic has empowered The Stones, and if questions need answering, we know to visit The Stones. This is what the Mystics prefer, rather than answering questions themselves, hence their negative reply to me.

Not so long ago, the sun had been shining brightly, albeit a chilly one. There had been no sign of the strange mist, cold wind, or the supernatural lights that now coloured the landscape. The lights were like no others I had ever seen. It wasn't the Mystics causing this phenomenon. I knew this was not their time for worship. I trembled at the thought that perhaps this was a sign that we had angered the gods in some way. Shivering now, with fear as much as with cold, I motioned to Grandmamma and Trieainia that we should make haste away from The Stones. I was very frightened, fearing the anger of the gods and wondering what would happen to us. Certain that this was a sign of danger; I knew we needed to find a place of safety as soon as possible.

Seeking shelter and safety for my young sister and Grandmamma was now my top priority. My head was whirling as fast as the eerie mist as I tried to think of a secluded place that we could go to. Suddenly, my heart seemed to freeze with fright as I remembered one Elder telling me many years ago: 'Beware of the lights of The Stones,' he had uttered in a deep fearful voice, 'Anyone seeing the lights within the vicinity of The Stones is doomed.' He had gone on to say that, very few people had lived to tell the tale of the lights at The Stones. They simply disappeared. He added that the lights were rarely seen hovering over The Stones, but when they appeared, they always foretold evil. Recalling his words, my whole body went weak. I knew Grandmamma had also remembered the prophecy. I realised now that she was shivering with fright as much as the searing cold.

'Why, Grandmamma? Why us? What have we done wrong? Have we angered the gods in any way that you know of?' I asked this of her quietly, not wishing young Trieainia to hear me. I knew my sister was pretty near the edge now; her young face was unnaturally pale and I was becoming very concerned for her and my Grandmamma.

Grandmamma did not reply. Her fragile body was shuddering and trembling; I wrapped my arms around her again, feeling apprehension emanating from her delicate bones. She felt like a tiny bird wrapped up in her winter cloak.

'Perhaps the Mystic is wrong?' I queried in a small tight voice.

'It is true my little one,' she said, uttering a small gasp and very nearly tripping over a stone. I clasped her tighter. I did not want her to fall into the thick sandy mud that was covering our feet, making walking

9

so difficult, our shoes almost ruined. Trieainia was struggling to hold back tears and my heart went out to her.

My sister has always been a gutsy young girl. Constantly happy, she seems to have sung and danced her way through life. Everyone loves Trieainia. Her long blonde hair seems almost too heavy for her slight body at times; it is so thick and curly, the colour of ripened corn; on seeing her for the first time, people always remark on her beauty, and in particular her hair and smiling face. It takes Mamma an age to tame it in the mornings; before sending her on her way to the house of the Elders where she loves going for instructions. There, she meets her contemporaries, who all have the same love of learning as she does.

Grandmamma's voice brought me back to the present with a jolt:

'I have known people disappear any number of times when the lights shine at The Stones.'

'Really?' I cried out in fear.

'Yes Elvaennia, I am afraid so. Whenever we are at the settlement and see the lights hovering over them, we immediately take shelter in our homes. Anyone out near The Stones at the time the lights shine is rarely seen again. Some people are even killed.'

Her voice trembled as she spoke the words.

I was really shocked and wondered why she and the others at the settlement had never told me in detail what happened when the lights appeared.

'It would not have helped if you had known, Elvaennia. Until now, we have always managed to keep the full knowledge from you; we knew you would forget the words of the Elders as you were so young at the last disappearance.'

I understood her reasoning but felt concerned that they did not think I was mature enough to have been given the knowledge. Nevertheless, this was not the time to think about the past. My chief concern was to keep them safe from the evil emanating around us.

I had started to quake; couldn't help it. I had always felt I was emotionally strong and had a strong spirit, but oh, the thought that I might be going to die along with my dear young sister and Grandmamma

– both of whom I had unwittingly led into danger! Now I was going to be responsible for their deaths if I did not find a place of safety fast. How could I have allowed this to happen? They are much loved by everyone at the settlement. All this has happened because I wanted to ask The Stones for their thoughts on Deimuiss, my lost love. I felt truly dreadful at what I had done. Also knowing I might not see my dearest parents and my other siblings again was too shocking to consider. I know that eventually all souls are reunited with their ancestors at the Time without End, but I had led two members of my family into danger. Would I be sent to the Winter of Despair to join the dark winter trees and other sinister souls in their isolation?

Sensing my despair, Grandmamma pulled me to her; 'We will be all right little one. You are not to blame. We are together. We will be safe.' She kept repeating the words like a mantra.

I was not convinced, but tried to put a hold on my anxiety for the sake of Grandmamma and Trieainia. 'Wesh not my little one.' I smiled briefly at Grandmamma's words; she knew it was one of my favourite childhood sayings. No one in our family could ever remember what it meant, or indeed, where it had sprung from, but they all knew that the words comforted me.

'Wesh not,' I murmured; and true to form, I smiled and felt a little comforted.

Praying to all the gods and goddesses, I could think of, we slipped, slithered and squelched our way across the muddy wet heath land, trying to put as much distance as possible between The Standing Stones and us. We clung desperately to each other for comfort. The wet sandy soil stained our cloaks and tunics with clods of red mud, dragging at the hems. Our shoes were saturated; they were useless in conditions such as these. Stones pushed their way through the thin soles and my feet were feeling so sore, wet and cold. Oh, for this awful episode to end and everything to revert to normal.

'How could I have brought my grandmamma and sister into such danger?' I questioned myself relentlessly, desperately trying to hold on to Grandmamma, knowing that if she slipped, she could easily break one of her delicate bones.

Suddenly, I remembered there was one place in our vicinity where we could take shelter. It was a bivouac, and I decided we should head for it as fast as possible. The strange lights were almost surrounding us now. Dark threatening clouds were hovering just above, the strobes of light breaking through and striking the ground. They seemed to be following us. I was filled with the fear that one or more of the strobes would strike us. I felt sure we would die, here and now, if they did. If only I knew which of the gods we had offended, I could make a suitable offering at the Silver Spring near to the hunting cave. We were chillingly cold, our feet squelched onwards across the heath, our breath changing colour in the eerie glowing mist. The wind was north-easterly and was cutting through us like a knife. Suddenly, we heard a strange sound. Immediately, we all drew closer together.

'What noise is that Grandmamma?' I asked. 'What animal makes that strange sound?'

'Granddaughter, I do know not that sound,' she murmured, the wind snatching her words on the mist, whipping them back to the gods.

I was convinced now that we had offended the gods of Earth and Winds and vowed to make an offering at the Silver Spring near to the bivouac. The noise came again, this time louder, roaring and screaming, rushing by at a great speed. We felt a strange heat from whatever passed us. No animal we had ever heard or seen made such a shockingly loud noise. We all screamed and clung to each other, a strange smell assailed our nostrils and we coughed and coughed. It was stronger than the taste of the eerie mist. Our lungs were bursting and burning in the clinging mist. Yet again, another roar rushed past us, sounding even louder, and the awful smell that it emitted had us all doubled up, retching to ease our lungs. Looking at poor Trieainia, I knew it would take her a long time to recover from this disturbing experience. As for Grandmamma – I feared for her life. I prayed they would be strong for a while longer. Suddenly, Trieainia's young voice piped up:

'I know what the noise is Grandmamma. It is the dragons; remember? I told you we saw their skeletons last year when we went on a visit to the distant camp of our tribe.'

I remembered what she was talking about. Papa had shown us the skeletons of dragons from ancient times. I had sensed evil emanating from them, seen the black aura that surrounded them. My brothers had held no fear whatsoever and had clambered high up on one of the enormous skeletons shouting to me to join them. I refused, as did Trieainia; and Jennia our youngest sister. We had just watched as the boys climbed even higher up the powerful animal's skeleton; their strong, young limbs making short work of the climb. I knew these dragon-like creatures had once ruled the earth, and I was full of foreboding sensing that their spirits would return and take their revenge. Now, it seemed they had. When Father had returned from the nearby spring with the water he had been to fetch, he remonstrated with my brothers at their lack of respect for the dead creatures' spirits. Why had we not thought to make an offering to the spirits of the dead dragons? Perhaps if we had, the awful situation we were now in might have been avoided. I murmured words asking for forgiveness to the gods of the animals' spirits in the vain hope that the winds of the ancient spirits would take my words of apology back to them.

Trembling now with the cold and fear, whispering to each other about how we must surely have offended the gods, I was certain now that the spirits of the ancient creatures were indeed returning to take revenge for my brothers' disregard. We hurried down the heath towards the cave. Oh no! We could hear the eerie howling of the wolves, echoing through the mist. This only added to our fear. Glancing behind us, we were horrified. The lights seemed to be gaining on us; they were glowing ever brighter. We feared for our lives.

Gently urging Grandmamma to hurry if she could, we slithered and slipped our way down the hillside to the bivouac. I knew how they were both suffering from the cold and wind. Their poor feet looked as bad as mine did, and my heart ached for their discomfort.

Almost pushing Grandmamma and Trieainia into the cave entrance, I was more than pleased to feel a little warmth emanating from the campfire. Hunters had obviously used the cave earlier that day, lit the fire for warmth, and to ward off the wolves and other dangerous prey. With relief, we held our freezing cold hands over the faint glow of the dying embers, seeking the only warmth and comfort within our vicinity. I noticed a small water vessel left by passing travellers, and told Grandmamma that I would fetch water from the nearby Silver Springs. Once we had warmed it on the warm cinders, we could use some of the herbs from our pouches to make a warm drink. She nodded and slipped off her gold and amethyst ring and passing it to me, she said, 'Give this as an offering Elvaennia.' I acknowledged her gift with a nervous smile. Trieainia was worried that she had no offerings to give me but I told her not to worry. I would give something for her. Telling her to look after Grandmamma, I again braved the eerily glowing mist and cold northeasterly wind. I went as fast as I could towards the spring, thinking anxiously, 'I will make the offerings to the gods, collect some water then return to the cave as fast as possible,' all the while praying my dear sister and Grandmamma would be safe.

Worriedly, I thought how wrong the signs were today. In fact, they were extremely frightening. I had never experienced anything like it; but whatever was happening, I vowed to do my utmost to rescue my relatives from this danger. Reaching the springs, I slipped my gold bracelet off my arm then hesitated for a moment. Deimuiss had given me this bracelet. Our initials were engraved and entwined inside the circle of gold. 'For all time,' he had whispered softly as he gave it to me with a loving kiss. For a moment, I was reluctant to part with it, but then surely, I reasoned with myself, if it saves our lives, I have no choice. I removed a small brooch from my cloak as an offering from Trieainia. I threw these things along with Grandmamma's precious ring – I knew she treasured that ring above everything else she owned as my Grandpapa had given it to her not long before he died – into the springs, praying to the gods in the hope that they would find our offerings acceptable enough to appease their anger. Quickly, I glanced through the strange glowing mist. I could see no signs of life. Despite this, prickles of fear ran up and down my spine, as if something or someone was watching me. Again, I glanced nervously around me. Suddenly, I thought I heard a scream coming from the direction of the cave.

Oh no, were they in trouble back at the bivouac?

I wondered what on earth was happening, heart thudding loudly in my chest, my blood chilled in my bones. I headed back up the hill as fast as I possibly could. The ground was treacherous, the red sandy mud slowing my progress. Any second now, I thought I was going to fall over and I did not want anything to delay my return to my grandmother and Trieainia. I was fearful that they might be in serious trouble. Had my instincts proved correct? Were they now in danger? Once back at the cave, I wanted to be able to tell them I had made the offerings of the bracelet, brooch and Grandmamma's precious ring. They would both be pleased and relieved that we would now escape the danger that was surrounding us, and our lives would hopefully be spared. After hearing the scream, the terror seeped back into my bones again holding me in its grip and I made my way back towards the cave through the dragging, clinging red mud as fast as I possibly could. How I wished we were all safely at the settlement, surrounded by family and friends; instead, here we were seeking shelter in a gloomy, fast darkening, cold, hunting cave.

Chapter 2

Drawing near the bivouac, I was relieved to see the faint glow of the fire through the gloom. Glancing behind, my heart leapt with joy. The strange lights and mist had disappeared. Overjoyed that the offerings had been acceptable to the gods, I reached the cave, stepping round the hearth, almost exploding with delight, calling out, 'Grandmamma, Grandmamma, Trieainia, the gods are...'

I pulled up short, horrified. The welcoming smile froze on my face. My body stiffened with fright. I saw my grandmother lying sprawled on the floor. She was still and silent. Deathlike. No breath came from her lips. Her eyes were open wide, staring, her whole face frozen in time, forever in terror. 'Grandmamma, Grandmamma?' I cried out, dropping the container of water. Stooping down, I reached out towards her deathly still body. Then, horror struck again. I saw she was laying across my sister's still, lifeless body. A strange light entered the cave, swirling round us. I glanced towards the entrance, saw the sky was dramatically lit up with the lights, and mist again. Terrified, I pulled Grandmamma's frail body further inside the cave, sobbing as I did so. My sister lay still, in death's icy grip. I knew that she and my dearest Grandmamma were dead. Her body was lifeless. Cold as the coldest winter. I knew that already the gods of death would be fighting over their spirits. I prayed they would be returned to our ancestors. I was beyond despair. I had killed my sister Trieainia and my grandmother. 'If only I had not left them alone,' I sobbed. For this misdeed, my spirit would languish in the Winter of Despair for eternity. There was no escape. I was as guilty as whoever had killed them. My soul would never be released to the Time Beyond.

'Who but our enemies would have murdered an innocent old lady and young girl?' I cried, hugging my sister's cold dead body to me. I felt that I had killed her and my dearest grandmother with my bare hands. 'If only I had not left you both,' I cried, stroking her soft golden hair from her face. My hand touched a lump on the back of her head. Obviously, this blow had felled and killed her. I dragged her body into the cave and lay it on the cold, grey, sandy earth beside Grandmamma, sobbing in despair. I knelt and felt the back of my Grandmamma's head. The same telltale lump was there. 'How could they kill them? Two innocent women. Why?' Filled with remorse and deep regret, I remembered that I had not bothered to see if our tribe had left any warning signs when they had visited the cave. I had been so traumatised by the lights that fear had made me careless and forgetful. Tribe members will always leave our secret sign if they know enemies are in the area. I had failed them; I berated myself as tears flowed relentlessly down my face, soaking my cloak far more than the mist and rain had done. I felt defeated, wishing it had been me they had murdered. How would I ever forgive myself?

Suddenly, hands were grabbing at me. Rancid smells assaulting my senses, and my hair was grabbed and pulled hard almost from its roots. I screamed loudly. Glancing down, I saw the red arrow sign of the Delph Tribe on the back of the filthy hands that were pulling at me. They were trying to break the gold circlet of jewels from the top of my cloak. 'Oh no!' I thought. 'They're our sworn enemies. They will kill me as they have killed my Grandmamma and sister. I'm going to die in this little cave on a desolate hillside. My parents and siblings will never know what became of us.' As I fought desperately for my life, I regretted not making a larger offering at the Silver Springs. This would never have happened if only I had taken more time and trouble to appease the gods. I kicked out, finding a strength that I did not know I possessed; fear replaced by anger so forceful that I felt I had the strength of ten fighting men running through my body. These men of The Delph Tribe were extremely fit from years of fighting and hunting. In addition, there were three of them:

a small hunting party, far stronger than I, a mere girl of 17 summers. Kicking and punching out as hard as I could, I managed to knee one hunter. He fell to the floor, groaning and shouting, 'No, no.'

Suddenly, I realised who he was. 'Deimuiss! You turncoat! You traitor.' I screamed, in sorrow and a riotous anger. Filled with hatred at his treachery, I kicked out again, all the while lashing out at the other warriors. My mind was filled with fear, abhorrence, and now betrayal. I knew these men planned to rape and kill me. I could not believe that Deimuiss, who had been my betrothed since childhood, would consider murdering me. Repugnance and loathing swelled in my throat, almost choking me. With a scream of rage, I kicked out at him once again as hard as I could. He doubled over, clearly in agony. I was glad. Having loved him all my life, his betrayal filled me with utter disgust.

Why, I had even been to the top of the Hill of the Spirits for the ceremony of sending his spirit to safety on his last journey to the ancestors. (This had just been a precaution in case he had died; his spirit needed to be taken care of). I must confess that I did not see his spirit transcending. In fact, I had no sense that he had died. Moreover, as we were so close, I firmly believed that the moment his spirit left his body, I would know immediately. However, I had taken the precaution for the sake of propriety. Strangely enough, the Mystics had not performed the ceremony for his soul; now I knew why; obviously, they knew he was not dead.

Now he lay on the cave floor at my feet. I saw that his deep blue eyes held an icy, angry look. For a moment, I felt guilty. I found this disconcerting to say the least, but there was no time to even think of how he had always been the one for me; how I had loved him all the years of my life; how I had thought he had loved me; until that awful day he had disappeared on a lone hunting trip. I was heartbroken and that's putting it mildly. In fact, it is an understatement. When he had disappeared, I really thought I would die at the thought that he may have died alone in some abandoned, isolated place, his bones chewed by the marauding wolves and other wild animals. My heart quailed at the thought.

Deimuiss and I had been inseparable from the time we started to walk. His dwelling was next to ours at the settlement, and when we could, we spent every waking hour together. If the weather was bad, we would run back and forth through the underground passage that linked our homes. We had shared all the good times, growing up loving and knowing each other's likes and dislikes. Our families also shared strong relationships forged by our love for each other. I adored his dark, good looks; he was so tall and strong, his long, black, spiralling, curly hair shone in the sunlight, reflecting the sun's rays in a myriad of lights. I envied him his long, dark eyelashes. His deep blue, almost navy eyes were the colour of the lakes on a sunlit summer day. If ever we were apart, I pictured myself reflected in those eyes as he rode his black stallion through the ancient forests of the Chase, the sunlight sending sparkles of light that surrounded him, making him seem indomitable. In fact, wherever he was, I would see a golden light surrounding him. It was his aura and I knew instinctively that he was a natural healer. He had proved this so many times, as whenever a member of the tribe was ill, it was always Deimuiss who was sent for. It was fascinating to watch him work; from the time he entered a patient's home, his whole demeanour changed. A look of authority took over his normal self; he appeared older, more mature, authoritative and capable. He had the appearance of a professional man; his deep blue eyes would immediately be drawn to the patient and I could almost see his mind assessing the patient's illness; a piercing look came into his eyes and it was almost as if he 'saw' the illness through the skin of the patient.

Watching as he healed people mesmerised me. His hands would hover just above the patient's body; never touching them. He had no need to. His inner sight would diagnose the problem, and Deimuiss would then tell the patient or immediate relative, at great length, what they needed to do to make the person whole. When his healing work was finished, he would always wash his hands immediately, telling me that despite not touching his patients, the illness was 'drawn' into him. By washing his hands, the illness was dissipated. I often wondered if the small gold circle on the back of his left hand was a sign of a great healer. I had never mentioned it to him, as I am certain he would have laughed at my thoughts. Deimuiss was Deimuiss and he would never think he was any greater than the man standing next to him was. He looked on 'the healing' as his life's work. Out walking, he always knew the names of the herbs that grew in abundance in and around the settlement; he recognized instinctively which plant would help to heal a particular illness. When we were out, he would always be pointing out various flora to me, telling me of their healing properties, what illness they would cure and the appropriate way to give it to a patient. He made me so proud to be with him. I had always known that he was an extraordinary person and how fortunate I was to love him, and at times, when I thought how much he loved me, I was awestruck.

I had never thought or imagined a time when we would not be together; his sudden disappearance had left me bereft.

Explaining his gift to me, he had told me that he actually 'felt' the pain his patient was suffering, and instinct guided him in the way he should heal them: by exercise, rest or medicine. I was enthralled by his words and hoped that his natural ability would be passed on to at least one of our children.

I had always accepted that we would marry and have children. His gift surpassed the powers of the Mystics in the field of healing, but Deimuiss was always careful never to overstep the mark and brag about his greater power. The Mystics respected his healing powers and acknowledged that his healing abilities were far greater than theirs were. I also hoped my gift of 'seeing' would be passed on to our children. I have known all my life that I have the gift of 'seeing' the future and, occasionally, the past. At first, I was frightened whenever it went misty around me and I found myself in another place when the mists cleared. I would see strange buildings and people dressed differently from us. Nevertheless, as I grew older, an inner knowledge had taken over, and I knew that in the fullness of time my 'visions' would be de-mystified.

Deimuiss made me feel safe and loved. I knew there would never be another man for me; he was my life, my love, my soul mate through time and beyond. Now I was shocked beyond measure that he was here with these savages from The Delph Tribe; trying to kill me. My worst nightmare was unfolding around me. For pity's sake, he was out to rape and then kill me. Now as he writhed on the floor doubled up with pain, his long, dark curls falling across his handsome face, he at least posed no immediate threat. I felt vindicated that at least I had stopped one of them in their tracks. Moreover, I had seen the small gold circle on his left hand, so I knew it was definitely him and not another that resembled him.

My heart was shattered, scattered to the four winds by his deceit, but I had no time to think of that now. One down, two to go. They would not find me such an easy kill as they had Grandmamma and Trieainia. The remaining men were still trying to wrench at my clothes, their hands grabbing at whatever part of me they could. I felt defiled by their filthy, nail-bitten hands. I tried circling round them, hoping to reach the cave entrance, twisting out of their grip as best I could in the confines of the cave. The mere smell of them made me feel nauseous; never mind feeling their awful hands on my body.

The trouble was, I was being pushed further and further back into the narrower recesses of the cave and I knew from visiting this place many times before, there is no way out. The men were now advancing on me, evil shining from their faces in the gloom. Their smell was disgusting. It hung in a black cloud around them. I knew that even when I went to the Winter of Despair, I would never forget their barbarous faces filled with their lustful intent. 'No!' I screamed, as lurching towards me, their hands outstretched like those awful tree branches I had seen earlier, they lunged, trying to seize me. 'No! Oh no!' I screamed again. By now, my panic was a living, pulsating thing, my voice hoarse from my desperate screaming and cries for help. The air was vibrating with my fear, anger and hopelessness. My back was up against the far wall of the cave and I was filled with desolation. There was no escape from these loathsome hunters. I knew I was going to die a horrendous death. I tried once more to escape from them, pushing backwards against the cave wall with every ounce of my strength, ready to kick out with all my might; I felt their evil rancid breath brush my face. Horror filled me. Suddenly, the strange lights lit up the whole cave; brighter and brighter, they shone as the eerie mist began to fill the cave. Pushing myself against the rear wall of the cave even harder, to avoid the men and also the eerie lights and mist, I suddenly found myself being pulled upwards by some strange force, through, it seemed, time and space.

Chapter 3

Strangely, I could hear Deimuiss's voice calling to me as if from a great distance. I saw his deep blue eyes looking straight into mine. 'Elvaennia, you have got it all wrong. I would never betray you.' Then, the vision faded and I was spinning ever upwards through a darkness that was blacker even than the darkest night. Voices and noises kept attacking my ears so much so that my head began to ache; I shook with fear, my thoughts filled with the horror of the small, dead bodies of my grandmother and sister. Who now would care for their mortal and immortal remains? Their spirits must be sent to our ancestors from the top of the Hill of the Spirits, their souls from the Hill of Souls. Why, oh why, hadn't I lit a flare to see if a warning message had been left on the side of the cave? How unforgivable of me. The need to find out about Deimuiss had made me negligent of my duty to protect them. I had killed my poor, defenceless Grandmamma and sister. Now, I too was going to die. What great sadness and despair I have brought to my family. Now that I have discovered Deimuiss has betrayed us. I am mortified.

Swirling upwards through the inky blackness, my despair almost as tangible as my tears, I knew I was going to die. In addition, I realised, because of my failure of care to my family, that the gods were prolonging my agony before the final blackness took me to the Winter of Despair – where I would grieve for eternity for what I had done. No way would my spirit be sent safely from the sacred Hill of the Spirits. No, the people from the settlement would probably send me first to the Cave of Lost Spirits, a great distance away, from where my spirit would make its final journey to the eternal Winter of Despair. They certainly would not allow me to be returned to my ancestors after what I had done. I knew I deserved the fate that awaited me at the end of this journey. The Mystics definitely would not be taking care of my soul.

So many spirits of my family and friends had made their last journey from the Sacred Hill where we gather to say our final goodbyes at the parting ceremony. At times, I could swear I saw the spirit break free from the body, and make the final journey when the silver cord was finally severed. A dazzling white light spins the spirit ever upwards into the waiting arms of relatives and friends where they are reunited at the Time without End. Now I knew my spirit would go to the blackness of the Cave of Dead and Lost Spirits, and then ever onward to the Eternal Winter of Despair, to be frozen forever in the black ice of the forests. I sobbed with the inky blackness of depression as I swirled upwards. To where, I knew not.

By now, I was feeling nauseous and my head was swimming. I had never felt so ill. My body ached from the assault by the hunters, and I could still smell their rancid stench in my nostrils. Not only that – I was freezing with cold, I clutched my cloak and tunic to my shivering body; I needed my cloak now more than ever, despite its dampness. I was so angry with myself for my negligence at not taking greater care of my beloved relatives. My negligence would haunt me throughout eternity: I felt anger and utter abhorrence at the huntsmen (including Deimuiss) more than hatred for the murder of a defenceless old lady and a young girl. If I should meet the evil killers as I travelled to the Caves of Dead Spirits, woe betide them. I made a solemn vow that eternity would not be long enough to wreak my revenge. Rage and a murderous fury filled me again. It was frothing inside me like a burning, hissing, spitting cauldron, knowing that Deimuiss had turned traitor and gone over to our sworn enemies. This heinous act hurt me more than I could say. How I had loved and adored my tall, blue eyed, dark haired man. Never had I thought he would leave me to be with our enemies. How I had missed seeing and talking to him - the only time we were ever apart was if he went on hunting trips with other warriors from our tribe; or on trips to heal the sick when I could not go with him. That day, when he had left on his lone hunting trip, never had I in my wildest dreams thought that he would disappear without trace. I wondered now: had he planned to leave and join the Delphs? My thoughts were veering crazily to and fro as my mind whirled and swirled like my body, as I was pulled higher and higher on this crazy journey ever upwards.

Offerings had been made to the gods for his safe return, but he had not been seen since that fateful day. Members of the tribe had travelled great distances, asking at other settlements whether 'the healer, Deimuiss' had been seen. All at the outlying settlements knew his great skills. I often travelled with him, as I have the 'sight' – a special gift of being able to see the past and the future. I use it to help people with their problems. At times, people travelled to our settlement in the anticipation that he could help them. Not one person had seen him from the time of his leaving our tribe to go on his hunting trip. It has been a big mystery; and as the weeks and months, and finally, 18 months passed, I had begun to accept that my soul mate had possibly gone to the Time without End. Anger smouldered inside me. I railed against a fate that had taken such a wonderful man from me. I felt all was lost. I knew my future with Deimuiss was now fated never to be.

We had carved our initials into logs that we were going to cover with furs and then use as seats in the home we were building together. Mamma had given us animal skins and furs for our bed and furniture; Grandmamma had passed on various cooking utensils, wooden plates and cooking implements that, since Grandpapa had died, she no longer needed as she now shared with us. Thinking of her kindness and gifts was unbearable, and again a great sadness and anger mingled throughout my body as I thought about our lost lives and the children we were now fated never to have. Carpets were being woven for us; Grandmamma was making lace for us and for our children, 'particularly for your daughter, Beth,' she had said. The name had startled me as I had heard that name whispered on the summer breezes and heard it in the chattering waterfalls that run alongside the Chase Way. I had wondered who the name belonged to. Now Grandmamma had unwittingly told me.

My shock at seeing Deimuiss with our enemies in the cave was almost too much to bear. And to think my poor Grandmamma and sister must have seen his treachery was another bitter blow for me to bear.

I had been desolate for months after Deimuiss had disappeared. It felt as if part of me had gone forever. I found it so hard to come to terms with the fact that he had simply disappeared, as if he had fallen from the edge of the World; just as if he had died. Now, to have seen him alive – and obviously he must have been living with our sworn enemies – was equally as heartbreaking. Why was he with the Delphs, betraying not only me but also the tribe he professed to love as much as his family and friends? The scene in the cave replayed repeatedly in my mind as this strange force pulled me even harder, constantly upwards. The more I struggled against it, the tighter the grip became, tugging me ever onwards. I sobbed, shivering with cold, and thinking of Deimuiss's deceit and how he had betrayed me.

My situation was now unbearable and just as I reached the point of thinking I could not bear any more, I was suddenly flung at an incredible speed on to the sandy surface of the cave. Everything went black for a few minutes. When I recovered, I lay on the dirty floor, trying to catch my breath, wondering what on earth I was doing back in the cave. I was terrified that The Delphs would be waiting to rape, attack and kill me.

'No,' I sobbed. 'Please, no more.'

I felt even more confused. I was battered, bruised, cold, wet and frightened. Was this going to be my punishment? To be whirled ever upwards and then flung out, back into the cave, attacked again, and then have to keep repeating the whole episode for eternity? I groaned with the pain of my bruises and carefully got myself into a sitting position.

Timidly, I gazed around my surroundings, checking to see if The Delphs were waiting to pounce. It slowly dawned on me that I was not in the same cave. This must be a different one. 'My goodness,' I thought. 'Where am I? This cave is not one I have ever been in before.' It was familiar, but then, on the other hand, it wasn't. For one thing, it was so much smaller. Scanning the area close by me, I saw something glinting. Reaching out, I carefully picked it up. It appeared to be gold. I was perplexed – the gold-coloured item was as light as air. I did not recognise the material it was made of, and there was some strange writing on it. I turned it around in my hands, then lifted it, and sniffed. 'Ugh.' It smelt unlike anything I had ever smelt before. I slipped it into my pouch, thinking I would examine it later. In fact, on closer inspection, there were many strange objects littering the cave floor. One looked like a strange-shaped transparent object. Was it some kind of water carrier? I picked it up. It was extremely light, and sniffing the open top, it had a sweet almost cloying scent. Definitely not water, I mused. Perhaps it was some type of herb that I had not yet come across. I was tempted to taste it, but thinking it might be some kind of poison, decided not to.

Then, I heard some very strange noises that made me almost jump out of my skin. I realised they were animal noises, the same as the ones we had heard on our way to the cave. However, they sounded louder here, and far more menacing. I was afraid now, alone in this strange lonely cave with no one to talk to or give me advice. How could I protect myself? Who knows the Dragons of the Dead might be waiting outside the cave to attack me? My thoughts were in chaos. I huddled into my cloak, finding comfort in the images it gave me of the herds of deer and bison that have roamed the lands of my ancestors for so many generations. I pictured their beautiful, gentle faces as they grazed the heath lands and raised their young; each season of the year bringing its changes to the herds. The seasons are the invisible golden threads that link the animal kingdom to humanity. I felt something sharp pressing against my hands. Looking, I realised I was holding a small flint knife with Deimuiss's initials engraved on it. Was Deimuiss here too? If so, where was he? How had he become separated from his knife, his most precious possession?

I must still be in the bivouac, but why was it so much smaller? Moreover, what were the strange objects lying around the cave floor? Wrapping the knife in some strange looking material from the ground, I tucked it into my pouch, wondering how Deimuiss had come to lose it. Glancing down, I could see faint markings on the ground. But there were scuff marks over them, as if small animals had walked across the cave. I could not make the marking out. Had Deimuiss been here? My heart leapt in my throat. Had he been here before I arrived? But then how could he? I decided he deserved to lose his precious knife. 'Serves him right,' I thought bitterly. 'I hope he misses it!' My thoughts were indeed turning increasingly unforgiving.

The noise outside the cave had stopped. Slowly and carefully, I crawled towards the entrance; pausing to take a deep breath, I separated the grasses that partially covered it. Taking another deep breath, I looked through the gap. What I saw astounded me. Hastily snapping back the grasses, I scrambled to the back of the cave in astonishment. Where on earth was I? What was this place outside the cave? I had never seen anything like this at the settlement, or anywhere else for that matter. I huddled into the darkness at the rear of the cave. It gave me a strange kind of comfort, making me feel more secure. I felt safe within its confines. Outside was a strange alien place. Not only had it looked out of the ordinary, but it also smelled very similar to the odour we had smelt at the bivouac. I thought I could hear sounds comparable to what we had heard on the way to the cave. I told myself to stop imagining things and snuggled deep into the warm fur that lined my cloak. Strangely enough, it was now completely dry. I found this very odd, but I was comforted by its warmth and did not dwell on it. I was just grateful for its soothing warmth.

My thoughts turned once again to Deimuiss. Swallowing hard against the lump within my throat, trying not to cry, I remembered our years of love and laughter. From early childhood, we had been constant companions. Living next door to him, it was obvious that we would be great friends from the outset. The attraction was instant. Mamma said that we were friends from the word go. She could never remember us ever having an argument or an angry word. Unbelievable really, as I constantly disagree – in a friendly way of course! – With my brothers and sisters.

Deimuiss showed me the hidden pathways of the Chase lands and forests, the nearby bivouacs, the Holy Springs and mysterious haunted caves, the magical haunts of the Druids, hidden waterways and waterfalls.

I knew we lived in a mysterious mystical land. I so admired his knowledge of where we lived and also his understanding of the ancient laws of the gods and goddesses.

One day, he had taken me to the Cave of the Sacred Spirits, high up on the side of one of the steepest hills on the Chase. It was a long walk. I took jewellery and gold coins (our families are of high status, the wealthiest on the settlement) as an offering to the gods and goddesses. We had to visit the spring and make the offering before we could enter the cave, otherwise the gods would indeed have been very angry.

On entering, we stopped to let our eyes adjust to the inky darkness. Slowly, very slowly, my vision cleared and I gasped aloud at the remarkable drawings and paintings on the cave walls. Images of beautiful people, some with wings, ascending to the skies, and drawings of animals I had never seen before. The expressions on the people's faces showed their happiness as they neared the sacred cloud that was depicted high up on the walls. They held their offering in their hands towards the gods, who smiled benevolently at them as they approached. I saw the drawings had been painted gold. They were truly beautiful. I wanted to stay all day, just looking at the wondrous sights. They filled me with awe. The cave shimmered in the light reflected from the gold of the paintings.

On our way home, Deimuiss told me that he felt quite emotional when he saw the wonderful drawings and paintings; saying he experienced a great sense of peace, and that his spirit was renewed after a visit. I agreed, telling him that I felt the same. We vowed to return in the near future. He mentioned that he would take me to the Crystal Caves soon. My eyes sparkled at the thought. It was a place I longed to visit, as did my friends. They had often mentioned it to me. It was legendary. Generations of our tribe had discussed it, but no one knew where it was. Seemingly, to my utter delight, Deimuiss knew. Hugging the invitation to me, I looked forward to paying a visit, feeling privileged and special indeed.

One cave intrigues me more than any other. It is a long walk from the settlement, and high up on the moorlands. You enter it between a cleft that runs between two enormous rocks. We had to crawl in along a long, narrow, winding, dark entrance. I often wondered how Deimuiss discovered these caves. Once inside, it was strangely light and airy. Brushing the dust from me, I glanced up and was amazed by the drawings on the walls of the caves. I gingerly stepped my way across the uneven floor of the cave to take a closer look. I glanced back at Deimuiss and pointed to one of the drawings – 'I have seen that place in one of my visions.' He nodded, but made no comment, which I must admit was very unusual for him as he was rarely at a loss for words. Moving around the cave, I became more and more intrigued as many of the drawings reminded me strongly of my dreams and visions. Other pictures made no sense to me whatsoever, and I was at a loss to understand them. Strangely enough, I could see myself depicted in some of the artwork, it was startling to say the least. I saw myself inside a strange looking house that had what looked to be wood on the floor; and had a high sheen. I was dressed in very different clothing to what we wear in these times. Beautifully coloured cloth made up the clothes I was wearing. I looked happy, smiling, and was in the company of a man who the artist had made very apparent was extremely handsome. He had greener than green eyes, and springy, brown hair. In addition, there was an older plump woman. In the drawing, she had a beautiful smile and the artist had drawn particular attention to her snow-white hair. This and other pictures showing me in various situations puzzled me. Nevertheless, what worried me was there was no sign of Deimuiss, only the man with the wondrous green eyes. There were many other paintings showing me in different times wearing clothing I had never seen, and situations I could not understand; I was at a loss to understand the paintings. Were the paintings giving me a message? Were they telling me part of my future? 'No!' I cried out, upset. I was shaking, thinking that I was going to lose Deimuiss and find myself alone and frightened in a very different world.

'Elvaennia, do not cry.' He ran across to me and enfolded me in his arms. 'Do not distress yourself my love, my dearest heart. Everything will work out, I promise you.'

Comforted by his words, I waited for him to explain the artwork to me. But he made no comment at all. I found this strange, as at other caves we have visited he would go to great lengths giving me long explanations about the history of the subjects portrayed.

For some unknown reason, I made no further effort to engage him in conversation regarding the paintings. I knew he had his reasons for bringing me to this cave. No doubt, in the fullness of time, he would make everything clear. For now, I had to be patient, something that did not come naturally to me.

A number of the drawings mystified me. I could not understand the subject matter at all, and wondered at the artist's imagination and versatility in portraying so many different happenings.

There were huge buildings (as in my young dreams), strange houses and ribbons of tracks with strange animals seemingly moving along them. The youths and younger children were dressed in similar attire. They were indeed strange pictures, telling of a different lifetime to ours, so why was I depicted in some of these paintings?

On leaving the cave, Deimuiss told me that on no account should I ever tell anyone of this place. Nodding in agreement, I did ask him if he could tell me what the broken lines within the paintings meant. These had puzzled me greatly. Shaking his head, he told me that I would discover the reason in the fullness of time. He was so serious and unlike his normal self that I agreed immediately. Again, I did not ask him for an explanation, but I did recognise that I was very privileged to be allowed to see this extraordinary cave. The descent seemed harder to navigate than the ascent and I was clinging on to Deimuiss's tunic for dear life. Again, I wondered how he managed to discover these caves.

At other times, we would go hunting in the forests, often catching a wild animal and taking it home to be shared between our families for our evening meal. I was proud of my love, and it was accepted by all that, one day, we would marry and have the children that we desperately craved. How I needed him with me NOW, needed the strength of his strong arms to hold me safe from the monsters that were roaring beneath the hillside – unknown creatures that were frightening me half to death. At this moment, remembering the strange drawings in the cave, my heart missed a beat. The animals in the paintings were at the bottom of the hillside. We had heard this noise on our way to the Mystical Standing Stones. Fear of the unknown was preventing me from exploring my surroundings any further; I drew my cloak closer for warmth and comfort. I felt so alone and frightened. What if the strange animals beneath the hillside made their way up to the cave, how would I cope? My heart raced with fear. I needed Deimuiss to give me strength and confidence. I was thirsty and hungry and I needed food to fuel my body. I sank deeper, relaxing into the soft fur, Deimuiss's face swam into my line of vision. I thought I heard his voice 'I love you Vinny. Be brave. I will find you.' It was him. I was convinced. Only he had ever called me Vinny. I struggled to open my eyes, convinced he was here in the cave with me. I could smell the scent of the ancient woods and heather that he always brought with him. Yet, the more I resisted the deeper I began to sink into an exhausted sleep. The further I drifted, the sharper the images of home at the settlement became. I could smell the roasting meat, hear the crackling of the fire, and smell the apple wood smoke. My brothers' voices, raised in one of their constant arguments, reached out to me across the void of time and centuries. Try as I might; I could not make my brothers see me. I shouted their names: 'Tomissia, Diaviadia, Piettra, please, please look and see me, my brothers.' They did not even glance in my direction, continuing to argue amongst each other. That is, Tomissia and Diaviadia did. My poor small Piettra just sat lost in his own little world, looking but apparently not seeing his surroundings. 'If only I could help him,' I thought, 'unlock the door that shuts him out.' I longed to see him respond and join in with our world. My eyes alighted on my sister, Jennia, who was sitting working at the weaving loom. I called her name as loudly as I could. 'I am here! It's me, Elvaennia, your sister.' Jennia started and glanced around the house as if she had heard me. 'Over here,' I cried, 'Please look. Look!' But, she returned to her weaving, obviously unable to see me. Watching as she bent to her work, I noticed tears streaming down her face. Jennia, my little Jennia, was crying – for Trieainia, our dearest Grandmamma, and me. This was my worst nightmare: seeing my family and being unable to make contact with them. The horror of what had happened enfolded me once again. How I longed to turn back time.

The awfulness of what had transpired awoke me and I thought of my family. When would I see them again? What would they think of me neglecting Grandmamma and Trieainia so badly that they had been murdered; and even worse, that the man they thought so highly of had participated in their killing? For some reason I could not accept that Deimuiss had been a part of such a travesty. Thinking of my lost love, tears slid down my cheeks. What treachery had led him to join The Delphs? How could he ignore me? Remembering those ice cold, blue eyes when he had looked at me in the cave, I shuddered. The dark cloud of depression entered my mind like the thunder that broods darkly over the hills of the Chase at times. Snuggling deeper into the warm folds of fur, my thoughts once again turned to Deimuiss. How could he leave our tribe and join The Delphs? When the Elders of our settlement heard of his defection, a hunting party would be sent in search of him. My heart quailed at the thought of what would happen to him should he be found. He would be tortured, no doubt of that, and then killed. In addition, his body, spirit and soul would forever be outcast, a fate worse even than the Winter of Despair. I shuddered at the thought.

How could I love him, I still did, if the truth were told. I adored everything about him, remembering my heartbreak when he disappeared as if the very earth we trod still had the power to fill my heart with tears of sadness. Swallowing hard now, trying not to cry again, I remembered our years of love and laughter. From early childhood, we had never really wanted other close friends. The attraction had been instant; I had truly believed our pathways through life would be joined as one. How wrong had I been?

I was torn emotionally, thinking he had killed my relatives but swayed by the thought that he could not possibly be a murderer. Surely, I would have seen the tiniest chink in his aura or glimpsed it in his eyes? All my instincts cried out, saying he is not a killer, but I had seen him in the cave with our enemies - proof enough, surely.

Awful thoughts of dying on this alien hillside filled my disturbed mind. I was so afraid of leaving the comparative security of the cave.

33

Soon I would have to face it, but not now, as a deeper sleep claimed me, and my thoughts drifted back to Deimuiss. Perhaps he had an accident and lost his memory? Could this be the reason he had joined The Delphs? Maybe they had captured and enlisted him as one of their warriors. If he had lost his memory, then he was not responsible for his actions, surely. The Deimuiss I knew would never be capable of murder.

The thought that he may well have lost his memory cheered me considerably as I drifted back to consciousness. Again, I thought of the time when he would regain his memory, then return to the settlement, and explain everything to the Elders. What then though? He would discover I had disappeared along with Grandmamma and Trieainia. What would he do? I wondered what he would think of my carelessness in deserting them. All this supposition was becoming too much for me, my head was beginning to ache even more; I was cold, tired, hungry and very afraid.

Wiping my tears away with the back of my hand, reason began to reassert itself. I could not stay here forever, could I? I would need food and water to survive. I had nothing with which to hunt or fish. I could perhaps use Deimuiss's flint knife; but where would I go to get my food? The world outside the cave was a threatening place, with the constant noise and smells lingering on the air. Also, the strange buildings that I had seen in the distance worried me considerably. If I waited until it was dark, I would not be able to track the wild animals, as I had no light. My head felt fuzzy and I was so confused. My thoughts were in chaos but I had to be practical to be able to survive. I needed water urgently; fuel and flint to light a fire to heat the water and cook whatever food I was able to find or steal, plus extra fuel to keep the fire going through the coming night to keep the wild animals and any enemies away. If only my head would clear. It felt so muzzy.

Deciding that I had to be brave, to go outside and find food and water, otherwise I would become weak and useless, I ventured to the cave entrance. Parting the grasses, I nearly fainted. A man's face was staring back at me. I screamed at the top of my voice and fell backwards into the shelter of the cave.

Chapter 4

I heard the man's voice laughing at my fright. This angered me so much, I again approached the entrance, only to be shocked as his head and shoulders appeared through the entrance.

I backed away as fast as I could. The man continued to crawl into the cave. I was so scared;, after all, he could be one of The Delphs or from another tribe of our enemies.

Shaking with terror, I scrambled as far back as I could. Why didn't I get out of this cave earlier? Berating myself angrily, thinking surely, now I was going to die at the hands of this man, I vowed, 'I won't go without a fight.'

Lifting my head high, I looked at the man and was surprised to see he was young and good looking (that registered immediately), but anger spurted up inside me. He had a huge grin on his face. That annoyed me intensely. How dare he think it was funny to go around frightening innocent people! Opening my mouth ready to tell him exactly what I thought of him, I suddenly noticed that he was dressed – from what I could see – in very strange clothing indeed. However, his eyes held me in thrall. They were the most alluring green colour that I had ever seen. As green as the lakes on the Chase under a moonlit night, particularly when the Northern Lights appeared and Deimuiss and I would dance as they shone and flickered, changing the landscape into a mystical, magical world. As we danced, he would murmur in my ear, 'We are dancing with the Spirits Elvaennia. What more could we ask for?' Snuggling up to him, I always agreed.

He also had thick, springy, brown hair. 'Very nice indeed,' I thought. Suddenly, the man spoke, jolting me back to the present.

'Please do not be frightened.'

His deep voice reverberated around the cave.

'I was wondering why you are in the cave. Are you in some kind of trouble?'

Concern showed on his handsome features; he sensed how fearful I was.

By now I had managed to get to the very back of the cave, and I prayed that whatever mystical force had brought me to here would take me straight back to the settlement. I pushed against the rear wall of the cave as hard as I could. To my utter disappointment, nothing happened. I had hoped I might be transported back to my time, anywhere away from this stranger.

'Look,' he said with a disarming smile, 'I promise I mean you no harm. I am leaving the cave now and I hope you will follow me.' With these words, he disappeared, shuffling backwards out of the cave. After a few seconds, I began to follow him. I had no choice really, thinking that perhaps it might be in my best interests to get out, as he was less likely to harm me outside the cave than inside. Taking a deep breath, I slowly crawled out of my shelter. I tried to stand upright. This presented a bit of a problem: my legs felt like jelly; in fact, my whole body was shaking; the man took hold of my arm to steady me.

'Tell me, why you were hiding in the cave?' he demanded.

If only the muzzy feeling would leave me, I might have been able to think up a suitable reply; but as soon as I ventured outside, my head began to feel very strange indeed. My thoughts were chaotic, there was a whirring noise inside my brain, and I felt most peculiar. Taking some deep breaths, shivering with cold and fear of the unknown, I managed to stop trembling and gave the man a sideways glance. Gosh! He was wearing a strange outfit. I wondered which tribe he was a member of. He wore a white short-sleeved top; and some strange looking, blue material covered his lower limbs. I had never seen any clothing like this before.

'Tribe?' he uttered loudly. Oh dear, I must have spoken aloud. I could hear a smile in his voice. Oh, if only my head would clear!

'I do not belong to any tribe, young lady. In a short while, everything will become clear to you. Just be patient.'

I was so confused, and wondered what on earth he was talking about. I hoped he was right and that my head would clear fast and stop aching.

He pointed to himself with a tanned, slim hand saying, 'My name is David, Dave for short. Now, at least tell me your name.'

'Elvaennia of the Calegi Tribe,' I managed to stutter, very aware what a sight I must look. My cloak was dusty and dirty, as was my tunic. I knew my hair was dishevelled, to say the least, after the episode with the hunting party at the cave. I dreaded to think of how I must appear to him. My eyes were sore and puffy from crying, my cheeks tear streaked. In fact, overall, I must have looked a sorry sight.

He shot me what can only be described as a quizzical look.

'Calegi? Mm, never heard of that name before.'

My head was beginning to clear a little now and I thought it strange that he misunderstood what I had told him. But no matter – pulling my cloak around me, I was just about to ask him the way back to the settlement when a loud noise reverberated all around us. Suddenly, it seemed to be almost overhead. I screamed, throwing myself at the young man. As his arms encircled me, and a wonderful warmth ran through my body, I felt secure, safe; my loneliness abated. Wherever I was, it had to be better than fighting off a murderous hunting party in a dark, cold cave on a lonely hillside. The noise became much louder. It was now directly overhead. I huddled even closer to the man (I quite enjoyed the feel of his arms holding me tightly). 'Is it the dragons?' I whispered fearfully.

'Pardon, did you say dragons?'

'The noise, the smell, what is it?' I choked in fear as I spoke.

'Noise?' he queried. Clearly, whatever it was, he was not afraid of it. 'The only noise I can hear is the traffic: cars, lorries, buses, and yes, I can smell the fumes, unfortunately.'

Still shaking, I pointed upwards.

'Oh, that's just a helicopter, probably the police looking for a criminal,' he laughed. 'Traffic fumes and noise linger longer on still, warm days. Now stop worrying, everything will fall into place very soon.'

None of this made any sense to me and again I wondered where on earth I was. It certainly was not the Sacred Cave of the Spirits, and certainly not the Winter of Despair. His words made me realise that, yes, it was very warm outside the cave. It felt like summer, yet back at the settlement it was early spring. In fact, it had been the Equinox, I suddenly remembered. How strange! My fear had blocked out everything but sound and smell. I moved away from the man – David, Dave for short – and looked fearfully around. My heart thumped loudly. Could he hear it? This landscape was so alien to me. There were strange buildings at the top of the hill. At the very bottom of the field, just beyond the hawthorn hedge, I could see a wide track and the peculiar objects were moving at great speed, hurtling towards each other. How on earth, I wondered, did they miss each other? Obviously, these were what the man referred to as traffic. But how were they able to move? They had no wings like the birds, those huge airborne things that David (Dave for short) had called a helicopter, and no bird I had ever seen made that noise. The sound carried to the top of the field and I could hear the same swishing noise that I had heard on the hillside in my time. Therefore, it was not dragons that we had heard and smelt; it was cars, helicopters, and lorries. How had this happened, and how did I know?

Things were beginning to make sense to me as he had said they would. His name for instance was David – not *David, Dave for short*. How stupid of me!

I glanced at David and recognised that he knew his world was now becoming my world. He smiled, looking relieved that I was no longer quite as terrified as the person he had found in the cave; still scared and very worried admittedly, but happier now that a few things were beginning to make sense.

I scanned the view, to see if there were any recognizable landmarks, but there was nothing to indicate that I was anywhere near to the settlement. The sound of sparrows twittering in the hedgerows with their young ready to fledge reminded me of home. Tears began to choke me. I had to swallow hard and concentrate on my present situation. Despite feeling excited at the thought of time travel, I ached for familiarity. I knew I had left my world a long way away, all that was known had gone to be replaced by these new surroundings in a different time. I did not want to be in this situation with this man with the unusual green eyes (they were truly amazing) and strange attire. I wanted to be at home with my family and friends. How I longed to see Deimuiss as he used to be, not the treacherous man I had last seen lying in the cave. I looked behind me to the West and my heart flipped.

The Hill of the Spirits!'

I cried out the name in my excitement. Strange, it was the same but different, now it is covered in trees. I could see hazel trees, bushes of broom and silver birch trees covering the hillside. It was our hill – the rocky outcrop still hung at the top – but it was different. David looked stunned at my words, but I ignored him. I was so happy at seeing a place I recognised from my world. For a moment, the landscape misted in front of my eyes and I was back in what was being whispered to me as my own time. I blinked in astonishment at seeing my father working at the settlement. For a second, I saw Mamma and my brothers walking towards our house. I gasped in shock. Surely not? How could I possibly see through time? The picture disappeared as quickly as it had appeared. Bewildered by everything, a tear slipped slowly down my cheek and I felt the man's hand gently wipe it away.

'Come with me, little one.'

He held out his hand, and like a child I slipped my hand trustingly into his large, tanned hand. 'Why, you are as tiny as a sprite,' he remarked in a joking fashion as together we slowly walked across the field; my feet were still sore from the stones on the heath land.

'Look, my little sprite.'

He gestured in the direction of a strange, low, rambling building, not far away.

'That is the farmhouse where I live with my mother. I will take you to meet her and I am sure she will help you. You will be able to talk to her.'

I knew how kind he was being to me. After all, I was a complete stranger who he had only just met. Different scents assailed my nostrils as we walked past the swaying, beautiful, nodding heads of the cow parsley that laced the edges of the track. Dandelions and daisies bowed their heads as if acknowledging my presence in their world. Buttercups shone their yellowy glow all around, lighting the pathways for travellers old and new.

Murmuring my thanks, I decided to keep silent and try to absorb all I could of the new place I was in. The man, David, had no knowledge of my culture. I was as strange to him as he was to me, but I was not fearful of him. I was, however, very wary of the situation I found myself in, and hesitant of where the man David was taking me. Slowly, very slowly, my head was clearing and I thought I might have to bluff my way through this situation. For now perhaps, I thought, I should take on another persona, but I had no idea who I could be in this new world. After all, without thinking, I had already told the man, David, my name and tribe. Therefore, on second thoughts, I could hardly pretend to be someone else. I was extremely confused and nervous; my head still felt as woolly as a sheep. We were about to enter his home and I was completely unprepared for this state of affairs. Surely, I reassured myself, it could be no worse than what I had already been through at the hunting cave.

Chapter 5

Taking a deep gulp of air, I coughed and spluttered, trying to clear my lungs. I had a rank taste in my mouth. This air was nothing like the air of my time, which had been fresh and pure. Following him in through a blue painted door that had a strange metal shape cut into it, we were in a dark, shadowy hallway. What hit me first was the heat. Despite the warmth of the day outside, in this hallway I was almost overwhelmed by a deep, cloying heat. Shadows of people appeared, pressing closely in this enclosed space. Dust motes clouded the air - even they seemed threatening. It was so claustrophobic! I knew this hallway contained many dark secrets of the past. The shadows pressed closer. Instinctively I knew they wanted to share secrets with me. They were whispering, telling me that they had come from other times; and now they were ensnared in this place, unable to move on.

'Listen to our stories, Elvaennia. We have much to tell you. We know you can help us escape. Do not allow yourself to become like us, just a shadow trapped here in this dark, forbidding place forever more. Listen to us, please, Elvaennia. You are in danger.'

I could not cope with them. Not now. Everything here was so strange, and as the shadows clamoured closer and closer it became too much. Head spinning, I knew I was going to faint, and I swayed, reaching out to the wall to try to stop myself from falling. At the same time, I was trying to convey to them that I needed time to adjust. 'When I am stronger, I will help you,' I murmured faintly, hoping this gave them some comfort as I began to slip into an all-encompassing darkness.

I found myself in a comfortable old armchair in a light, airy room. David was crouching in front of me, chaffing my hands. He sighed with relief. 'There you are. You will be all right now, thank goodness. It all became a bit much for you. Not to worry, you will be fine now.' He walked away and I heard the sound of water running. He re-appeared in front of me, passing me a glass of water. Instinct told me it was a glass but, how I knew, I did not question; just accepted it. The water tasted vile as if it was full of impurities. It also stank, but I gratefully drank it down and felt better for it.

The kitchen door suddenly swung open and a plump matronly lady with snowy white hair entered. She came towards us with a startled look on her face, which she quickly replaced with a smile. 'Welcome. So, you are a friend of my David?' She nodded towards the young man who was obviously her son. Her eyes were identical in colour to his; and despite her plumpness compared to his slim body, the similarity was there for all to see.

'Mother, this is Elvaennia.'

Now, did I curtsy? Did I hug or kiss her? What did I do? Truth to tell, I still felt too weak to move and was at a loss what to do, but the woman resolved the problem by hurrying around a huge, wooden, scrubbed table and she hugged me where I sat. 'Table?' I thought, amidst the biggest cuddliest hug I had ever had in my life – where did I get that name from? We have no 'tables' at the settlement. The woman's brow furrowed. Clearing her throat:

'Erm, Elvaennia, what a pretty name. If you are feeling better, would you, erm, like to change out of your dusty clothes? My daughter, Joanna, is away at Birmingham University and I am sure we could help you out with something of hers, mind you are tiny aren't you? I'm sure they will fit you though.'

I felt, rather than saw, Deimuiss grin widely at her words. I knew that he couldn't possibly hear her. Could he? How I wished I could get him out of my mind. Was my imagination playing tricks on me or was he with me in spirit?

I nodded my assent to Mary, trying to assimilate her words. Oh dear, this was not going to be easy. I told myself to put Deimuiss firmly away out of my mind while I concentrated on the here and now. Everything was so confusing, my head felt as if it would explode at any time. How could I come to terms with all that had happened when I could not even think straight?

'Call me Mary,' the kindly plump soul said, escorting me upstairs to a room that she intimated was her Joanna's, 'Who I mentioned is away at university.'

'My other daughter, Angelina, is married and lives in Lichfield with her husband Michael and their four children,' Mary chattered on, explaining as she moved swiftly round the room, patting and straightening the bedclothes, moving trinkets around on the dressing table. 'Angelina is from my first marriage and is a few years older than David and Joanna, who are both from my second marriage. Unfortunately, their father, my husband died a number of years ago.' She looked sad for a short time, and I was about to commiserate with her, when she suddenly beamed at me; going on to describe, in a loving way, the ages of her grandchildren and how perfect they were and how beautiful. 'On the other hand,' with a sigh, she said, leaning against the dressing table for a second, 'Don't all grandmothers say the same?' Nodding in agreement, I thought what a nice close family they appeared to be. This, of course, sent my thoughts winging to my own parents and family back at the settlement. A longing tugged at my heart - how I would love to be with them all, but instead, here I was in an unfamiliar house and world feeling very strange and uncomfortable indeed.

How odd that the names Birmingham and Lichfield meant something to me. I stored them in my memory for later when, hopefully, I would have time to think more clearly. Opening a highly polished wardrobe door, Mary told me to look through the garments hanging inside and feel free to help myself to whatever appealed to me. I was amazed that any one woman could own so many clothes. The wardrobe was huge, and the array of clothing was quite overwhelming. The garments shouted, 'Choose me, choose me,' nearly jumping off the rails into my oh-so willing hands. I wanted to examine each and every one, never having seen anything like them in my life; I was overwhelmed to say the least.

'Take your pick, my love, and when you have changed, come back down to the kitchen.' David's mother was certainly a kindly soul. Making her way through the doorway, she pointed to the room facing, saying 'This is the bathroom, if you would like to tidy yourself first; come and see.' With a kindly beckon of a plump finger, she trotted across the corridor.

Taking a peep through the bathroom door, I was astonished at what I saw; I felt that I needed to lie down before I fell as I looked at the extraordinary objects that hit my eyes. Mary went around the room pointing out what she called the 'guest's cupboard'. 'You will find everything you need in here,' she remarked. I noticed her looking at me a couple of times when she thought I was unaware; it was as if she recognised me. What a stupid thought I told myself, taking a stealthy look at her from the corner of my eyes. Then, just for a second, I thought, she looked a little like a relative or a member of our tribe: Pranny. I took another surreptitious glance. No, the resemblance had disappeared as fast as it had appeared. Shrugging my shoulders, I thought I had probably imagined it.

Mary gave me a quizzical look. I felt as if she was reading my mind.

Dear me. I was becoming paranoid. I smiled across to her. 'Thank you so much, Mary, for your kindness.' A beaming smile creased her jovial face. Giving me another hug, she hurried away back to her light, airy kitchen.

I wondered how I could have thought Mary resembled Pranny. What a stupid idea, I told myself. Pranny? The original man-eater? Never! What connection could there possibly be between Mary and Pranny? My thoughts made me smile, nevertheless. Pranny was one of the biggest flirts I had ever known – she would eat any man in her vicinity for breakfast. No man within 50 miles of her radar was safe from her clutches; apart from, that is, my Deimuiss, and also Carnaan – but I was not going to think of him now. No way, not Carnaan. A sudden thought hit me like a kick in the chest. With me here, away from the settlement, what if Deimuiss was to return there? Would he be able to resist the temptations of Pranny's charms?

Now I was being stupid, I told myself as I walked around the room known as the bathroom. Mary could not possibly have anything to do with Pranny. I grinned at the idea. I mean, Pranny! Pushing all thoughts of *her* and her ways from my mind for the time being, I set about the tasks of mastering the bathroom and the new clothes.

A long time passed as I acquainted myself with everything and their various uses. Mary and David both called up, querying whether I was 'okay'. I determined they meant all right, never having heard that word before. Reassuring them that I was fine, I grappled with the new clothes. I quickly realised what was for what, and I enjoyed the look and feel of the garments. I selected a top – it wasn't a tunic, I couldn't find one, but it was pretty with embroidered flowers down the front – and a matching skirt. How did I know what it was called? The same way that a good many things were being told to me. The same way as when I was young....

As a vision of Deimuiss's wonderful blue eyes seared my brain, I stopped. Oh, how I missed him, but this was not the time or place to think of him. I had to sort myself out. I slipped the gorgeous clothes on and chose a beautiful belt that had a wonderful butterfly clip on it. It was amongst a vast selection of belts that Joanna had hung on a rail just inside her wardrobe. Thankfully, my head had lost the muzzy, confused feeling. I now knew the names and uses of all the various objects surrounding me; but I still felt quite overwhelmed.

The clothes felt good. The material of the underwear was wonderfully soft and silky against my skin compared to the clothes I normally wore. Looking at the wreckage of my belongings lying in a heap on the floor, I felt quite ashamed. The smell of them was quite objectionable. They looked so out of place in these opulent surroundings and I wondered what to do with them. It suddenly struck me how well these clothes fitted me and also that they were new - they had never been worn. This was all very strange and I began to suspect that all was not as it appeared to be. I began to worry, as, looking around the room, it looked as if it had been recently made over and there were no signs of it ever having belonged to anyone – let alone one of Mary's daughters.

This was yet another problem I needed to add to my list to think about later.

I picked up my pouch. It felt good to hold something familiar; a link with my past. I peeked inside. The smell of the herbs and spelt wheat assailed my senses again. The spelt had a nutty, sweet smell and I was drawn back to the settlement, into the room where we stored the winter supplies along with the herbs. I touched the jewels that Deimuiss had given me; his flint knife. He was so near, yet so far away. Tears stung my eyes as again his handsome face swam in front of me. I slipped the pouch into my skirt pocket, needing to keep a tangible reminder of my other life about my person for comfort. My situation was intolerable and there appeared to be no way of finding my way home.

Clipping the beautiful belt around my waist, I muttered, 'If only someone would tell me what I am doing here.'

'You have work to do Elvaennia.'

My heart flipped. Now, I was really confused. How could Myllaou, the Chief Mystic, break into my thoughts from so far away? What work? When? Where? Why? Or even, how? More questions than answers. I tried to make contact. 'Tell me more,' I pleaded, but wherever the voice had come from, it seemed that was all I was going to be told as no reply was forthcoming. All was now stubbornly silent. 'Please,' I yelled back through the centuries. 'Don't leave me to work this out for myself, please.'

'Did you call, Elvaennia?' Mary's voice carolled cheerily up the stairs.

I realised, in my anxiety, I had shouted out loud; I hoped she had not heard what I had said.

'Just coming,' I rejoined.

Bracing myself, knowing this was going to be far harder than anything I had ever done before, I sat on the soft, cosy bed for a moment to collect my thoughts. Suddenly, depression again swept across me. Deimuiss was lost to me forever; as were my family, it seemed. Would I ever see them again? Were our lives destined to be spent centuries apart? Wherever I had been brought to, my soul mate would not be here. If he were still alive, that is. I grieved for our lost futures. Now, it would seem, our two worlds would never meet and we were as far apart as ever. Neither time nor distance would ever kill my love for Deimuiss. I truly hoped that one day we would meet again. Tears were again threatening, but I had to be careful and not, at any cost, talk about my past. Somehow I could not think of a story as to how I came to be in the cave. I knew nothing of this world.

I longed to sleep, to escape my predicament. In sleep, I had hope. A vision of my future would enter my dreams. I would be with my family, happily living at the settlement and retaining a deep enduring love for Deimuiss. I dreamt of the happy hours that we had spent building what was to be our new home. However, sadly, it seemed, never again would I see my tall, dark haired man; the man I had pledged to spend the rest of my days with. How hard we had worked, building our house. With the help of my brothers, he spent days knocking in the wooden posts and weaving the hazel and willow branches through the posts. Each branch was, Deimuiss said, 'a symbol of the love we hold for each other.' We were happy working together; Deimuss whispering words of love, exchanging kisses and loving glances as the house gradually took shape. Soon, we would have been spreading the mud and straw on to the walls, plugging any gaps to keep out the cold north-easterly winds. We had been looking forward to placing the wooden struts to form the slanting roof. After that, we would add the final touches of straw, reeds and heather that would make a strong weatherproof roof for our first home. The job of building was nearly completed. We had been planning our shared future, talking of the children we were going to have - they would complete our perfect lives.

Thinking of our home reminded me of the name I had heard whispered on the winds and chattered to me by the silvery waterfalls. I had heard it a few times, as we were building our home. The name had been whispered to me on the summer wind repeatedly. I heard, 'Beth, Beth.' The name was whispered and spun like a golden thread through the hot summer days. When I went to fill the water vessel at the waterfalls, the name tinkled downwards into the shining stream, eddying in swirls and making beautiful patterns on the surface of the Rising Brook. Once, I thought I saw the face of a beautiful, dark haired, blue-eyed child looking at me through the water spray; but as fast as it appeared, the image faded into a rainbow spray of beautiful summer flowers that kissed my cheeks and laughed on a mystical cloud that formed and drifted over the stream. One summer night, I told Deimuiss the name that had been whispered to me on the summer winds. He thought it beautiful, but, like me, had never heard the name before. How strange that Grandmamma had mentioned it when she was making the lace. Dearest Grandmamma and Triennia had now gone to the Time Beyond because of my carelessness. Was that why I had been brought to this strange world? Was this to be my penalty? Living amongst strangers in another lifetime, my sentence: a life spent away from my family and the life I loved.

Deimuiss's strange disappearance on that fateful day had left our plans in disarray. At first, I had thought he had met with an accident, and soon he would return to the settlement; tired but happy to be back, laughing at his unfortunate experience; no doubt full of the different adventures that had occurred during his absence.

The days and weeks had turned into months and my hope for his return began to fade little by little as no sign of him or his horse had ever been found.

I could not bring myself to even think that I would never see him again, and as each new day dawned, hope would again flare like a shooting star. Hope that today he would be back with us. Each sunset, my hopes dipped as the sun dropped beyond the horizon. I would again cry myself to sleep.

My parents urged me to go out with Carnaan – a young man who lived at the settlement – who I knew had loved me from a distance for many years. To please them, I had gone out walking with him a few times, as a friend, but I felt no attraction to him. Deimuiss set all my senses on fire. Not only was he the love of my life, he was also my best friend. He made me laugh, we shared our secrets, our hopes, dreams and fears, and we even cried together when one of our pets died. We turned to each other for the comfort we knew we would find in each other's arms. To me, Deimuiss was my perfect man and always would be, but I could not forget his treachery to me at the cave. It kept returning to haunt me, and for a few moments I felt as if I hated him. There had been no real sign of recognition whatsoever in his ice cold, blue eyes. In fact, there was shock and puzzlement now that I thought about it. He had definitely lost his memory, I thought. When I return, I will tell Mamma everything (what a story!) then we will visit the Mystics and Elders for their advice. I felt certain the Mystics would want to hear my story; something told me they would not be sending me back to The Standing Stones.

Thinking about that day, I wondered if they had known what was going to happen; surely not, I thought. They would not knowingly have sent Grandmamma and Trieainia to their deaths.

Taking a last look at my outfit, I thought of the gold item I had found in the cave. I now knew that it was, in fact, a cigarette carton, and the smell was of tobacco. I would keep it though, as it was the first thing I had picked up that belonged in this time. Fortunately, the herbs seemed to have dispelled the strange smell that had clung to it. Making my way along the passageway, I nervously started to descend the stairs. Now that my head had cleared, little things did not look quite so black, and hopefully I would be able to find out exactly where I was and why Mary seemed so familiar to me. Surely, she could not possibly be related to Pranny? The thought of Pranny made me smile yet again. What a flighty piece she is. No man in the settlement or for miles around was safe from her clutches. 'Look out, look out, Pranny's about,' the youngsters at the camp would cry whenever they caught sight of her. A giggle escaped me as I thought of how her black eyes would flash with fire and anger at the youngsters' words. Hands on generous hips, she would screech shrilly, 'little demons,' back at them. It did not take much to upset her, and the youngsters, knowing this, would always try to get her rattled and generally succeeded. 'Who you after today then Pran?' their words floating joyfully on the wind as they took to their heels, knowing full well that if she caught them, one or more of them at least would get their head slapped.

The young ones were right though. Not many men escaped her clutches. Her eyes would alight on the next man on her list to conquer and the invite was there for all to see. How could they refuse? Pranny is so beautiful: her red blonde hair flows in waves and curls around her beautiful face and down her back like a fiery stream; her strange black eyes glint like chips of obsidian; the majority of men are like putty in her hands. Travelling men and hunting parties from other settlements vie for her favours, and many a fight has erupted over her. A few drinks of mead of an evening, and men, hungry for hearth and home comforts, know they will find their comfort with Pranny. She has no shame. I smiled thinking about her. Knowing that Deimuiss and Carnaan have never submitted to her enticing ways gives me a warm feeling. Suddenly, the thought struck me yet again: I was not there! What if Deimuiss returned, and Pranny stepped into my place? Not only with Deimuiss but Carnaan as well? Jealousy seared me like a knife. Would they be able to resist her charms, with me out of the scene?

The injustice of life churned my insides around like Mary's washing machine. Now where did that name come from, I wondered? I knew immediately what it was despite never having seen or heard of a washing machine before; and it seemed, the longer I was in this household, the more knowledge I was gaining by the minute.

Placing my hand on the carved (it was of an owl) newel of the banister, slowly, I descended the stairs into my new life.

Chapter 6

David was deep in thought as he waited in the kitchen for Elvaennia to come down. Earlier that day, knowing that Elvaennia was going to be in the cave sometime during the day, he knew it was up to him to meet her and escort her to the farm. He hoped the journey through time would not prove too difficult for her. It was always a nerve-wracking occasion when one of the 'others' was due to arrive; he never knew what state they would be in or how long it would take for them to recover enough to be taken to the farmhouse. He truly hoped she would not be too exhausted.

This time traveller was different; in so much as he knew the girl was to be the last to be transported to the cave that was under their watch. It would be strange, he thought, once their job had finished. What would they do? Perhaps they would return to their own time. He would have to ask his mother what she had planned.

Now he was approaching the cave. He knew it was too early for the girl to be there, but headed in that direction just in case. Glancing towards the cave entrance, he saw a glint of silver sparkling in the sunlight. It disappeared almost immediately, but he knew straightaway that the girl was here earlier than he had expected; and was pleased at his forethought in arriving early.

He hurried along the dusty field track, knowing she would be frightened, at finding herself alone into a strange environment.

He was shocked when he saw the beautiful young woman cowering in fright inside the cave. His heart went out to her and one look into her beautiful, silvery grey eyes and he found, to his astonishment, that he was falling in love with her. Never had he been so impressed by a woman's beauty and delicate fragility before; he wanted to protect this frail-looking female and take care of her forever, to take away that desperate lost look that surrounded her very being. Sadly, he knew she was not for him; that another held her heart and always would. Like the girl, he had a job of work to do and he could not allow himself to become emotionally involved with *anyone*, let alone a girl from another time. However, to his dismay, he knew she had stolen his heart forever when he had looked into her wonderful eyes framed beneath the longest eyelashes he had ever seen. Her eyes held the secrets of time in their hauntingly beautiful depths. He knew, without doubt, he would love her for eternity.

He looked forward to having a long chat with Elvaennia at sometime in the future, about the settlement from where she had travelled. Not yet though. He had to wait for his mother's permission, as she was 'The Boss'. Suddenly, he was roused from his musings by a sound. He jumped from his seat and strode towards the door. His jaw dropped in admiration when he saw Elvaennia standing on the wide staircase. She looked so stunningly beautiful; the young man was temporarily speechless.

He swallowed hard. 'Are you okay? Would you like a drink? Tea, coffee or fruit drink?' He was embarrassed to hear his voice squeaking. Catching a look of puzzlement chase across her beautiful features, he sensed her nervousness. Drawing her into the kitchen, he motioned towards a straight backed, wooden chair that had a beautifully embroidered cushion pad on it. He promptly presented her with a soft drink. 'As it's so warm, this will cool you down. It's freshly squeezed oranges.'

Smiling her thanks, Elvaennia sniffed the glass, warily taking a sip; never having tasted oranges before, she was pleasantly surprised at the piquant taste and swallowed the glass's contents in one gulp – much to David's amusement. He quickly fetched another drink.

Elvaennia wondered what on earth was going to happen to her now. Was she to return to the cave? Looking around the well-appointed kitchen, she realised this was the hub of the family's life; and while she was not a part of this family, she did not feel particularly out of place. In fact, in a strange way, she felt she belonged. Obviously, she reasoned with herself that she would have to find somewhere to settle before nightfall, and try to form a plan of how to return to the settlement. She needed time to herself, to think and absorb all the knowledge she had acquired in the last few hours, and also, to come to terms with all that had happened. She was exhausted in both mind and body.

Placing the empty glass on the table, Elvaennia gave David a beautiful smile that he found heart-stoppingly wonderful. Thanking him for everything that he and Mary had done for her, she headed for the door.

Bounding after the slim, young girl – how he longed to stroke that silvery fall of hair and gaze into the silver grey depths of her eyes – catching her by her arm, he asked:

'Where are you going?'

'Back to the cave.'

'You cannot return to the cave, young lady. Come, it is time we talked.'

'My people at the settlement will be wondering where I am. I am lost and have to find my way home immediately.'

'Well, tell me the name of the place where you live.'

Hesitating now, Elvaennia was reluctant to say, but then why not? She had nothing to be ashamed of. Gazing at him, silver eyes shining as brightly as her hair, she replied, smiling with pride. 'It is known as the Calegi settlement near the Hill of the Spirits.'

For a second, Elvaennia thought he knew exactly where she meant, but then his handsome face went blank to be replaced immediately with a smile.

Chewing his lip, David said:

'Wait, let me find a map.'

'A map? What on earth is that?' she wondered? She could hear him running up the stairs along a passageway. She heard a door slam, followed by a few bangs and thumps and there he was, back again.

Spreading a large sheet of paper across the table, David pointed out the farmhouse (this clearly meant nothing to her) in relation to the cave.

Concentrating hard on the map details, suddenly, everything became as clear as crystal to her and with a finger she traced a line back from the cave; past what she called the Hill of the Spirits – David's eyebrows shot up when she mentioned it again – and her finger pointed to an area near an old quarry on Cannock Chase.

'This is it. This is where the settlement was.'

Her eyes lit up – a mysterious silver grey. Her beautiful eyelashes swept the blush of her cheek as she looked up at him with a huge smile.

'Yes, this is the place. I know it from the landscape on the map. It is the exact area.'

He was perplexed and sat at the table pondering on the problem. Running his fingers through his mass of brown hair, he thought, 'Yes, now that I think of it, she is right. That's exactly where it was. But I cannot tell her, so I will have to fob her off somehow.'

'Are you sure, Elvaennia? Certain you have the right place? Personally, (he swallowed hard on his lie) I have no knowledge of this place you speak of.'

Nodding excitedly, her hair swaying as silver as her eyes, she asked longingly, 'Let me show you David. I know exactly where it is.'

Now he knew he was in big trouble, and regretted showing her the map. He knew his mother did not want him discussing anything of Elvaennia's past. *She* was the boss, not him.

Watching the emotions chase across his face, Elvaennia acknowledged to herself that the settlement was no longer there. She could tell by his face that he had no wish to discuss her past life. After all, thinking about it, why should it mean anything to him? She was a stranger who he had happened upon in an old, sandy cave. Why should he be interested in her, let alone her past? This was hard to accept but she had to recognize that she was in the year 2007 now. Her world had disappeared centuries ago. How could she possibly expect anyone to believe she had led a previous life, and that she knew where the settlement had been? Knowledge was being constantly fed to her. She longed to retire and sleep the exhaustion away.

Her eyes misted over and David felt a rush of sympathy like no other he had ever known. Her hurt became his hurt and he ached to comfort the stunningly beautiful, young girl sitting facing him.

Only an iron will prevented him clasping her to him. He wanted to whisper words of love and endearments to her, but he knew that Elvaennia could never be his. Nevertheless, he ached to take her in his arms and hold her close. If he physically could, he would erase the name Deimuiss from her mind and replace it with his. For a second, a cruel smile stole over his face. Elvaennia caught a glimpse of it and drew back, momentarily startled. Realising what had happened; he gave her a beaming smile and turned his hypnotic gaze on her.

For a second, Elvaennia felt a longing for the comfort of his arms, wanting the strength and security of this man wrapped around her.

The spell was broken, as, hearing his mother coming down the stairs; he gently squeezed Elvaennia's hand. 'Come, little one. Time for you to take a rest. We can talk later.'

Giving him a grateful smile, she got up from the chair as he called:

'Mother, Elvaennia is going to rest for a while before supper.'

Mary literally bounced back into the kitchen; much to Elvaennia's amusement. How light she is on her feet, she thought. For such a small, plump person, she dashes about like a 12-year-old. 'Oh Trieainia, my dear sister,' she gasped, remembering what had happened to her beautiful 12-year old sister at the cave.

'Elvaennia?'

Seeing the ghastly pallor of her face, Mary quickly ushered the younger woman to an easy chair by the window.

'What ails you child? You looked fit to pass out for a minute.'

Knowing she could not tell Mary what had upset her, Elvaennia quickly thought to say she had felt dizzy again.

'If you're sure you are okay, lass.' Nodding, Elvaennia got up from the chair, and slowly, with Mary's assistance, made her way back upstairs to her bedroom.

Lying on the bed, she thought how wonderfully comfortable it was;

comparing it briefly to the bed of sweet smelling heather and soft grasses, she was more used to back at home. However, she barely had time to think of this, as she drifted off into a deep, healing sleep. No spirits of the past haunted her dreams. Nothing of the present or the future intruded. The sleep she had craved to heal her shattered body and senses took over her completely, preparing her for the important work that lay ahead in her future.

When she awoke, Elvaennia replayed everything that had happened that day and eventually led her to this rambling farmhouse with its huddle of outbuildings and barns, not far from the Hill of the Spirits.

~

Downstairs in the kitchen, David and Mary sat over a cup of tea, talking about the beautiful, young girl who had entered their lives.

Having retrieved Elvaennia's few clothes from her bedroom, Mary held the cloak up for her son to see.

'Beautiful, isn't it?' she asked, running her hands over and through the soft red layers of fur. Her fingers strayed to the gold chain. Seeing it hang loosely down the cloak front, the couple could see the precious stones that were interwoven into the chain.

Raising his eyebrows, David took out his glasses to take a closer look.

'My goodness, mother,' he breathed in shock, this chain is worth a fortune.'

Nodding her head, Mary again ran her fingers lightly over the chain.

'So beautiful – like its owner.'

She glanced across at him, her eyes dark with anxiety.

'Now what do we do?'

Looking round to make sure she was not overheard, Mary repeated, 'She will be the last one, you know.'

'Yes mother. I meant to talk to you about that. What do we do when she returns?'

'How do you mean, David?'

Sighing, David rested his elbows on the table and head in hand he said wearily.

'You know exactly what I mean mother. Where do we return to?'

Mary hesitated, her eyes clouded over with worry for a moment; then her natural resilience re-asserted itself.

'Let's not worry yet awhile son. Something will turn up for us. It always does.'

With a huge sigh, David got up from the table, knowing full well that he would get no more information from his mother that day.

'We will discuss it again soon then mother. I have plans to make, as well you know.'

Hearing a note of impatience in her son's voice, Mary started flitting around the kitchen, moving ornaments and vases of wild flowers a few inches then putting them back in their original places. 'Course we will son. Everything will be fine.' She scurried on, getting cooking utensils together for the next meal.

'Sure sign she is worried,' David thought, making his way towards the door. 'She's scatting round the kitchen like a demented cat. Mother is always like this when she is worried. This all needs a great deal of thought. I will go to feed the animals and lock up as I go round. Maybe I will find the answer on my rounds.'

He slammed the door louder than normal.

'Well, really!' she called indignantly.

Then, immediately regretting the sharpness of her tone and not wanting an atmosphere to develop between them, she shouted after his retreating figure:

'I'll get supper ready while you're out and keep a check on Elvaennia, if that's all right with you?'

'Okay.' His voice floated through the open window as he strode across the farmyard.

Mary pottered around her homely kitchen, preparing supper for the three of them. 'Hope Elvaennia likes beef pie,' she pondered, placing a small vase of the wild flowers in the centre of the table. I know she will like these cornflowers; they will remind her of the settlement. If there was one thing Mary liked, it was the wild flowers that grew in abundance in her garden and many other areas of the farm. They brightened her days as the wonderful scents drifted in through the kitchen windows, bringing summer into the house. After the blooms died, Mary collected the seedpods and left them to dry, ready to plant out next year.

Mary also enjoyed embroidery, and was always trotting out into her garden and around the farm with her digital camera – taking what she called her 'heavenly photographs'. She used these in her embroidery designs, mainly stitching them in the late autumn and winter months when she was not needed quite so much on the farm. Numerous embroidered pictures adorned the walls of the farm. Visitors to the farm often remarked how beautiful they were, much to Mary's astonishment – she was an extremely modest person. Of course, there had been hers and Davids other work that had kept them even busier over the preceding years. She hoped Elvaennia would be the last visitor to the farmhouse, as she felt she strongly needed a rest; though she had to admit there was something about Elvaennia that was different from the other visitors. But of course, she ruminated – she was from the settlement; so obviously, that was a huge link in the chain. She hoped things would work out right for her. Worry lines creased her brow as she thought of David. She had not missed the furtive glances he had been casting Elvaennia's way. 'She is not for you son,' she muttered beneath her breath as she sliced the beef pie ready for their supper. Dishing up the vegetables, worry etched the sides of her mouth:

'She's the last one, thank goodness and I hope David doesn't get involved with her – we can't have last minute complications at this stage of our lives.'

The smell of the herbs and Worcester sauce she had used in her beef and onion pie drifted across the kitchen and she sniffed the air, appreciating the delicious aroma.

Mary prized her wild herbs and had a huge stock in her kitchen cupboard. Years ago, her mother had passed all the family knowledge of the herbs' medicinal properties on to her. She rarely visited the local health centre in Sandy Lane, preferring her own 'dispensary' – as she called it. Members of her family and friends called on her frequently to ask what she recommended for their various ailments. It seemed to them that she had a herb for every problem they asked about. She was always willing to give advice and distribute a herbal remedy to them. On the rare occasion when she did not know what to prescribe, she would look through her great grandmother's book of herbal potions. She had long admired her ancestor's beautiful writing and wished her own was as good.

Thinking of all she knew, Mary's thoughts skittered about in her head; could she risk telling Elvaennia now, or would it be best to tell her at a later date? She thought the latter would probably be better. After all, she reasoned, the young woman had gone through a lot in the past 24 hours; so it might be best to let her come to terms with the loss of her relatives and her journey into this time. She would leave the talk for a while and perhaps let her know a little at a time. Nodding her head, as if agreeing with her decision, the woman gave a small, self-satisfied smile and, if Elvaennia had seen it, she would again have been convinced that she had seen a glimpse of someone she knew.

Chapter 7

A few weeks later:

Rubbing my eyes, I awoke with a jolt. This place was so noisy. You just could not seem to escape it. Inside or outside, there was always noise; so different from my other life where, in the early mornings, there were only the sounds of the birds singing and the animals out in the reserve. Lying in bed at the farmhouse, I could hear the sweet sound of a blackbird singing in a tree outside my window, and the sound of the animals in the fields; but in the background there was the whoosh of the car tyres as they sped along the busy A51. I heard the sound of an ambulance rushing towards the hospital at Stafford with its precious cargo. I knew the baby would arrive safely, much to his mother's joy. Now and again, a police car would speed its way up Swift Lane, past the farmhouse, intent on helping some poor person in trouble.

Smiling to myself, I snuggled back down beneath the soft and fresh-smelling lavender duvet; recalling my fear of the previous evening, when once more I had seen the strange lights through my bedroom window and heard again what I had thought was the swish of horses' tails – identical almost to the sound I had heard that last day in my time. I now knew what we had seen and heard was this time breaking through into our time. I shuddered at the thought. It was almost as if they – whoever they were – had come to collect me. I still did not understand why I had been 'taken'. Surely, there must be a reason for bringing me through into this century.

It was like the huge jigsaws that David tackled sometimes late of an evening. I had seen a few, but he kept the majority of them in the loft, saying they were too large to keep downstairs. He had promised that one day he would show them to me. I thought the missing pieces were like my life: disjointed and out of place, with huge areas missing.

Pulling the sweet smelling duvet over my head to shut out the noise of the traffic, I thought of all that had happened in the last few weeks. It was amazing, to say the least. Here I was, a Calegi girl from a time some thousands of years ago, living a life (quite privileged compared to some people I had met) in 2007. Unbelievable! What would my family think of this? I still lived in hope of meeting Deimuiss and returning to our home. I kept these thoughts to myself, not wishing to upset my hosts, Mary and David, who, though they were more than kind to me, I sensed knew far more than they were telling me. I am more than convinced that Deimuiss is here somewhere, and I long for my instincts to be proved right.

Suddenly, remembering that Mary was taking me to Tamworth today, 'to acquaint me with another town,' she had said, I leapt out of bed, showered, dressed (skinny jeans and top) and flew downstairs. I think I could get used to wearing jeans and tops for ease-of-wearing; plus I now owned a pair of wonderful comfortable trainers – how I loved them! I must admit to missing my beautiful clothing and jewels from my other life at the settlement. Nonetheless, I prized these clothes also.

Mary had just finished cooking a huge breakfast of bacon, eggs, tomatoes and fried bread – delicious. I thought how easily I had adjusted to the food and drink of the 21st century. It was so different from anything I had ever eaten before, but I loved it. In particular, I adored McDonalds and their delicious McChicken Sandwich, or their Beef DeLuxe with bacon and fries. In addition, the ice cold, fizzy pop was something else. Mary would watch me tuck in and her eyes would open wide.

'Where do you put it all Elvaennia? You are so tiny and you eat like a horse. Where does it all go to?'

She would gasp in astonishment as I wiped up the last of the tomato sauce I had put on my fries.

I could quickly become a fast food addict, but kept myself in check as much as I could, which was difficult because Rugeley town is full of food outlets. It amazes me how one small town can have so many. Every other shop seems to be selling take away food of some description or another. The number of charity shops also astonished me when I first went into the town, but I must admit to enjoying a browse around them. Some of the stuff fascinates me, particularly the old jewellery. A few of the designs are reminiscent of the jewellery we made at the settlement while the men were out hunting for food.

'You're as thin as a rake, so get that down you girl.'

Mary's voice cut into my thoughts as she placed an enormous pile of toast in front of me. It is delicious, particularly when spread with Mary's thick, chunky, homemade marmalade – another taste I had acquired. One thing I missed more than anything was the sweet, nutty taste of the spelt wheat. Mamma often used it to make soups and flat biscuits. It was delicious and I longed to taste it again. When added to stews, the white of the grain gives a wonderful flavour. Idly, I wondered what my family would think of the world I now lived in. They would be amazed, and unable to comprehend it without having the knowledge that I had acquired on arriving.

'No time for going down memory lane.'

Mary interrupted my daydreaming. It was as if she knew I had drifted back into my past, but how could she have? She had no idea where I was from. On the other hand, did she? Maybe David had told her that I was from the Calegi Tribe, but surely, she would have mentioned it? I often thought how extraordinary it was that she and David had accepted a complete stranger into their family without question; and some of the looks she gave me, led me, at times, to think she knew more than she cracked on. What an expression I thought, smiling to myself 'cracked on indeed!' Why on earth, I wondered again, did they never question me?

'Make haste, lass. We haven't got all day.'

Hardly drawing breath, she went on,

'If I have time when we return, I am going to make a fruit cake with wholegrain flour. I know you are going to love it. It will do you good after all that fast food you've been eating.'

Not quite spelt wheat, but I did enjoy wholegrain flour, particularly the bread, so the fruitcake would be interesting to taste. I looked forward to it.

Hastily finishing my breakfast, in no time at all, I was ready to leave. I didn't want to miss a minute of this day out. I knew it was going to be interesting but I did not realise how much.

I was looking forward to going to Tamworth. I had heard it was a pretty town with a long history. Moreover, of course – I remembered 'seeing the castle'; not once, but twice. Once was when I had been playing with the other children as a young girl, and the other time at the cave with Deimuiss where I had seen some of those extraordinary paintings. I jumped suddenly as I remembered: of course, I had 'seen' the farmhouse and barns depicted, and also Mary and David. I recalled how the artist had depicted David's green eyes. How true the painting had been. Mary interrupted my train-of-thought again.

'Quickly, Elvaennia. We haven't got all day you know.' From her voice, I knew she was joking. Nevertheless, I followed her out to the car, not wanting to delay her unnecessarily.

It did not take long to reach Tamworth. The roads were fairly traffic-free and we were soon bowling along. I admired the scenery, the wild flowers bursting forth; the hedgerows were aglow with white and pink flowers; blood red poppies swayed in the fields; cow parsley (Queen Anne's lace, Mary informed me) and ragged robin vied for a place in the picturesque scene. How different everywhere was from my time, I thought to myself. The houses fascinated me and I wanted to explore each and every one of them. All the different modes of transport had my head spinning at times – cars, buses, trains – their noise, I am more than certain, I would never get used to! All these new words tasted so different to me. Mary had trouble understanding my meaning when I said I tasted them, but it was the only way I could describe what I meant.

Mary had told me she was going to give me a few driving lessons then pass me on to an instructor. She said she wanted me to have my independence; that it would be good for me. What a lovely, kind, generous person she is! I am looking forward to my lessons – another challenge. She mentioned there was a car going begging in the garage, and I was welcome to it when I had passed my test. Independence beckoned.

When we reached Tamworth, we were fortunate enough to be able to park on the car park at the Ventura Trading Estate. It was crowded, and the shops looked very inviting. My eyes were on stalks as we drove around looking for a parking space. Mary told me how busy the trading estate became at weekends, bank holidays and Christmas. She said, 'Don't even think about shopping here then.'

We strolled out of the car park, crossed a busy road – I enjoyed pressing the crossing buttons that stopped the traffic – and we headed off towards the town. Walking over a bridge that spanned a river, I was delighted to see so many swans, such beautiful creatures. Mary mentioned that she had been fortunate, in the past, to see black swans. I envied her that. As we walked towards the castle gardens, I thought how attractive they looked from this distance, filled with red geraniums and other colourful flowers. I was eager to see the castle and I urged Mary on. She quickened her pace, remarking, 'Anything for a bit of peace. I expect you have something else planned afterwards?'

'Erm, no, I haven't actually.' I grinned at her, almost stopping her in her tracks for once.

'Nothing planned. That's not like you at all.' Her mouth curved into one of her beautiful, motherly smiles. I gave her a hug, thinking yet again how lucky I was to have met her when I 'arrived' in this time.

As soon as I saw the castle, my heart missed a few beats. It was the castle; not as I had seen it in my other lifetime, but I recognised it as being the same from seeing it as a painting in the cave. Obviously, all traces of the early wooden construction had long since disappeared. The castle had been rebuilt since those times. How, and why, had I seen it so many thousands of years before as a wooden structure, and a few years later in the cave? Of course, the name Tamworth had been given to me – but again, I wondered why?

Walking up the steep incline and around the perimeter of the castle was very impressive. I was disappointed to see that it did not open until after midday. Shrugging my shoulders, we agreed we would pop back at a later date. There was always another day to see inside the castle. On leaving the castle area, I decided to see if I could see the black swans on the river that Mary had mentioned earlier. I felt drawn towards the riverside.

She told me she was just 'popping' into Tamworth, and would catch up with me by the river. 'Don't get straying too far, lass. I don't want to lose you.'

Spotting a bench in a recess in the castle wall, I decided to rest my feet for a few minutes before walking to the river. It felt strange but right somehow. The bricks felt mellow and warm; welcoming, drawing me back into their history. I felt part of the castle's history. Looking across towards the river, I tried to imagine how the scene must have looked centuries ago. I watched the people walking past me, intent on their daily lives. I wondered who they were and where they were hurrying. I could hear children chattering away to their mothers, and I wondered if I would ever fulfil my longing to be with Deimuiss and have his children. Behind the children's chatter, I could hear the canter of horses' hooves. Everything around me became shrouded in mist. Then, as it slowly began to clear, I heard angry voices shouting about an invasion. Suddenly, a strong pair of hands wrapped themselves around me. A man's voice whispered, 'Whesh not my little one. You are safe.' Opening my eyes in terror, wondering what was happening, I found to my utmost delight I was looking into Deimuss's deep blue eyes. Where on earth was I? How was I with Deimuiss? Was I dreaming? Was this one of my visions?

'Oh my goodness. My love. My life. Where have you been?'

Deimuiss was here with me. I had found him again. He was alive, here with me. Happiness bubbled up inside me like the waterfalls that leap and sing across the Chase. I could not remember a time I had ever been so happy.

'I thought I had lost you forever.'

Then, I remembered what he had done. Stepping back, I pointed my finger accusingly at him.

'Why Deimuiss? Why did you murder Grandmamma and Trieainia?'

Tears spurted from my eyes as memories of that awful day returned to haunt me.

'Elvaennia my love, whatever are you talking about? I would never harm another person. How can you think such a thing of me?'

'But you left us and joined The Delphs.'

He took a step towards me; I stepped backwards away from him until my back was against the wall.

'I certainly did not!' He remonstrated loudly, 'I am no murderer of women and children.'

I suddenly felt panicky, asking, 'Where on earth am I?' I gazed wildly around me; suddenly realising I was high up inside the castle. Looking through a window slit, I could see we were indeed very far above the ground up in the old wooden fortress that I had seen all those years ago. Gazing down, I could see pigs, cattle, geese, hens. It looked as if there was a market being held in the compound. Men were calling out their wares, and women were competing with them as they shouted at their children to behave. It was dank and cold inside this small room. It smelt of the green mould that was running down the walls. I shivered in shock as well as astonishment at finding myself in this ancient stronghold.

Deimuiss smiled. Stepping in front of me, he reached across and began stroking my hair, trying to calm me. He nuzzled his face into my neck.

Drawing back, I realized he was wearing very strange clothing indeed. Looking up, I saw that he was studying me with a strange look on his face.

'What are you wearing Elvaennia?'

'I could ask you the same,' I retorted spiritedly.

'Always my little sparkler, aren't you my sweet?'

Drawing me closer, I felt the warmth of his body. For the first time in nearly two years, I felt at peace within the shelter of this wonderful man's presence.

'I have been fighting for Hereward at the Isle of Ely, my little one;

helping to save the treasures of Peterborough Abbey. But my main job, as always, is healing the sick and wounded.'

Now I was more confused than ever as I did not understand what Deimuiss was telling me.

'You mean you are working in this time? You are no longer living in our time?'

He nodded, his long, black, curly hair shimmering and dancing even in this light.

'Yes my love. The healing is my work for all my lifetimes.'

How did he know these things, I wondered and what's more, why had he never told me? Was I now going to stay with Deimuiss in this century and not return to 2007? Mind racing, I wondered what Mary would think when she couldn't find me by the river. Would she think I had fallen in and drowned? Maybe she might think I had been abducted. My thoughts were in disarray. How on earth had I found Deimuiss in this tiny room in the fortress? What's more, was I now going to lead a life in this century? Life was certainly getting more and more complicated by the minute.

'Oh no,' I sighed, reluctantly pulling away from him I walked around the small room, my footsteps echoing loudly on the uneven wooden floor, I noted how sparsely furnished the room was. It contained a small table, a couple of ancient, three-legged wooden stools, and that was all. No wonder my footsteps echoed.

'Deimuiss, we need to talk.'

Placing my hand on his arm, I drew him close again, longing to be near the man I loved. I felt out of my depth yet over the moon. To be reunited with my lost love; was all I asked. However, I was extremely concerned to find myself in an alien landscape once again. I desperately wanted to know everything he could tell me of where he had been and what he had been doing.

'That much is true, my little one.' He gave me a heart-stopping smile. No wonder I loved him; his beautiful, black, curly hair and deep blue eyes; he was so tall, when he wrapped his arms around me I felt so safe and protected from everything and everyone.

Nevertheless, I had to know what had happened. Why had he disappeared and then turned up at the hunting cave with our sworn enemies?

'Tell me what happened to you, Deimuiss. You simply disappeared the day you went hunting. I have been out of my mind with worry for you, as have your parents and everyone at the settlement.'

Taking a deep breath, I continued, 'We searched and searched in vain, then something so awful happened to Grandmamma and Trieainia at the bivouac on the hillside. You were there with the treacherous Delphs.'

On hearing my words, Deimuiss pulled away from me.

'No, no, my sweet. I have never been with The Delphs, never. I will tell you what happened, and then how I came to be here, but first, tell me how you came to be here at the castle when you went to 2007.'

'How on earth did you know that?'

My mouth dropped open in amazement. I was unbelievably shocked that he could stand here in a distant century and know that I had been living in 2007.

Striding across the small room, he put a hand over my mouth.

'Be careful my little one. The flies are even more dangerous in this era than in the 21st century. We don't want you dying of some foul disease.'

'Deimuiss, we are just talking round each other. Please let us sit down and talk.'

As much as I wanted to be hugged and kissed by this beautiful man, first, I wanted to hear his story. My head was beginning to spin like a merry-go-round. Pointing at one of the three-legged, battered, old stools, I made my way to the other one.

Holding hands across the small table, I shivered. It was so cold and damp in this old tower. It also stank to high heaven, and I hoped against hope that we would soon be in a warmer environment.

'Please tell me Deimuiss, from the beginning, what has happened and more to the point, what is happening. You are right; I have been living in 2007. Let me show you what I found in the old hunting cave; it belongs to you.'

Feeling in the pouch that I wore constantly around my waist, my fingers found the gold package. The mist descended, swirling around me. Deimuiss was disappearing into it. I screamed, 'No, no, come with me please Deimuiss. I cannot lose you again.' I held my arms out, imploring him to come with me. Tears streamed down my face, as I was whirled upwards once again, through the mists of time and space.

I was distraught, beyond words, to have found him after all this time, only to lose him yet again. Was he lost to me forever? Would I ever see him again? Depression again settled its murky, black cloud over me and the way ahead seemed bleak indeed. My head felt heavy and cloudy; my brain was clogged with my tears. Life would never be the same again. How could this possibly happen? To find, and then lose him, within such a short space of time was unbelievable.

Where was I being taken to now? Fear clasped me in its tight jaws. Oh, please not another century where I would be unknown and not know a living soul. I would be so afraid. 'Oh, please,' I prayed, 'take me home to my family.' How I longed to be with them, not drifting through time and space with no real family or home. I sobbed, heartbroken at the loss of Deimuiss and now I had no idea where I was going. Life seemed suddenly unbearable and, for a fleeting moment, I wondered if the Winter of Despair might be a better place to be. But reason quickly re-asserted itself and I stifled that thought as quickly as I had thought it. Anywhere was better than that awful, living hellhole.

'Elvaennia, Elvaennia!'

A voice was calling me as I spiralled upwards away from Hereward's time in the 11th century.

'Wake up child. Are you ill?'

Mary was gently shaking my shoulder.

'Mary? What is it? What's wrong?'

I shook my head, trying to clear it of the fuzziness that had befallen me.

Oh dear, this was so unnerving. I was back in the 21st century and poor Mary was looking extremely worried. Glancing down, I was relieved to see I was still dressed in the clothing I had donned that morning. Phew, that was a relief to say the least.

'I'm fine,' I said brightly, feeling anything but fine. I was certainly not going to tell her what had happened to me. I could not share my joy with anyone else now; meeting Deimuiss again had been nothing short of wonderful but I had lost him yet again. How could I have been so stupid?

I remembered what he had said about healing people through time, and wondered: how many other lifetimes he had lived or was going to live? Were we doomed to be forever apart? What was my part meant to be? Why was I living in this century? I remembered the shadows in that strange little hallway at the farmhouse. I puzzled for a moment. Thinking about it, I had not seen that hallway since. I had to find it, I resolved, and talk to the poor souls trapped within its confines. Why were they trapped, unable to escape? Maybe I could help them leave; move on. It must be horrible to be ensnared in such a small space. I felt quite ashamed that I had forgotten about them, and responsible for prolonging their suffering. 'Poor things,' I murmured. 'I will go to them when we arrive home.' I thought it was strange that neither Mary nor David had ever picked up on them, but then I reasoned that perhaps the shadows had not approached them. I decided not to mention them to either Mary or David, feeling it wise to keep quiet about the shadows. On reflection, the shadows might be able to tell me a lot.

Mary slipped her arm round me comfortingly. 'We will go home, my luv.' She almost crooned the words to me. 'The summer heat must have disorientated you.'

I agreed with her, knowing full well that the summer heat had nothing to do with it. I was determined, now, to unravel this mystery. How had Deimuiss travelled to Tamworth Castle? For that matter, why was I living a life in the 21st century? Now I wondered were there others who time-travelled to different eras? How could I find the answers to all my questions?

Mary stowed me safely in the front passenger seat and we were soon heading back to Rugeley. I dozed off for a few minutes, the latest time travel experience having exhausted me.

Waking from my nap, I sensed, rather than saw, Mary keep glancing towards me. I knew she was longing to know what had happened, but I was determined to think about it first – and do a little research. I wondered anew what Mary and David actually knew. Many times, I sensed that they understood far more than they had ever told me and sometime soon, I was determined to ask them outright. For now though, I needed time to think.

My longing for Deimuiss had returned tenfold and I berated myself at wasting those precious minutes at the castle. I ached to be back in his arms, gazing into his deep, navy blue eyes. To speak to him and see him smile had been blissful. Now I was desolate at losing him again. Then, remembering his treachery, I realised there was no way we could ever be together again after what he had done. I could not love a murderer. The small voice intruded into my thoughts:

'You still love him, Elvaennia and always will.'

Perhaps I was wrong and it had not been Deimuiss in the hunting cave. I was so confused.

Looking across at me, Mary said, 'If you are feeling okay, Elvaennia, we could go back the pretty route?'

'Fine.' I nodded. I did feel a bit more settled and it would be good to see more of the area where I now lived, and to see how much it had changed since my time at the settlement. I decided to do what I normally did – think about my worries later when I went to bed.

Chapter 8

Driving down various lanes and through numerous small villages, I was impressed by the beautiful cottages and the countryside, as we swept past. We came to a village called Mavesyn Ridware, when something made me say, 'Turn right here Mary, please.' Without a murmur, she indicated and proceeded along a narrow, winding lane.

'Stop! Stop!' I shouted. Slamming the brakes on, we came to a hasty halt outside a small, ancient looking church. Mary lifted her eyebrows. With a smile in her voice, she said, 'This is as bad as taking the driving test.'

'It was here, wasn't it?' I said dreamily.

'What?'

'Come on Mary, you know.'

I really thought the time for pretence was now long past, but Mary obviously did not seem to think so.

'What are you talking about Elvaennia? What was here?'

Sighing, I decided not to quibble with her for now.

'There was a settlement here in my time. They had a large wooden henge, and the causeway was over there.'

I pointed across the fields, from the church, in the direction of the river. I saw, through the mists of time, the roundhouses and tribe members going about their daily tasks. I could taste the smoke from their fires; hear the sheep calling across the fields; see the wild horses running, filled with the joy of freedom; the cattle grazing in the fields – far larger than today's cows. Everything looked so normal. The tribe's people certainly looked happy as they worked industriously in the different work places around the settlement. Young children were playing happily together. I knew their names and their families. Dogs were running around looking for mischief no doubt. Our settlement was no great distance away and we would often get together to socialise. At times, we would take goods along the river to other settlements, to trade or sell. The river provided a good mode of transport as, at times, the tracks became impassable due to awful weather conditions, and the traders could become stuck for days on end. Furthermore, many tribal outcasts waited to prey on the unwary travellers. Using the river was a much faster and safer method to visit and trade with our contemporaries. Not that there weren't river thieves, but there was far more chance of escaping their clutches along the waterway.

I knew all the people who lived here; they were our distant relatives and friends. My eyes filled with tears as memories returned of long, warm summer evenings spent beside the river with family and friends.

I recalled that one morning, as the sun was rising through a pink dawn, I had taken myself for a walk along the riverbank. Pausing, I sat on a log; drinking in the beautiful scene, smelling the warmth of the summer earth. Thinking I had heard someone or something, I glanced to my side and was astonished to see a group of ancient Druids approaching the wooden henges in the field. It was half-light, and I watched, amazed, as the Druids walked around the henges. At each one, the group would halt. One man would then leave the group and stand in front of a henge, head erect, facing towards the East. Each Druid knew their particular henge. When the last one had taken his place, they began a mystical chanting. As the sun slowly became more visible, no birds sang, no animal sounds could be heard; just the mystical chanting travelling towards the sun as it rose higher through the dawn light, its rays touching the white of the Druids robes, turning them into shimmering gold. A mist descended over the henges, the air became colder and colder. I shivered, despite the growing summer warmth. As suddenly as the mist had appeared, it dispersed, leaving the mystical site deserted. The Druids had disappeared. I blinked in disbelief. Where had they gone? Had I imagined what I had just seen? No, they had definitely been there and I knew I would see them again at some time in the future. They were a force for good, and they respected the earth and its secrets. The scene had haunted me through the years, and now, as I recalled it, I realised that I had travelled far back that morning to a distant age – almost, I should imagine, to the beginning of time. A great sadness stole across me, remembering how beautiful this land had once been. Now, its resources were being used so fast, it was frightening to think of how it might end.

Sensing my gloom, Mary switched the engine on, and we headed back through the pretty country villages to Rugeley.

'Come on Elvaennia, we're home.'

Mary's sing-song voice brought me back to the present and I clambered wearily out of the car.

It was hot and I ran upstairs to my room, and threw myself on the cool lavender scented duvet cover. Tears slid down my cheeks as I remembered the love in Deimuiss's eyes. Where was he now? Was he riding back into danger, going to fight in some pointless war for goodness knows what, or who? Turning over, I tried my hardest to think my way back to his time. I reached for my pouch; I always carried it with me, wanting to keep my past with me in the present. Slipping my hand inside, I tried to find something of my time at the castle inside the bag. Stupidly, of course, I had not thought to pick anything up. Oh, what an idiot, I now suspected if I had some item from a century I wanted to visit, I only need touch it to enter that time at will, assuming the elements were right. Of course, making certain I entered the correct time zone needed to be worked on, as I hadn't a clue how to do this. I was uncertain whether this would work. Maybe it had been a coincidence, my touching the gold packet and being transported back here. Only time would tell.

I realised I must be careful what I touched in my pouch in the future. Taking a peep inside, I saw the herbs were so dry they were turning to dust. The wheat seeds were fine; the scent remained, reminding me strongly of the settlement. I wondered whether there was a certain time to touch the dried herbs, wheat or my jewellery and thus, transport myself back to the settlement; although, all the other times I had touched them, up to now, nothing had happened. My theory looked a bit dodgy, I thought, but maybe if I checked a calendar, or a diary, then certain celebrations – such as Beltane, the Equinox, Midsummer's Eve that I knew of, and possibly, there are others I am unaware of – might be highlighted. If I discovered this, I could then put my plan into action.

I was hugely excited thinking about this, and I tried to remember where Mary kept a calendar. It is strange – I could not recall ever seeing one.

Hearing her working in the kitchen I thought I ought to offer to help. I would also keep my eyes peeled for a calendar.

'There you are Elvaennia,' she called out. 'Feeling better?'

'Yes thanks Mary. Wondered if you needed some help?'

'That's thoughtful of you. Perhaps you could have a quick tidy round for me?'

Delighted to be needed, I gave her a hug and quickly set to tidying the room, keeping my eyes alert for a calendar. I loved the kitchen. Despite its size, it was so warm and homely, unlike the missing hallway. I had never revisited the hall since that first unpleasant experience on my arrival. Now, remembering my earlier promise, I worked my way towards the kitchen door and walked past the staircase, along the passage and into the hallway. Yet, strangely, it was very different from when I had arrived. I remembered it as being a small, enclosed, unpleasant area. No wonder I had forgotten it. This present hallway was as light and airy as the kitchen with a highly polished floor, just as I had seen in the cave paintings. Remarkable! How strange I had forgotten. However, recalling, the state I had arrived in, I guess it's understandable. I could hear Mary busily working at the sink, so I stepped into the hall. I noticed a small door in the wall that somehow looked out of place. Certain that this was it; I began to make my way towards it. Now I would be able to help the poor, trapped shadows.

'Elvaennia, can you just whisk the cream for me please. We need it for the apple pie.'

Mary's voice floated along the hallway, stopping me in my tracks.

'Yes, on my way Mary.'

Oh, I would have to investigate another day; and keep my eyes open for a calendar, I promised myself, as I headed back to the kitchen.

Whisking the cream brought back memories of life back at the settlement and using wooden paddles to make cream and butter: the hours that had taken; and it took some strength as well. Now look at me, using an electric whisk for the cream – a few seconds and it was done! How life has changed.

As we were eating, David mentioned that he was going for his usual Friday drink with the boys. Mary chipped in, asking whether I would be okay, as she had to pop and see a friend who had been rather poorly.

'I won't be long. She lives this side of Stafford.'

As an afterthought, she added that she had to take me to the local health centre for a health check and some injections, in the near future.

Injections? Scary thought indeed.

Trying to hide my delight that they were both going out, I reassured her that I would be fine; and scurried around, rinsing the crockery and placing it in the 'washing up' machine. I smiled at this modern-day wonder, remembering washing our pots in the stream and drying them in the sunshine. Weather permitting that was. I wondered also about the injections she had mentioned; they did not sound altogether inviting. It also posed the question: how did she know I needed injections? Giving the kitchen a final clean and tidy, I listened out for mother and son. Hearing them leave the house together, I waited with baited breath, listening for the sound of their cars exiting the gravelled drive.

Waiting just a few minutes longer to ensure they hadn't forgotten anything, I put Cederic, the cat, outside so he could have a good old prowl around. Calling Pip, the family collie, to follow me, I dived into the study, immediately switching the computer on. I felt my heart begin to race with excitement. Now, I thought, I could have an uninterrupted search.

One of the most brilliant things David had introduced to me was the computer. What a marvellous invention!

David showed me all the programs, from writing in Word, to email, to accounts, and the Internet. I was truly amazed watching him surf the Internet. Given the chance, I could easily, spend endless hours reading about this world on Internet sites. But David refused to let me use the PC without him sitting beside me.

'Too much knowledge is a dangerous thing, my Elvaennia.' I worried that at times he sounded quite possessive of me.

He had said this so firmly, I knew he would brook no argument.

His words infuriated me and I could not wait until the time came when I could log on without him being around. What secrets were hidden from me in his computer, I wondered? With him watching my every move when he allowed me to use it, I felt forced to look at all the women's magazine sites like *Heat Magazine* and *Hello*. I enjoyed them at first, but celebrity culture is not really for me at this time. Something tells me that, in the future, I will be meeting with the 'stars'. However, not now, at this point, all I want to discover is the history of Rugeley and the surrounding areas that are inexplicably linked with my past. I need to discover how they are related. Now's my chance while Mary and David are out.

Logging on to the Internet, I quickly typed 'RUGELEY' into *Yahoo!* (the online search engine). 'Wikipedia' was the first site to catch my eye, it's an on-line encyclopaedia. It was an interesting read, giving a history of the town, then and now. A quick read informed me that Rugeley was listed in the Doomsday Book; and that in medieval times there were iron workings, and a glass-manufacturing site – interesting! In addition, there was more: at one time, the coal industry provided work for a great many of the town's people before it closed down in 1990. Apparently, the town suffered severe hardship due to this, and has never recovered. The pit employed a huge number of local people who have had great difficulty finding subsequent employment.

Reading more, I discovered that, a Doctor William Palmer of Rugeley was executed in Stafford in 1856 – for poisoning a John Parsons Cook – and was implicated in the killing of a number of other people. Not a pleasant character at all! A young woman, Christina Collins, was found murdered in the Trent & Mersey Canal on June 13th 1839. A boatman was later convicted of her murder and executed. Her gravestone is still in the local churchyard of St. Augustine. All very interesting, but I could not relate myself to this information. It certainly seemed that Rugeley had a chequered past. The River Trent and the Trent & Mersey Canal run through the area. Thinking of the river took me back to Mavesyn Ridware and my 'vision' of the Druids. My sixth sense told me I could always call through time for their help, should I ever need it. This thought gave me great comfort. I clicked on the next site: www.rugeleyonline.co.uk now this looked as if it would be a really good read.

There were many excellent photographs of the town, and some interesting history. In fact, I found it fascinating to read of Rugeley through the ages and about the lives of some of the well-known people who had lived here in times gone by. I hadn't realised so much had happened in such a small town. I noticed that the site mentioned a lady who collected and wrote ghost stories. She would be interesting to chat with. I clicked on her website (www.staffordshireghostclub.co.uk). It was interesting and I thought I would contact her soon.

There was a page showing how many people resided in the town. In 2001, the population was around 23,000. I was startled to see that in 1851, the number of residents was well below 5,000. For a few seconds, I tried to imagine how different the area had been in that time, and then, even more striking, compared it with the population in my time.

Still looking for any reference to the Calegi settlement, it seemed so strange that nothing was mentioned about it in any of the links. Surely, we could not have just lived and died, leaving no imprint on the area whatsoever. I knew it was a long time ago but it seemed so odd.

I continued my search but the information evaded me and I felt so frustrated. I logged on to 'eBay'. David often visited this site, looking at all the electronic equipment that was up for auction; but I much preferred the girly things and immediately clicked through to the jewellery site.

My eyes were on stalks. There wasn't just new stuff for sale. There was a vast selection of old jewellery up for auction, and somehow, I didn't think I would ever get to look at all of it. Nonetheless, I was going to have a good try.

Looking at all the different items took me back to when my sister Trieainia and I used to make jewellery together. I pictured her wide, cheery smile and happy chatter as we worked. The two of us had created the gold circlet of jewels that I wore on my cloak. I recalled the day we had made it. We had been so happy working on the design and chatting happily together about our family and our lives. Now I was haunted by my beloved sister's happiness and lightness of spirit. Our closeness had always been a joy to me. Trieainia was such a special person; she would live on in my memory forever. I could not believe I would never see her again. I missed her so much, and always would. Oh, how I longed to return to my family, and grieve for my poor, dead relatives. Perhaps this was to be my punishment, remembering all that I had lost.

The memory of that day faded and I was left with a deep sense of loss. If only I had never visited The Standing Stones that day, I would not be in this time, and my dear relatives would still be alive. Thinking of the gold circlet of jewels, I wondered where they were; and my cloak. I knew Mary had my cloak and other clothes, but she had not mentioned their whereabouts. I needed to know, because when I returned to the settlement (I clung to the fact that one day, I would return to my time), my clothes, my pouch and its contents, were my only links with the past. I yearned to see my family and friends. A deep sadness took hold. Thinking of Trieainia and my Grandmamma, killed by our enemies, The Delphs, I hoped that their deaths would be avenged one day. How awful that they had died through my negligence. I physically ached to hold them, and my remaining family, in my arms. Sadly, I knew that I would never see Grandmamma and Trieainia ever again. I would give up this lifetime in a second if I could return home to a time when they still lived and I could alter the day I walked to the Standing Stones. My thoughts turned to Deimuiss. Had he, by some miracle, returned to the settlement? Briefly, I thought of the man my parents had suggested I take as a friend, Carnaan.

Chapter 9

I had always known that Carnaan loved me, but I had never loved him, not even for a second. For me, there was never any man other than my beloved Deimuiss (still aghast at his treachery!). I had never, to my knowledge, given Carnaan any sign that I was attracted to him in any way whatsoever. My parents often suggested that I should walk out with Carnaan, pointing out that it was bad for me not to have any social life. After all, they said, there was no sign of Deimuiss ever returning. I refused, as I was still in love with Deimuiss. I would occasionally chat to Carnaan if we should meet during the day. Sometimes when I looked into Carnaans pale blue, lustreless eyes, I shuddered and remembered Deimuiss's deep blue eyes filled with love for me. What more could a girl want? One thing that did disconcert me was that Carnaan had no eyelashes. Now I know this is not his fault, but for some reason, it deeply disturbed me. Even when I pretended he was Deimuiss, if I looked into his eyes, I would quickly return to Earth with a huge bump.

My first and only love was so tall and strong. Whenever we met, he would enfold me in his powerful arms, draw me close, and whisper words of love, telling me that I was his for all time and that no one would ever take his place.

'Even in death, you will be mine.'

'And I yours,' I would reply, snuggling deeper into his loving embrace. Then he would kiss me and again I would be lost in his enduring love that would sweep our time together on Earth and onwards through death into the Time Beyond.

It had taken me a long time to accept that perhaps, just perhaps, I would never see Deimuiss in our time again. My parents would urge me to go out and meet with friends, encouraging me to go walking with them across the heath land. 'Make new friends,' they encouraged me, 'you are young and beautiful. Do not waste your youth.'

They would suggest that I could maybe meet with the story group. This was just one of a number of our social events where a group of us young adults met up in one of the homes and exchanged stories that had been passed down (and no doubt embroidered on) through the generations. Alternatively, one of us might make up an original story and share it with the group. Favourite stories were retold, and sometimes added to, in particular, ghost stories. This had been one of the meetings I enjoyed the most, the best stories being the ghost stories. After the meetings, I would hug Deimuiss tightly as we made our way home, praying we did not meet a ghost. He would laugh at my fears and gently chide me saying, 'You have more to fear from our enemies than any ghost you know. Ghosts can't hurt you but the living can.'

'True.'

I would agree, nervously looking around. 'But, I would still prefer not to see one.'

Reflecting on my parents words, I resolved to start going out and about again, to visit the dancing group and release some of my pent-up energy. Perhaps by dancing, I would leave some of my sadness behind. I had always loved dancing with Deimuiss. He was my perfect dancing partner. Often, we would go dancing out on the heathland near the waterfalls. The tinkling sound of the falls was like music to our ears and it was magical, dancing under the summer night skies with the man I loved. The time that is imprinted on my memory forever is dancing into the Northern Lights – never has anything affected me so deeply. We knew the spirits of the lights danced with us; each light brings its own being who joins in this wondrous night of joy, sharing their secrets of the time before and the times yet to come. We were welcomed into their mysterious world as they embraced us with their lights. We danced with them until they faded and returned to their world as dawn broke, leaving us suffused with knowledge and joy at having danced with the spirits of the lights.

Mamma and Papa reassured me that they were only trying to help me to return to the World, and in turn, I told them I was grateful for their advice.

My parents had even sent me to ask The Standing Stones if I would ever find true and lasting love. The Stones' reply was unclear. The more I asked, the more difficult the answer became to interpret. The same had happened when I visited the Mystics; they prevaricated, avoiding question after question that I asked; as is their way. They prefer us to visit The Standing Stones. I know this, but when I am seriously worried, I forget and pay them a visit. The Elders are not as learned as the Mystics but they try to be helpful. Unfortunately, their knowledge is limited. The Mystics are all-knowing and they understand the secrets of past and future times.

My visits left me in more of a quandary than I had been in before. No one had mentioned Deimuiss. From the Elders I had gleaned I would be making many journeys into places and times unknown. Their words gave me a real jolt, but no mention of my lost love returning or of my finding him.

My thoughts were chaotic and they left me undecided about what to do. Obviously, at this point in time, my future was uncertain. I decided that it would be best to follow my own star for the time being.

Discussing the situation with Mamma later, I concluded that eventually I would find the man who would fulfil my destiny. I knew it was Deimuiss, but I didn't tell Mamma that. Feeling easier in my mind, but wishing I knew when we would meet again, and try to understand what had actually happened to him, I decided to take my parents' advice and spend a little time with Carnaan – strictly on a friendship basis.

Deimuiss had been gone for what seemed forever. There had been no sign of him since he rode off on that fateful day, 18 months ago. Time moved on and I wanted him back here where he belonged. More than anything, I wanted to marry him and have his children. All my life I had known we would have two boys and two girls, all would have his beautiful, black, curly hair and deep blue eyes. My girls would be dainty but strong, and have our loving nature; the boys would be big and strong physically – like their father. They would be hunters and warriors, of that I was convinced. Brave fearless men like Deimuiss. They would, I knew, become leaders of men as Deimuiss was. On the other hand, had been. As reality crept over me, I thought, sadly, that perhaps he had gone forever; this man that I loved beyond life itself.

'Surely I would know if he was dead?' I had asked of the Mystics. Shaking their heads, the six elderly Mystics would reply evasively, 'We think he will appear dead in your eyes my child, but you also have important work to do.' Now what did they mean by that? Perhaps they had meant Deimuiss would be dead to me once I had witnessed his treachery in the cave. I had questioned myself many times over this since arriving in this other time; querying how I could continue to love a man who was capable of committing such heinous crimes. Despite seeing him in the cave with my own eyes, I still could not accept he would willingly kill two innocent people. The Deimuiss I knew would never commit evil against another.

'I am here to cure people, not kill them.'

I had heard him use those words many times over the years. Moreover, I knew he hated hunting, but accepted that it was the way of things. Like the other tribe members, he would only kill what was necessary. Never would he take part in hunting for the fun of it. That would go against all his principles.

I had no answer to this. My adoration for him was total, all encompassing. I just knew that whatever he had done, or would do in the future, my love for him would endure for eternity.

Again, I visited the Elders. 'What sort of answer is that?' I had chaffed at them, repeating what the Mystics had told me. 'He is either dead or he is alive.' The more I questioned them, the more stiff-backed those ancients became. In the end, I could not break down the stone wall they had erected between us. Not another word would pass their lips.

I was assured that Carnaan was a good, kind, generous man, and that he would provide for me if I should decide to marry him. On numerous occasions since Deimuiss had disappeared, family and friends had urged me to join my life with Carnaan's.

'He is a very caring man and be assured he has always loved you.'

They would advise me to at least consider him and leave the past behind. I had hesitated for many months, never wanting to give up on Deimuiss, my first and only love. I was certain he was still alive. Also, despite their reassurances, there was a certain something about Carnaan that I did not trust. Sometimes I thought I saw a possessive glint in his eyes when he looked at me; then on occasions, a sly look would cross his face to be immediately replaced by a huge grin when he saw me looking at him. Somehow, I did not trust him.

In the end, for the sake of my parents – who I knew longed for grandchildren – I accepted Carnaan's invitation when he next offered to take me out walking. I was pleasantly impressed by his conversation, and the attention he showed me. I realised just how lonely and depressed I had become in the time since Deimuiss's disappearance. We reached the top of Green Hill and sat scanning the surrounding countryside. It was a beautiful day. Soon the first day of spring would be here and all the trees, wild grasses, flowers and herbs were beginning to show their heads through the ground. The earth seemed to throb with the news that spring was nearly upon us. A light, southerly wind brought the beautiful sound of pipe music drifting up from the settlement. I realised one of the music group was practicing for the coming weekend's musical get-together. The haunting tune added to the magic of the morning and my blood quickened. Suddenly, I wanted Carnaan to kiss me. Seeming to sense my thoughts, he put his arm around me and then we were lying in the lush green grass, kissing and murmuring endearments to each other.

Oh, how I had missed the touch of a man; it felt so good to be in a man's strong arms once again. For a moment, I pretended that Carnaan was Deimuiss and kissed him passionately. I felt his response immediately and gasped in pleasure as he returned my kiss. How I now regretted never allowing Deimuiss to fulfil his love for me. Lying on the warm grass with the sun overhead and life springing forth from Mother Earth, I wanted so much to become a real woman. Carnaan whispered his love for me and I was jolted straight back to the here and now. What was the matter with me? This was not Deimuiss. This was another man who I did not really know at all, let alone love.

'Take what he offers,' whispered the treacherous voice inside my head.

'Pretend it's him, your first love.'

I relaxed again, momentarily liking the effect of his lips and his arms around me. No; I shot up off the grass, dusting the grasses from my clothes, smoothing my hair down, straightening it where Carnaan had ruffled it as he whispered words of love. I stood for a minute, trying to calm my thoughts and, body trembling; I slowly became aware that we were being watched. I looked around, trying to see who it was.

'Who's there?' I called. 'Come show yourself.'

Running across the top of the hill, I peeped over the brow and saw a woman run behind a bush.

'I know who that is,' I shouted to Carnaan.

'Who?' he called from the other side of the hilltop where he had run to take a look.

'It's Pranny, the spying bitch!' I spat.

I had recognised the red blonde of her hair – it was unmistakable, as she is the only one in the settlement with that colour hair. I had actually always admired it as it shimmered and cast beautiful red lights when the sunlight caught it.

'I know it's you who was spying on us Pranny.'

I shouted angrily down the hillside but she did not reply. Actually, I was really cross with myself for kissing Carnaan and being caught doing so; Pranny would gossip about me with the tribe's women. The thought of how embarrassed I was going to be quickened my pace as I ran down the hill at full pelt, breathlessly reaching the bush she had disappeared behind. I ran around it, hoping to catch her, but she had disappeared. There was no way she could have climbed through to hide in the centre of it, so she had obviously crawled away on all fours until she had reached the shelter of the trees. Frustrated at her disappearance, I turned to Carnaan who had joined me.

'She's gone!' I remarked quite unnecessarily as it was obvious she was not there. 'Now the whole settlement will know we were kissing and cuddling on the hill.' Stamping my foot in anger, I glanced up at Carnaan who to my surprise looked quite pleased with himself. Almost, I thought as if he relished the idea of being gossiped about. Blow Pranny and her nosy ways I chuntered to myself.

Carnaan wrapped his arms around me again, drawing me close, raining butterfly kisses over my face. I felt his need for me return. How I longed for him to be Deimuiss. I felt deceitful in this man's arms, wanting him to be another, and again I almost reached the point of not caring, thinking: even if Pranny had returned to watch us, I just wanted to be loved. I broke away, ashamed of betraying Deimuiss and for acting like that slut Pranny. I would be just like her, I thought. She did not care how many men she went out with or what she did with them. That is, of course, if you believed the local rumours. Men did find Pranny irresistible with her long, red gold hair and curvaceous figure, which she did not mind putting on display every day. What is it with some women, I thought, who were never satisfied with one man. They had to have every man they saw. The only two young men she had never had, to my knowledge, were Deimuiss and Carnaan. I knew that made her angry and even more determined to have them. She knew that both men desired me and they had never really cast an eye in her direction. I laughed to myself at the thought of her jealousy – she even had to follow me up the hill! I could never understand a woman being so jealous that she could not stand the thought of someone else being the first woman to have a man.

I knew I did not love Carnaan, but I also knew I did not want Pranny to have him. How selfish was that? Perhaps I was more like her than I knew.

Now sitting at the computer in Mary's home in another time and place, I realised that, although Mary had a look of Pranny on occasions, she certainly did not act like her. Thinking about the two of them, Mary did have certain mannerisms that reminded me of Pranny. Then at other times, she reminded me of Mamma and other women in the tribe. Life seemed to be becoming more of a mystery every day and my head was awash with so many thoughts.

A stab of jealousy went through me like a knife. I was not at the settlement. Pranny was, and would soon get Carnaan in her clutches. Furthermore, should Deimuiss return then victory would be hers. Tapping my foot restlessly on the floor, I was suddenly jolted from my reverie. The computer was bleeping.

Looking at the screen, I could see a small, silver light moving steadily across it. Strange as it sounds, it appeared to be beckoning me to follow it. I gasped and blinked. The silver light had stopped and was hovering over the settlement; the houses and outbuildings had appeared on screen. How could this possibly happen?

'Impossible!' I murmured. This could not be happening. Sure, I had travelled through time, but no way was it possible to log into my own time through a computer. On the other hand, was it? 'Don't be stupid Elvaennia,' I told myself, blinking my eyes hard. Surely, that could not possibly be the settlement. It had to be a film set or television drama. But no, I realised I was looking at the houses, barns, workshops and stores – I could even see the granary – that made up the settlement where I lived. I rubbed my eyes hard, still not believing what I saw. I looked away and then back at the screen again. There were curls of smoke coming through the roofs of the houses. There was my home, and dearest Mamma on her way to tend the animals. I zoomed in and was saddened to see how unhappy she was. A tear ran down my cheek.

'Oh Mamma, if only I could tell you how sorry I am.'

My breath caught on a sob; her sadness reached out and touched me through the centuries. I longed to hold her in my arms, hug her sadness to me and take the burden from her. Suddenly, she looked up and straight at me. I could swear that, just for a second, she knew I was there. Her eyes lit up through her tears and she seemed relieved, as if she knew that wherever I was, I was safe and secure. I saw movement and looked across the settlement to the children's play corner. They were feeding the piglets, and others were having a good time together playing 'chase' and 'tag' games (just like those still played today).

I spotted my youngest brother Piettra. He was sitting rocking himself with his puppy, Breenia, cuddled in his arms. I so loved Piettra. He was different from all the other children. Since he turned three, he had seemed to slip away from us. Now, he would never make eye contact, and would rarely communicate. He had trouble expressing his needs and in his frustration would end up screaming at us. It was shocking, because he had always been such a bright and bubbly little lad. He was very intelligent, and Papa always remarked what a fine warrior Piettra was going to become.

Then, as he approached his third birthday, he began to lose his speech and became unaware of anyone around him. He simply stopped playing with us and the other children. It was heartbreaking, watching him regress back to babyhood. I was the only person who seemed able to understand him. Just occasionally, I had managed to look deep into his eyes as he normally avoided eye contact at any price. In fact, any type of contact seemed hideous to him. Physical contact was unbearable and he would retreat deep into his psyche or become terribly upset – screaming, shouting and flailing his arms and legs around. At other times, he would simply stiffen his little body and just stare. That was the scariest thing to happen. I was shocked at the raw pain and suffering I saw in his eyes. For a second, we linked. I had enfolded him in my arms and he had responded to me with a small hug. That was magic. It was the first time in many months he had accepted human contact. It only lasted a minute, but to me it was a wonderful breakthrough into this little lost soul's world. If only I could help him, I often thought watching him just sitting, rocking backwards and forwards lost to the world. How sad I felt thinking of his lost childhood and the life he might never know as a warrior, husband, and father so many things would be lost to Piettra, unless a cure could be found for him.

What would he do now, I wondered. I was so glad I had suggested to Mamma that we get him a puppy; it had been another breakthrough. I smiled as I watched them lost in each other's world. I knew they went to another time and place. I could swear I saw him smile. How I longed to be beside him. I knew that it comforted him if I was near; which was good, but strangely enough he gave me a feeling that is hard to define: a sense of peace and love. I knew he walked in another world with Breenia. In one of my visions, I had seen him running and chasing with his small puppy. Neither of them had a care in the world. It was a different time and place, one I had never seen or would ever enter. This was where he lived with his friends, those like him, who shared his world. It was so wonderful watching him running and laughing with his dog; so carefree, and most of all happy.

Looking towards the settlement dwellings, I spotted Pranny. As usual, she was wandering around. 'Probably looking for today's man catch,' I thought, smiling to myself. She was certainly a striking girl. Mind you, looking at her again, she seemed to have piled on the pounds. She couldn't be, could she? Trying to catch sight of her again, I was disappointed. She had disappeared from view. I was probably wrong anyway. She wouldn't be pregnant. After all, she wasn't married. I idly wondered what she would have done with herself if she had lived in this time – more than likely become a barmaid. Thinking how happy she would be serving behind a bar made me chuckle to myself. She would have all the men she could possibly want to flirt with. Looking around the settlement, the longing to be back in the peaceful surroundings made my heart ache and I hoped and prayed that I would soon be back in the home where I belonged. I looked for Mamma again but to my despair, the picture began to break up, disintegrate before my eyes. Then it disappeared. I felt terribly sad and hoped against hope that one day soon I would be able to see my home again. Strange about Pranny, though. I was obviously wrong in my assumption – unmarried mothers-to-be were thrown out of the settlement- she would never have been so careless, would she?

Glancing around David's study, my eyes fixed on some framed photographs that were hanging on the wall to the side of me. Jumping up, I took a closer look. I was so astonished; I had to rub my eyes. I was looking at a photograph of the settlement; I did not recognise the people, they were quite elderly, the older men were holding walking sticks. The group were standing outside one of the houses. I could not believe my eyes. I shook my head and looked again; I was not imagining it, the settlement photograph was still hanging there.

How was this possible? It wasn't, was it? Yet the photograph was there for all to see. A long forgotten memory surfaced in my mind of an incident from when I was young. I recalled seeing Mamma holding some kind of picture in her hand, and staring very hard at it. I had tried to grasp the unfamiliar object from her but she had sternly said:

'No, Elvaennia, this is mine and Papa's. You will no doubt see it one day when you are older.'

Remembering how puzzled I was, I watched Mamma place it in a wooden box beneath an upturned hollow log. This was where she kept all her various treasures, and we children were firmly warned never to open the wooden box on pain of a severe punishment. That warning worked. Despite being tempted many times, I had never once peeked into the box of treasures.

How I had managed to forget something so important was beyond me; but then I had been very young at the time, and other happenings had crowded it out. As I had grown up, the memory had faded. I wondered how Mamma acquired it.

Hearing a car coming along the drive, I rushed to switch off the computer, and then ran into the bathroom. Turning the shower on, I prepared for bed. I certainly did not want either David or Mary discovering that I had been using the computer during their absence.

Later waking from a deep sleep, I was aware of someone or something in my room. I was terrified, wondering who or what it was. Pulling the duvet up, I tried to burrow beneath it to hide from the intruder. My mind was racing, my heart thumping loudly in my chest. Could it be David? I did not think so, I did not think he would risk Mary's wrath should she hear him in my bedroom in the early hours. I heard a creak as if whoever was there was moving towards my bed. Shaking with fear now, I peeped over the top of the duvet, ready to scream my loudest. My eyes were on stalks. There was a Druid standing at the foot of my bed, and in the shadows behind him, I could see the outline of another man.

'What do you want?' I whispered in fear, but too late, they began to fade into the mists of darkness. I was very afraid; not of the Druid but of the shadowy figure who had been standing behind him. Druids don't hurt you, do they? They protect you. But who was the shadowy man? Was this a warning to me? Is that why the Druid had appeared, as some sort of guardian angel? Nevertheless, who was he trying to warn me about? I wasn't just afraid, I was petrified. Why should some man be with a Druid in my bedroom? It was unnerving, to say the least. I lay awake, too scared to go back to sleep. What if the man returned without the Druid? I called on all the gods from my time, and any other god that might be listening, to protect me.

Never, to my knowledge had I had any enemies, so who was the man who came with the Druid.

Chapter 10

After a sleepless night, Elvaennia rose at first light. Dressing swiftly, she ran lightly downstairs, calling softly to Pip, Mary's dog to follow her. She grabbed her jacket and hurried out through the kitchen door.

Making her way through the back of the farmyard, she headed in the direction of the old cave.

'Keep close,' she whispered to the dog, glancing fearfully over her slim shoulder. How she wished that Vionny, her wolf dog from the settlement, was here with her now. 'Vionny would protect me,' she thought. 'One look at her, and no one would come near me.' Elvaennia had cared for Vionny since she was a cub. When she was out in the forest one winter's day, Elvaennia had heard a low squeaking sound and found the young wolf half dead in the snow. Scooping her up, she had taken her home, weaned and reared her. Since that day, the wolf had barely left her side. One look from Vionny's haunting lantern eyes would stop anyone in their track, and now Elvaennia longed for her comforting presence. She remembered the shadowy figure of the man. Not knowing who it could be frightened her, and dread held her in its grip. As the sun rose steadily in the sky, she crested the brow of the hill where the ancient cave stood. For a moment, she stood mesmerised. The sun was casting a strange light over the cave, bathing it in a golden glow. 'I knew I was right to come here,' she thought, watching the long fingers of the sun painting the cave a shimmering gold. 'I know I will find what I have come for.'

The dog running beside her was panting with the excitement of his early morning run. Elvaennia hastened down the hillside to the cave. Squatting on her heels in the cave entrance, she spread her hands wide, feeling just beneath the sandy surface. A satisfied smile spread across her beautiful face. She began collecting the tiny stones she needed to perform her task. Jumping to her feet, stones safely stowed in her pockets, 'task accomplished,' she called happily to Pip.

'Race you back!'

Silver hair swinging, the golden sunlight cast a magical light around the girl and dog as they raced happily up the hillside. Neither noticed the Druid standing across the field watching them and just behind him in the shadows was the outline of a man. Across the field, another man watched her running towards the farm. His longing for the girl showed in every fibre of his being. 'She is so totally unaware of her beauty,' he thought, 'and I find that so beguiling.' His eyes followed every move the young woman made as the sunlight traced her progress back to the farmhouse. One day he declared she will be mine and no other will ever have her.

After helping Mary with the breakfast, Elvaennia washed the stones she had collected, and then laid them in the sunlight on her bedroom windowsill. She wanted the sun's rays to warm and bless the small collection before she made a casting. She knew preparation was everything if she wanted to discover the truth.

The magic of the early morning walk to the cave was still with her. The terror of the previous night was beginning to recede but still she decided to proceed with casting the stones. Taking a silk scarf from her wardrobe, she spread it on the floor. Then, picking up the sun-warmed stones, she felt empowered, knowing they had come from her time and had been blessed by her gods and the sun god – who had shone his rays so powerfully this morning.

Saying a short prayer to all the gods, Elvaennia scattered the stones gently in front of her on to the silk scarf.

Looking at the way they had fallen sent a shudder through her body. Fear returned a hundredfold. The stones foretold a time ahead when she would be in danger: from someone she knew in this time, and someone from her past. But she could not tell who they were or the reasons for their malevolent feelings.

'I need some tarot cards,' she thought. 'The ancient cards will point me in the right direction. The stones have helped, admittedly, but the men are still hidden from me. If only Deimuiss was here, he would protect me, I know he would.'

'No time like the present. I will ask Mary to take me to Lichfield if she is not busy. I need the cards now. These men are not going to go away.'

She re-cast the stones. Again, they fell in exactly the same pattern. Knowing she had to help herself, she quickly wrapped them in the silk scarf. Glancing up, she caught sight of the Druid who was watching her, from across the room, with a strange expression on his face. His robes were shimmering, white edged with gold. He was extremely old as if he had lived for many centuries. Before she could stop herself, she asked, in a voice trembling with fear, 'who is the man you brought with you last night?' Too late! Again, the Druid began to fade as the bright sunshine disappeared; the room became dark as clouds blotted out the sun. Elvaennia felt her earlier happiness dissipate. Coldness clenched her heart. She worried: 'Why does he keep appearing?'

Running down the stairs, she shouted anxiously for Mary.

'What is it child? Why are you so worried and nervous?'

Shaking her head to clear her muddled thoughts, Elvaennia asked if Mary would take her to Lichfield.

'Of course, you know you only have to ask. Come, we will go now, and then you can tell me on the journey – why all the anxiety?'

Despite everything, Elvaennia had to smile. Mary was doing her favourite thing, ending every sentence with a question.

Walking through the main shopping centre in Lichfield, Elvaennia hesitated, wondering where she could purchase some tarot cards. Mary had no clue either. After walking around the shopping area, Elvaennia realised – much to her disappointment – she was not going to find a shop in Lichfield that sold the cards.

Needing to consult the ancient tarot was paramount to her peace of mind now. All of a sudden, Mary remembered that she had seen a small shop that sold items to do with magic in Corncrake Lane, not far from where they were.

'It might not be there anymore, but let's go and see, if it is you will be able to find what you want.'

They made their way quickly to where Mary remembered seeing the shop. Much to Elvaennia's delight, it was still there.

Entering the premises was an experience Elvaennia would never forget. There were candles of every description scattered around the shop area; many were lit. It gave the shop an eerie atmosphere, and she wandered round, looking at the many different items on display.

There was a display of witchcraft items: spells, candles, books of spells, even tiny broomsticks. 'Quite amazing,' she thought moving on to the next area – the cards. She easily made her choice. The deck of cards seemed to jump off the shelf into her hands. Sighing with relief, she paid for her pack of 'Angel Tarot' and happily left the shop. Arm in arm, the women made their way to a nearby café, where Elvaennia immediately opened her new purchase. Gently lifting the gold edged pack from the box, a sense of peace and tranquillity flooded through her. 'They are beautiful Mary,' she murmured, reaching a hand across the table and touching her friend's hand in thanks.

Mary smiled at her delight, assuring her that thanks were unnecessary.

'Pleased you got what you wanted, Elvaennia and I hope they tell you what you want to know.'

Watching Elvaennia inspecting her new cards, a worried smile played around her lips as she thought, 'Though, I hope she does not discover too much too soon.'

'I know...' Mary said brightly as they finished their welcome cup of coffee.

'Let's go for a walk up to the cathedral.'

Elvaennia agreed happily.

'Oh yes, that will be nice. I would love to visit such an ancient building.'

'I thought you might enjoy a walk around it.'

Mary's rosy cheeks smiled as they strolled along the old paths towards the cathedral.

'Walking through history again Elvaennia,' she chortled. Elvaennia smiled, agreeing with her, thinking sardonically it was very different to the way she arrived.

Making their way through the ancient city streets, Mary pointed out various buildings and points of interest, drawing the young woman's attention to other sites of local importance. The old buildings fascinated her, and she longed to be able to walk around some of them. But time was getting on and she wanted to see inside the cathedral that towered above the city.

The nearer they got to the cathedral, the more drawn towards the ancient church the young woman felt.

On entering through the heavy latched door, Elvaennia was awed by the sight of the interior.

'This is beautiful, Mary. I have never seen such an imposing building before.'

Nodding in agreement, Mary proceeded to walk slowly down the north aisle. She was surprised when Elvaennia hurried past her, seemingly intent on an urgent destination. Hurrying after her, Mary hissed 'Slow down, there is no rush.'

Brushing her hair back and looking directly into Mary's green eyes that were so like David's:

'But I have to hurry Mary.'

Shrugging away from the older woman, she quickened her pace past the vestibule that led to the chapter house. Down the north aisle she plunged, as fast as she could. Mary, following in her wake, found she had difficulty keeping up with the flying figure of Elvaennia, hair drifting around her like a silver cloud. She actually seemed to glide over the tiled floor.

Reaching the far end of the north aisle, the young woman turned right, making her way into the Lady Chapel.

Elvaennia stood at the table where the candles were glowing, flickering brightly and mysteriously into the shadows of the cathedral.

Picking up two candles, she lit them and carefully placed them in the holders.

Mary sat watching her, aware that something mystical was taking place. There was no sound to be heard around them. Everything had faded away. There was just Elvaennia looking into, and through, the candlelight. A ghostly light descended into the Lady Chapel. Mary watched as Elvaennia's face lit up as if by a thousand candles. Elvaennia saw someone who was just outside of Mary's vision. She heard a whisper.

'Deimuiss, I knew, I just knew you would be here.'

Then, Mary saw him – a tall, dark haired man dressed in a reddish coloured fur cloak. She watched as he gazed into Elvaennia's eyes, as if she was the only person in the world who mattered to him.

The candlelight shone on Elvaennia's hair, sparking silver lights along its length with a myriad of other jewel-like colours. Stretching out her arms, Elvaennia tried to take the man into her embrace. Fingers touching for a brief moment of time, the two of them were reunited. Suddenly, a cry of pain escaped Elvaennia. He had gone! Disappeared as if he had never been there.

Mary took a deep breath of relief, realizing that Elvaennia had not seen the shadow of a man standing behind the Druid not far away. The shadow was a menacing figure and she knew the Druid was keeping the young man and woman safe from him.

Hurrying across, Mary hugged the young woman tightly.

'You saw him, didn't you Mary?'

'Yes, I did.'

'But where has he gone?'

'Now, there's a question I cannot answer my sweet, but come with me. I know somewhere quieter where we can sit and think about what's happened.'

Together they headed up the south aisle. Turning right, Mary beckoned Elvaennia to follow her up the stone steps, along a short balcony, then up another short flight of steps into a small chapel.

Sitting together, facing the beautiful altar cloth of two golden embroidered angels, Elvaennia experienced a healing peace. She heard

Deimuiss's voice whispering to her, 'Wesh not little one, we will meet again.' A tear slipped silently down her cheeks at his words. Remembering him in the Lady Chapel, she now understood why he could not enter this century – he still had work to do in, what was at present, his time.

'I've seen him twice now, each in a different era,' she thought. 'How much longer before we are reunited?' Knowing the time was fast approaching for the 'big' talk with Mary and David, she took a deep breath and whispered to Mary, 'I'm okay now. Shall we leave?'

Taking a last lingering look at the beautiful embroidered angels, the two women wended their way out of the cathedral to make their way home. Not a word passed between them of the experience in the cathedral.

After supper, Elvaennia hastened upstairs. Taking the cards from their box, she carefully shuffled the pack and drew three cards.

Laying them face down, she took a deep breath and turned them over.

'Amazing,' she breathed on reading these words:

'Follow your own intuition and divine guidance. The angels and the gods are with you. Eventually your goal will be achieved. Love will be your guiding light and whatever you accomplish will be through love and the guidance of the shining light. A new beginning will lead you to help many people along life's pathways, bringing you closer in touch with your inner being. Your life's journey is soon to begin, and all will change beyond belief.'

Elvaennia was surprised at what she had read. Yes, it was a good positive reading, but there was no mention of the man who had appeared with the Druid.

'Strange, very strange,' she muttered. 'Perhaps I need to use the cards in a different manner.'

Shuffling the cards carefully, she again drew three and placed them face down. Slowly turning them over, she read the messages. Again, the cards focused on her new beginnings. 'Maybe I need to do a longer reading,' she thought, and proceeded to reshuffle the cards and withdraw

12. Having placed them face down in three sets of four, Elvaennia then turned them face up.

On reading them, she saw that two men would cause disruption in her life. Her frustration at being unable to divine the identities of the men really annoyed her; and the more readings she tried, the more frustrating it became. 'Mmm,' she thought, 'I have found them, but still I am no further forward than this morning. The stones predicted exactly the same.'

On a sigh, she packed the cards away and placed them, wrapped in black silk, on her bedside table. She stood looking across the field towards the ancient cave. Deep in thought, it took her a few seconds to perceive that there was movement at the site. Opening the window quickly, she practically hung out of it, eyes fixed on the distant bivouac.

What was happening? Was there someone at the cave? Another traveller in time? Who was it? Was it someone from the settlement? Questions were churning and tumbling through her mind. Perhaps, just perhaps, Deimuiss had come through?

Excitement sped through her body as she rushed down the stairs, through the kitchen, not stopping even to change her shoes or grab a jacket. She ran through the kitchen garden into the farmyard and almost vaulted over the gate into the top field. Picking up on the excitement, Pip was racing hard on her heels as she ran along the track in the direction of the cave, the summer grasses swaying and bending as she rushed along.

'Please, please, let it be Deimuiss,' she prayed as her feet hardly touched the path. Across the far stile, she jumped, as Pip crawled beneath it, almost tripping her up as he scuttled between her feet, anxious to lead the way.

Chapter 11

'Perhaps it's as well,' she thought, that her favourite daughter would never love another man as she had loved Deimuiss. 'Maybe we are wrong to interfere in her life,' Elvaennias mother pondered as she tidied their living quarters.

Thinking of Deimuiss, she felt really unsettled. Some instinct told her he was not dead, and she had decided to ask the 'runes' later that day. Perhaps they would give her the answer. She decided she would cast them when Elvaennia returned from her journey. Eiluiniad loved her eldest daughter deeply; she loved her spirit and her laughter. The sound of her voice in itself would lift anyone's mood, she thought, and to look at her was sheer delight. Her beautiful, silvery hair that tumbled down her slim back; her laughing, silvery grey eyes were like a beautiful moonlit evening. Eiluiniad thought everything about her daughter was perfect. Concern, though, was beginning to rear its ugly head. Elvaennia had not returned from The Standing Stones with her sister and Grandmamma. She knew her daughter would not delay their return, aware of how her mother and family would worry if they were late. 'It's the Equinox,' she thought worriedly. 'We have preparations to make to thank the gods of winter for bringing us safely through the dark time.'

Making her way to the sheep enclosure, she thought, 'Elvaennia is a sensible girl. She won't keep them out late.' Feeding the animals, still she worried. Darkness was beginning to fall and the evening chill was beginning to make her feel cold. Hurrying through her tasks, she headed home to prepare the evening meal and gifts for the ceremony of thanks.

Each family conducted this ceremony in their own home on the eve of the Equinox. She knew Eppill, her husband, would be back soon and he, as well as the others, would be in need of a warm fire and food. But she knew that he would be so worried if Elvaennia had not returned with the other family members. She hurried faster, feeling quite distracted and now hoping against hope that her daughters and mother were waiting at the house.

Pushing open the heavy door, darkness greeted her; a thick pitch-black darkness that somehow foretold of dark happenings. She put her hand to her mouth to stifle her fear. No cheery voices greeted her, telling of the day's exploits; no welcoming fire warming the air, just an aching empty silence. Turning, she ran back down the track to the home of the chief mystic, Myllaou. Knocking loudly on the door, she called out in her fear:

'Please, please, something awful has happened to my daughters and mother. I know it. Please help me. Please.'

The tears she had been holding back now poured unheeded down her pale cheeks. Head bowed, she acknowledged the mystic, Myllaou, as he opened the door.

'Come in daughter of Matealdia. Be seated and tell me what has happened.'

Entering this house, Eiluiniad always felt slightly awed. She knew he was a mystic of the first order; the mysticism was tangible in the very air around her. Bowing her head as much in awe of him as ever, but now bent almost double with sorrow, she sat on the long log that was not too far from the fire in the centre of the house. Smoke circled in strange swirls as it rose in the air. If she had not been so unhappy, she would also have noticed the different colours in the smoke rising in spirals, merging together as it passed through the roof-space on its way to other worlds. Urging her to tell her story, the mystic settled himself as near the fire as he could. He had begun to feel his centuries of late: his bones ached with stiffness in the early hours of the morning, and he felt his many years on this Earth more so than ever now. He found himself looking back far more often nowadays than forwards. His rheumy eyes registered

Eiluiniad's great distress, and calmly he asked her once again what it was that he could help her with.

Taking a deep breath, the mother tried to hold back her tears as she told him her fears for the safety of her family. The mystic sat deep in thought for a few seconds then, taking a bundle of short sticks from his pouch, whispering an incantation, he threw them on the ground around him. Eiluiniad watched him and a cry escaped her as she saw the look of disbelief and horror that spread across his face. Realising that for once he had let his emotions show, the elderly mystic quickly returned his features to their normal state. But he was too late. Elvaennia's mother knew beyond doubt that disaster had struck her family. 'They're dead, aren't they?' She cried out loudly in her distress. She began to feel breathless. Her heart raced with anxiety as she thought of the awful possibility that her mother and two of her daughters were dead. A loud knocking came at the door, and not waiting for an invitation to enter, Eppill burst into the fug of the smoke-filled room.

'What is it Eiluiniad? What ails you? Where are our daughters and your mother?'

Eppill's presence seemed to swamp the room. He was a huge bear of a man, not only in size but also in personality. Eiluiniad knew, though, that he would never harm a soul unless pushed beyond endurance. The mystic, realising that Eppill was not being disrespectful, motioned him to the log where his wife was now weeping uncontrollably, her breath coming in short gasps as her grief threatened to overwhelm her.

The mystic explained what had happened. He also said that he had not much good news to offer that night, but remarked it was by no means all bad. In the fullness of time, Elvaennia would be returned to her tribe once she had completed the tasks ahead of her.

Noticing that he had not mentioned her other daughter and mother, Eiluiniad began to keen as she realised she would never see them again.

'All is not lost my child,' the mystic said. 'Your eldest daughter will be returning.'

He repeated his words, trying to reassure the distressed woman.

Putting his large arms around his wife, Eppill drew her close as they sat together on the wide log. Filled with a great sadness, this bear of a man was distraught at the thought of what had befallen his family. 'Hush my darling,' he whispered. Drawing her slight body to him, he stroked her hair, wondering how he could ease her great sadness. He suddenly realised what the mystic had said – that eventually, Elvaennia would be returning.

'She is safe then?' he asked him.

The mystic avoided the direct question, saying, 'Elvaennia will return in the fullness of time. You must go tomorrow to seek out the remains of your mother and daughter and commit their souls to the Time Beyond.'

Sadness flooded his soul, but knowing his wife was destroyed by grief, Eppill realised he had to be strong – for her, his sons and remaining daughter. Gathering her close, he whispered the good news that their daughter would be returned to them in the future.

'Now we must go home to impart the news to our sons and young Jennia. They will have returned from their friend's home and will be worried as to where everyone is. I must make plans for tomorrow.'

Nodding, too upset to speak, his wife leant on his broad shoulder as they took their sorrowful leave of the mystic. Eiluiniad felt distraught; not only for the loss of her daughters and mother, but also because she now had the job of telling the three boys and Jennia. Why were the gods so angry with them? She wondered anew what they could possibly have done to induce so much horror on her small family. Leaning closer to her husband, she tried to take comfort from the warmth of his body as they struggled home, a flickering flare lighting their way through the darkness, their thoughts as black as the night surrounding them. No stars or moon broke through the blackness. It was as if the gods of darkness were still waiting to send further anger and desolation to their family.

No words could describe their intense grief as they informed their sons and daughter of the family's loss.

Piettra was the only one of the family group who, but for a quick flash of recognition in his eyes, seemed untouched by the tragedy. He sat rocking himself faster and faster, occasionally hitting his head on the wall. Eiluiniad rushed across the room and gathered him as close to her as he would allow. She tried to impart some comfort to this small, lost soul. However, he rejected her advances, pushing and flailing against her to be put down on the floor so he could continue his rocking to and fro, to and fro.

Looking at Piettra only added to Eiluiniad's misery. 'My poor son,' she thought. 'If only I could reach into his hidden world and help bring him back to our world. Help to take his pain and loneliness away, now Elvaennia, Trieainia and my mother are lost to me. Tomissia, Diaviadia, Piettra and Jennia are all the children I have left to care for.' This was such a terrible time, but she knew she had to be strong for her remaining family. She hadn't a clue how she was going to achieve this, but the thought that Elvaennia might return helped a little.

Grief filled this once happy home. It felt as if a huge, black cloud had enveloped them – each separate from the other. Words were too difficult to speak, and as the evening wore on it was as if the very shadows in their home were threatening them. Eiluiniad even thought that the shadows were drawing towards them, ready to stretch their greedy fingers out and take the remaining members of her family from her. Tears poured down her wan face. Eppill left his seat and drew his distraught wife towards the bed. Wrapping the furs around her and gently kissing her wet cheek.

'Be brave wife. The sun will shine on all of us again.'

So saying, he returned to his seat to keep a vigil for his family.

Following a restless night, the family rose, and having done the most important chores, they gathered outside their home with the rest of the community. En masse, they made their way to The Standing Stones. After a ceremony of commitment, they split into small groups to search for the two missing women.

After two hours of searching, Eiluiniad was beginning to despair, thinking the mystic must be wrong. No one had found any trace of her family. She and Eppill headed towards the ancient hunting cave.

'Look!'

Eppill pointed out the footprints in the wet soil.

'They were here,' he cried. Calling out to the other groups, he hurried his wife down the hill to the cave.

'Oh, no!' they both cried out together, at the sight of the two bodies inside the cave.

Eppill quickly dropped his stick and went into the bivouac. He felt despair, realising that the life force had left both of the women. There was no hope. They were dead, and he and Eiluiniad murmured a prayer for their souls.

The search parties arrived and they quickly wrapped the women's bodies in their cloaks; and between them, carefully carried them slowly and respectfully back to the settlement, chanting their sadness on the winds of time.

Despite their relief at finding the bodies, Elvaennia's parents knew they would have a real struggle to come to terms with their awful loss. Their thoughts were in turmoil: wondering what had happened, and where Elvaennia could be. How would they manage without their beautiful daughter? Her spirit was in the air, all around them, but they could not make any contact. Not even knowing where she was broke their hearts; their very souls were in torment. Over and over their thoughts reached out, asking where she could be. Eiluiniad asked her husband, 'When will we see our beloved daughter again? Is she safe from danger? Is she happy?'

'The Mystic told us we would be reunited with her so we must trust his words,' he rejoined comfortingly. He was worried at how ill his wife looked; dark shadows were crowded beneath her eyes; her skin looked sallow and she stumbled as she made her way back up the hillside. Placing his arm around her slim waist, he knew the only thing to bring her a glimmer of happiness would be the return of their daughter.

Although he did not show it, Eppill was beside himself with worry. The loss of his family weighed heavily on his soul. Anxiety was tearing him apart. Like his wife, he had had no sleep the previous evening. He knew he had to be strong for his remaining family but tiredness and depression were making him desperate. For now, he clung to the thought that, as far as he understood it, Elvaennia was still alive somewhere in the universe. He prayed silently to all the gods that she would be returned safely to the family. It was the not knowing where Elvaennia was that hurt so much.

How she would cope was beyond Eiluiniad's comprehension. She so loved her eldest daughter. The only shred of comfort was from the mystic who had told them that Elvaennia would return. Standing on the desolate hillside, Eiluiniad faced east and affirmed she would find her adored daughter. She prayed to the goddess of Morning Light for her daughter's safe return.

Having made her plea, Eiluiniad made her way home with the others who had accompanied them. She stumbled a few times and Eppill drew her close, whispering encouraging words, hoping to help her along the grieving path.

Back at the settlement, they set about the duty of preparing the dead women for their final journey. 'Deimuiss would have helped,' Eiluiniad thought as she went about her tasks. 'He would have known exactly what to do and say to comfort us. He is well versed in matters of the dead and bereaved.'

Determined to help her remaining family cope, Eiluiniad went to her store of herbs and busily made tinctures of chamomile to help soothe their worries away. She made many offerings to the gods and goddesses, pleading with them to comfort her family and help the departed souls on their way. She felt better for doing these positive things, and began to prepare an evening meal of venison with vegetables. Opening the clay oven, she lit the fire and placed the pot of food over the heat. She knew the food would be a comfort for the family if she could get them to eat it.

Glancing round at the sad faces that surrounded her, they tugged at her heart. Crossing the room, she gathered them together, telling them they would get through the sadness. More tears began to fall and the hopelessness of their situation hit her afresh, but her inner strength reasserted itself and she sent a silent word of thanks to the goddess of light as she knew she was constantly with her.

Only young Piettra remained remote, outside of the circle of his family, rocking himself with his puppy clutched tightly to his chest.

Occasionally, a silent tear slipped down his cheek as if, in some strange way, he was well aware of what had happened. His mother longed to comfort her poor, lost son but knew he would not tolerate her intrusion and decided not to upset him.

Wrapping the cleansed bodies of her dead family in their death robes, the mother called the family together to say a final farewell. At first light, men of the tribe would collect the bodies and take them to the cave of the dead some five miles away. Eppill would lead the way. Women were banned from seeing this ceremony. While the men were making the sad journey of the dead, the women made their way up the Hill of the Spirits. Eiluiniad would lead the women and would perform the ceremony to release the spirits to the Time Beyond. The Mystics would make their way to the mysterious Hill of Souls and perform their sacred ritual.

Once the ceremonies had finished, relief would flood through the villagers, as they knew they had done all they could for the dead. Some of the sadness would begin to ebb slowly away, and life would gradually begin to return to normal over the ensuing months.

Eiluiniad found the day of the dead very difficult to deal with; and her family grew concerned at her grief, worried that they might also lose her. Eppill was a tower of strength to her, bringing warm drinks of herbs and strengthening berries that he found in the food store. After sleeping, wrapped tightly in his arms, Eiluiniad awoke knowing that she had to face up to life without her mother and two daughters. She promised to be strong and to watch her remaining children like a hawk. 'No one will ever take them away from me,' she declared. 'I could not face losing another child. I love them all so much.'

Silently, she began her day. Whereas normally, just like Trieainia, she had filled her days with song, now the days ahead promised to be empty of happiness and laughter. She longed for the past when they had all been together.

The men stated they were going to avenge the deaths of the women and would gather at night in one of the huts, discussing and making plans around the smoking fire as to how they could catch the persons responsible. Often the talk would turn to Deimuiss and Elvaennia, wondering if the lights had taken them, and wondering where they might be. Nevertheless, if Eppill was with them, they did not dwell on it, seeing the sadness steal across his face at the mention of his daughter's name.

Late one afternoon, as the daylight was fading fast, Eiluiniad saw a silvery light hovering over the track. Puzzled, she followed the light as it hovered in the air just in front of her. It was as if it was inviting her to follow. It was dark now and very cold. Elvaennia's mother followed slowly, wrapping her cloak tightly around her thin body. The going was very difficult, as, apart from the silver light, everywhere was black. She had no flare to light her way. Stumbling along the rutted track for a while, Eiluiniad decided she could go no further and turned for home.

'Mother, is that you?'

Eiluiniad jumped on hearing Elvaennia's sweet voice breaking through the darkness.

'Where are you child?' She called out, a desperate longing in her voice. Unfortunately, all she could hear was the night calling of the birds and the eerie howling of the wolves. The wind suddenly gathered into storm-force and Eiluiniad found herself bent almost double by its enormous strength. Clinging to the words she had heard on the edge of the wind, Eiluiniad made for home feeling more comforted than she had in a long while. She felt happier, as she was now convinced her daughter was alive; but she was also disturbed that she had no idea where exactly her daughter was. Even as a child, her motherly instinct had always told her exactly where Elvaennia was. At any given moment, her intuition would take her straight to her wherever she happened to be – be it in the settlement, or even if she had strayed outside of what was considered the safe area. She would always home in on her offspring. Now, every waking minute, Elvaennia was in her thoughts, and so was Eppill. She was so close to her husband that she knew his every thought. Eiluiniad recognized how terrible his suffering was at the disappearance of their daughter. His consolation was remembering the words of the mystic that Elvaennia would return. Regrettably, he had not said when. Now she would be able to tell Eppill of the mysterious silver light that she had thought might take her to their daughter; and of hearing her daughter's voice. She knew he would derive comfort from her words. Having now made the first contact with Elvaennia since her disappearance, Eiluiniad was convinced she would hear or even see her again.

Vionny, Elvaennia's wolf dog, spent her days wandering the settlement and surrounding areas, looking and howling out her grief at her young mistress's disappearance. Eppill had said, 'If Vionny cannot find her; she is not to be found in this world.' It was also strange how the wolf had not tracked the women to the hunting cave. They had all found this very odd, as she was normally wonderful at tracking. They knew something extraordinary had happened and wondered about what it could be.

The following afternoon, Eiluiniad was feeding the animals when she sensed Elvaennia was again nearby. Gazing around, she felt certain that her child was watching her. Her instinct told her that her daughter was nowhere near the settlement, but was, in fact, many ages away. 'If only you were here my daughter, safely back home,' she murmured. Looking into the distance, she felt comforted, knowing that she was alive.

'Mother?'

Eiluiniad jumped on hearing her daughter's voice.

'I am lost to your time mother.'

The words seemed to be a sigh on the winds, rippling over the streams that gurgled across the Chase lands.

'Elvaennia, come back to me.'

The mother knew instinctively that her utterances were lost in the waters of the streams. For some reason, the gods of the waters had dropped her words like pebbles. She could almost see them sinking down and down, deep into the depths of the stream, to be lost forever in the Lands of Lost Words where no human ever entered.

'Elvaennia, my sweet daughter of light I know you will return in the future. Do not be afraid.'

Eiluiniad kept these comforting words firmly in her mind, hoping against hope that somehow Elvaennia would pick them up wherever she was. Firmly reassured that Elvaennia would return, she made her way back to the settlement feeling more comforted than she had been in a long time.

Lately, thoughts of Deimuiss had been coming into Eiluiniad's mind, as he too – along with Elvaennia – had disappeared without trace.

'I wonder if whoever took Deimuiss also took Elvaennia; so strange that they should both go missing.'

Chapter 12

Sitting outside his home at twilight, Eppill surveyed the scene. He sighed, thinking how much he missed his family.

'Life goes on,' he ruminated watching the people go about their night tasks of feeding and securing the animals for evening. The hunting dogs were howling, no doubt longing to be chasing across the heath lands. He could hear mothers calling their children in from play, the cows were lowing softly in fact it was a typical evening at the settlement as the sun was setting on another day, 'but not so typical for my family,' thought Eppill, 'three beautiful women gone from our midst. If only I could turn back time, and they were here, safely beside me. Now they are scattered to the four winds, and I do not know for certain if I will see my beloved daughter again despite what the mystic said.'

'I so miss them, each one of the three beautiful women who have disappeared as if in on a breath of the wind. Two, I know, I will not see again until I go to the Time Beyond. But my Elvaennia – who knows if and when I will see her again?'

He wiped tears from his eyes, sadness emanating from every fibre of his being.

'All I can do is pray to all the gods of the Earth and Skies that they will take care of Trieania and her Grandmamma until we meet again. And I pray that Elvaennia returns to us soon to help ease her mother's grieving heart.'

He sent prayers to the gods on the wings of all the birds in the skies, praying that his daughter would soon be returned to them.

In the gathering gloom, everywhere went suddenly silent, even the sheep in the fields were quiet. The horses and dogs emitted no sound; it was as if they had homed in on the family's sadness.

Chapter 13

It wasn't him!

I thought I had seen Deimuiss from my bedroom window. Thinking that he had travelled through the cave to see me. Pip and I raced across the field, down the hillside, but there was no one there and no sign of anyone having been there recently either. I was so disappointed. I sat beside the cave wall and cried and cried. Pip came and snuggled up to me, licked my salty tears away and comforted me.

Strangely, though, I did not feel alone. I felt as if we were being watched. I felt disturbed, frightened, Pip pricked his ears up and started shaking. That was enough for me. We ran back as fast as we could. I even locked and bolted the kitchen door and went round closing all the windows.

Mary laughed at me when she came home but I couldn't find the right words to tell her how scared I had felt. I wished Mary and David would talk to me about what they know. Life would be so much easier. Why won't they talk to me?

Chapter 14

Surfing the Internet one evening, when David and Mary were out visiting friends, Elvaennia happened on the website of Stafford Castle. Immediately, she recalled 'seeing' the castle when she was younger.

'Why,' she almost spluttered aloud, 'I went to this castle in 1936 and remember hearing people saying it was haunted.'

'I heard people say that, as they walked through the woods at night, they heard the sound of horses galloping. In fact, they had to step off the tracks to make way for them as they sounded so near, but the horses never appeared and the sounds always disappeared.'

Remembering what a good state of repair the castle had been in during the 1930s, Elvaennia felt quite upset to see the disrepair it had fallen into in such a relatively short period.

While walking around the castle in the 1930s, she had joined a small group of visitors and followed them up to the tower. The views were breathtaking, and the guide had jovially pointed out the various landmarks stretching from the south and west: to the Wrekin, the Long Mynd, and beyond to the Welsh mountains; in the north to the Potteries; the east, over Stafford town to Derbyshire; and southeast over Cannock Chase.

There were a few dark passageways that she noticed and thought did not look particularly enticing. Still, she did glance into a few rooms along the way, and noticed the jugs and bowls on side tables – which people used for washing themselves in the mornings.

The atmosphere of the castle attracted her and she wished she could stay longer. The thickness of the outer walls of the castle was brilliant, she thought, helping to keep the cold away. Fortunately, it did have electricity, otherwise the darkness might have been a little overwhelming in such a large space; but then candles were still needed at times to aid the sparse lighting when going to bed. There were partitions in some of the bedrooms, which were not very high so privacy would have been at a premium. The banqueting hall was a lofty room about 70 feet by 40 feet with four long and elongated, elaborately fashioned, mullioned windows on each side. On the upper part of the walls, there were various colourful coats-of-arms and heraldic designs – all truly impressive. She noted the solid oak floor, and felt even more impressed by the quality of her surroundings. How she wished now she had been able to stay longer on her last 'visit'. 'All that beauty has gone,' she thought despondently, looking at the now dilapidated castle on the hill. Such a great pity to see history disappearing before our eyes, if only someone had thought to save it for future generations. Elvaennia hated to see links with the past vanish as if they had never existed. She was still trying to come to terms with the fact that despite her constant research she still had not discovered any trace of the Calegi Tribe.

Chapter 15

One day, while out walking Pip on the Chase, Elvaennia had been admiring clumps of late rosebay willow herb and the purple thistles swaying in the gentle breeze. She had noticed the bright yellow of the ragwort and hoped the horses would not snatch at it while being exercised, as it is highly toxic to them. In fact she knew it could kill them. She also noticed the bracken dying down where the forestry workers had sprayed it in their efforts to clear the ancient heathland. The forests looked dark and green in the distance, but in her mind's eye, she saw the ancient oaks of the Chase and the wide-open heathland covered in heather. Moreover, she thought, 'No wonder it was once the hunting ground of Kings. It has always been a mystical place.'

The young woman was surprised to suddenly see a group of people dressed in strange clothing. 'Looks like a uniform of some kind,' she thought to herself, 'and they appear to be carrying some type of weapons.' The sudden thought did cross her mind that maybe, just maybe Deimuiss might be amongst the group. Wherever she found herself he was always at the forefront of her mind. How she longed to be with him again.

Calling Pip quietly, she hooked him on to his lead and hid behind an oak tree, watching the men as they fell into line and started marching along the track. Wondering who on earth they could be, she made a note of their uniform; and on reaching home, she described it in detail to Mary.

'My goodness girl, from what you describe, those were First World

War soldiers. They were stationed on the Chase during the war. You must have had a time slip. Good gracious, I wonder why that happened.'

Elvaennia could not understand this herself as there seemed no rhyme or reason for it. She had not recognised any of the soldiers and she could only think that, once again, a point was being made to show that it was really quite easy to travel through time, unfortunately much to her disappointment, on this occasion Deimuiss was not with the group.

Mary remarked that one day she had been walking in an area not far from Birches Valley when she had seen two horse riders galloping along a bridleway. 'That's not unusual, I know,' she remarked with a huge smile, 'but they were dressed in 17th century clothing. Now, that is unusual!' She laughed. 'I just knew they weren't filming; those riders were almost flying along – their cloaks were billowing out behind them, as was their hair. It was an amazing sight. I could almost smell the sweat from the horses. It was so unexpected.'

Chapter 16

Carnaan's face was a picture of despair. He had been out looking for Elvaennia many times with the other warriors of the Calegi Tribe. His spirit was in turmoil. He loved Elvaennia with every fibre of his being. For so many years, he had looked on enviously at her relationship with Deimuiss. His pale blue eyes took on a brooding look thinking of Deimuiss. How he envied his height and strength, and his handsome looks. Next to Deimuiss, he knew Elvaennia would never give him a second glance. He thought he had won her over when Deimuiss had gone missing. Now, after all his efforts, she was no longer on the scene. He thought back to the time when he was sure she would be his forever.

Elvaennia – whenever Carnaan thought of her, his heart would quicken, his skin would flush, as thoughts, best kept to himself, raced around his head. Hands sweating, he would think of her slim, young body lying beside him; and he quickly had to think of other things. When Deimuiss had disappeared, Carnaan gave offerings to the gods, thanking them for giving him Elvaennia. Carnaan had always been obsessed with her for as long as he could remember. No other girl had ever attracted him. Since Deimuiss had disappeared, he had trodden very carefully, knowing that it would take a long time for Elvaennia to accept he was not going to return. He prayed that he would never ever come back, and that then Elvaennia would always be his. Slowly, she had come to accept him as a good friend and would confide her heartbreak to him as he gently wiped away her sorrowful tears. At times, he felt impatient with her, wanting her to see him as more than a friend, and to know that he wanted to marry her. Being so close to her unsettled him greatly, wanting to draw her into his arms and cover her beautiful face and neck with kisses. How he longed to run his hands through her beautiful, long, silvery hair. Every day he thanked the gods for giving him Elvaennia. She filled his every waking hour. Her graceful body haunted his dreams. Her smile set his heart racing. Each morning he awoke thinking of her beauty and that she was his. He vowed that nobody would ever come between them. She was his and his alone. He prayed every night that Deimuiss would never return, as he knew Elvaennia would never give him a chance if he did. Should members of the tribe so much as cast a look in her direction, the malevolence of Carnaan's look would quickly make them look away. The tribe now accepted that Carnaan had replaced Deimuiss in Elvaennia's affections. What they did not realise was that in Elvaennia's eyes, Carnaan was just her friend; there would never be another man to take Deimuiss's place in her life.

Elvaennia had felt lost, sunk in despair, lonely and sad since Deimuiss had disappeared. He had been her only love. She had never wanted any other man in her life. Just thinking about him set her pulses racing and her body tingled for his touch. Hearing his deep, rich voice would send her running to him. He would lift her up, kissing her eyes, her face, her lips so that she ached for him to marry her; to make their lives complete. When he had failed to return from his hunting trip, Elvaennia thought she would die of her anguish. For weeks, she could barely eat and her family began to despair that they would lose her because she lost so much weight from her already slim body. Slowly, she had become aware of Carnaan offering his sympathy and company through those days of anguish. She began to rely on him and lean on him. He listened so patiently to her outpouring of grief and agony at the loss of her soul mate.

Elvaennia was grateful to Carnaan, and together they would go to the Hill of the Spirits in the hope that she would be able to put Deimuiss's spirit to rest. What hurt her beyond measure was that she had never come to terms with, or understood, why she had never seen his spirit rising up into the heavens. Did this mean he was not dead? She wondered anew. If he was not dead then where was he? The more she thought about it, the more her thoughts tortured her.

This added to the sum total of her grief, and she turned to Carnaan even more for friendship and advice, worried that her lover's spirit was not at rest.

Carnaan was more than happy to share her grief and to offer her his support. After all, he had loved her for many years. He thanked all the gods repeatedly for giving him this opportunity and swore he would make her love him.

He would put his arm around her slim waist and draw her close to him. He adored the sweet smell of her skin – it reminded him of spring flowers - and the softness of her body that moulded itself to his. Her small breasts were soft and warm against his tunic. At times, it almost became too much for him, and he wanted so much to make her his own. He restrained himself, knowing that this was not the right time. He knew his patience would be rewarded in the end. Then, Elvaennia would be his for all time. Her beautiful grey eyes would no longer shed oceans of soft tears for Deimuiss; they would shine with love for him. No more sadness and despair, instead she would worship and adore only him.

Rising from his bed, he made ready for the day. Donning tunic and trousers, he tied his belt around him. Taking his small pouch, he slipped a small ring inside it along with charms and amulets.

'Soon, Elvaennia, my love, you will be mine. The time of mourning is nearing its end.'

A cruel smile suddenly crept across his face at the thought of how he would soon bind Elvaennia to him eternally.

'Not long,' he muttered, scanning the landscape for her. An underground passageway did not link their homes but Elvaennias house was only a short distance from his. This suited him because when he married her she would be his alone; no one could enter his house via a passageway. His thin lips twisted in glee when he thought of her becoming his and his alone. Walking across the open ground towards her house, he realised his day could not begin without a glimpse of her slim gracefulness. He longed for a glance from her grey eyes, which would change to silver when she laughed, igniting his whole body, filling him with a burning passion. Carnaan knew he was obsessed with Elvaennia, and had been for many years. The thought that his endless wait to possess her was nearly at an end excited him beyond measure. His jealousy of Deimuiss had reached gigantic proportions, and when he had disappeared, Carnaan had never been more delighted in his life. He prayed to every god that he could think of that Deimuiss would never return.

'I have to have her for myself. No one else will ever possess her. She will belong to me, never him or anyone else.'

Carnaan of course did not understand, or have any knowledge of, the invisible golden thread that joins two people together for all time. His jealousy of Deimuiss overrode logical thought. To him, possessing Elvaennia in physical terms meant that she would be his body and soul for eternity and beyond. Little did he realise what fate had in store.

Suddenly, she was there, walking towards him, a beautiful smile lighting her face. He stopped in his tracks, waiting for her to draw near.

'Good morning, Carnaan.'

Her small, white, even teeth were revealed through her smile. The sight and smell of her was almost too much for him and he stepped back. A look of surprise crossed her face as she asked, 'What's the matter? Have I offended you?'

'No, oh no. Of course not.'

Smiling, he reached out his hand, drawing her towards him, saying, 'Will you walk with me, Elvy?'

'A few minutes are all I have. Grandmamma, Trieainia and I are going to The Standing Stones.'

He nodded.

'Would you like me to accompany you, Elvy?'

'No, it's fine. Thanks for offering.'

Seeing his look of disappointment, she said, 'I will be back soon. Why don't you come to meet me?'

'Yes, that's a good idea,' he agreed, thinking that this would be ideal. He would then have her to himself once they had dropped her grandmother and sister off at her home. Then, he would ask her to go for a walk with him and give her the ring that would bind her to him for all time. His pulse quickening, he quickly turned away so she could not see the smug look that flitted across his face. How he longed to take her, even now, into his house and lay beside her on his bed. Quickly, he drove these libidinous thoughts from his mind. He was aware how perceptive Elvaennia was, and did not want her to suspect that he had anything but pure intentions towards her.

Carnaan knew he was lucky to have a home of his own. His parents and family had moved to a distant camp to be near his elderly grandparents. He refused to leave, making different excuses for not going with them. The real reason he kept to himself, was that there was no way he would ever leave Elvaennia. Now he pursued her ruthlessly. Anger would shoot through him like an angry flame when he thought his rival Deimuiss. Now, he thought, 'I have every opportunity and it won't be long before she will be mine for eternity.'

He was under no illusions about why she was visiting The Stones – she was obviously going to try to find out if Deimuiss was ever going to come back. 'He can return when she is mine,' he laughed. It was an evil sound. His thoughts sped along a happy track, thinking of how Deimuiss would feel knowing that Elvaennia was his, and that she shared his bed and life. For once, he felt elated. The cards were stacked in his favour. Nothing could go wrong now. Deimuiss was off the scene and his plans were made.

'I have all the advantages while he is missing,' he thought. Jealousy of Deimuiss flushed his face, and anger again filled his mind and body. 'I will never know peace of mind until she wears my ring.' Controlling his thoughts, and as much as it pained him, he bade her farewell and surprising himself managed to wish her good luck. He decided to work hard while she was absent – that would make the time pass quickly and help wear away some of his anger. After all, he thought, the animals needed tending and there were many jobs to do around the settlement. First he had the wood to cut, his stock of fuel having run low. Carnaan could not resist one last look at Elvaennia as she hurried away. 'How slim and tiny she is,' he thought, 'and so beautiful, and totally unaware of the effect she has on men.' What was more – she was his, and soon would be for all time. He began making his plans for later that day when she returned.

Turning towards the enclosure where he kept his sheep, goats and horses, he saw Pranny, a neighbour's daughter, watching him.

'My, you have it bad for her.'

Carnaan looked at her beneath lashless eyes.

'What's it to you who I speak to?' he asked churlishly.

'She doesn't want you, you fool!'

Her dark eyes burnt into his, the very air seemed taut around both of them. She lifted a well-rounded arm and stroked his face sensuously. Her shapely body suddenly came alive and he realised how much he needed her – to try to drive out thoughts of Elvaennia's slim beauty. Raking his eyes up and down her, she smiled invitingly at him. 'Meet me at the forest track within the hour,' he offered breathlessly.

'Why not now?' She pouted, bending forward so he caught sight of her voluptuous young breasts. Licking his lips in anticipation, he agreed.

'The Mystics and Elders must not suspect anything untoward is happening or we will be brought before them, you know, and they will throw us out of the settlement.'

'Yes, but that makes it even more exciting.'

With a coy look, Pranny mischievously swayed away, every step inviting him to follow her.

Making haste to tend the animals, Carnaan's thoughts were in tumult. He had never realised that Pranny held him in any regard. He thought, 'I have only ever had eyes for Elvaennia.' All the same, his young body was on fire with lust – and it was only lust he told himself – for Pranny.

Ensuring that no one was watching him, he quickly took a roundabout route to the forest track. Having only walked a few steps along it, Pranny stepped out from behind a tree, her red gold hair shot through with sunlight. 'Here,' she beckoned softly. Glancing around, worried anyone should see him with Pranny – after all he knew she had a reputation for enticing men – Carnaan stepped off the track. 'Follow me,' she encouraged him, making her way along an animal trail. He could smell the musky scent of her body, which only served to inflame his senses as he followed her shapely form through the full, lush, green bushes. She suddenly stepped off the trail. He followed, desire flooding all his senses. Within a few steps, they were in a small clearing. He reached out for her, his need almost spilling out of him. 'Wait,' she murmured, slowly removing her tunic to reveal her nakedness to him. His eyes hotly raked her body. She swung her long, red blonde hair, enticing him to come to her. He reached out, anxious to take his fill of her, but she stepped back. Licking her lips suggestively, she asked, 'What have you got for me then, Carnaan?' By now, Carnaan was beyond waiting for her, and taking two long strides, he flung her to the ground and despite her protests, within minutes it was all over.

Sated, he sprawled across her. Angrily, she declared he would pay for raping her, and made to get up. Too late. He was on her again, spilling his seed into her, calling out Elvaennia's name as he took the young woman again and again. The more she cried out in pain, the more excited he became, and all he could think was that the woman beneath him was Elvaennia and that now she was his. The forest clearing was silent. No leaves rustled. There was no bird song. The forest seemed to wait with baited breath for the man to finish his violent assault on the woman.

Just when she thought her ordeal was over, he took her savagely one last time, again calling out his obsession for the woman he had so desperately craved for years. Suddenly, he was spent and disgusted with himself for betraying Elvaennia with Pranny he roughly pushed her away.

'You bastard,' she cried out to him.

'You liked it, bitch,' he growled, 'and do not tell me you didn't or why else did you ask to meet me here.'

'You'll pay for this Carnaan, never fear.'

He laughed and a terrible look crossed his face, making Pranny fear for her life. She turned, grabbed her tunic and painfully pulled it on. Seizing her pouch, she noticed his pouch lying where he had carelessly thrown it in his anxiety to take her. She picked it up and very slowly made her way away from him. He was still lying on the grass, naked, staring up at the canopy of trees. 'I don't think he even knows I've gone,' she cried pitifully, wiping the tears from her face.

Up until now, all her little escapades with the young boys and men had been fun and enjoyable. No one had ever treated her as Carnaan had. 'He will pay,' she mumbled wiping the tears away. Stumbling through the forest, every inch of her ached and she longed to be lying safely in her bed.

Resting against a tree, she opened his pouch and found the ring.

'Got him,' she crowed triumphantly, slipping it on her ring finger.

'Get out of this, Carnaan.'

She also removed the amulets for good measure. Throwing his pouch on the track, she made her way back home.

'Just a couple of days, that's all I need,' she vowed, 'and he will be tied to me forever. That will be punishment for him. He will never have Elvaennia, now that I have the ring and I have the seed of his first born within me. I will tell the Elders and the Mystics. They will make him wed me. He will never get Elvaennia. No man treats me like dirt and gets away with it.' These thoughts comforted Pranny as she slowly and painfully made her way home, her face still wet with tears. 'But once we are married he will never live with me, I will never divorce him though, that will ensure he never marries Elvaennia. Revenge can be very sweet; he will spend a lifetime regretting this day's work.'

Chapter 17

The alarm woke me. Jumping out of bed, I quickly showered and dressed in a pair of jeans and blouse plus my trainers. Mary had told me the previous evening that we were going to Birmingham and would be doing a lot of walking, and I wanted to be comfortable. How easily I seemed to have settled into this lifetime. Although, at times, some things were still rather strange to me, they quickly fell into place as my memory switched up a gear. That is the best and easiest way I can describe it. Brushing my hair until it sparked silver; I decided I had no time for make-up today. Taking a last look in the mirror, I hurried downstairs.

'Morning, Mary.'

I greeted her with a smile as she placed the, by now customary, huge plate of bacon and fried eggs before me.

'My, where you put it all is beyond me. You're nought but skin and bone, just like…'

She gasped and spluttered on her words and ran towards the sink where the tap was fast filling the bowl.

'Like who, Mary?' I queried innocently, wondering who I could possibly resemble that she knew.

Noisily, she clattered the pots in the bowl, ignoring my question. Again, I knew she was holding on to secrets about others and possibly me. The quizzical way she looked at me at times made me aware that she knew far more than she let on. Things she began to say, like just now, then hastily changing the subject. I wondered how many other time travellers had been rescued by Mary and David. There, I had admitted it to myself now. I was more than convinced that this was what they had been doing over the years, and I longed to able to get into her or David's mind. I really wished I could break through the wall they had erected to stop me reading their secrets. I did not pursue her with more questions. I knew it would all come out one day. Why did they make their home available for time travellers? For what reason did people come from other times? Why was I here? I knew I had been told several times that I had some work to do – but so far, no work apart from helping Mary in the farmhouse had come my way. No time to think of that now. Ascertaining from Mary that we were due to leave in the next half hour, I picked up the tea cloth and helped her finish the chores. Mary rarely used the dishwasher during the week.

'Looking after our carbon footprints, you see.'

This was another one of her pet subjects: saving the planet. I agreed with her when I see all the waste scattered around compared with my time this centuries' waste is horrendous. The air smells obnoxious; everywhere is so dirty; plastic bottles litter the streets; the countryside is strewn with waste of every description. It saddens me to see the world being destroyed by humanity.

Driving towards Birmingham, I was amazed at the amount of traffic on the roads. I had thought the A51 through Rugeley was bad, but the roads to Birmingham were something else. There were coaches, heavy goods vehicles and seemingly thousands of cars streaming along in different lanes. I should not have been as shocked as I was, because I had watched enough news bulletins on the television. What a huge learning curve that had been! Finding myself in the midst of so much traffic was a whole new experience. It was daunting, and made me feel claustrophobic. I found it overwhelming, to say the least. After all, I was used to horse power of a very different kind. I was taken aback at times. Whenever the traffic was brought to a halt, it felt as if I was sitting in a huge poisonous car park. No wonder the planet was dying. If only I could go forward in time, I thought, to see if the world carried on or whether it died as it began with the big bang.

'Look Elvaennia, Spaghetti Junction.'

I looked out of the passenger window expecting to see spaghetti straddling the road. All I could see was traffic piling up and down roads on different levels; and at strange angles as well. It dawned on me very quickly why it was so-called, and thank goodness I had not made an idiot of myself by asking Mary. I'd embarrassed myself several times before and I was now learning to think before jumping right in with any comments.

Now Mary was pulling into a car park, and we were going round and round and up and up. 'Hold in there,' I thought. This was like the journey I had made from the settlement to this time. I had to take some deep breaths because I felt quite panicky at remembering that occasion.

'Okay Elvaennia?'

Mary's kindly tones brought me swiftly back into focus. A weak smile was exchanged, then she announced.

'Now for the shopping experience of your life, young lady.'

I had been shopping with her in Rugeley several times. Perhaps that had been the preparation course? I was amazed at the amount of food people packed into their trolleys. At first my eyes were on stalks, looking at shelves and shelves of foodstuffs on sale. Staring into the baskets at the array of food and the sheer amounts left me open mouthed. Did people really manage to eat that much? Mary had to poke me in the ribs, telling me not to be so rude. She glanced and apologised to the lady trolley-pusher whose basket I had been studying, then tugged me away.

'So much food for one person!'

'Elvaennia, people have to eat you know.'

'Whoops. I didn't mean to be rude. Sorry.' I gulped. 'It's just that particular basket looked overstocked, but obviously, she is shopping for more than one person I should imagine.' Thinking quietly to myself, I hoped she was.

'Take the toothbrushes and toothpastes for instance.'

I pointed towards them.

'How many teeth have we got in our mouths for goodness sake? There are so many different shapes and sizes, colours and prices, and that's just the toothbrushes! Now look at the toothpastes. I'm amazed and just know I would never, ever be able to choose on my own. Oh Mary, it was so much easier when I used a leaf or some grass.'

'Shush Elvaennia. I don't know what on earth you are talking about, but people will think you are very strange coming out with things like that.'

Oh dear, poor Mary had gone red with embarrassment.

I apologised, as I certainly did not want to upset Mary. She had become a dear friend despite her being so much older than me. But still, I could not stop being amazed at the amount of food stocked in the supermarkets. There was really no comparison with my own time. Whereas we would stock herbs, seeds, meat, fish, birds and rabbits, leaving them hanging to dry for the cold winter months, here, people seemed to shop daily and buy enormous amounts. We never took more than we needed, and always tried to put something back; whereas in this time there were massive amounts of waste.

This was going to be a wholly different shopping experience. I knew it, because Mary had told me we were going clothes shopping. Whoopee! I knew I was going to love it.

After collecting the parking ticket, we went through the swing doors and I jumped in amazement to see a flight of stairs moving as if on their own volition.

'Come on now.'

'Walk down them?' I stuttered.

'No, just stand on them. This is another new experience for you, part of your education,' she hissed, grabbing my arm and hauling me on to what she called an 'escalator'. (From time to time, I had noticed Mary could get a little off-hand with me). What with going up to the car park, and now down an escalator, I wondered what else the day would bring for me to contend with.

I soon found out. At the bottom of the second escalator, I wanted to run back to the car park. There was so much noise everywhere, and thousands of people milling around. My head felt fit to burst. I really was awestruck by everything that hit my eyes and my poor ears. Yes, I had seen cities on the television, but this was a real life experience and it was unbelievable. It did not seem to bother any of the crowds of people who were rushing here, there and everywhere like swarms of bees. My head was swimming.

Taking my arm, Mary pulled me to one side.

'Take some deep breaths Elvaennia. You will be fine in a few minutes.'

I did as she bid, and it worked. Everything quickly fell into place just as it had the day I arrived. Only faster this time.

My head cleared and soon I was strolling past the shops, arm in arm with Mary as if it was something I did daily. I simply did not know where to look first; clothes of every shape and description filled the windows of the big department stores. It was a good thing Mary had hold of my arm, or I would not have got very far.

Leaving the Pallasades shopping centre, we found ourselves on an extremely crowded walkway – talk about sardines in a can (Mary's expression not mine)! We went past McDonalds. I had visited one of these outlets before at Cannock and enjoyed it immensely. Once again, Mary had said it was part of my education. And then we headed across a set of traffic lights into the city.

What held me in thrall were the Christmas decorations – despite Christmas being quite a few weeks away – strung across the streets; shop windows full of glitzy glamour, the sides of the buildings decorated with magical figures of elves, fairies, angels and Father Christmas. It was so wonderful. I would so liked to have seen them at night. I could imagine the whole city transformed into a winter wonderland. A notice caught my eye – 'Ice skating in Centenary Square'. 'I bet that's a wonderful sight to see,' I thought, remembering how Deimuiss and I had skated across the frozen lakes of the Chase.

Where Mary got her strength from was beyond me. After an hour or so, I was dead on my legs. My feet throbbed, my legs were sore, my back ached, and still Mary looked as fresh as a daisy and managed to keep a conversation going continuously. Not that I was complaining – I had bought some great jeans and tops and was well-pleased, but badly needed to rest my aching legs. In the end, I dragged her into a café and ordered us both a cup of coffee and a sandwich.

This was far more tiring than a day's hunting in the forests. I've hunted with a party of five men, stalked the wild boar for hours, made the kill, skinned the beast and helped carry it home and still felt full of life and energy. Two hours shopping in this city had left me tired out.

'I'm worn out, exhausted, Mary. Where do you get your energy from?'

'Practice my dear. All women love to shop and I'm sure you will get used to it.'

A man walked past our table and handed me a sheet of paper. Reading it, my heart skipped a beat. It was advertising a psychic fair being held today. At the venue, there were clairvoyants, mediums, tarot-and angel-card readers and healers, along with people selling crystal balls, cards and crystals, runes, books and many other things.

Excitedly, I drew Mary's attention to the flyer.

'May we go, please?' I pleaded with her.

Mary did not seem to be very keen on the idea; but she agreed, her face full of misgivings. She quickly finished her coffee, grabbed the carrier bags, and off we trotted in the direction of the hotel.

My tiredness had vanished like magic and I easily kept apace of Mary, helping her with the carrier bags.

I didn't know what to expect but was amazed on entering the room where the fair was being held. It was so crowded.

Walking around, I saw people sat at small tables with various items used for the task of predicting the future: from tarot cards to runes, from runes to crystal balls and playing cards, so many different items – and even sand readings. I was not tempted to ask for a reading. This surprised Mary and she offered to pay for one, but I refused her kind offer.

I approached a table where a gentleman was reading the tarot cards for a lady. He was a small, elderly, Indian gentleman dressed in an old fashioned manner. I hovered nearby, intrigued by his cards. They were extremely old and I was fascinated by the pictures and by the interpretations the man was putting on the reading. He glanced up at me and smiled. Suddenly, I blushed, realising I was invading their space. I intimated that I would wait for a reading but he shook his head saying in a gentle voice, 'Later my dear, but not here.' I shook my head, wondering what on earth he meant. I hastily scurried away but the memory of the cards was imprinted on my mind, as was the kindness of the expression on his face when he had smiled at me. I walked around the hall but I did not see another deck of cards resembling the ones the elderly reader had been using. If I had, I would have been very tempted to buy them. I had felt very drawn to the cards. I wondered why I had not waited to have a reading from him.

A stall at the far end of the hall drew me to it. There was a notice that said simply 'Spiritual Healing'. I helped myself to a leaflet. Some instinct told me that it would be of significance to me.

The Angel Tarot Cards also fascinated me. I had always known that angels walked beside me, so to actually see people giving readings intrigued me; and I wondered how their style of reading compared to mine. Again, I was not drawn to anyone for a reading.

Passing one stall, my hand was suddenly grasped by the lady owner who pulled me into a seat beside her.

'Now deary, the cameras will be on us in a minute. As they start reeling, I will give you a quick reading!'

My eyes were like saucers. A reading!

'Oh well, cool,' I thought. 'Why not?'

'Draw three cards now,' the lady instructed me. I looked at her and could see what a good person she was. Honesty shone through her eyes. She was such a hard worker, I thought, her eyes a wonderful dark chocolate brown and I could see how much she had suffered through her life. She realised what was happening and immediately the veil was drawn and she pushed the cards closer. 'Three,' she repeated firmly.

'Ah, you have drawn the Snowflake Angel, a good positive card,' she said loudly for the cameras. 'There are many new beginnings but also changes around All Hallows Eve next year. You will have to prepare for it Elvaennia, in the coming months.'

How did she know my name?

'Many truths will be made known to you.'

Turning my next choice of card over, a puzzled look crossed her face and she gave me a quick look as if to say she didn't believe it. Clearing her throat, she started to say, 'Elvaennia, where you have travelled from is a place unknown to us mere mortals. You have seen and experienced things unknown to mankind today.' She stumbled on her words. Realising what she had been saying, she quickly said, 'You will take up a new profession and help many people in this lifetime.' Hesitating for a heartbeat, the words seemed to be out of her mouth before she could stop them. '...and in other lifetimes.' I looked behind me, hearing gasps of astonishment at her words and was astonished to see groups of people gathered around the stall, the cameras panning round their shocked faces. Oh my goodness, this lady reader had blown my cover. How was I going to get out of this?

Muttering a sarcastic, 'Thanks very much indeed,' I scanned the faces around me and was so relieved to see Mary almost bouncing up and down at the back, waving me to follow her. I pushed through the milling crowds as fast as I could, ignoring their shouted questions and the man with the microphone who was trying to get me to speak to him. No way did I want or need any media attention. Almost running from the hall, to my utter relief, I found Mary waiting for me outside.

'Oh dear, Mary. That was awful. Let's hope it doesn't make it to the television screens.'

'Too late for that Elvaennia. I think we may have to lie low for a while. Come along. We will head for home.'

After making certain we weren't being followed by anybody, we headed for Corporation Street by a roundabout route. Mary popped into Rackhams, 'for one last item.' I waited outside with the shopping. I'd decided there was a limit to this shopping experience after all, but kept my eyes skimmed for any lurking journalists. Looking across the road at a group of buildings that included 'Mothercare', 'New Look' and what looked to be a sports shop, suddenly, as if from nowhere, a mist clouded my vision and my head felt really muzzy. I tried to shake the feeling away but it did not help at all.

As quickly as it had arrived, the mist dispersed and, to my utter astonishment, I suddenly found myself sitting in front of a small, elderly, Indian gentleman who seemed very familiar indeed. It appeared as if he was about to tell me my fortune. Scanning his desk, I saw that the deck of tarot cards in front of him was an exact replica of the cards I had seen at the psychic fair. Taking a further look, I realised I was right – this was the same gentleman I had seen at the psychic fair. What was happening?

Looking around, I saw we were in a small, wood-panelled room. Glancing out of the window, I realised we were on the second floor. I could see horse drawn carriages going up and down the street where not long ago there had been buses. In fact, I realised that I had time travelled yet again and arrived in the Edwardian age. The manner of the man's clothing, as well as the room, spoke of the time I was in. This was just too confusing for words. He was at the psychic fair a mere 10 minutes ago. And just now, I had been outside Rackham's. Whatever was happening?

Glancing down at myself, I saw I was dressed in a very regal manner; my dress was electric blue and made of shot silk. A beautiful, pale blue parasol rested against my chair and on my lap was a marvellous, dainty blue, embroidered reticule. I felt really elegant, not like my normal self at all.

I looked at the gentleman facing me with astonishment imprinted on my face. How on earth had I time travelled to this era?

The man proceeded to read the cards as he had predicted he would earlier.

'I see you have lived many previous lives and there are more lives to live before your journey is finished. Then, you will travel to the Time Beyond.'

I frowned at his words, wondering what he meant. As if reading my thoughts, the kindly gentleman proceeded to explain.

'The first life you remember was spent at a place known as the settlement.'

At his words, I gripped the edge of my seat. How on earth did this stranger know where I had lived in my own time?

'You were exceedingly happy in that lifetime until your betrothed disappeared as if into thin air. I am correct Elvaennia,' he stated in a firm voice.

I merely nodded. By now, I felt extremely nervous, agitated, and wondered what he was going to say next.

'You eventually found yourself in a different lifetime but you still sadly missed your beloved. But, I would be correct, would I not, in saying that you briefly left that lifetime and met up with your betrothed in a past century?'

This was making me tremble with shock. What extraordinary gift did this little man have? Nodding again – I seemed to have lost the power of speech – I suddenly pulled myself together to ask him, 'Will I ever see him again?'

A beatific smile flickered across his kindly features. 'Of course you will my dear, but I'm afraid the road ahead will be rocky – to say the least.'

'Will I eventually marry Deimuiss?'

'Ah, now, that is outside of my time and remit.'

'Pardon,' I whispered. 'You cannot tell me?'

Shaking his greying, almost white head of hair, the elderly reader added, 'You will soon return to 2007 my child, where fame and fortune will be knocking at your door.'

I groaned, remembering the psychic fair. One thing I did not want was fame and fortune. I wanted to be with my long-lost love.

As if reading my thoughts, the man laughed saying, with a twinkle in his eye, 'You cannot avoid fate. If it is written in the cards, then it will happen whatever you say or do. That's all I can tell you for now, but wesh not. All will become clear in times yet to come.'

I sat up straight-as-a-dye as Grandmamma's expression hit my ears.

'Where did you hear those words?'

'I felt you needed more proof of my gift, my dear. I have another client waiting in the wings for a reading, so I will say goodbye for now.'

'Just one more question, please? Will I be happy?'

'In time, Elvaennia. In time.'

135

That was all I needed to hear. I began to take my leave, and then it hit me – how on earth did I get back to 2007? Was I now going to be stuck in Edwardian times? Life was beginning to get very difficult.

Sensing my confusion, the gentleman jumped from his chair and opened the door for me.

'Goodbye my dear. All will be fine. Try not to worry.'

He smiled as I walked past him on to the landing. I began to descend the stairway.

Hearing a sound, I turned quickly and could not believe my eyes. A man was greeting the reader. It was Deimuiss. I called out.

'Deimuiss, Deimuiss, it is I, Elvaennia.'

I almost jumped back up the stair towards him... when I found myself being pulled upwards by an invisible force, just as I had been torn away from my own time before. Now, it was happening again.

'Oh, I have lost him again,' I sobbed, realising my love was lost to me yet again.

The mysterious force pulled me relentlessly upwards. I wondered where I would find myself and I hoped that if it was not back with my family, then it would be with Mary. I could not face another century and another disappointment. I felt myself being pulled downwards, spun around, and with a thump found myself sitting outside Rackham's department store, on the pavement. Highly embarrassed, I looked around to see if anyone had noticed my fall from grace. Fortunately, no one was staring at me. I quickly stood up, dusted myself down, and felt relieved to see I was back in 2007 attire. I gazed around, and just ahead of me saw a man dressed in a very smart suit talking to a group of young people who I took to be students.

The well-dressed gent noticed me watching him from the corner of his eye and called out, 'Hello,' in a very pleasant manner.

I was impressed by his friendliness and moved in to hear what he was saying. He was speaking with great authority to the students about the history of the buildings in Corporation Street in the early 20th century. I found it fascinating. Suddenly, he pointed down towards the end of the street and said, 'Here's a quirky bit of information one of my listeners sent me – In chambers 2 and 11, a Professor Burton used to do what he called psychology readings for members of the public. He published a number of booklets dealing with phrenology (head readings), physiognomy (face readings), palmistry, and many other forms of interesting readings all aimed at helping people overcome their difficulties in a psychological and psychic way.'

One of the students interrupted him asking, 'Professor Chinn.'

'Call me Carl,' he chipped in, with a big grin as the student went on to ask his question.

I was astonished at hearing what the Professor had said about the very building I had just visited, all-be-it by accident in another time. Wanting to hear more, I lent an ear only to become aware that Mary was bustling towards me with another couple of shopping bags.

'You okay, Elvaennia?'

Not waiting for an answer, she swept me down the busy street towards the Pallasades Shopping Centre. I couldn't resist taking another peek at the building I had just visited.

Chatting to Mary, I mentioned that I had just overheard a Professor Carl Chinn talking to a group of students about the history of the area.

'Never! You mean THE Professor Carl Chinn? Wish I had seen him.'

'Oh, you know him?'

'I know *of* him.' She corrected me. 'He is one of the most famous people in Birmingham. He is a brilliant historian. I call him the 'Brummie Treasure'. He even has his own show on Radio WM, and he does an unbelievable amount of work for charity.'

'Really? Mm, that's what he meant about listeners. He's a radio presenter. I was lucky to catch sight of him and hear him teaching the students.'

'Yes, I envy you. I would so love to meet him. Come along then Elvaennia, we'd better get home before the evening rush hour starts. We don't want anyone recognising you, do we?'

She scurried ahead as I took a last lingering look at the city. Somehow I didn't think I would be returning any time soon, but I was impressed that I had met two professors in one day. Not bad considering I had never even met *one* before, apart, of course, from the Mystics back at the settlement. They, and the Elders, were definitely the professors of their time. I'd also loved the Christmas decorations. They were indeed beautiful, even if Christmas was some time off.

Hurrying after Mary, I agreed with her: the last thing I needed was any one of the people who were milling around to recognise me. Fame and fortune beckoning me? Not a chance, I thought, but then what did I know?

Travelling back to Rugeley, I was determined not to be downcast at missing Deimuiss yet again. I rustled through the leaflets I had picked up at the psychic fair. One in particular caught my eye, and brushing my hair away from my eyes, I read it quickly.

'Oh Mary, listen to this – Lichfield Spiritualist Church is holding a psychic evening.'

Before I could say another word, Mary gave a deep chuckle saying, 'Yes, we will go if we have nothing else booked. When is it being held?'

Scanning the paper, I told her, 'Saturday.'

'Mmm. I have that evening booked, but I will take you and arrange a lift home. Don't worry.'

'Oh Mary, you are a 'Rugeley Treasure' just as you called Carl Chinn the 'Brummie Treasure'!'

She laughed loudly.

'Ah, but I wish I had Carl's knowledge. That makes a huge difference you know.'

Chapter 18

Deciding I had to find out more about the history of Rugeley, I asked Mary if it was okay if I visited the local library in town.

'Fine!' she trilled as she busily polished the furniture. Catching the scent of the 'Pledge' polish she was spraying reminded me of the wild lavender that Mamma picked at the settlement and used in her cooking. She also made up small sachets that she placed beneath the furs if we were having restless nights.

'Okay.' I smiled, thinking how fast I'd picked up that word. 'Won't be long. Off for the bus now. Have my mobile with me.'

The first time I had heard a mobile telephone ring, I had jumped, and then when Mary explained to me that you could speak to people you could not even see, I was awestruck. 'Even dead people?' I had asked. I had been thinking of my dead relatives and wondering about my family at the settlement and ancestors in the Time without End.

'Erm, no. Only living people, and they have to own a telephone as well,' she had pointed out. 'If you like, I will get you one. I think you will find it useful.'

Feeling very embarrassed by my stupid mistake, I readily agreed to having one, thinking that if you could contact people so easily, I would soon find Deimuiss. Never thinking, of course, that I would need his number first. Another silly mistake!

Jumping on the local bus, the houses flew past in a flash. Before I knew it, we were pulling into the bus station. I walked through the shopping precinct, past Smiths' bookshop, and then swung down the

High Street heading in the general direction of the library. I was still amazed at how easily I had settled into this lifetime. If only Deimuiss were here with my family from the settlement. Then, I think, I would be more than happy – apart from the noise that is! I would, of course, be far happier living back at the settlement with him beside me, planning our new life together, but it seemed that this was not to be.

Passing a couple of card shops and the local Woolworths made me remember that I would soon be needing cards and gifts for Christmas, and I determined to have a good look round the shops one day soon. Not that I needed too many really, as I knew so few people. But I was looking forward to my first Christmas, never having experienced this celebration before; and the fact that you exchanged gifts was an added enticement. I found it interesting that only one God was worshipped – because, back in my time, there was a god for everything we knew.

Walking through the marketplace, my eyes were drawn to a stall selling rich displays of beautiful flowers: pinks, russet reds, lilacs, white. So many colours and different varieties were on sale. I thought to myself that I would buy some for Mary as soon as I had finished at the library. She had been so good to me. Thinking about how good Mary and David were, I was more than convinced they knew far more than they let on, and I wished they would tell me what it was.

Mary would still cast the odd thoughtful look in my direction. As for David – did I imagine the secrets hidden in the depths of those oh-so-green eyes? I think not.

One day soon, I was going to sit them both down and ask them to tell all.

Entering the library, I was overcome by the huge number of books on display and I wondered how on earth I was going to find out anything about the towns past. I hadn't a clue where to start looking.

I made my way to the reception area and had a word with a small, pleasant-faced, grey-haired lady. She told me to, 'ask Julia, she deals with local history. She's just over there.' She pointed across the room.

'Oh great! A local history assistant.'

I was delighted. I approached the young lady who had truly

beautiful, long, curly, light brown hair with wonderful highlights. Her elfin face lit up when I asked her if she had anything in the files about the early history of Rugeley.

'Follow me,' she said gaily, running lightly up a flight of stairs and entering a room to the left of the staircase. I noticed she was married, and instinct told me she had two youngsters: a boy and a girl, the boy being the oldest.

'I wonder how I know these things,' I mused, settling myself on a chair by the Formica topped table.

Enthusiasm shining from her eyes, Julia headed for the shelves at the back of the room. 'How far back do you want to go?' Her voice floated cheerfully back to where I was sitting. It took me a minute to register that she was speaking to me, because I was still admiring her beautiful hair.

'As far as possible,' I called, slipping the handle of my denim (embroidered with flowers, by Mary) bag on to the back of the seat and slipping off my jacket. I certainly looked, and felt, ready for business.

'Here you go then. Here's some to be getting on with.'

Smiling, Julia cheerfully placed a huge pile of files in front of me. As she made her way to the door, she glanced back saying, 'Give me a shout if you need any more help.' With a swirl of skirts, she was gone, her high heels tip tapping down the flight of stairs.

I could tell from her enthusiasm she enjoyed her job enormously.

Nodding my thanks, I immersed myself in the files piled up on the table. This was going to be such fun.

I perused the early history folder. It stated briefly that there were signs of early settlers on the Chase. Burnt hearth stones had been found along with other small finds at a Mesolithic cave. I nearly fell off my chair with excitement. This was it – what I had been looking for. My eyes were on stalks as I read about the flint and arrow finds, also animal bones, but my eagerness abated fast when I read about two skulls discovered outside the cave, one of an older lady and one of a young woman. Blinking my eyes, finding it hard to stop the flow of tears, I read on, but there was no mention of our tribe. A huge lump in my throat threatened to choke me.

But, apart from that article, I could not find any more information. I shuddered, wondering if the skulls were of my relatives. But, on reflection, I did not think they could be, because surely Mamma and Papa would have discovered them and they would have sent them to the Time Beyond.

Disappointed at the lack of any more information, I sought out young Julia, asking if she knew the lady who wrote the ghost books that I had read about on the Staffordshire Ghost website.

'What a helpful person,' I thought, strolling across the supermarket car park, heading towards the lady's house. Julia had phoned the lady for me and Caroline (that was the lady's name) had told her to send me straight across.

Walking across the bridge that spanned the brook, I headed down the old lane towards the lady's house. As I opened the gate that led into Caroline's driveway, I happened to glance up at the bedroom window of the empty house next door. I was surprised to see an elderly gentleman gazing back at me. He didn't smile or in any way acknowledge my presence. Why should he? He was a ghost.

The door to Caroline's house suddenly swung open and I was greeted with a beaming smile by a slim, golden-haired lady in her late twenties. She wore glasses that magnified her amber coloured eyes beautifully. I also noticed that she had attractive, black eyebrows and long, black eyelashes. I immediately took to her and felt really comfortable in her presence.

'Do come in and make yourself at home.'

She ushered me into a pleasant living room and sat me on a wonderful, old, brown and orange tweed-effect sofa. Sinking into its depths, I felt immediately at home. 'Now what can I do to help?' she asked.

I explained how I had come across her name on the local Rugeley website and seen that she collected and wrote ghost stories; and that I had visited her website. Suddenly, I hesitated, thinking she might think I was foolish when she knew my reason for visiting.

Encouraging me with a smile, she said, 'Go on. Don't be

embarrassed. You won't shock me in any way.'

Plucking up my courage and taking a deep breath, I stuttered, saying.

'Have you ever seen or heard of any ghosts by the old cave on the hillside off Swift Lane?'

Caroline's eyes opened wide and she did indeed look surprised.

'The Mesolithic cave?'

Nodding in agreement, I watched various expressions flit across her face. Suddenly, she sighed and muttered, 'I knew this day would come.'

'You know of it?' I asked eagerly, leaning towards her.

Nodding, she sat twisting her hands as if wondering what to tell me.

'I've only heard rumours, you understand.'

'Anything you may have heard will help me,' I whispered, pushing my hair back from my eyes.

'It was about two years ago. A middle aged man knocked on my door. He was in a real state. He was pale and quite shaken; wouldn't even come in the house. He told me that he had been walking down the A51 – he was going to a local garden centre near the Wolseley Bridges – when he happened to glance up the field that adjoins Swift Lane. The man was stunned to see quite a large group of people standing beside a rocky outcrop on the hillside. He knew there was a Mesolithic cave there.' She paused to light a cigarette and offered me one. I shook my head then smiled, encouraging her to tell me more.

'The amazing thing is, they were all dressed in strange clothing. Not of this time, more like,' he said, 'clothes worn in prehistoric times but unlike any that I have ever seen in any history books, and I studied prehistory at university.' He thought they were being filmed for a television programme or film, or maybe rehearsing for some local play or other. He stopped to watch. 'There were so many of them,' the man stuttered, clearly still traumatised by what he had seen. Men, women, teenagers and toddlers had all been grouped around the rocky outcrop. He went on to say that he could see them clearly. The men were holding spears; and as they talked together, a group of men on horseback rode over the hillside, heading straight towards them, screaming words in a language he did not understand. He had watched horrified as the horsemen attacked the people on the hillside. He saw them swinging wooden clubs, and throwing spears and axes at the people. Some were even hurling large stones. The people were screaming in terror. It was horrifying to see and hear. He could taste their fear, smell the blood, and hear the terrified cries of the women and children. Then the scene disappeared in the blink of an eye. He couldn't believe what he had seen and heard and that it had disappeared as fast as it had appeared. He told me he was shocked beyond measure, and had to return home. He could not visit the garden centre after that experience. He had found it horrifying to think that he had just witnessed a mass murder – albeit one that happened many centuries ago. He could still hear the screams, especially of the younger ones. The man was visibly shaking as he told me his story. I offered again for him to come in, but he refused.'

Caroline then continued in a quiet, sad voice, 'After hearing the man's story, I did some research and discovered the history of the cave and passed it on to him. Apparently, it is an old hunting cave known as a bivouac. It has been excavated, and bones, teeth and flints had been recovered. Also, the skeletons of an older lady and young woman were found outside the cave. Why the skeletons were outside the cave has never been discovered. The archaeologists said the cave was the most important discovery in Staffordshire history. Unfortunately, they could not do a full dig as animals had burrowed deep into the soil and there was a danger of the site collapsing. That was some time ago, but since then, I have found out even more of the cave's history. He was quite correct about the people. The remains of many people – bones, teeth and hair – have been found inside the cave. They did identify with the group of people the man had seen. Obviously, he had experienced a time slip, and witnessed the killing on the hillside that day. I could only think that the murderers had put the bodies into the cave. They must have destroyed a whole community; otherwise the bodies or remains would have been removed for burial.'

I was horrified on hearing the story of the massacre. It was bad enough that the two skulls had been found – though, on reflection, I was still convinced Mamma and Papa would have found our relatives and buried them. Who were these other two murdered women? I thought that if I smoked I would be smoking non-stop all that day, and forever more. What a shocking story the slaughter of the people had been. I wondered again if they were my relatives. My blood ran cold. A terrible thought entered my head: had the villagers gone to the cave, searching for us, and been killed by our sworn enemies The Delphs?

My thoughts whirled around and I felt quite sick, thinking of what had happened at the cave. Another thought scampered into my head – no wonder the cave was smaller if animals had been burrowing into it on the hillside. But, that was of no consequence now. I could not get the scene of the massacre out of my head.

I thanked Caroline for her time and, as I was leaving, she mentioned that she ran the Ghost Club from her home; and she invited me along. Caroline also gave me one of her books, telling me she had included the story of the cave in it, just in case anyone else had witnessed anything in that area. Maybe they would then contact her. I didn't know what I had been hoping to hear, but it certainly wasn't the carnage I had just heard. Saddened beyond measure, I walked slowly back to town, wondering if I had been the cause of the murder on the hill. Tears threatening, I bought the flowers for Mary and decided to walk back to the farm in the hope that my head would clear.

I spent hours in my bedroom thinking about the story of the battle on the hillside. Well, hardly a battle, more a massacre. Wondering exactly what had happened, and whether the people who died were my family and friends. I shuddered at the thought of it and started to sob not knowing what to do.

Later that evening, lying in bed still wondering and worrying, I could not settle down to sleep. In the early hours, I was disturbed by a slight sound. I sat up, gazing around my room, heart thumping, and then I saw him. It was the Druid. 'What do you want?' I questioned him. Despite knowing he would not hurt me, I still felt unnerved by his presence.

He glided across the room intimating that I should not be afraid of him. Then, he spoke and his voice sounded amazingly like that of the Chief Mystic.

'You have to rescue them, Elvaennia.'

I nodded, quickly agreeing. 'The shadows, yes, yes, I will.' I gabbled. He nodded his head, sagely.

'Yes, those poor souls must be helped but you must rescue your people.'

Then, he disappeared as fast as he had appeared, leaving me puzzled at his words, and relieved that the shadowy figure of the man was not with him on this occasion.

Rescue my people? How did he suppose I would do that? We were separated by centuries of time for goodness sake. But reflecting on his words, a spasm of fear hit me hard – obviously, it was my people who were killed at the cave.

'No!' I screamed silently to myself, by now pacing up and down the room. 'I cannot let them be killed. I have to help them but how, I have no idea.'

I went to the window and gazed towards the ancient cave, looking for answers. Dawn was beginning to break as the sun rose and the early mist began to shimmer, and then cleared leaving the cave bathed in a pink, unearthly glow. It's strange how whenever I looked at the cave, I always seemed to sense movement in and around it. I felt a pull towards it as if it was trying to speak to me or tell me something. Then, suddenly out-of-the-blue, the answer came. Of course I had to rescue my family, and the only way to ensure their safety was to bring them to this time.

Relief flooded through me. Obviously, I was the key. But how could I possibly achieve this?

I needed to make a plan, to ensure I had everything in place in readiness for the rescue – when the time came.

Chapter 19

A few days after my visit to her house, Caroline telephoned and invited me along to the Ghost Club meeting. She said I would be really interested, and it would widen my circle of friends.

I was thrilled, and agreed immediately.

The meeting was being held in the lounge at her house, and there were quite a number of people spilling over into the conservatory. There were also a few members having a chat in the garden. I sat on the conservatory steps for a few minutes, gazing around the garden. It was chilly, but the lights scattered around added a certain warmth and nuance to the scene. I was surprised to see Connie (Caroline's dog) playing with a large, black, furry, lovable looking dog. The two were chasing around having a wonderful time together, almost as if they were playing tag. Watching them have fun made me smile and I was on the point of calling them across for a hug when a call from Caroline made us make our way into the house – followed by Connie. The other dog had disappeared altogether. Not a sight of it anywhere. He had disappeared into thin air. I knew he had been a spirit dog.

Calling the meeting to order, Caroline settled everyone with a cup of coffee. She gave a brief résumé of the last meeting and introduced me to the members.

It was fascinating to hear all the different ghost stories the people contributed to the meeting, and I sat wide-eyed with astonishment on hearing some of the tales. I could still not get the story of the hillside massacre from my mind though, and I was determined to help my family at all costs.

I decided to relax, for now, and enjoy myself.

Melanie, one of the younger members of the group, chipped in with a story:

'A few weeks ago I was walking through the woods near to the old Brereton tip, with my dog, when a sound alerted me that someone was nearby. My dog's ears went up and off he ran in the direction of the noise. I hurried after him calling, Buster come here at once.' Of course, he disobeyed as per usual.'

This invoked some laughter, and Melanie continued:

'All of a sudden, a man appeared just ahead of me. He had run out of a clump of trees. I must say I was scared, as he had a huge cloak wrapped around him. He wore no shoes and when he saw me, he jumped. I just stood staring in amazement, my feet frozen to the ground. Then, Buster appeared and started yapping at the man, running round him and having a really good sniff of the stranger.

What I remember more than anything is that he had wonderful, long, dark, shiny, curly hair. It was beautiful and he was incredibly handsome.'

Melanie's hazel eyes had a distant look as she described the man from the woods. It was clear she would never forget her encounter with the handsome stranger. Shaking herself, she said:

'The man bent down, patted Buster on his head, and whispered in his ear – whereupon Buster turned and ran to me. The stranger nodded towards me, and then disappeared back the way he had come. I have been wondering ever since who he could possibly be. I know there is an old hunting cave at the top of the woods but I decided not to go and investigate. Well, you just don't know what could happen, do you?'

From her brief description, I was more than convinced she was talking about Deimuiss, and I longed to go and look – right there and then. My heart was racing in excitement at the thought that he was here in 2007. He had found his way. He had come to rescue me and take me home.

I was having a hard time containing my excitement and I took a few deep breaths. I wanted to ask Melanie some questions but the group was breaking up. The get-together was over, to my acute disappointment.

After the members had left, Caroline and I settled down with a coffee in her cosy sitting room. I decided not to jump right in and ask her about Melanie's sighting straightaway. Instead, I asked her tentatively if she thought her house was haunted.

She chuckled throatily, saying that I was only the second person who had ever picked up on the ghosts that 'resided' in her home. She told me that the first time someone had mentioned the ghosts she had denied it. 'Why I did,' she chuckled, 'I will never know.'

I was relieved that she knew, as there was no way I would have told her about the ghosts if she was unaware of them.

'The first ghost I saw was not long after we'd moved here a few years ago,' she said, offering me one of her cigarettes from a gold packet. I noticed she smoked the same brand as the empty packet I'd found in the cave. I wondered if she had visited the cave herself. Did she know more than she had told me? I shook myself. I really was getting suspicious of everyone. Still, once the thought entered my head, I knew it would stay niggling away until I resolved it. Being a non-smoker, of course, I refused her offer and settled back in my chair to listen to her ghost story.

'One spring morning, I was washing up the breakfast dishes when I thought I heard footsteps upstairs. As there was only myself and Merlin, my dog, at home – 'Merlin's gone now,' she added sadly, '– I was, to say the least, worried. Looking round for my dog, I saw he was shaking with fear. That made me even more scared, I can tell you.'

She flicked her cigarette in the ashtray and I saw a flash of remembered fear in her eyes.

'For some reason or another, I knew that it was not an intruder. Maybe it was because the dog was shaking in fear. He had done this before when there had been ghosts about. I mean, he was quite a large, black, woolly dog and the only things he was scared of were ghosts. Wish you could have seen him; he has not long gone over to the Spirit World.'

I hesitated wondering whether to say that I had seen him in the garden.

'Do you know,' she continued, settling herself more comfortably in her easy chair, 'there are certain areas around Rugeley where, when I took him out walking, he would make me cross the road. Big brave dog he was not.'

Flicking her cigarette again, she leant back in her chair and continued:

'Since I have had Connie, the strange thing is that she re-acts in the same way. She even refuses to walk past the areas that Merlin refused to walk past. I wonder whether she is picking up the feeling telepathically from me, or whether evil spirits haunt the places.'

Caroline grinned, suddenly saying, 'Sorry, I've lost the thread of the story. I'll carry on with it. Now, where was I? Yes, I remember:

I went to the bottom of the stairs and I admit that I was a nervous wreck, as I could not be one hundred per cent certain that it was a ghost. I glanced towards the landing and saw a small boy and girl holding hands. They were grinning at me. I was surprised, to say the least, and took the bull by the horns so to speak, and started slowly to climb the stairs. I hoped the children would stay, but of course they disappeared as quickly as they had appeared. As to their style of clothing, I would guess at about 1905. They certainly weren't well-to-do by any means but they were clean. I was disappointed that they vanished so fast. I would have loved to have had a chat with them. Even Merlin did not seem so worried; which I admit was unusual for him, but he did love children.

As you well know Elvaennia, the lane and the town have an extremely long history,' she said with a very mysterious smile.

'One day, you and I will have a good chat, but for now, let me reassure you that you will find Deimuiss.'

My heart nearly stopped beating at her words. She was oh-so matter-of-fact as she said it. I was stunned beyond belief, and was about to ask her what else she could tell me, when the doorbell rang and in bounced Mary.

'Come on Elvaennia, it's getting late. We farmers have to be up and about early.'

We were back at the farm within minutes. I'll say this: when Mary moves, she moves fast.

Chapter 20

Elvaennia hardly slept that night, wondering about the man in the cloak that Melanie had seen, but she was determined to go and look in the area that she had described. 'If I can find Deimuiss,' she thought, 'He will be able to help me return to the settlement and bring my family back. I must keep them safe.' Her thoughts of what might happen to them all were tortuous and sleep was impossible.

At breakfast the following morning, she asked Mary where the old tip at Brereton was, and if it was within walking distance.

'Tut, child, it's too far to walk from here – unless you plan on staying out all day. Why do you want to go there?'

'Hmm, a lady mentioned that there was an old hunting cave near the old tip. Sounded interesting, and I thought I would like to go and see it.'

Mary gave her a quizzical look as if she didn't quite believe her.

'Best if I run you up and come with you. Never know who you might meet up there. Pop and get ready, and we will take Pip with us.'

'Really? Oh thank you Mary.'

Elvaennia's face was a picture of delight. She felt guilty at not being completely honest with Mary, but shrugging her slim shoulders, she thought, 'I just forgot to mention the sighting of the man dressed in the cloak who might possibly be Deimuiss – that's all.'

Parking up at the entrance to the woods, the women strolled down the forest track.

'It's beautiful here Mary, despite the leaves dropping fast. Reminds me of my time in a way, you can smell the autumn, though it's definitely

151

not so wild and there aren't the wild animals either!'

'True, thank goodness,' Mary said on a laugh. 'If there were wild animals here, apart from the deer and the foxes, you wouldn't catch me walking on the Chase.'

'Shhh, Mary. Stop, don't move.'

Grabbing Mary's arm, she motioned her to stand still and pointed ahead.

Mary gasped and pulled Pip close to her. Fortunately, he was on his lead. She was amazed to see running down the track, away from them (luckily) was a huge black cat. Mary's legs turned to water and she found herself shaking as the cat disappeared from view.

'Phew, Mary. Thought you said there were no wild animals apart from the deer?'

Elvaeninia's eyes were dancing with glee as she looked at the older woman.

'Aren't you scared?'

'No, the cat has gone. He won't be back. He's old and past it. We won't see him again.'

'Strange,' she thought, 'Mary never picked up on when I mentioned my time – how very peculiar.'

Shaking her head, Mary muttered, 'I'm not sure about this, dearie. That's the biggest wild animal I've seen outside of a zoo. And I don't like it!'

Worried that her trip to the cave was fast slipping away, Elvaennia sought to reassure Mary that they would be fine; and reluctantly, not wanting to disappoint the girl, Mary agreed to continue with the walk... looking left, right, and behind her every few minutes. She was scared.

Deciding to employ her tracking skills, Elvaennia kept scanning the path as they walked, telling Mary she was keeping her eyes open for the black cat while really she was looking for signs of Deimuiss having been in the area. At one point, she sank to the ground. She was certain she could see a man's footprint (shoeless, of course) but it was almost invisible. 'If only I could spend time looking around the area, I'm sure if it was him, I would find a trace,' she thought. But unfortunately, Mary was becoming agitated, thinking the black cat was still hanging around, so she decided not to worry her any further and they made their way home. Elvaennia kept wondering if it had been Deimuiss, but was undecided because she had had no sense that he was close when they were in the woodlands. This had probably been a false lead and she had no idea who the man Melanie had seen was. Of course, he could have been another time traveller, or an actor, or part of a film crew. The Chase and surrounding areas are popular venues for film and television companies as it is a perfect backdrop for historical settings. She felt dejected but reassured herself that, eventually, she would find Deimuiss. After all, Caroline had said she would. Also, the Mystics' words had cheered her considerably. She knew Deimuiss would help her eventually to bring her family to safety.

She longed for the day when Mary and David would talk openly with her about her past. She could not understand their reluctance.

Chapter 21

The following evening, my head was still full of ghost stories and the trip to the woods. I settled down and read Caroline's book. I was enthralled by all the stories. One in particular caught my eye. The story concerned a ghost investigation by the West Midlands Ghost Club. I was hooked, and after finishing the book, I logged on to the W.M.G.C. website. It was so interesting and professional that, spotting the mobile number, I quickly sent a text to the founder, Nick Duffy, asking if it would be possible to go on an investigation with the group at some time in the future.

The next day, my mobile bleeped and it was a text from Nick inviting me to an investigation. I was overjoyed and rang him to confirm details.

Bubbling with excitement, I ran to find Mary to tell her.

'Well done,' she said, one of her huge grins splitting her face. 'I will take you. Just let me know the date and time.'

'Thing is Mary, it's tonight! Is that okay for you?'

'Sure, not a problem. Might join you, if that will be okay with Nick?'

'I'm sure he won't mind. He sounded so friendly and helpful.'

I dashed back upstairs and began to sort my clothes out for the coming evening. I just knew this was going to be a great night out, plus I would be mixing with like-minded people. What could be better?

Arriving at the investigation site, Nick introduced himself to us and then to the other group members who were taking part in the investigation. What a friendly bunch they are.

The group members began setting up the tools of their trade: video cameras, digital cameras, audio recording equipment, still cameras, some thermometers and other instruments. Nick also went on to say that they sometimes used what they call 'trigger objects' too – crosses, or other items that they have specifically brought with them to the site, or they might possibly use some object which has 'a history of moving by itself' in the property concerned. Such objects would be left somewhere, usually drawn around (outlined) on a piece of paper, and checked every so often during the investigation – on the off-chance that they had been moved. Some members do not necessarily agree with the non-technical side, but they like to be open-minded and cover different angles in order to be truly objective.

I found this fascinating and could not wait for the investigation to start. I hovered around the members, watching everything they did. Chatting away to Nick, I was amazed at his knowledge of ghosts, and admired him for his dedication to his subject; never giving up despite never actually seeing a ghost since founding the W.M.G.C. in 1991. I was impressed by the group's approach to the investigation because, when I'd been doing research on the Internet, I had visited certain sites that seemed less-than-professional.

The investigation was now underway.

The venue was being held at a large, old house in Wolverhampton, and both Mary and I were intrigued by the research.

The group members were very skilled and took their work seriously. Sitting beside Nick in the sumptuous lounge I was careful not to interrupt the proceedings. My heart was in my mouth a number of times as I noticed the extra sensory activity in the room. The group seemed to take it all in their stride and told me later that, despite getting readings on many of their instruments, this did not confirm for definite that the building was haunted.

They assured me that they needed far more proof than that, before they could ever say a venue was definitely haunted. Sometimes, they needed to return to the 'haunted' site many times before they were convinced.

Later on though, as they left the Hall, the 'medium' in the group saw the figure of a man running through the grounds and was able to give a full description of him. He said he was dressed in the style of a youngish man of the nineteenth century. The man was well dressed as befitted the status of a well-to-do gentleman who had obviously lived at the Hall in that era.

I nodded my agreement as I had seen him but wasn't about to let on to the group. After all, I was there as a guest and they were obviously well in touch with the 'other side'. They certainly did not need my input. Plus, Mary had given me a huge nudge when she realised I had seen the young man. Since living in this lifetime, I had noticed my psychic powers had developed greatly. I was even more aware of the 'other' side and no longer afraid of ghosts!

Chapter 22

Mary had really enjoyed the night out, and chatted away to David about it the following morning as she was preparing breakfast.

'Very nice people they are at the W.M.G.C. Elvaennia enjoyed it enormously. Took her out of herself for a while.'

'Mmmm, pleased it went okay,' David grunted as he read his post. He was only half listening to his mother.

'Hello?' he murmured, looking across the table at Mary, 'There's a letter here for Elvaennia.'

Mary's eyebrows lifted in surprise, her green eyes wide with astonishment.

'Who's it from? Does it have a return address on the back?'

'No. Here, take a look.'

He passed it to her, a puzzled expression on his face, wondering who on earth could be writing to Elvaennia. She knew very few people, and he doubted if any of them knew where she was living.

Just then, the kitchen door opened and the young lady in question swung into the room, silver hair drifting across her shoulders, smiling her morning greetings to both of them.

'Morning Mary, morning David.'

Pouring herself a coffee at the breakfast bar, she made her way to the table. Mary silently passed her the letter.

~

'For me, how exciting,' I gasped as I opened it quickly. 'It's from Caroline, the lady who gave me the ghost book and who runs the Ghost

157

Club.'

I scanned the letter quickly.

'She says she has some information for me about the old cave, and has asked me to pop in when I can. Her telephone has been out of order, so she thought she would drop me a line. Wonder why she hasn't got a mobile?'

Slipping the letter back into the envelope, I was about to jump out of my chair to go and get ready.

'Have your breakfast first deary. Go and see Caroline in a while.'

Shaking her white curls at my impatience, she said, 'Calm down. It's nothing that can't wait.'

Mary and David exchanged a quick look, and again I got the suspicion that they knew more than they let on. 'Somehow,' I pondered, 'I think they know Caroline.'

Nodding in agreement, I proceeded to make short work of my eggs and bacon. In between mouthfuls, I remarked to Mary:

'You know, I didn't know that Caroline is a friend of Nick from the W.M.G.C. I am going to have a chat with her about last night's investigation when I pop down. It was so interesting, don't you agree Mary?'

'Yes, my luv, it was,' she said, glancing at David as she replied.

Following her gaze, I suddenly registered how quiet he was this morning. So far, he had added not a thing to the morning conversation, which was very unlike him indeed.

Catching Mary's eye, I nodded as Mary intimated that I should not say anything.

David suddenly gathered his letters together, jumped up from his chair and made for the kitchen door with the words, 'see you later.'

'Well, really,' Mary huffed quite crossly – which was unusual for her. 'He's hardly had a decent word to say to anybody today.'

'Must be worried about something,' I remarked, wondering what on earth had upset David that morning.

Outside in the yard, David shuffled his letters together and put them in his jacket pocket. He too was wondering why he was so angry, but he acknowledged that if he was truthful, he was jealous of Elvaennia's night out where a number of other men had been around. His green eyes sparkled with jealousy. Drumming his fingers angrily on a field gate, he was filled with a black depression.

'If only she were mine,' he thought bleakly. Knowing that she would more than likely find Deimuiss filled him with dread, as he knew they would return to the settlement and she would never be his.

Jealousy seared him, remembering his feelings last night when the two women had gone out. He could not understand why he had not been invited. After they had left, he had gone to his local pub, 'The Horns', to drown his sorrows and had then spent a sleepless night wondering if Elvaennia had met someone else.

'What am I to do?' he wondered. 'I love her, and know it's an impossible situation. When she is out of sight, I am filled with jealousy and longing for her.'

Shaking his head, he became aware of the chickens pecking away at his feet. Shooing them off, he opened the gate and went down the field to inspect the pigs and clean them out. 'This job will keep me grounded, if nothing else,' he thought wryly, trying to lighten his mood.

Mary offered to run me to Caroline's, 'but first,' she said, 'let's get those injections out of the way.' I felt the colour drain from my face. Mary laughed aloud, 'Come now Elvaennia, they won't hurt you. Then, I will pop you along to Caroline's.'

It seemed as if I had no choice. So, putting a brave face on it, I succumbed to the injections thinking it made sense to protect my health. After all, I had no immunity whatsoever against this century's illnesses. Obviously, Mary knew this too, but still chose not to discuss anything with me.

Relieved when the minor ordeal was over, and pleased that Mary seemed so reassured, we made our way to Caroline's. Along the way, she reminded me about my driving test. I was thrilled that there had been a cancellation and, despite being highly nervous about the coming test, I looked forward to being independent if I passed, of course.

Caroline greeted me with a beaming smile as I slipped through the door.

'Nice to see you again. Want a coffee?'

Nodding, she motioned me to take a seat while she busied herself in the kitchen. Returning with two steaming mugs, she settled herself in a seat facing me.

'Now, Elvaennia.'

I could tell by her face she had something serious to discuss. I tensed ready for her words.

'I have received a message for you.'

Thinking it was a letter or note from someone, I looked around expectantly wondering why they should have sent it to Caroline.

'Sorry to confuse you. I meant a message via a medium.'

My eyes opened wide in astonishment. 'For me?' I squeaked breathlessly, 'From a medium?'

Her face held a serious expression as she went on to say, 'I hope you will understand it. I did not want to put it in a letter, not knowing who might read it. That is why I said I had information about the cave. I do apologise if I have misled you.'

'Not a problem,' I responded, leaning towards her and hopefully reassuring her that I was not bothered. But, I was really.

Sensing my anxiety, she quickly continued.

'A friend of mine was talking to a medium a couple of nights ago. She was told that your betrothed had said you should not become entangled with the man with the green eyes.'

'Whatever does she mean, and where is Deimuiss? How come the medium received a message from him but not me?'

I stuttered again. Truth to tell, I felt a bit guilty as I knew she obviously meant David; and at times, I do feel attracted to him. Heavens, I certainly didn't want to be receiving messages from people who didn't even know me regarding my personal life. I also felt more than jealous that someone else could make contact with my fiancé. 'What a flipping cheek,' I spluttered under my breath. Gosh, I was picking up the local slang as well.

I glanced at Caroline and she grinned at me.

'It can be unnerving I know, but hey, don't worry. The medium doesn't know you or either of the men.'

I was more than relieved when she told me that, and I hoped I didn't receive any more missives from the medium. But perhaps I should close down my thoughts; not be so open to everything. I asked Caroline her opinion.

'You're right Elvaennia. You should protect yourself more. Not just physically, but mentally as well, from the unwelcome elements of the psychic world. You know the Druid is helping you and keeping the man from your past at bay. You can help him by shutting your thoughts down so he cannot get into your psyche.'

Oh dear, this was all getting complicated, but I knew Caroline wanted to help me, so I listened intently to her words as it was such good advice.

'Use your Angel Cards everyday and wrap yourself in gold.'

'Pardon?'

'I don't mean literally,' she laughed loudly, lighting another one of her endless cigarettes. I worried for her lungs but she seemed healthy enough, albeit a little husky voiced.

'Whenever you feel threatened, or see the Druid (how she knew about him beat me, but I decided not to question her), think of a gold cloak or blanket and wrap it around yourself. That way, you will protect yourself from any evil, okay? Alternatively, remember when you saw the Angels?'

I nodded, convinced that she was more than psychic. She grinned, saying, 'Well, think of them. They are your guardian angels. You are so lucky Elvaennia. Most people only have one guardian angel. You seem to have a host! Almost one for every occasion.'

I had to laugh at her words, but the evening that I had looked up into the sky and seen the angels would stay with me forever. I had only been a young girl and had been walking back home after a meeting when I had glanced up and seen the beautiful sight of a host of heavenly beings. Hovering in the sky, it had looked as if they were watching and guarding me. A sight I had never forgotten, and now, amazingly, Caroline had brought it up. Not that I minded. I realised that she knew a whole lot more than she was letting on. So, with a smile, I thanked her and got ready to take my leave.

'Sorry about the small deception, but some things are best kept private.'

I nodded.

I rose from the lovely old sofa but she put her hand out saying, 'Just a minute dear, before you go, I have received another ghost story that you will find more than fascinating.'

My eyes opened wide in anticipation and I settled back into the comfort of the sofa. Lighting up yet another one of her never-ending cigarettes, Caroline settled back once again in her chair.

'I was in two minds whether to tell you this story, but I thought 'yes', you should hear it along with details of a couple of other sightings.'

'A young man, well I say young, he is in his late twenties, watches the night skies as he has a great interest in U.F.O.s. In recent months he has noticed an increase in strange lights, and they are always hovering over the field that runs behind Crowsfoot Farm, where the old cave is.'

My heart leapt at her words and I wondered again whether there were 'others arriving'. Was that what the lights meant? Was it connected to the strange feeling I got when I looked towards the cave? Of course, I could not say anything to Caroline, but if others were arriving, where would they go? Or, were the lights a precursor to my family arriving? My head was spinning at all the differing thoughts running around it. Perhaps after all, I would not need to rescue them. Maybe they were being brought by some other force. But, this thought did not last long. I did not truly think that they would all be arriving in the cave without my assistance.

Caroline said the man had mentioned this further story to her a few weeks earlier:

'A lady had told him that she had been sitting in her car at Stile Cop, a local beauty spot high up on Cannock Chase, in the early hours of one morning. 'It was mid-summer', she told me. It was one of those nights that never got particularly dark and she was sitting watching the skies, when all of a sudden, she saw the Northern Lights. Talk about astonished. She told me she had never seen anything so beautiful as the wonderful curtains of green, yellow and pink lights dancing upwards and downwards all across the sky. As she watched, hypnotised by this glorious spectacle of colour, the lady suddenly saw a man and a woman dancing within the curtains of the lights. She said they danced so closely together, as if they were one. The amazing thing was the young woman who was dancing was dressed in a deerskin cloak with a beautiful circlet of jewels holding it together across the neckline. Through the opening of her cloak, you could see she had on a beautiful, white dress edged with silver and crystals. The woman's hair was a wonderful silver colour and seemed to glow as if crystals were also encrusted in it. They sparkled in the Northern Lights. The man was dressed in a darker coloured cloak and deerskin trousers. His long, curly, black hair was a sheer black, and the lights reflected blues from it. He was very tall and she was tiny like a night nymph but you could see the light of love surrounding them as they danced with the spirits that night. She had never seen anything so beautiful in all her life. They were so in love, it took her breath away.'

I sat still as Caroline described the scene of Deimuiss and me dancing within the Northern Lights. 'How amazing,' I managed to whisper, keeping my eyes downcast so she could not see the truth of her words reflected in my eyes.

'Elvaennia my pet, your secret is safe with me for all time. Have no fear.'

Looking up at Caroline, I believed her, but still found myself unable to speak as, in my mind, I was still dancing with Deimuiss and the Northern Lights were enfolding us within their night-time magic. The stars were like stepping stones weaving a pathway of love. I could feel his warm breath on my cheeks, his arms holding me tightly. I could hear his whispered words of adoration. The clouds were soft cushions of air. The moon lit our way as we danced across the stars with the spirit beings. 'Together forever,' he murmured softly in my ear. I nodded, ecstatic to be with the one man I truly loved for all time.

We said our goodbyes at the small wooden gate. Glancing up, I saw the man's face watching us from his bedroom window. Caroline followed my gaze. 'Bless him,' she said, 'He was a lovely man.'

It was a beautiful, early winter's day. I decided to walk back to the farmhouse. My arm was aching a little from the injections but I consoled myself that it was far better than becoming ill. As I headed back to the farm, I thought hard about everything Caroline had mentioned, and I wondered where she received her information from. A thought wriggled its way into my head – that she was one of the 'Listeners.' Instinct told me that certain people received 'messages,' not unlike a medium, but on a different sphere. There were 'listeners' who could hear way beyond normal hearing abilities, picking up information. They knew instinctively who to pass the information on to. Mediums channelled the dead but 'listeners' were a channel for the living; they passed warnings to people who were in dangerous or difficult situations.

As I turned through the gate of the farmhouse, I quickened my pace remembering that I hadn't checked my horoscope on the Internet, or in magazines or papers for a couple of days. This would never do. From reading all of them, I did glean a certain amount of information of what lay ahead. I intended to have a good read of all of them over a cup of coffee. My favourite astrologer was Russell Grant. He writes for the local paper, The *Express & Star*.

Chapter 23

I couldn't believe my luck: David and Mary had just left for a local farmers' meeting. Now I could use the computer yet again unsupervised. Getting comfy, I clicked straight on to 'search'.

Glancing at the screen, the small silver dot started bleeping as before. I followed its progress excitedly. Was I going to see the settlement and my family again despite the centuries that separated us? A map appeared on screen. It said 'Google Earth.' The silver dot began zooming in on an area of the country named 'Wales'. Wales? I hadn't heard anything about that region at all. I watched its progress. The dot zoomed in on a place called Llandrindod Wells, highlighted in red. My goodness – what was the meaning of this place to me?

I was now looking at a photograph of a hotel. It was huge and situated almost in the town centre. What was the significance of this to me? I was mystified. Now the silver dot was zooming in to the large sign near the entrance gates of the hotel.

The silver point hovered over a notice that read:

THE LINKS HOTEL, LINK WAY, LLANDRINDOD WELLS

Reading the notice I learned:

'Spiritual healing by Desmond Kelly, world famous. Everyone welcome. No entrance fee. Do come along and let Desmond introduce you to the healing arts, and also give you a demonstration of his amazing healing skills in the conference centre.'

It was the small photograph that enthralled and gripped me. It couldn't possibly be Deimuiss, could it? This man had short, black, curly hair. I couldn't zoom in close enough to see the colour of his eyes or his facial features, but from what I could see, the smile looked familiar. Surely it was him. Was it? Could it really be Deimuss? Was he really living and working in the 21st Century? No, I thought it couldn't possibly be him. But what if it was? I had to go and see for myself. There was nothing for it. I had to own up to using the computer.

Suddenly, it hit me. I minimized the site – I didn't want to lose the information, did I? – clicked back on to the Internet and typed 'Desmond Kelly' into 'Yahoo' search engine. Oh my goodness, there were hundreds of links. I started clicking on them and found he was really famous for his healing skills. From what I could make out, he was celebrated worldwide. Could this man be Deimuiss, the man I loved? I was upset that for all the many sites I visited, I could not find a decent photograph of him.

The sites talked of his amazing healing skills, and his intuition. His dark good looks were mentioned numerous times, by the lady journalists in particular. Well, I knew that, but I couldn't help a stab of jealousy searing my heart when I read their words.

Site after site reiterated his astonishing ability to heal, but also pointed out how humble he was. That certainly sounded just like Deimuiss, I thought, and also indicated that he made no claims or promises – just the offer to try and heal. I knew it was him. Everything they said about him was the man I had known back at the settlement in our time. I was convinced.

But, how had he arrived in the 21st century? Surely it was impossible for him to have achieved so much in such a short period of time. I had left him lying in the bivouac after kicking him – not once, but twice. Must admit I felt ashamed at my actions now. But on reflection I was, after all, fighting for my life; and I suspected him of killing my Grandmamma and Trieainia. I wanted to know if he was involved in their murders and why he had gone over to the Delph Tribe. Yes, I had a lot of questions to ask Mr. Desmond Kelly if, of course, he was indeed Deimuiss of the Calegi Tribe.

Realistically, of course, it could not be Deimuiss. How could it? The last time I had seen him, he was doubled up in pain. The Internet showed that Desmond Kelly had been doing his healing work for 18 months. Well, that fitted in one way. It was the amount of time that Deimuiss had been missing. His fame had quickly spread and he was being feted almost as a celebrity. I was intrigued and needed to go and meet this man, if only to satisfy myself that it wasn't my Deimuiss. But, should it be him, then we would have so much to talk about. My heart leapt at the thought that possibly, just possibly, I had found him. The question remained – how was I going to get there? The event was not for another two weeks. I would have liked to have gone the following day. The thought of waiting was awful. Tapping the ballpoint pen on the desk, I clicked off the Internet and made my way down the stairs to make myself a coffee. My brain was in overdrive, trying to sort out my emotions. Was this man my Deimuiss? Suddenly, I remembered we were going to Lichfield Spiritualist Church. Surely, someone there would be able to tell me about this Desmond Kelly. If his name was splattered all over the Internet, then his reputation obviously went before him.

While making the coffee, I remembered that I hadn't switched off the PC. I shot back upstairs, not wanting David to know I had been logged on. I knew the time was fast approaching for 'our talk' but I needed to sort this latest information out first. Not that I could hide the evidence for much longer as the time was drawing nearer to when I had to confess my culpability. Perhaps this would then lead on to the discussion I longed to start with Mary and David.

The following morning after breakfast, I took the bull by the horns and admitted my misdemeanour to David and Mary, telling them that I had been using the computer in their absences.

'I know you know who I am.'

I had decided to be frank from the word go.

'You know about the settlement, in fact, almost everything about my life, but I truly do not understand how you know... or who you are.'

Mary was clearly taken aback. David just nodded then took my hand.

'Elvaennia, you are correct. We do know a lot about you and the fact that you are looking for Deimuiss.'

167

He looked grave for a few seconds, thinking deeply.

'At the moment, I would prefer not to tell you about Mary and myself. I would like you to trust us.'

Surprised and disappointed, my heart sank. However, I knew I had to accept the situation. After all, I could not force them to tell me anything.

Timidly, I asked if I could use the computer now.

David nodded and we went upstairs to his study, where he logged on for me. Turning towards me, he reached out and gently stroked my hair, pushing it back from my face. I looked into his wonderful, brilliantly green eyes. For a moment, my heart skipped a beat as I saw my thoughts mirrored in his. The look disappeared as fast as it appeared, to be replaced by his secrets hidden in sea green depths. I tried my hardest to read his thoughts but they were impenetrable.

Sniffing, trying my hardest not to cry, I moved my chair closer to him and confessed to finding the site at Llandrindod Wells. I did not want to tell him my real reason for wanting to go, but somehow, I sensed he knew.

He didn't want me to. I could see it in his eyes. He knew far more than he had let on but I had seen the look in his eyes. Was it fear? Why should he not want me to go? What did he and Mary know? I was determined I was going to find out.

I looked deep into his eyes again and saw the secrets emerging and chasing round. What was he trying to disguise? To my disappointment, I could not catch them.

'Elvaennia, my child, my little fairy, you told me yourself that you had left Deimuiss curled up on the cave floor and you seemed to think he had lost his memory?'

I nodded.

'How can he be here then? You said he was with The Delph Tribe: the butchers, the murderers, the sworn enemies of your tribe.'

Nodding again, I thought my head would drop off soon. I felt pathetic sitting here, knee to knee with David, crying unashamedly. I began to doubt myself. Suddenly, I sat up straighter. 'Just a minute

David, when did I tell you about Deimuiss?' I could have sworn I had never ever mentioned Deimuiss to him or Mary.

Before he could reply, Mary came bustling into the room in a swirl of white apron and green skirt, her cheerful face plastered with her usual grin.

'Whatever's to do Elvaennia? Are you poorly? Are you in pain?'

Rushing across the room, she clasped me in a hug. Oh, that felt good. It had been so long since I had had a motherly hug. I sank into her warmth and comfort.

'Son, go and make some coffee – and put extra sugar in for Elvaennia. She looks as if she needs it.'

Relieved, David clattered off down the stairs. I was certain that he had slipped up mentioning Deimuiss.

Mary gazed at me. I guessed she wanted to tell me something, but she restrained herself, saying only, 'Do you want to talk about it deary?'

I quickly explained how much I wanted to visit Llandrindod Wells.

'Mmm.'

Cocking her head to one side with a very sympathetic expression on her round face, I could see her thoughts whirring round in her head like a windmill.

'Elvaennia, why do you want to go to this place? Have you a particular reason?'

I could not bring myself to tell her, in case I was wrong.

'I just feel drawn to it. That's the only way I can explain it Mary.'

'That's fine. Let's have our coffee and see what we can sort out shall we?'

Patting me on the head, she grabbed my arm and nearly lifted me out of the chair.

'Come along. No more surfing the Internet today. We will take Pip for a walk across the Chase, go to the Forestry Centre, and choose a Christmas tree. We will go after our coffee. How do you feel about that?'

I had noticed that Mary was ending her sentences with a question again, and I gave a broad grin while agreeing to go out walking.

I enjoyed walking with Mary. Her energy astounded me because from the moment she left her bed, she was like a mini tornado – a busy, busy person who was forever on-the-go. At times, I had a hard job keeping up with her.

Chapter 24

The Chase fascinated me. Obviously, it was nothing like it had been in my time. Now, there were wide open spaces whereas in my time it was heavily wooded with a few areas cleared for settlements and livestock.

Mary said we would walk across a wooded area not far from Stile Cop. There was something she wanted to show me. I was intrigued. I made haste to get ready, and soon we were on our way.

My eyes drank in the beauty of the countryside. It was hard to imagine that I had hunted for the wild boar and deer here in the dark mysterious forests where the wolves and black bears had hidden. Nowadays, the Chase is an area of outstanding natural beauty. There are no dangerous animals. It is also illegal to kill the deer. I'd seen a few herds of deer running wild when we had been out and about in the Chase area, and my hunting instincts had come to the fore very quickly. These days, of course, food comes from all over the World – usually pre-packed. My time is definitely well and truly consigned to history, as will this time be... eventually. I mused on the fact that every age becomes history but there was no point following that route. I wondered what Mary had in store for me today.

It was a wonderful day for walking and we soon reached our destination on the outskirts of Longdon.

'Follow me Elvaennia.'

With these words, she quickly headed off up the track with Pip hard on her heels, and I hurried after her. She is unstoppable when she is on a mission.

Following the narrow track, we walked through the woods, over a small stream, and then proceeded to follow a blackberry-hedged track. 'The fruits of summer,' I murmured softly, remembering the time I used to gather them with my brothers and sisters. Piettra came with us, but he did not help; just watched us from his own private world. Piettra is such a lovely boy. I desperately longed to rescue him from his many fears, but it seems an impossible task.

Mary suddenly stopped and pointed across a stile a delighted smile on her face, 'Not far now pet, for a minute I thought I had taken a wrong turning.'

Again, I marvelled at her energy and agility for someone who is, to put it mildly, quite mature and rather overweight. She rapidly scrambled up and over the stile, up the hillside through the dead bracken. Broken branches, twigs – no obstacle bothered her at all. Despite my background with the tribe, I found it difficult to follow her and Pip.

Nearly at the top, she halted. She was puffing and panting a little. So was I. Her face was bright red as she pointed and wheezed, 'Look over there Elvaennia.'

'Are you okay?' For once, I was a little concerned; the exertion seemed to have knocked her about a bit.

Nodding her white head, 'You carry on, go that way.'

Following her lead, I walked in the general direction, wondering what was so mysterious. What was I looking for?

Mary began directing me from a distance. I found it amusing at first, but suddenly it came to me in a flash: 'I had been here before!' My pace quickened. I wasn't walking over bracken anymore. I was following the old track way. Not to the settlement, I knew that much. I was walking eastwards away from it.

Mary and the Chase faded into the distance and I began to hurry. I was on my way to meet Deimuiss. We were going to the Cave of the Crystals. It was one of the most spiritual places we knew of and always discussed, but no one knew where it was. Deimuiss had asked me to go with him. I was so looking forward to this day. My heart began to hammer. Soon, very soon, I would be meeting up with the man I loved, and that was all that mattered. 2007 could take care of itself. All I asked of life was to be with Deimuiss and my family. It had been months since I had felt this happy; more than that, in fact, since Deimuiss had gone missing. Somehow I had managed to slip back through the mists of time into our time when we were together. What joy! What happiness! My feet seemed to have wings as I sped as fast as I could to our meeting place.

Suddenly, Mary's voice broke through time.

'Elvaennia, Elvaennia. Not yet, the time isn't right. Come back at once. You will be in danger.'

Crack; the bubble of time exploded around me in a million pieces of jetsam. It had become a shattered world. Disappointment lay deep inside me. I was back in 2007 amongst the high bracken, fallen trees and goodness knows what else. Suddenly, I heard a soft bark. My hunter ears pricked. I knew that sound. A rustling to the right of me alerted my senses. I parted the bracken and there, standing watching me, was a young doe. Her soft brown eyes looked into mine and we both shared the wisdom of the centuries between us. I reached out and stroked her soft fur. She showed no fear, and I knew that she sensed I wished her no harm. Licking my hand with her rough tongue, I felt our connection; it was as strong and as enduring as time itself. I was more than convinced that the doe knew I had time travelled, because she too carried the genes of her ancestors. With a gentle pat, I let go of the bracken that surrounded her small den, leaving her in safety. I knew my scent would not worry the others in her herd; the scent I had left behind was of another distant age.

'Elvaennia, carry on up the hillside. You are nearly there.'

Mary's voice again broke the late autumn peace and I scrambled up with difficulty.

'Stop. You are nearly there. Just look around you Elvaennia.'

She sounded excited now, and I peered around trying to get a fix on whatever it was she wanted me to see.

'Got it,' I grinned. There it was – an old sandstone cave. I could see the ground had been disturbed and there seemed to be a faint echo of writing on the cave floor. I could not distinguish the words, as animals had scuffed the earth, just the same as the cave near Swift Lane. Somehow, though, I did not think it was Deimuiss who had visited this cave recently. I knelt and sniffed the floor. I was right – he had not been here, because his scent would have remained. The man Melanie had seen must have travelled through time to this cave and been exploring the woods when she had seen him. His scent was still quite strong. I wondered who he was and, more to the point, where he was. His scent was not even of our tribe.

'Everything all right Elvaennia?'

Mary's voice sang out again, setting the birds off squabbling between themselves. A fox appeared from nowhere and scuttled away. 'Looking for food,' I thought to myself. A bird of prey screeched high above, making the birds in the trees call warnings to each other through the woodlands and onwards to the skies.

'Yes, thanks Mary. On my way back now.'

My descent to Mary was quite easy. I simply followed my ascent; the track through the bracken was quite visible.

'So, you found the cave then?'

'Yes,' I nodded.

'Not many people know of that cave. It was used in the Mesolithic period, the same as the one near the farmhouse.'

Mary cast me a couple of curious glances.

'Penny for them Elvaennia.'

'Just thinking how lovely Cannock Chase is, Mary. It has some history though; hasn't it?'

'Certainly has my love; as has Rugeley.'

Mary never stopped impressing me with her local knowledge. She would make a fantastic guide for this area, I had no doubts.

'You will have to give me a potted history one day,' I said as we were getting into the car.

Nodding, she nosed the car into the road and we headed back to Rugeley. Personally, I was chuffed that I had discovered the hidden cave with Mary's help. I would be able to tell Caroline and Melanie – at the next meeting of the Ghost Society – exactly where it was.

I was disappointed that there had been no signs of Deimuiss in the cave, but I knew that other time travellers had used it. I felt very curious about whom they were and also where they were, but on reflection, I thought that now was not the time to concern myself with the others. None-the-less, who knew, at some point in the future I may well meet up with them. My pathway was clear – I had to find Deimuiss and get my family to safety.

I hoped Llandrindod Wells would be the answer to my prayers. If the healer was Deimuiss, then we could begin to make plans.

Mary's voice interrupted my thoughts.

'There is another old cave at Brereton too,' she mentioned casually as we drove through the beautiful scenery of the Chase, past the old pit site and the new bungalow that replaced the Old Holly Bush Inn, down the lane where my knowledgeable friend pointed out the site where the scrap merchants used to be. Proceeding down Coalpit Lane, we headed towards Brereton.

'Really, another old cave?'

I was all ears again. 'Perhaps we could visit it one of these days?' I asked.

'Of course pet, but I'm not certain if we will be able to locate it because at one time it went under the road.'

Again I thought: what a thoroughly nice, helpful person Mary is.

She giggled, suddenly making her plump body shake.

'We forgot to go and choose the Christmas tree. Not to worry, I will get David to pop up to the forestry in the pick-up; save them delivering it. I must be getting old – fancy forgetting the tree.'

Still laughing, she headed home.

Chapter 25

That evening, David was working in the barn and on asking him if I could use his computer, he immediately said, 'Of course.'

Turning to go to the study, I felt his eyes burning into my back. I glanced back. Then, as if hypnotised, I found myself walking back to him. I looked deep into his wonderful, green eyes and he wrapped me in his arms. It felt so right. I relaxed against him. He lowered his head and I thought he was going to kiss me, and what's more, I wanted him to. Tightening his arms around me, I felt the heat from his body pulsing through me. I felt so alive, loved and wanted. I pushed myself deeper into his embrace. I knew, in that instant, that I had become a part of his very being. I felt light, as if I had no substance. All I could feel was the heat of his body; and a wonderful, floaty, ethereal feeling overtook me. I wanted this moment to last forever. A great joy suffused me as I felt myself melting into him. I relaxed completely as his body gradually took over my will. I felt we were as one.

Suddenly, he released me and said tersely, 'Let's go inside, have a chat and a coffee, see what we can work out.'

I shook myself. I was shocked at my reaction to David's hug. I had wanted him to kiss me. It seemed as if he had woven a spell around me and my body ached to be back within the comfort of his arms. Once again, my sense of reason and free-will had deserted me. Gone was my all-consuming love for my childhood friend. All that filled my thoughts, my very being, was David.

I followed him into the kitchen, shoulders sagging, ashamed now at my reaction. Was I such an easy woman that, when a man hugged me, I lost the power of sensible thought? What was wrong with me? How could I fancy another, when I was so in love with Deimuiss? David was an added complication that I could well live without. I desperately hoped I was not becoming wanton – like Pranny. I felt guilty at betraying my love for Deimuiss.

Sitting in the kitchen over coffee, Mary joined us saying her feet were aching – that was a first for her! Not even a question attached to it – another first. I noticed she had given us a suspicious look, but surely, I reasoned, she could not possibly have seen us hug.

'And nearly kiss…'

A little voice whispered as my heart jolted, remembering how much I had wanted David to kiss me.

'…and more', the voice whispered again.

I blushed at the thought, and yes, I was convinced Mary knew how we felt about each other; from the look, she was casting in my direction.

Suddenly, a thought hit me.

'Don't forget we're going to Lichfield Spiritualist Church tomorrow, will you?'

'Yes,' Mary nodded. 'I have cancelled my other arrangement so that will be fine, something to look forward to.'

'Yes,' I agreed. 'I am looking forward to it.'

'I think you called mediums 'mystics' in your time, Elvaennia.'

'I don't think today's mediums are as advanced as the mystics though, Mary.'

'You're probably right Elvaennia,' she acquiesced, scuttling around, preparing for the next meal.

'Mmm,' I thought gleefully, 'She's just mentioned my past and not realised it.'

David chipped in:

'Okay, then Lichfield it is for all of us. Now, I'm off to check the horses, have supper and then to bed.'

He hurried away and I curled up in one of the large, comfy chairs thinking how strange it was that I had the gift of seeing, yet I hadn't seen any of this coming – and certainly not the added complication of fancying David.

'It's his eyes,' I thought, 'His voice. He is so good looking' and I could not forget how good it felt to be held by him. I wondered if I had developed a crush on him. But no, this had to be the real thing, and I didn't want to fight it, but I would. Not that I intended anything to happen between us. After all, I trusted myself. I was promised to Deimuiss; always had been. And there was not a man on this Earth who could come between us.

'Come now Elvaennia, let's get supper ready.'

She eyed me keenly. I became convinced she sensed the change in the relationship between David and me.

Later, lying awake, I was thinking of Deimuiss and David as I flitted between wakefulness and sleep. Trying to understand my emotional turmoil, I concluded that my attraction to David was because he was here, now, in the present, someone who obviously found me attractive and desirable. Just the thought that he did, stirred my emotions greatly. Deimuiss was not around; could not offer me the comfort and support that I so needed in this world. I longed at times, for the feel of Deimuiss's arms around me. No wonder I had found David irresistible earlier. Remembering how aroused I had felt within his arms, I blushed again, telling myself that nothing would have happened.

'Are you sure Elvaennia?' a voice whispered loudly in my ear as I drifted off to sleep. I shut out the voice, determined to concentrate on Deimuiss and on rescuing my family.

Chapter 26

Parking outside Cruck House in Lichfield, all three of us hurried inside, shaking heads, brollies and coats. It was pelting down with rain, making it feel colder. The late autumn leaves were slippery underfoot.

Introducing ourselves to the burly man at the door that led into the hall, we were made to feel like old friends.

'Welcome.'

He greeted us in a very deep voice, a huge smile cracking his florid face. Take a seat inside.'

'We will be starting soon.'

The small hall was nearly full. We were lucky to find three vacant chairs at the back, and quickly settled ourselves down.

A lady appeared on stage almost before we had time to take in our surroundings.

'Welcome to you all. It's so nice to see you, and also to welcome so many new faces. We will commence with a prayer, and then our first guest, Mr. Andrews, will give a short reading. This will be followed by Mr. Henry Adams, the respected medium. Then, we will take a short break before the healing takes place.'

I glanced at my two companions. Mary looked interested but David definitely looked uncomfortable. He was shifting around on his seat and he seemed to be in some discomfort.

'Oh dear, he looks to be in pain.'

My heart went out to him. I wanted to soothe the pain away for him.

179

After Mr. Andrews' reading, Henry Adams gave an interesting talk on mediumship, explaining how he was used as a channel for the spirits. He was adamant that he was not a fortune teller; his job was to prove life after death. After his introductory talk, Mr. Adams got in touch with various spirits, linking them to different members of the audience who seemed satisfied with what he told them.

He looked at me for a few seconds and I returned his gaze with a steady stare, wondering if he would be able to make a link for me.

He hesitated, and then a curious expression leapt across his face.

'Young lady, you made a remarkable journey not so long ago. I am correct, am I not?'

I felt the colour drain from my face. My goodness, he wasn't going to divulge about the settlement was he? I nodded quickly, hoping against hope he would then move on to his next victim, thinking, no publicity, please. Birmingham had been bad enough, but, so far so good, not a thing had happened since we had returned from the city – much to my relief.

'You have work to do, young lady. Only then will you be able to return to your people. It won't be easy. I wish you every success. The first stage of your work will commence shortly.'

Nodding my thanks, highly uncomfortable at being singled-out, I looked down at my hands wondering what on earth his words meant. There it was again – someone else telling me I had work to do. Why couldn't they be more specific? I hadn't a clue what type of work they meant, and could only surmise it was to do with clairvoyance and healing.

I heard a low murmur go around the hall and could swear I heard voices saying, 'It is her, you know, the girl who was caught on film in those news bulletins. She's been mentioned in the papers as well. They say she's from another time.'

'Heavens, no,' I thought. They were catching up with me. I kept my head down. At least there were no journalists here, thank goodness. No prying cameras.

The medium had left the stage and I became aware of poor David wriggling and squirming about on his seat. I nudged him with my elbow, and then – I couldn't help myself – I slipped my arm around him, drawing him close.

He sighed and I felt the warmth of his body through my clothes. I wanted this man, and he knew it. Oh my treacherous heart! After vowing to distance myself from David, now I desperately wanted to kiss him. At times, I found my emotions difficult to understand.

'Bad back,' he muttered. 'Must be these hard chairs.'

I squinted at him from the corner of my eyes, twitching my lips.

'You can have healing later then.'

He whispered in my ear, 'you are all the healing I need Elvaennia.'

Delighted, my cheating heart danced about and I nuzzled closer to him.

I felt – rather than saw – Mary's steely eyes fixed on us, and I moved away from David whispering, 'I hope the pain goes soon.'

'Pain,' Mary scoffed. 'Don't be fooled Elvaennia.'

I raised my eyebrows in query but Mary had spotted a couple of friends: John and Pat, a couple in their early fifties. She sped across the hall to say hello. I turned and looked at David. His magnetic green eyes looked steadily into mine. I was mesmerised. It was as if he held me in a spell and I did not want anything to break it. Next thing I knew, Mary had brought her friends across the hall to meet me. We were soon having a very interesting chat about spiritualism and psychic matters in general, when we were interrupted by a lady's voice saying:

'Mom, Dad, Afreionnia and I are off now. Sorry we can't stay, but we have a table booked at 'The George Hotel.'

I jumped on hearing the man's unusual name. It reminded me of home at the settlement and the Calegi Tribe.

Looking up, I saw a man of medium height with mousy brown hair. There was nothing distinguishing about him at first glance apart from a sudden recognition. But then, I shook myself.

'No, it couldn't possibly be, could it?'

I looked into his eyes and what I saw turned my stomach upside down. Never in all my life have I felt such horror and repulsion for any person I have met before, apart from, that is, The Delphs in the cave.

181

And by now, I was more than certain that this man was one of the men from the cave. He was evil personified and I drew back with a gasp. Feeling quite nauseous, I sat down quickly on a chair, trying to keep myself on an even keel. I was trembling. My whole world had turned upside down. I looked at the young woman who was chatting blithely away to her parents, completely unaware of the awfulness of the man standing beside her. She looked to be around 23 years of age, a small, plumpish woman. The one remarkable thing about her was her beautiful skin – what I've heard described as the English 'peaches and cream' skin. This she had in double measure, her beautiful complexion surrounded by a bubble of blonde, highlighted curls. Despite her tendency to plumpness, she was a striking looking woman, and I felt really sorry for her being in the company of such a vicious, evil man. I determined to help her if I possibly could. I looked at my hands and saw that I had steepled them together, which is a sign meant to protect me against evil. I had unknowingly done this as I sat down.

'Elvaennia, may I introduce you to our daughter Maria. Maria, this is Elvaennia.'

Jumping up, I acknowledged Maria with a smile and said, 'Hello, pleased to meet you.'

Maria returned the greeting with a bob of her curls and said, 'Elvaennia, meet Afreionnia.'

I noticed him putting his hand out to shake mine. 'Hello,' I greeted and then deliberately dropped my bag to the floor. 'Whoops!' I bent to pick it up, thus avoiding any physical contact with him. He had extended his hand towards me and my heart sank to my shoes as I had seen the red arrow mark of The Delphs. This young woman was in grave danger. Obviously, this man had time travelled; disastrous for her and her family. I took a deep breath, determined not to let him see I knew who he was and where he was from. As I glanced at him, I saw the other man (who had been in the cave) standing in the shadows behind him. He was a spirit I knew. My heart flipped in terror for Maria, but what could I do at this stage? Simply nothing. I knew I had to bide my time before I could take any action. I wondered how many more of The Delphs walked the earth in this century.

'Nice to meet you Elvaennia. See you later Mom and Dad,' Maria's voice sang out as she and her friend (followed by the spirit shadow) made their way towards the exit.

I shuddered with a sense of relief when the couple had departed. Hopefully, I would get an opportunity soon to help rid Maria of the danger she was in. I had to help her. I knew she was keeping dangerous company.

Soon it was time for the healing to begin. A lady stepped forward and introduced herself as 'Glenda.' She looked straight at David and told him he was in some discomfort with his back.

The look of shock on his face was something else. A small giggle escaped me.

I received a nudge for that; but already the lady was calling him out to the front. Slowly, he unwound himself from the chair and wended his painful way to the front of the hall. The lady stepped down from the stage, ready to meet him.

'You'd think he was going to be hung not healed,' Mary chirpily remarked.

A louder giggle escaped me. 'Ah, you would indeed.' I smirked unfeelingly.

The lady healer was in her fifties, and was a little brusque in her attitude: tall, upright, and despite not having a coat or jacket on, she still wore her hat.

David looked extremely self-conscious, but I admired him for having the courage to stand in front of the fifty or so people in the hall.

Holding her hands a short distance from his spine, she quickly located the point of pain. She stood for a few seconds, her hands stretched above the troubled area.

'Give yourself ten minutes and you'll be fine, young man,' she said in her no-nonsense voice. 'You are undoubtedly under a lot of tension.'

'Thank you,' he replied and made his painful return to us.

The healer spent a lot of time helping other people with various ailments, and we were all surprised to find that a good hour had passed when the lady host popped up saying, 'A huge thank-you to Glenda, our healer for the night,' and asked for a round of applause.

'Before you go, we have a few seats left for the evening at Llandrindod Wells tomorrow. It is free, but a ticket assures you of a seat.'

'Tomorrow!' I breathed in excitement. I thought it was the week after next. I looked pleadingly at Mary. She nodded and I made my way through the departing crowd to ask the evening's host for three of the spare tickets and more details.

I couldn't wait for the next day to arrive. I thought it was fate that had led us to Cruck House, otherwise I would have missed Llandrindod Wells. I wanted to hug everyone in sight, but I thought better of it.

Glancing round, I could see a group of people heading our way and I knew they were intent on finding out if I was the person who had been on the television.

'Quickly Mary, let's leave. I think they know who I am.'

Mary looked at the fast approaching group and almost pushed us out of the hall.

Much to my relief, we were leaving the car park as the crowd of people came outside. Was this a taste of what was to come if I wasn't careful? I hoped not.

David admitted to feeling much better as he drove us home. 'Of course, it could have been coincidence,' was all he would say. I smiled to myself, thinking 'typical man'.

Maybe, just maybe, it was Deimuiss who would be at Llandrindod Wells tomorrow, and this was how it was meant to be. We would then be together for all time. Hopefully, we could return to the settlement and take up our lives again.

I pushed all thoughts of David from my mind. I was mystified how I had suddenly become attracted to him. There was something achingly familiar about him but I could not put a finger on what it was.

I became lost in troubled thoughts of Deimuiss and my family until the voice interrupted, 'He will have you Elvaennia.' I jumped at those words and replied, 'He won't!'

David's voice called, 'Come on Elvaennia, we're home.'

He was holding the door for me. As I passed him, I felt his presence so strongly I was drawn into the circle of his aura. He drew me into his arms.

'You are so beautiful my little sprite. I don't think I can let you go.'

I didn't want him to. Ever! Such was the power of his charisma. I was hypnotised by him. All thoughts of Deimuiss, the settlement, anything that had gone before, disappeared. All I wanted was to be with David – now and for- evermore. I was convinced that my destiny lay with him. Looking into his wonderful, green eyes, I saw my desire for him reflected strongly. The silver of my eyes was intertwined with the sea green of his. Encircled in his arms was the only place I wanted to be, forever. Such was his power over me that I knew, in that moment, that he held my body and soul for eternity.

It was dark on the drive beside the car, and David held me tightly, whispering endearments to me as he ran his hands through my hair, kissing my face and nibbling my ears. I shivered in anticipation, wondering what had changed my feeling for him. Had he cast a spell over me? All I knew was that felt powerless to resist him

'David, Elvaennia.'

Guiltily, we jumped apart.

'Coming mother.'

Disappointed, but greatly relieved, I ran through the front door of the farmhouse straight into the small hallway that I had been in once before when I had arrived. My body was still aching for David's touch as the shadows reached out to me crying, 'We told you Elvaennia, beware of that man. He is dangerous. Set us free and we will help you get rid of him. We want to be free and return to our own time.'

'No,' I thought, to my utter shame, 'Not yet.' I wanted David's touch more than anything I had ever wanted before. Nothing else mattered. He filled my senses so that everything and everyone was distanced. My whole body ached for him. My head was spinning. I had never felt so confused about a man before. What had changed between us? I did not know, but he intoxicated my every thought and I longed to be with him forever.

'Elvaennia, he is not for you. He will destroy you. Let him go.'

The shadows were trying to overpower me when, suddenly, the door was flung wide and David's arms enfolded me again. I sank into his body. I had no control over my feelings anymore; he possessed me – body and soul. I didn't care about Deimuiss now. David was all I wanted. He was the centre of my world.

'No, Elvaennia.'

The shadows were trying to press between us as I was elbowing them out of the way. They were trying to separate us but David moulded his body to mine. There was no separating us, we were as one.

I felt a nip on my heel. 'Ouch,' I cried pulling away from David. 'Who did that?'

The shadows had gone, disappeared. We were standing in the wide, airy hallway with the highly polished floor. Pip was sitting, looking up at me, and wagging his tail innocently. Mary came rushing through from the kitchen.

'Come along you two, I have made a little supper and a warm drink. We have a busy day tomorrow so best we have an early night.'

David met my eyes with a quirk of his eyebrow. My heart jumped. He wanted to come to my bedroom that night.

I ignored the question. Strangely, the nip on my ankle had brought me back to my senses. Whatever was I thinking? Letting another man hold and caress me when I was to marry another? David had bewitched me, and if this was a test, I was obviously 'losing it'. Determination took over. I had to fight. I moved away from the circle of his aura, knowing I had to keep my distance. My future lay with Deimuiss. It had to. I had come too far to let my life be ruined by an affair. Again, I heard the voice.

'That's what you think, Elvaennia.'

I jumped. Who on earth was it that kept passing these messages to me?

Walking towards the kitchen, I suddenly felt David's arms encircle my waist. Turning me round, he held me close. Stroking my hair, he whispered endearments to me. I realised I was putty in his hands.

Looking up into his eyes, I was sure he could read the naked longing in my eyes and I saw the same reflected in his.

Hearing Mary's footsteps approaching from the kitchen, we separated and hurried to the supper table. Not that I had much appetite for food – it was David I wanted, in my bed, not just in my life. I shuddered at the thought of him making love to me and realised that this was probably a challenge laid down for me to fight and overcome; part of the journey I had to make in my search for Deimuiss. How to be strong though? David's attraction was all powerful. How was I going to stand firm against him?

As soon as I had showered – made certain first that David was outside locking the animals up for the night – I hastened to my room and locked the door. I felt very strong-minded indeed doing that. I then retired to bed, pleased with myself for being tough and for facing up to my shortcomings.

'He will have you Elvaennia.'

Again, the voice challenged me.

'No, he won't,' I vowed, stronger now, more determined than ever to fight him.

Chapter 27

Taking our seats at the conference centre, I was awash with nerves. Oh my goodness, I would be seeing him soon. I had convinced myself by now that it was HIM, and that David definitely had no part to play in my future. If the healer was Deimuiss – I just knew he was – then how would I react? I hoped I would be able to contain myself and not rush up to him.

There was a stage at this venue. It was all very professional. Our host for the evening was a genial gentleman with a cheerful looking face. He introduced himself as Colin Hoggs.

('Mmm, don't giggle at his name Elvaennia!')

I gave myself a little kick, biting hard on my bottom lip.

'First let me welcome you all and give you a programme run down.'

'This is it,' I thought, 'Soon I will be seeing him…'

My heart rate had increased, all thoughts of David erased from my mind. Deimuiss was here, I knew he was. Soon, very soon, I would be in his arms, never to be separated again. How I longed for the moment to arrive.

Reading the programme, I saw that the healing was at the end of the meeting. There were five speakers before it started. All that time to wait. I was so impatient and I wondered why I hadn't attempted to try and see him before the show started.

At times, I felt myself beginning to drowse and Mary nudged me awake. I must confess, I'd been awake with excitement since five a.m. Now the time was dragging. I must have nodded off again as they were announcing the interval. Not long now. A quick rush to the toilet, a cup of coffee to wake myself up properly and then back to our seats, I would see him then, after all this time. I could hardly contain myself.

We were only a couple of rows from the front and I could hear a lot of to-ing and fro-ing, whispering voices behind the dark red curtains. My hands were hot and sweaty and I was jigging up and down on my seat with excitement. People were returning. The hall was filling up fast.

'Not long,' I exhaled and took a very deep breath. My torment would soon be at an end.

Our evening host, Mr. Hoggs, suddenly popped through the curtain. He was holding a sheet of paper.

Every eye was watching him expectantly; none more than mine.

I could feel my mouth gaping open and I snapped it together, biting my tongue sharply – damn! Another mouth ulcer, but hopefully it would be worth it.

Clearing his voice, the speaker gazed around the hall.

'Ladies and gentlemen, first I have to make a sincere apology.'

'What?'

I nearly shot off my seat. He's not coming. He's let everyone down. Oh no, I couldn't bear it if he had let all these people down, me in particular. I felt devastated. What, no Deimuiss? I felt like crying.

'Elvaennia, listen pet, the healer hasn't cancelled. It's someone else who's arranged another date in the future. They have re-booked.'

Mary curled one of her plump arms round me in half a hug. As far as I knew, she did not realise that I thought the healer was Deimuiss. Or did she?

Relief! I wiped my sweaty hands down my jeans, getting a reproving look from Mary as she surreptitiously passed me a couple of tissues. Mr. Hoggs cleared his throat.

'Ladies and gentleman, before our healing session begins, I would like to introduce our last medium. Please give a big welcome to Polly Smith.'

The clapping quickly subsided as a slim, young woman with wavy shoulder length brown hair walked out on to the stage.

I was drawn to her immediately. She was dressed very circumspectly for such a young woman. Her clothes were all in subdued colours, nothing that would attract your attention to her at all, but around her shone one of the brightest auras I had ever seen (it was almost pure gold). Deimuiss's aura was the purest one I had ever seen. It sparkled as gold dust all around him. Never once had I seen anything around him that signified he would go over to the enemies. Now I saw someone of a similar ilk. I was transfixed by the golden light around her and the luminosity of her blue eyes.

Smiling, she greeted us and immediately went to a couple sitting at the back of the hall, giving them a message from one of their children who had died not long ago. The child had passed-away when he was just 11 years of age. My heart went out to the mother and father. I could feel their grief as an impenetrable black wall. I didn't need to turn around and see them. I could feel their desperation from where I was sitting; I could hear it in their monosyllabic replies. I wanted to reach out and help them as I had helped others in my other life at the settlement. I sent them healing thoughts and hoped they would help them.

The medium moved quickly to a young woman sitting at the end of a row. Her message was that she (the young woman) would eventually leave her past behind and move on, re-marry and have twins. I could hear the smile in the woman's voice as she thanked the medium for her words. From the guarded conversation, it wasn't difficult to work out that the woman had been in an abusive relationship.

Again and again the young medium gave out messages of hope to members of the audience.

Suddenly, she looked directly at me. I jumped when she said:

'You have certainly come a long way for one so young.'

I gulped at her words. It was as if she knew my life story, just as Mr. Adams had 'tuned in' last night.

'You have a lot of work to do, before your time to return home comes. You will be well-known on the so-called 'celeb circuit.''

Oh no, the very thing I did not want to happen. No way did I want to be well-known.

'You cannot stop it.,' she went on to say. 'It has already started. You will receive help, but…'

She shook her head at this point.

'You do have a lot of important work to do here and elsewhere. You will come to understand what I mean as time passes. It will all take a very long time, but eventually everything will come right.'

Oh, this was confusing. Nevertheless, before I could question her, she gave me a nod, and then moved on to the next person.

So that was it, no more explanations – The 'thing' had started, it would seem. I had no choice in this matter. Goosebumps sped up and down my arms and my heart thudded in my chest. How did the woman know this? I glanced surreptitiously at Mary and David and caught each of them slowly nodding their heads. People around us were looking at me. I wanted to curl up and die from embarrassment.

I looked directly at the young woman as she was leaving the stage, and mouthed my thanks to her politely. With a smile to me, and a 'thank you' to the audience, she left the stage. It was as if she had been waiting to give me the message and accepted that her work for that evening was done.

Still mulling over the medium's words to me, I missed Mr. Hogg's introduction; so deep in contemplation, was I. Suddenly, a voice broke through my thoughts and I looked up at the stage. My poor heart – it couldn't really take any more shocks that evening. I gave a gasp of surprise and quickly covered it with a small cough. That *was* Deimuiss up on stage, wasn't it? My childhood friend was standing confidently, speaking to this group of people, explaining 'his gift'. He went to great lengths, telling the audience how he was directed by an 'invisible' force, to what was causing the person's illness. It was him, wasn't it? His hair was fairly short but I could see the dark curls springing up uncontrollably. He looked so handsome and tall in his smart, dark suit and white shirt, complementing his navy blue tie and the colour of his eyes. But, there was no way I could kid myself any longer. This man was not my Deimuiss – his aura was wrong; everything about him was wrong for me. I felt myself beginning to cry. The man on stage definitely was not my Deimuiss.

I ran out of the hall, tears of disappointment pouring down my face. I had been so certain that the man was Deimuiss. All my hopes and dreams had been centred on it being him. Now I was cast down, lost and lonely and filled, yet again, with despair. Another false lead – was I never going to find my lost love?

Was he even now back home at the settlement in Pranny's arms? The thought was almost too much to accept.

Leaning against a wall, crying, silent tears slipping down my face, an arm snaked around my waist; David drew me towards him, whispering words of endearment, asking why I was crying.

I snuggled closer, welcoming the warmth of his strong, lithe body, glad of the security he brought to me. I ran my hands through his brown, springy hair, feeling the warmth of him flooding through my fingers.

He bent his head murmuring, 'I will always be here for you Elvaennia.' My heart lifted at his words and I felt him nuzzling my neck. I turned towards him, welcoming his kisses. It was so good to be wanted and not to feel so alone in this strange alien world. I felt David was the only person who truly understood me. I twined my arms around his neck, whispering loving words to him. I felt his whole body respond to me. His hand was inside my coat, stroking my breasts. This felt so right to me and I drew him even closer, whispering words of love. His mouth and hands were doing wonderful things to me. more than anything, I wanted, to belong to him and feel safe and secure.

The familiar voice broke through our wonderful love-making.

'David, Elvaennia, where are you?'

A giggle escaped me. 'A repeat of last night,' I whispered, laughing then I shivered realising how cold it was.

I felt David smile as he hastily stepped away from me. 'Later Elvaennia,' he promised, kissing me lightly on the cheek.

'Over here mother, I think we will book into the hotel for tonight. It's rather late to return home.'

'Yes, that's fine son. I packed a bag for us all just in case we stopped over.'

I was impressed by her forethought. I had not given a thought to what would happen after the meeting. If I'm truthful, I had envisaged being with Deimuiss – nothing else seemed worth considering.

Bookings made, we ordered a light meal in the dining room. As we were eating our food, I was surprised when a small crowd of people approached our table. Raising my eyebrows, I asked if we could help them.

'We saw you on the news the other night and wondered if we could have your autograph.'

I felt myself go hot with embarrassment.

'Pardon, what did you say?' I said almost choking on a very hot chip.

'We saw you on the national news last night and wondered if you would sign our programmes?'

'But, I haven't done anything to warrant signing your programmes.' I protested, aware that the whole dining room was now watching us.

'Oh, but you have,' one of the young girls cried out. 'You have travelled through time.'

'Sign it Elvaennia,' David almost hissed, 'then they will go.'

Knowing it was pointless to argue, hands shaking at this unexpected turn of events, I signed the programmes. The leader of the group lingered. 'Could I ask you a few questions?' she murmured.

'No questions, it's late,' David insisted firmly and watched the group leave the dining room.

'Quickly now, we will go to mother's room.'

He whisked us to the lift before I could blink.

'Now then, what do we do?' he asked as he roamed around Mary's room. 'It seems that your secret is about to break, Elvaennia and we have to make plans.'

He began pacing to and fro, to and fro, clearly thinking hard about which road we should take.

After a few minutes, he stopped and stood in front of me saying, 'Here's my thoughts for now – you could follow the pathway opening up for you and take the 'fame' road. Alternatively, you could settle for what you have. It's up to you Elvaennia.'

As always, within the sphere of his aura, all I wanted was to be with him; but a thought wormed its insistent way into my brain. If I followed the 'fame' route, it would bring in lots of money. Wouldn't it? Money that I could put to good use when I had found a way to bring my family here.

'You will help me David?' I asked, clenching my hands nervously together.

'Every step of the way, my little one. Whatever you choose to do, I will be there for you.'

Looking at her, thinking how beautiful she was, he again thought how surprising it was that she did not realise how attractive she was. Already jealousy was rearing its ugly head at the thought of all the attention she was going to receive now that the road to fame beckoned. He was determined that no other man, but he, would have Elvaennia.

Mary cleared her throat, clearly shocked.

'Excuse me, who will manage the farm?'

David smiled at her.

'I will find a good manager for it, mother, have no fear. Elvaennia needs caring for. We cannot just throw her out into the world.'

Mary's lips pursed and she did not look happy at all at this turn of events. For once, she did not say anything – apart from, 'Best be getting some sleep then,' I realised she did not want to lose me, nor I her either, but my future was calling me on the winds of time and I knew that this was the right road to follow. I had to rescue my family, and I had to have the means to look after them. This, I told myself, was what the Mystics had meant all those months ago. Quite how I was going to earn this money, I had no idea, but I thought I would worry about that later. My head was whirling with everything that was happening.

I hugged her, wished them both 'Goodnight,' retrieved my night bag from Mary, and made my way to my bedroom.

Alone with my thoughts (I'd locked the door, just in case!), I was astounded at the turn of events and remembered the reading that I had at the psychic fair. Was it all going to come true? Would I really be famous? That wasn't what I wanted at all. If I was truthful with myself, the lure was David. Whenever I was near him, I wanted him. I was unable to think straight whenever I was around him. I realised that this could be my downfall, hence the locked door.

Slipping into bed, I lay awake, wondering what on earth was going to happen. How I was going to be famous, I hadn't a clue. Celebrities acted or sang. I did neither and certainly had no wish to be on the so-called 'celebrity circuit'. It did not appeal to me at all. The idea of being well known appalled me, but if a way to earn money from being famous presented itself to me, then I knew I would do it for my family. I drifted off into a restless sleep where 2007 became entangled with my time. And we lived, 'world within world'.

Chapter 28

At breakfast the next morning, Elvaennia was embarrassed by the surreptitious glances of some of the guests, and also the outright stares of others. As they were about to leave, one of the waiters asked her to sign a table napkin, 'for my girlfriend,' he confided, while idly casting a lustful look over her tiny figure. Signing as fast as she could, Elvaennia beat a hasty retreat, followed by mother and son.

David drove the car, with Mary in the passenger seat. Elvaennia sat relaxing comfortably on the back seat of the car, thinking of all that had happened in the last few days. Disappointment still rode high on her list, having had her hopes dashed to smithereens at once again not finding Deimuiss. But she consoled herself with the thought that she would eventually find him, and all would be right between them.

She had deliberately chosen to sit behind Mary so that David could not watch her through the driver's mirror. Having spent time by herself last night, she had made a firm decision not to become entangled with him at any cost. She had taken out her pack of Angel Cards and drawn the Angel of Help – sending prayers via the angel to help her have the inner strength to resist his charms. She remembered the voices of the shadows in the hallway, insisting she see him for what he was – a bad person. As she thought of the voices, Elvaennia realised what a fool she was being in allowing herself to be distracted from her search. She was determined that at the first opportunity she would talk to the shadows and find out what they had to tell her; also, if it was within her power, she would free them. Again, she felt ashamed for not helping them.

'If I can't help free them, I know Deimuiss will know how to.'

With a sense of renewed responsibility, she began to think about what her life ahead held.

For the first time in many weeks, Elvaennia acknowledged that she had made a strong decision and had taken control of her life. It was when she was close to David, that his attraction drew her into his aura and her resistance slipped away immediately. It really felt as if he had hypnotised her. She understood that the charm he exuded was like no other she had ever experienced, but recognised he was wrong for her. 'David is definitely not the man for me.' She concurred, 'and that's all there is to it.'

Settling back in her seat, her thoughts turned towards the prediction that she would become famous and would become a celebrity. A small chuckle escaped from her and Mary glanced round asking, 'What's tickled you lass?'

Explaining with a smile, Mary replied wisely, 'what will be, will be.'

'You are correct as always mother,' David chirruped, glancing to Elvaennia in the back of the car, flashing his magnetic smile at her. She felt her heart and stomach flip in an astonishing manner but managed not to go overboard and returned the smile with a nod.

'Be strong Elvaennia,' she kept repeating to herself. 'Think of Deimuiss – he truly loves you.' She kept reiterating to herself as she drifted off to sleep into dreams of her childhood sweetheart.

She was woken suddenly by Mary's cry of, 'what is happening David?'

For the first time, Elvaennia heard David swear. It was far from polite. 'What is it? What's happening?' she called drowsily from the back of the car, tiredly rubbing the sleep from her eyes.

'Look! The farm is surrounded.'

Sitting up and leaning as far forward as her seatbelt permitted, Elvaennia was shocked to see what appeared to be the World's press surrounding the entrance to the driveway of the farmhouse.

'My goodness,' she whispered, 'whatever can they want?'

'To be blunt, it's you they want,' David said breathing heavily, 'but they are not going to have you.' The words were spoken so savagely, the two women were astounded.

Reversing quickly down the lane, David turned the steering wheel viciously and headed towards the A51.

'I'll fox them!'

He almost spat the words out as he headed down the lane. Glancing through his rear view mirror, he indicated, then turned sharp left up a narrow lane. Never having seen this hidden side road before, Elvaennia wondered where he was taking them.

Reaching the end of the lane, again David steered left, parking in front of a farm gate. He leapt out, opened the lock with a key and after driving through, jumped out again and relocked it. All the time, rage was exuding from him. It was almost tangible.

'Nearly home,' he beamed across at his passengers seemingly having recovered his equilibrium in the blink of an eye. He followed the track across the field to the next gate repeating his unlocking and locking procedure. His spirits seemed to lift when he climbed back into the car. The back of the farmhouse loomed into view. He stopped the car.

'Pass me the binoculars from the glove box mother please.'

Scanning the area, he nodded, satisfied.

'Safe to return – they haven't infiltrated the back of the farm.'

Then, in a dark undertone, he muttered, 'They hadn't better either.' Again you could hear the underlying savagery in his voice and both women shuddered as more of the darker side of his character emerged.

Ascertaining that all was well within the house, they met around the well-scrubbed kitchen table.

'What happens now?' Elvaennia appealed to David.

'Don't worry little one, I have friends. You will be protected. Drink your coffee and I will make a few telephone calls. Please Elvaennia, make me one promise?'

She nodded, captivated again by the greenness of his wonderful eyes. Despite trying hard to resist him, she began to feel herself slipping under his spell yet again.

'Do not speak to anyone unless I am with you. This is very

important. Promise me this one thing.'

'Of course,' she replied with a brilliant smile that made his heart race so fast he had trouble breathing.

'I must have her for myself,' he thought, beguiled by everything about this young enchantress. He vowed to himself again that she would be his forever. 'No one but me will ever have her,' he promised himself.

Tearing himself away from her, he headed into his study to make the phone call that would shape Elvaennia's future, thus changing her life in this time forever.

From her bedroom window later that evening, Elvaennia could see the lights of the cars parked on the drive and road. She could not understand why people should be so interested in her, but having spoken to David at some length, she felt a little more reassured about her future. He had told her that the following day a friend of his was going to land on the back field in his helicopter, and whisk her off to his home, Wythefield Castle, from where her future would eventually be mapped out away from the prying eyes of the media.

'You could become very rich, little one,' he stated, turning the full force of his charm on her. His words failed to impress her.

'Money disinterests me David' (Did he know me at all?), 'I will go along with the plans you mention but really, I am hoping that if Deimuiss is in this time, he will see me and will make contact.'

Obviously, she wanted money for her family; but not a fortune – just enough to tide them all over.

Nodding, David tried to mask his jealousy while seeming to go along with her.

'Mmm, yes I understand.'

He agreed on the surface, but underneath he seethed angrily – 'No way will he ever reach her now she is mine. She's in my power, and there is no man on this Earth apart from me who will ever possess her body and soul.'

Watching the different transformations racing across David's face, Elvaennia felt a flash of fear. What was he thinking to make his face so ugly and frightening? She shuddered, worrying that perhaps, she had made the wrong decision and she should have returned to her own time.

Sensing her withdrawal, David got up and lifted her out of her chair. Wrapping her in his strong arms, he hugged and kissed her fears away.

'Pack your clothes Elvaennia, ready for tomorrow. Peter will be arriving shortly after breakfast.'

Hearing Mary pattering towards the kitchen, he drew sharply away from her.

Entering the kitchen, Mary exclaimed, 'What about Christmas? If Elvaennia is away at that castle of Peter's, she will be on her own. Peter and his wife always go away.'

'Stop worrying mother. Elvaennia passed her test remember? She can drive here to us, or we can fetch her. That's a minor detail. Don't start panicking for heaven's sake.'

Remembering the thrill of passing her driving test, Elvaennia felt a huge grin steal across her face only to be replaced by the thought that maybe she had lost her new found freedom already – if she was going to be locked up in a castle. 'I'll be like a heroine in a children's story,' she thought wryly. 'I just hope they don't forget me or lose the key.'

She nodded slowly, worried even more now about what her future held. How had the media tracked her down? Who had contacted them? Now she was to go into hiding at a strange place until the unwanted interest in her hopefully quietened down. Looking out of her window, towards the cave, she was startled to see coloured lights hovering over it again. She wondered if someone else had arrived. And was this why David was moving her out? Suspicion clouded her thoughts. Why did she not trust anyone? – 'Because of Deimuiss's betrayal', the voice whispered in her ear.

'How can you ever trust anyone ever again?'

She longed to run to the cave to see if anyone was inside, worried they might be feeling as she had, lost, lonely and afraid. However, she knew there was no way she could risk it with the media pack surrounding the farm. Someone would see her, of that, she was convinced. She hoped against hope that if someone was inside the cave, they would not have long to wait before being found.

Mary had left suitcases ready for her to pack her possessions. Heavy hearted, she began to fold and pack them ready for the next day. Elvaennia knew she was going to miss the farmhouse badly. Not only had she come to love the house, and Mary – away from David, she was uncertain of her feelings for him – but also the house's proximity to the cave gave her a sense of security, as she knew instinctively that it was the link to her returning home to her family.

She desperately wanted to stay near it.

Chapter 29

Hearing the helicopter coming into land Elvaennia grabbed her suitcases and made haste back to the kitchen where Mary was dashing around the kitchen clattering the pots and pans, looking extremely worried. Elvaennia went to her.

'I will keep in touch every day, Mary. Really I will!'

Close to tears, she hugged her closely. She was so going to miss this wonderful woman who had become like a mother to her.

'I know lass but I am going to miss you so much.' Pulling some tissues from her apron pocket she blew her nose noisily.

Wiping a surreptitious tear away, she almost pushed Elvaennia out of the farmhouse door.

'Before I go, Mary, can I ask you something?'

'Of course. Anything, my luv.'

'Why do you keep that old shoe by the Holly Tree?'

The young woman pointed to a very old shoe that had obviously belonged to an elderly lady.

'Oh, that,' she said airily, patting her hair and trying to appear unconcerned, 'it's an old wives' tale that says it keeps the evil spirits away. Don't know why it's still there.'

'I see,' said Elvaennia, smirking, running towards the helicopter on the field. She noticed, as she turned to wave, that Mary hadn't picked the shoe up.

Safely in the helicopter, after greeting Peter, Elvaennia looked down as the farmhouse receded into the distance. 'Another new experience', she mused, settling into her seat, wondering how long the journey would take, she was more than surprised that after five minutes they began the descent.

Seeing her startled look, Peter laughed, shouting above the engine noise, 'It was to fool the media Elvaennia. I know it's nearby, but if we had used the car they would have followed you. Hopefully, they will be thinking you are many miles away now.'

Looking across the field, Elvaennia saw what looked to be a fairytale castle, all turrets and floating magical spires; it was at the top of a hill. Gulping, she glanced at Peter who nodded, 'Yes, this is going to be your home for as long as you need it. I hope you will be happy with us.'

His brown eyes crinkled at the corners under his huge shaggy eyebrows. His tanned face held a warm welcoming look as he picked up the cases, and they headed off towards the castle. She began to feel safer.

Drawing near to the building, Elvaennia felt a huge surge of excitement. The castle was so inviting. The brickwork glowed red in the wintry sunlight and, despite being old, a welcoming ambience seemed to reverberate across its ancient ramparts.

Within the walls, it was a truly amazing place, just how she imagined a modern day castle would be. The great hall had been divided into spacious rooms with luscious, comfy sofas, chaise longues and huge leather chairs scattered around. Her feet sank into the deep pile of the carpet. The curtains were of thick, heavy damask silk that complimented the furnishings. Strangely enough, she did not feel at all out of her depth. She felt right, as if she belonged here in this castle. Despite not being many miles from the farm, in truth, she felt a million miles away. It was as if her other life back at the settlement had never existed. Here in this castle was real. Any other life seemed to have faded from her sight. A strange anticipation bubbled up inside her. She sensed great changes were about to happen soon, and she wanted to embrace them with open arms. Nothing else mattered. Her whole being was now centred on what was going to happen in her future.

A few of the rooms had been furnished in keeping with the age of the edifice, and were a delight to the eye. Despite the fact that the suits of armour had made her jump a few times, Elvaennia adored the whole castle on sight; in particular, her suite of rooms.

When Elizabeth, the resident housekeeper, had shown her where she was to stay, Elvaennia's eyes had nearly popped out of her head, and it took a while for it all to sink in.

'Goodness me', she thought, 'I have a whole floor to myself.'

Walking through the rooms, Elvaennia felt almost overcome by all she was seeing.

'How lucky am I?'

She had thought that the farmhouse was beautiful, but this was beyond anything she could ever have imagined. It was truly delightful. Her feet sinking into the deep pile, she continued her tour of the rooms. A sitting room, a study, a television room with a huge plasma screen television, the most luscious bedroom – her rooms just went on and on. The bathroom was out of this World. 'I am truly being spoilt here,' she muttered to herself gazing around at the sumptuous bathroom, and the wet room with a power shower to die for and the most luxurious bathroom accessories you could want. She almost screamed out loud with excitement on seeing a sauna.

'All this luxury, just for me, I can't believe this is happening!'

Her eyes were almost on stalks as she drank in the sheer lavishness of it all.

Looking through the windows filled her with pleasure; marvellous views of the lake - there was even an island in the middle of it - with fields rolling down to the water's edge. There were sheep grazing along the sandy shores at the water's edge. Canadian geese pecked amongst the shale and sand. Beautiful swans glided across the lake's surface. Birds swooped across the rippling waters, hunting for food. Rooks swirled around in a black cloud on a distant field.

The fields were a beautiful patchwork of greens. All around her, the views were simply stunning. Elvaennia told herself she was indeed very fortunate to be made so welcome in what was, after all, a stranger's home. True, Peter was a good friend to the family, but she had never even heard of him until yesterday. And now she was ensconced in their lap of luxury.

Finding her way back down to the ground floor, she felt rather awkward, not knowing where to go or even what was expected of her. Hearing chattering voices in the distance, she followed the sound, finding herself eventually in an extremely large kitchen.

'My,' she gasped, 'and I thought the one at the farmhouse was large. It would be lost in this one.'

'Cup of coffee, Miss?' a pretty, smiling, young girl called to her.

'Yes please,' she responded, feeling rather shy in the presence of a group of four women and an older man who she assumed was some kind of manager.

Looking around the kitchen, she could see that it obviously had every mod con you could imagine, even an electric Aga. The shape of the Aga reminded her of the oven they had back at the settlement. Only slightly, as of course, they never had electricity, but the oven was the same shape and had certain similarities. Wistfully, she gazed at it, remembering her mother struggling to cook food within the confines of the one they had. Looking at the girl cleaning the silver, she remembered the pottery she had used along with oyster shells to scoop the food up with, or pieces of slate or polished wooden scoops, slices of dried skin to hold hot food on so that it would not burn you, certainly not this type of plate. 'We used wooden ones,' she thought, remembering how they held the heat, 'or just plain fingers to eat with,' she recalled, smiling at her memories.

Drinking the delicious coffee, her attention was caught by all the gleaming saucepans hanging around the kitchen walls. They did not look to be well used, but then her eyes had wandered to another two huge microwaves and she realised where most of the cooking took place. Again, her mind wandered into the past, remembering the huge cooking fires, the smell and the fug of the smoke within the houses. The smoke had never bothered her, as she found it added to the cosiness of their homes, particularly during the winter months. She suddenly tasted the delicious fish they used to bake in the fires. The fish, wrapped in herbs and grasses, had the most delicious taste in the World, unlike anything she had ever tasted in this time. Memories of apples, stuffed with wild fruits gathered from the hedgerows, baked in the clay oven, set her taste buds on edge and she longed to be home at the settlement. However, knowing this was a pipe dream; she thanked the kitchen staff for the coffee and decided to explore some of the grounds. Making her way down the hill to the edge of the lake, she stood for a few minutes, allowing her gaze to wander over the picturesque scene in front of her, watching the wading birds dipping their heads into the water. On her way back, she could picture how the grounds must look in the summertime. She imagined the wondrous scents that would hang in the air in the rose gardens on heady summer days. A cottage garden caught her eye, and she thought of the lupines, delphiniums, poppies shaking their tall heads, shedding their seeds ready for following summers. She imagined how beautiful it must look in full bloom. She felt quite heady as the remembered scents filled her nostrils for a few seconds. Wonderful she breathed. Scattered around the pathways now were wild winter pansies and grasses enhancing the wintery garden. Passing through into the conservatory, she noticed the Norlina plants standing proudly, displaying their white flowers along with an Aloe Vera plant silently guarding its position. She liked the Aloe Vera's healing properties, remembering that Mary also kept this particular plant at the farmhouse. The many different varieties of plants on display in the conservatory impressed her no end, and she spent some time studying each one and reading the labels of the ones she did not recognise. Many of them were from abroad; she realised and wondered if Peter and his wife had brought them back from their travels.

Shaking her head in admiration at everything around her, she felt quite choked, remembering the bad time in the cave and how she had miraculously been transported to this century. Having read on the Internet about some of the things that had happened throughout history, she was more-than-delighted to have been brought to this time, and indeed this place.

She adored the castle, although a few of the darker corridors spooked her – particularly if she happened to bump into a suit of armour at the end of some of them, but overall, the castle was a light and airy building that gave off positive vibes.

Returning to her suite of rooms, she noticed that her suitcases had disappeared, and on looking in the huge wardrobe in the dressing room, again she was startled to see not only her clothes hanging inside, but also whole rails of women's clothing arrayed before her eyes. She knew, without trying them on, that they would fit her. She then remembered how the clothing had fitted her at the farmhouse, and never once had Mary mentioned her daughters. 'How strange is that?' she thought, realising of course that there were no daughters and never had been. Mary had created her daughters to make her feel at home.

'One day, I will find out the truth of all this,' she thought, trying to decide what to wear for the evening meal.

Chapter 30

Christmas had been and gone, and Elvaennia had enjoyed all the celebrations, the exchange of gifts, and the delicious food. The sense of happiness the season generated was really overwhelming. She had even enjoyed David's kisses under the mistletoe and could still remember the gorgeous feel of his springy, brown hair between her fingers. She had managed not to become entangled emotionally, despite him trying his best. It had been difficult for her to resist his many advances but thinking of her family gave her strength and she knew her future did not lie with David.

Now, Elvaennia found herself back at the castle and at a bit of a loss. The weather had turned inclement in the last few days. Peter and his wife, Ann, had gone off in his helicopter on a business trip. Time was hanging heavy this morning. Turning the television on out of sheer boredom, she began to flick around the daytime shows and soon found herself deeply engrossed in the 'Trisha' show. This had been her favourite programme when she had lived at the farmhouse. She found it enthralling, as she always found herself being drawn into the lives of the people appearing on the show. She'd watched 'Jeremy Kyle' a few times, but always returned to 'Trisha'. Elvaennia always had empathy with 'Trisha' and with the people she had on her show. She knew the shouting and swearing did not mean anything. After all, the people were extremely unhappy – that's why they were on the show. They had to express themselves, and this was the only way they knew how.

In a flash, Elvaennia knew exactly what she had to do. It was blindingly obvious! She had to help people with their problems. To do this, she thought, she had to have her own television show. This was her destiny. She knew this, and she had to grab it with both hands. 'How strange,' she thought. She had always believed that the 'work' the Mystics had predicted would be 'healing,' and that she would be assisting Deimuiss. Now, she understood. What she had to do was heal people – but more on a psychological and psychic level. The two disciplines are intertwined, and she knew she held the key to the knowledge required to make the show a huge success. 'No wonder I enjoyed watching 'Trisha' so much,' she thought. 'It was the path that was to lead me to my own show. No wonder I used to record it,' she mused. Sky+ came in very helpful. She had quickly realised that she was not very technically minded, but Sky+ was cool, it was so easy to use. Wherever she had been, as soon as she returned home, she would settle down with a steaming cup of coffee and would lose herself in the day's show. The realisation that she had the gift of 'seeing' the problem a particular person had, as well as the solution, without the need for lie detector tests, counselling or anger management, had suddenly hit her the last time she had seen the show. She had realised she could 'visualise' the problem, even at a distance. The person did not even have to be in the same room as her. 'These people need me,' she thought. 'I will have a chat with Peter. He knows many influential individuals.'

Thinking of all the people she could help, Elvaennia immediately crossed to her desk and began writing a format for her show. 'This is going to be terrific,' she thought, her ideas coming thick and fast.

'With only me presenting it, there will be no need for any extras. I just know this is going to work. Nothing like it has ever been on the television before. It will certainly make people sit up and take notice. They will soon realise it is not the usual run-of-the-mill programme. Moreover, I can – just for effect, if the producers want me to – use my Angel and Reiki cards. I don't really need them, apart from reading for myself, but then they will add that bit extra to the show.'

In fact, as excitement gripped her, she thought, 'I can design and publish my own set of Angel cards.' Her enthusiasm knew no bounds, and after a few hours, she had typed up the show format. She saved it to the memory stick, knowing she would be more than disappointed if the PC crashed and she lost her day's work.

Reflecting for a few moments, she also thought that it would be a brilliant idea if she wrote a book of her life. Excitement gripped her again, knowing that she had the most brilliant story to tell. For a minute, she was back reliving her past at the settlement, grouped around the fire with her family. Sadness overtook her for the first time in many days, and the old longing returned. How she wanted a hug from her family, in particular her mother. How were they all? How had she escaped death twice?

First, The Delphs she had no doubt whatsoever that they would have raped and then killed her, and, if they hadn't, she would surely have died later as it seemed her family and the others had. Had The Delphs been waiting at the hunting cave, knowing search parties would be sure to look for them? Who knows? Maybe their original plan was to attack the settlement, but seeing almost the whole village so vulnerable at the cave was too good a chance for them to miss. Nevertheless, on reflection, she thought that, no, of course they hadn't killed them when they were searching for her. She had seen her family through the computer since that awful time, and also in her visions, since she had been in this time. Tears slipped silently down her face.

Knowing the heartache her actions had caused, she crossed to the window seat and thought of Deimuiss, still uncertain what he could possibly have been doing at the cave. Giving her head a shake, she resolved that she was now going to do everything within her power to earn as much money as possible in the shortest possible time – so that she could reunite her family and planned how this would finally be brought about.

'First things first, this was what the Mystics had predicted and they said I would meet up with Deimuiss again. I must have trust and faith in them and myself.' She resolved to put every minute of her time to good use.

'Maybe, this way, I can make recompense for my past mistakes and look ahead to a happier future,' she thought. Elvaennia realised she was growing up fast in this time. Smiling, she remembered the gauche girl she had been when she arrived. So frightened and afraid, so untidy too!

The most wonderful part of having her own show would be that, should Deimuiss be in this time, he would see her or hear about her. She clasped her hands in glee, thinking that everything was now falling into place.

Strolling across to the mirror, she looked at herself and knew her family would have a hard job recognising her in the clothes she was wearing. However, letting her hair free from the high clipped pony tail, she saw that her face, surrounded by the silvery fall of hair, was unchanged. And her eyes, of course, would never change. 'Yes,' she nodded. They would always know her, as she would never fail to recognise them.

After a quick sandwich at lunch time, she settled back down at her desk and started to design her Angel Cards. Sometime later, she felt her neck and shoulders beginning to ache and was astonished to see that it was five p.m.! Good gracious, the day had flown by.

Filing her printing in a loose folder, she decided to chat to Peter at the first opportunity; to see what he had to say about her decision. She knew he had contacts with television and publishing companies all around the World. She was certain he would help and advise her, and another spurt of excitement had her dancing around the bedroom. A knock on her door stopped her in her tracks.

It was Peter, just the man she wanted to see.

'Peter.' she stammered in surprise, 'I wanted to chat with you but thought you were still away.'

With a lift of his shaggy brown eyebrows, he nodded saying, 'Oh, we came back an hour or so ago, strange you did not hear us. Of course we can have a chat, just give me half an hour to get settled then come along to the study.'

Elvaennia decided to freshen herself up a little before the meeting; and to change her outfit.

'After all,' she thought, 'I need to look professional from now on – not like a young student!'

Chapter 31

Watching her TV show being promoted by the BBC made Elvaennia's head whirl with delight. 'I can't believe this is happening to me,' she trilled, speaking to Mary one day over the telephone.

'It's all so unreal, that I, a young woman from another time, should have a show on a major TV channel. I know I have a glittering career ahead of me.'

An ominous silence followed her words for a few seconds, and then Mary's voice came back at her in clipped tones.

'Pride comes before a fall my dear.'

'Ohhh,' she stuttered, her bubble bursting like shattered crystals, 'and I thought you of all people would be happy for me.'

'I am. Really I am. But please come back down to Earth. Remember your original idea? It was to help people. The job is not about YOU. It is about the people who will be asking you for HELP.'

'Oh dear, Mary, you are so right. Did I sound big-headed? I didn't mean to, really I didn't. Thank you for telling me, I do appreciate it. I would hate to get it wrong before I have even started. Thank you for your advice.'

Suitably chastened, Elvaennia replaced the receiver.

'Mary is of course quite right. I must think of my guests.'

Nevertheless, hearing the title music from her programme ring out around the room (she had the volume up high), her eyes fastened to the screen as a picture of her giving out details of the forthcoming show filled it. She danced with glee, punching the air around the television room, shouting aloud, 'Yes, yes. I've made it, I've really made it. I'm going to be a huge success. Woweeee!' No negative thoughts invaded her head, no warning bells chimed. All she could think about was being on the television and becoming famous. All thoughts of finding Deimuiss had disappeared.

'I know I am already famous, otherwise why else would I be living in this remote castle? What's more I know I am going to be really, really famous and I can't wait. Soon, I will be able to live in my own flat and be able to come and go as I please, earning my own money. What a thrill that will be.'

She was beginning to find it irksome, living as she was. True, the castle grounds were huge, but, at the end of the day, she often thought, 'I am young and need friends of my own age to talk to and to hang out with.'

Truly, her personality was changing. She had changed almost beyond recognition from the girl who had arrived at the cave last summer. 'March already,' she pondered, chewing the end of her hair (a habit she had acquired since living at the castle).

'Just a few more weeks and everything will change. How great life will be then.'

Flicking her ponytail back, she sauntered around the room and then decided to visit the 'Trisha' website. After having a look around – well, there was no stopping her – she immediately set about building her own website.

Her loneliness forgotten, she spent hours and hours carefully planning and evolving the site. 'More fodder for my book as well,' she thought, calculatingly as she recorded each move she made in her 'Word' document. The shy, awkward girl who had emerged from the tiny, sandstone cave had long since disappeared. A new Elvaennia was beginning to thrust her way eagerly into the world. 'From now on,' she thought, 'I will be the author of my destiny. Nobody, but nobody, will ever tell me how to run my life again. There is no way I want, or need, a manager.'

Ideas were churning around her head as she added and deleted items from her website. Writing a promotion for her proposed book gave her an enormous thrill, thinking how she was going to astonish the world with her story.

'The media have no idea, whatsoever, of where I am from or who I am. Once I have a publishing deal, this book will go global. There is no doubt about it I will be the most famous person in the world.'

She smiled contentedly and began to think of the fame and fortune heading her way.

'The first thing I will buy is my own home; then there will be no more living in other people's homes. How wonderful it will be – my very own home bought with my own money before I'm twenty.'

She hugged herself delightedly.

'…and a new car, of course.'

Thank goodness Mary had made her take driving lessons, and how fortunate had been the cancellation that allowed her to take her test early. Otherwise, she would still be waiting, no doubt about it.

Wriggling her toes in the deep pile of the carpet, her brain continued to run around itself with ideas. 'Maybe,' she thought, 'I had better invite Mary to be my assistant; and David too, when I am overrun with work. But I will impress on them both that I am the boss. After all, I know them both and it will save me interviewing anyone else for the time being. I can leave them to do the boring bits.'

No sooner said than done, with this new Elvaennia. 'Mission accomplished,' she beamed to herself thirty minutes later. 'I now have two more staff; just need to finalise hours and wages.'

She clicked on to her website. 'Soon,' she whispered. 'Once I have everything in place, I will float this on the Internet. Now for my 'blog' – so many ways of gaining maximum publicity, but of course, I need a first class media agent.'

She deliberated. The agent she had was okay, but she needed someone better known. She began to search the Internet. She was anxious to be out in the World. Impatience began to walk beside her, and she decided to go and have a good look around the castle. Climbing spiral staircases and running up long flights of stairs, she stood on the flat roof of the castle scanning the countryside with the dark woods of Cannock Chase on the horizon. Seeing the Chase brought memories of her other lifetime flooding to the forefront of her mind. Thinking of her family and Deimuiss, she gulped, trying to suppress the feelings of sadness that threatened to overwhelm her. How she longed to see them all again, to hold them in her arms, hug and kiss them; return to her old life.

'But, I can't. I am here and this is the work the Mystics said I had to do. I am certain of that.'

Her thoughts ran on, trying hard to forget her old life. Returning to her rooms, she again watched the promotional trailer for her TV show.

~

After a hard day of clothes shopping with Mary, the women decided to stop at the farmhouse on their return journey, for a cup of coffee. Re-acquainting herself with Pip, the horses, and all the other animals, Elvaennia felt a moment of sadness at not living there anymore. David suddenly appeared in front of her. Stepping back quickly – she was afraid of his attraction – she asked him if he was well.

'Come along to the study with me Elvaennia.'

He sounded gruff and she hurried behind him.

'Look!'

He pointed a long finger to sacks of letters lining the wall that led to the study.

'I would appreciate it if you would employ another couple of staff at least, to manage the office work.'

Nodding her head in amazement, Elvaennia began to realise just how big this thing was going to become – and it needed handling with care. 'I will find more staff as soon as possible,' she murmured, 'These people deserve quick replies. At the end of the day, they are future clients.'

David swallowed hard, thinking how much more mature she seemed, and sensed a huge difference in her since their last meeting.

'I will get them put in the car so you can take them back to the castle. Maybe you could find time to read some of them?'

'I intend to read every one of them,' she retorted quite sharply, making him step back in astonishment. He had never seen this side of her before, and he was impressed. 'Sorry, I misunderstood,' he stuttered, not actually knowing what to say. 'You are so right to take the job seriously and I admire you for taking hold of the reins from the start.'

A familiar voice trilled along the corridor.

'Coffee is ready!'

David was relieved. He felt a little unnerved by the changes in Elvaennia, and he determined to take things slowly and also, to discuss the situation with Mary later that evening. He found himself even more attracted to Elvaennia. She seemed taller, exuding confidence, and more beautiful than ever. Her wonderful, silver eyes glowed. Her hair shimmered around her lovely face and seemed to float in an ethereal cloud around her slim shoulders. He longed to hold her tightly in his arms and never let her go.

Over coffee, he watched as she quickly read some of the letters. Her expressions told him how affected she was by the suffering of the senders, and he knew that he would soon be relegated way down her list of important people. The clients were going to be her primary concern.

Elvaennia was dismayed at just how shallow she had risked becoming. Almost every letter and email she read told its own sad story, and she felt her determination to help growing by the second. Thoughts of fame and large houses fled away. 'I have to help these people now, while I can,' she exclaimed, placing the letters in her bag.

'See you soon,' she called. Her mind already dealing with the problems she had just read.

Watching her drive away, David thought longingly of the day she would be his.

'I will make her love me, and only me.'

At times, the need to possess her quite overwhelmed him. Since Elvaennia had arrived at the cave, his whole life had been turned upside down. Now, thoughts of her haunted his nights, and days, and he found it very difficult to concentrate on the day-to-day running of the farm.

Curled up in her chair that evening, Elvaennia, quite unaware of David's thoughts, began to read some of the letters. She comprehended the depth of people's suffering and her heart went out to them. 'I had no idea,' she said out loud, 'that such awful things happened to people. I am more than shocked; I am horrified.' Settling herself down at her computer, she started to reply to the first batch. There were a number of stupid letters. These, she quickly discarded. 'I've no time for idiots,' she muttered through gritted teeth. Knowing how busy she was going to be soon, she resolved to get more assistance immediately, but knew she would read every piece of important correspondence that was sent to her.

A few days later, filming began and she was fizzing with excitement. 'My life's work begins,' she whispered, and, taking a deep breath, she walked out on stage.

Introducing her first guest, she explained to the audience that Sonia had never had a good relationship with her family and, in particular, she felt nothing but hatred for her mother. This provoked a sharp intake of breath from the audience. 'It happens you know,' she called to them, 'not everyone has the perfect family, and that's why I'm here to help her sort it out. Come along Sonia.'

A small, dark haired girl walked on to the small stage and settled in the comfy chair facing Elvaennia. The girl stared at her. She had never seen anyone so beautiful in all her life. She also sensed the aura surrounding the presenter and thought that, if she just stretched out her hand, some of the magic that Elvaennia exuded would rub off on her. Looking into Elvaennia's beautiful eyes, she felt a sense of knowing that from now on her life was going to improve dramatically. She smiled with relief, thus transforming her worried features into an entirely different person. Elvaennia nodded quickly and then proceeded to identify all the difficult areas of her life. Sonia's mouth dropped open in wonder and she asked, 'How on earth did you know that?'

Elvaennia shook her head, making her hair move around her like a cloud of silver. The camera lights shining through it created a magical effect. Sonia related to her mother later, 'I don't know what happened in that studio, do you Mom?'

Her mother still appeared to be in shock, shaking her greying hair.

'No, I don't. It was uncanny. That lass knew more about us than we know about ourselves!'

'That is so true Mom, and I don't know how she did it. But the most amazing thing is, that just by chatting to us on the stage, we are now closer than we have ever been. I feel free of whatever it was that was messing up my emotions and making me hate myself and everyone else – including you. Though Mom, I didn't hate you, honest. I have always loved you.'

'I know you have, and like you, I can't explain it Sonia. I feel different as well – freer and happier than I have for years, and it's not as if she is a fortune teller either, but she knows what she's talking about. The lass never told us that everything was going to be hunky dory, did she? I just feel that she has brought goodness back into our lives; she is an extraordinary person. We must honour the agreement not to discuss it with anyone else until after the programme is broadcast.'

Nodding her head, Sonia went to hug her mother.

'You are so right Mom. That's just how I feel, and we can only thank Elvaennia for this...Mom, do you really think she lived thousands of years ago like the press say?'

Her mother looked thoughtful for a minute or two, and shaking her head, she admitted:

'I don't honestly know love, but there is certainly something different about the lass. That, I do know.'

Exhausted, 'the lass' was curled up in front of the television. Having recorded two shows that day; she was enjoying a well earned rest. Pleased that all had seemed to go well that day, she hoped tomorrow and the following day would be just as successful.

'Six programmes, each client with a different problem, then I can wrap up the show for the first series. It will be a huge success, I know. Next week, the first show is going to be broadcast to the nation.'

Her heart gave a nervous flutter but she quickly pulled herself together. Thinking she heard a sound, she glanced behind her and nearly fell off the settee. 'What do you want?' she asked loudly of the Druid who was standing in a pool of white light, his cloak shimmering in a myriad of colours, reflecting the pearly luminescent light. The Druid raised his hand as if to say, 'I come in peace.' He moved towards her.

'Soon Elvaennia,' he said quietly, 'You must rescue them soon.'

She jumped up.

'How can I?' she gasped in terror. 'I have no idea how to return to the settlement and then, how do I get back?'

She started to sob.

'You must help me, advise me. Tell me please, how can I possibly rescue my family?'

The Druid looked at her, saying, 'you will receive help Elvaennia, but you must now start preparing for their return.'

'I will,' she promised, 'as soon as I possibly can.'

The Druid seemed satisfied with her response and slowly faded from view, leaving her worried but determined to rescue her family as fast as possible.

~

Each programme's content was entirely different. She had discussed the content of the shows with her producer and had worked diligently on her scripts. But of course, not meeting her guests before each show, the scripts could change dramatically during filming. One such show was quite dramatic:

Jenny arrived in the studio looking exhausted. She was pale and drawn, with heavy shadows beneath her eyes. She looked anorexic; she was so thin it looked as if a gust of wind would blow her over. Seeing her for the first time, Elvaennia knew instantly what the trouble was. Settling her down with a coffee, she patted her hand comfortingly saying, 'The dreams seem real don't they? You cannot sleep or relax as they trouble you so much.'

The young girl's dark eyes widened in shock and her face seemed to pale even more. Nodding her assent, she whispered, 'You are so right Elvaennia. They terrify me.'

Nodding sympathetically, Elvaennia listened to Jenny describing, in a shaky voice, how practically every night the dreams came; and they were so vivid in content as to frighten her awake. Now she feared going to sleep, and lay awake rather than sleeping – which of course she eventually did, only to dream and awake, heart thudding in fear, sweating and clammy, shaking violently.

The worst dream was of a man dressed in an old fashioned army uniform chasing her through woods. The faster she ran, the closer he got to her. Just as he reached her, she awoke, crying out in fear and too scared to even attempt to go back to sleep.

'Always the dreams are of me being chased or followed by a man, Elvaennia,' she said pitifully, tears streaming down her thin face.

Nodding her head again, Elvaennia looked directly into Jenny's dark eyes saying 'But, you are still being followed in this lifetime, are you not Jenny?'

The young girl jumped violently in shock. 'How did you know that?' she whispered in a voice taut with fear.

'It seems that through every life span you have lived Jenny, you have been followed by the same man. Ever since your first lifetime, this man has attached himself to you despite your remonstrations that you did not desire him in any way whatsoever. He ignored you and has carried on stalking you throughout that life. Unfortunately, this has continued through many existences. He tracks you down and follows you continuously, causing you nothing but pain and hurt. You have never been able to have a successful relationship due to this man's obsession with you.'

The audience gasped in horror at her words and sympathy flowed in waves of compassion from the audience to Jenny. They were aghast at her suffering.

Elvaennia continued with her reading:

'Despite this man having a highly professional job in this lifetime, he is still obsessed with you, and if you had not sought me out he would have continued to harass you throughout your life. Now Jenny, we can put a stop to this finally, and I know you are going to go on and have a good marriage with a wonderful, caring man who will be devoted to you and to the children that you will have. For the first time ever, you will know real peace and happiness.'

Jenny's tear-streaked face lit up with happiness at Elvaennia's words, and she asked, 'What do I have to do to stop him?'

'Nothing my sweet, leave it to me. You will not see or hear from him again. Your dreams will only be good dreams from now on. There will be no more nightmares.'

Jenny was so relieved at hearing all this, the tears poured down her cheeks, but Elvaennia could see how her aura had 'lifted' from the black clouds of despair to the light blues of happiness.

As she took her leave, Elvaennia passed her a card to keep with her at all times. It was the Angel of Light. Jenny was so touched by the help she had received that she hugged Elvaennia and thanked her repeatedly in a choked voice. The audience were amazed at what they had witnessed, and clapped until their hands hurt.

After Jenny left the stage, Elvaennia was horrified to see the man she had met at Cruck House stroll across the platform towards her. Her skin crawled, and she knew she had to get rid of this disgusting Delph as fast as she possibly could.

He sat facing her, a nasty grin planted on his face. She saw the shadowy figure of the other Delph beside him. Immediately, she was transported back to the cave on the hillside in her time. All the fear and horror returned in one foul swoop. Her hands gripped the side of the chair, her knuckles turning white. She took some deep breaths to steady her nerves

'Keep calm Elvaennia,' she told herself sharply, 'Concentrate on the job in hand.'

'What can I do for you?' she asked frostily. Her eyes were hostile and her whole demeanour shouted, 'I dislike you intensely.'

Afreionnia seemed to pick up on her antagonism and came straight out with his question:

'Will I marry her?'

'Not if I can help it,' she thought, remembering how pleasant she had found Maria when she had met her and her parents at Lichfield

Spiritualist Church.

She meditated for a short time. She 'saw' The Delphs fleeing from her people. The shadow had been caught and killed, but his spirit had attached itself to his friend who had escaped to this century; thus, the shadow had avoided punishment for his horrendous crimes. Elvaennia was filled with loathing. Looking to the future, she suddenly smiled across at the man saying, 'Your life will be taking a really unexpected turn in the next few days and you will be really surprised at the outcome.'

'You can't tell me any more?'

Hair swinging in a silver fall, she shook her head as if wishing him goodbye. A secret smile hid the tremendous delight she felt having seen the terrible fate that awaited The Delph and his shadow follower.

Apologising to the audience for what she considered to be quite a secretive meeting, Elvaennia told them that all would be revealed to them in a future program. She was happy knowing Maria would shortly be safe.

Chapter 32

Word was spreading fast and Elvaennia was receiving more and more invitations to different functions. She refused most of them, telling herself that too much exposure in the media would only turn people against her. She wanted to be famous, but only for this work. She knew the need for restraint, and also, that keeping an air of mystery about herself would do her more good than too much exposure to start with. She was determined never to talk to the media about her life at the settlement. She knew that she could name her price to any television or film company, but she recognised that she never would. Her book was written, but it would not be published until she was ready.

Having looked on the Internet, she saw her name repeated over and over again on message boards and websites. Some were pure speculation, and she laughed at the things she was supposed to have said or done.

'Idiots, some of these people.'

She smiled at the messages, and often left a comment herself under a pseudonym. 'Make of that, what you will,' she smiled, moving on to the next site.

Her website had had over a million hits. At times, it crashed, as did her mailbox, but she soon had them up and running again. She did try to keep tabs on the emails but it was next to impossible. Therefore, in the end, she had her staff redirect the most important ones on to her so she could devote her time to them.

She had even been on a couple of dates, but found she did not enjoy herself very much. A small voice kept whispering to her all evening – 'He is not Deimuiss, is he?'– And she had to admit to herself that, 'No, he wasn't.' Its strange how no one matched up to her lost love, and despite her extremely busy life, Deimuiss had begun to enter her thoughts more often of late. She found herself longing even more for a sight of his face and the sound of his voice. Her desire for him actually hurt at times and she wondered how she could ever have thought that being famous was more important than him. But then, the small voice whispered, 'You do like the fame and glory Elvaennia, be truthful.'

One day she was working in the castle, dealing with her emails, when her private phone rang. Her eyes widened as she listened in amazement to the caller. 'Yes,' she agreed, jumping up from her seat and striding up and down the office.

'I'll be here, of course I will. Yes, you can land the helicopter not far from the castle. I'll be only too pleased to see you. I will respect your privacy, and as far as I can say, no one will see you land. It is extremely private here.'

More exchanges were made and she ended the conversation.

Elvaennia was stunned beyond words – almost, that is.

'Royalty? Royalty want a reading from me?'

Hard to believe, but there it was. They did, and they would be here within a few hours.

Knowing Peter's staff could be trusted implicitly, she ran down to the kitchen and explained about the guests due at the castle. First to arrive, would of course, be the security men. She politely asked if the staff would mind bringing coffee and maybe some snacks after the important guests arrived. The staff, looking suitably impressed, agreed and said they would be ready to greet the visitors on their arrival. She wondered what Peter would say when he heard that he had missed the expected guests. But thinking about it, she remembered he had mentioned meeting many of the Royals; and the ones she was expecting at the castle were, after all, not 'top flight' members of the family – but still, they were Royals, however minor, she told herself excitedly.

She knew that she could never disclose anything about her expected guests, but this in no way took away the glamour of the visit. Thinking about it, she realised that they were no different from any of the many people she had given readings to in the past, and she respected each and every one of those people, so why should these individuals seem any more glamorous to her, she wondered. 'Yes,' she concluded to herself, 'The Royals are no different from any of us. At the end of the day, they are people who experience the same problems with family, and wives, partners, and in business – exactly the same as everyone else on Earth. The only difference is that most of them are better off, and have to endure the press from the day they are born.'

Later that evening, seated at the computer, she ruminated on her day as she replied to some of her emails. Had she been impressed, she asked herself? Yes, they were so impeccably well mannered and they could not thank her enough for her time. And they were suitably impressed by the reading. She had felt awkward asking one of them to wait in the lounge while she 'read' for the first guest, but on this occasion, she felt it right that the readings were conducted on a one-to-one basis. And she had not wanted the lady concerned to learn of her partner's serious business troubles, which she had 'seen' as soon as he had been introduced. Many of these troubles had been caused by his lack of attention to management, because he spent so much time away from his business – preferring to lead the high life. Now, he was heading for financial ruin...if he didn't buckle down to some serious work.

Subsequently, she began to wonder again why she could 'see' for other people but not for herself. It seemed so strange that she got images and thoughts of the past, present and future on meeting other people, but rarely anything for herself. Even the cards were difficult to read when she panned them out for her own reading. The runes were also hard to interpret. Shrugging her slim shoulders, she returned to her work. She hoped and prayed that, one day, she would be with Deimuiss again.

The show was going from strength to strength and was getting top ratings. From being aired three times a week, it was now going out five days and it was even being mooted that a Saturday show was in the offing. She was having to extend her working hours even more, which was difficult because she had little free time as it was.

Elvaennia had more work than she could reasonably cope with, and Mary had come on side to assist her in the more 'delicate' cases.

'I couldn't leave these to the staff to reply to, Mary.'

She pointed to a pile of emails and letters that she had placed at the side of her computer. Picking them up, Mary quickly rifled through them. Elvaennia knew that Mary had a very astute mind, and thought, more or less, along the same lines as she did.

'See what you mean,' Mary replied, quietly scanning the contents.

'Pretty bad, some of these, lass, best we get our heads together about them.'

'I think I will telephone a couple of them. Something tells me that if I reply by email or letter, it could cause ructions. Perhaps, on second thoughts, I will text them on the business mobile first – to see if it's okay to call. They will maybe suggest a suitable time, after all, I don't want to call if it's going to cause even more trouble.'

'I agree,' the older woman nodded, her white hair dancing in a halo around her head. After conferring with Elvaennia, she sat herself down at the second computer and proceeded to reply to the emails.

She smiled to herself as she typed; not smiling at the emails' contents, but at the sound of Radio 1 echoing around the room. She groaned inwardly. She knew Elvaennia was not keen on listening to 'Today' on Radio 4 but my goodness, this was a huge change. Still, on the other hand, she had enjoyed listening to Professor Carl Chinn on Radio WM on a Sunday. Thinking back to their day out in Birmingham, remembering how she had just missed meeting him, it seemed a lifetime ago now, but she was looking forward to going to see him at 'The Mail Box' in Birmingham City Centre in the near future. She had been delighted when Elvaennia had asked if she would go along with her. She began thinking about what she was going to wear, at the same time keeping her mind focused on her replies. Thank goodness, as well, she thought to herself, that Elvaennia hadn't gone down the 'celeb' route. That way would have been so wrong for her. Now the young woman was fulfilling her destiny.

Suddenly, a tap at the office door made the women jump. The door opened and David entered the room. Immediately, Elvaennia sensed the whole atmosphere of the room change. She groaned inwardly. 'Not David, not today,' she thought angrily. 'I have more than enough to think about without him adding to the pressure.'

His eyes fastened hungrily on her as she perched on the edge of her seat. He could see that she did not wish to see him, but his longing to see her had led to him jumping into his car and driving at top speed to the castle. Taking in her fragile beauty, he longed to hold her close and to cover her beautiful face with kisses. He took a step towards her, but the look she flashed across the room to him stopped him in his tracks. He could almost hear her saying, 'keep your distance.' He felt the force field that she had surrounded herself with, and knew that, particularly with his mother in the same room, there was no way he was going to get close to her today.

'Just stopped by to say hello,' he said brightly, as if this was an everyday occurrence. Receiving no reply, he backed away to the door.

'Will call another day when you are not so busy then.'

Taking one last lingering look at Elvaennia, he called 'Goodbye' to her and a 'see you later mother.' He left them to their work. Gunning his car back towards the farm, he vowed that he would break down Elvaennia's resistance to him before too long.

'She's mine and no one else will ever have her.'

Stepping hard on the accelerator, he practically flew back to the farm, his thoughts and emotions in chaos. Flinging his car onto the drive, David hurried upstairs to the loft. He felt rejected, lonely, unloved and decided to seek comfort in his jigsaws. This hobby had held him spellbound for many years. He found he could lose himself for hours creating his beautiful pictures.

Elvaennia was only too well aware, now, how David felt about her. But she knew that if she kept out of reach of his aura, she was safe from his emotions taking over her life. 'He is not the one for me,' she told herself, finishing the last email for that day. Being away from him had allowed her to build up a strong resistance to him, and now she felt well able to cope. She realised that she was far stronger emotionally than

David, and now, having so much work to do, she did not need or want him (or anyone else) clinging to her skirts at this moment in time. Clicking on the Internet, she began to write her daily blog. Then, she began work on her website: *www.elvaenniaspace.com.*

She loved altering and adding to her site, and was amazed at how popular it was. Finishing for the day, she turned to Mary and offered to run her back to the farm.

'No lass, I have the car. You have a rest tonight as I know you have a full work schedule starting tomorrow; and don't forget that Saturday's programme is going out live.'

Elvaennia rolled her eyes in mock terror. With a giggle, she kissed Mary and thanked her for her help.

Despite being invited out to many first nights and celebrity functions, she refused – still preferring to stay at home and catch up on work. Something told her that changes were underway, and she felt the need to help as many people now as she could. But an invitation to an 'evening for television presenters' intrigued her; and she decided to treat herself. Donning a fetching evening dress of russet silk, she wore no jewellery at all and left her hair loose. Her stiletto-heeled russet coloured shoes caused her no problems whatsoever. She felt as if she had been born to wear this type of footwear. She felt right, dressed in this season's colours. She suddenly wondered where the summer and autumn had disappeared to. 'Working,' she thought ruefully, 'but then, that was my intention and I have almost achieved my aim to get enough money to bring my family back.' Worry creased her brow for a minute as she wondered how she was going to manage it. But remembering the Mystic's words, she knew things would work out for her and decided to let things happen.

All eyes were on her when she entered the room, but her new found maturity allowed her to smile gracefully and to nod greetings to all the presenters she recognised. Later, mingling with the crowd, she bumped into 'Tony Robinson' from the 'Time Team' programme. Having watched their show avidly many times, she was over the moon to meet him. 'He's such a dapper little man,' she thought, smiling happily at the

TV presenter. Soon, they were chatting away like old friends and she dropped a hint about the settlement. Tony was all ears, and pressed to know more.

Elvaennia was cautious in what she said, but managed to convey that the dig needed to be done soon. Tony was very interested but he said that 'Time Team' was booked for the next two years – so he wrote down the name of a Staffordshire archaeology group, telling her to contact them. He assured her they would be only too pleased to help her.

Talking about her other life had unsettled her, and her thoughts returned to the days when she had walked the Chase for miles with Deimuiss, and the time he had taken her to the Crystal Cave. 'I wonder if it is still there,' she asked herself. 'I would love to go and see.' A faraway look was in her eyes and many people noticed that she had a distant look about her. They weren't surprised when she suddenly turned on her heels and, nodding goodbye to people around her, she took her leave.

Going home in her chauffeur-driven car, Elvaennia's thoughts drifted back to the days she had spent happily amongst family and friends. She admitted to herself that this life was the unreal time, and a great longing to be back at home cut through her like a knife. She almost cried out with the pain of it. At times, she admitted to herself that she was lonely. 'I have no friends,' she thought, 'to share my ideas and thoughts with. In fact,' she contemplated: 'I've never really had a close girlfriend. Deimuiss was always my friend, and in this time Mary has been my closest friend; and Caroline has been helpful as well, but then perhaps it's as well,' she reflected.

'I have my work to do and really I never have the time for hanging out at coffee bars or clubs.'

She was more than relieved to be back at the castle, and quickly changed from her evening clothes. 'This is a false existence,' she told herself. 'I have no roots, no family and only Mary and David that really know who I am and where I am from.'

Depression hit her hard, and she wondered just where life was going to lead her.

Chapter 33

Elvaennia's Journal Entry, late 2008

It goes against the grain, but I somehow seem to have become involved in doing readings for celebs from time to time; just as I did for the not-so Royals. Still, my life is all about helping people – and this is just another spoke in the wheel.

I've got a room at the TV Studio and one at the castle where I give private readings to people who, for various reasons, it would be wrong to put on air.

Lady (celeb) client visited today. I started to read her cards, and saw immediately that she was having an affair. I didn't really need the cards to tell me this because her lover – his spirit, that is – actually walked through the door with her, closely followed by a very worried looking husband-spirit. She blushed crimson when I told her, sotto voce, that her lover was sat beside her on the sofa.

Stuttering, she said, 'But how can he be here? He is still alive.'

'My dear,' I replied with a smile, 'I see the living in spirit a well as the dead.'

This shook her. She went as white as a sheet but recovering very fast, she asked the usual question – 'Will he leave his wife and children for me?'

The honest answer I told her was that I did not know. My cards only show the very immediate future. I knew it was pointless to relay to her the statistic that only about one third of men leave their wives for their mistress. Her relationship was in the very early stages. She was convinced he would soon realise that it was her he wanted, and would soon be packing his suitcase and running off with her.

My cards were telling me that her husband already suspected what was happening, and her immediate future showed the upsets and disharmony ahead, and that, in fact, she was not going to run off with her lover.

I was in a very difficult situation.

Her husband clearly loved her. I could 'see' he was a good, hard working man and had been an excellent provider who dearly loved her and their two children. Since his wife had shot to fame six months ago on one of these 'Traffic Island Love' programmes (if you missed it, a group of people camped on a traffic island not far from Lichfield for eight weeks), his whole world had changed dramatically and he was in turmoil, suspecting (correctly) that his wife was having an affair – and that he was going to lose her.

They had been childhood sweethearts and he had never loved anyone else but her. Now he could see it all slipping away.

Despite trying never to get involved emotionally, looking at his troubled face, I felt so sorry for him, heavy eyed from lack of sleep, lines of worry furrowing his brow. The poor man looked much older than his 24 years.

Her 'lover' is also a 'celeb'. They had recently met on the 'circuit' and, in her words; she had 'fallen passionately in love.'

I did not think it was my job to disillusion her, but I know this man inside out and have met some of his various lady friends in the past few months – when they too have visited me for readings. They all asked me the same question, 'Will he leave his wife for me?'

I always think, 'Here we go again,' and I want to say outright, 'Not a chance my dears. He loves the thrill of the chase and then goes home to his nice, safe home with his wife and 2.4 children.' There is no way this (Traffic Island) rat is going to leave his cosy home set-up for one of his 'girlets'. Yes, indeed, that's what he calls them.

I could see why these 'girlets' would be attracted to him. He is

231

famous, extremely rich, good looking in his own way; but this man is never serious about his other women, and they would be so shocked if I told them that he often visits me for a reading. He gets concerned that his latest 'girlet' might spill the beans to a publicity agent. Then, he would have to read along with the nation about his latest affair in the tabloids, and he certainly would not like that. So far, he has been lucky; but I have tried to warn him that one day his luck is going to run out and one of his little 'girlets' is going to head for the tabloids, or someone will see them together and spill the beans. The one good thing in his favour is that he is seriously worried that his wife will find out about his liaisons, and he will then lose her. She has repeatedly told him that if she ever discovers he is having, or has had, an affair, then that will be that.

This scares the pants off 'lover boy', but he does like to live dangerously; hence the affairs.

He's a very likeable man and I can see the animal magnetism he has for the young women, but he certainly has no plans to leave his wife. He enjoys playing the field far too much. He knows there will always be a 'girlet' ready to fall for him – so he thinks, why not? As long as his wife does not find out. That's his only concern.

I think he truly loves her but there is that side of his character that makes him pull every young girl he can; especially those pretty blondes that win the reality TV shows.

What surprised me about him this time was his attraction to this particular lady celeb. She is so different from his normal type. Whereas he has always gone for the busty, bleached blondes in the past, this young woman is petite and very dark. Try as I might, I could not 'see' the reasons for his change of type in her cards.

Time, I thought, to give him a call and invite him over.

I knew he would make a beeline for my place as soon as I phoned him. He would wonder what I had 'seen' for him, and until he could pay me a visit, the suspense would kill him. As long as our meetings revolved around him and his massive ego, all would be well. And, of course, I had good news to tell him.

Obviously, as with all clients, I could not divulge that I had had a visit from his latest 'girlet fling'. I take my job very seriously. At times, it can be a bit tricky. I once had a very famous 'celeb' in the study where I give my readings, when I had an unexpected caller. I know – I should have foreseen their arrival. On opening the door, I was horrified to see it was his ex-mistress paying me a visit. Now, what should I do? I just knew that the sparks would fly if they met. I hurriedly put her in the lounge and made some outlandish excuse to the celeb so that he had to make a fast exit. This one had been a close call.

Back to the present conundrum.

I was honest with Cynthia (lover boy's latest conquest). I didn't hide the bad news; it's not my way. She was very surprised as I told her that things looked pretty bleak and she should be prepared for a number of disappointments in the coming months. I know she expected me to predict sweetness and light all the way to the altar with lover boy, but no way could I tell her something that I couldn't 'see'. It's best to be honest, I always say. Tell them what you 'see', and then the clients will always return for a further reading. Obviously, you do not talk about death or major accidents if you see them in the cards. To my way of thinking, they are going to happen anyway, and telling my clients about them will not stop them occuring. It will just give the client more worry and anxiety. In fact, if I 'see' an accident, by telling them, I could in fact worry them to such an extent they would lose their concentration – and cause a bad accident to happen. No way could I live with myself if this happened.

After she had left, I thought deeply about her situation and I determined to do what I could to 'help' her husband. Never before had I felt so sorry for a man involved unwittingly in a marital triangle. I was finding it so difficult to blot his unhappy face from my mind. Normally, I would never dream of stepping in and interfering in someone else's life. My job is to read the future, not to alter or to try and 'fix it', but there seemed to be an invisible cord pulling me towards the husband, and willing me to help him.

First, I resolved to contact 'Lover Boy', my pet name for this celeb. I also have a 'Casanova and Romeo' on my books – and other pet names; but more about him, and them, another time. Back to Lover Boy:

No time like the present, I told myself as I punched his number into my mobile. Blow! I got his answering service just when I felt on the ball, ready to have a good chat. I left my number, knowing that his vanity would make him definitely return my call as soon as he could.

I would then tell him that I had 'seen' that a petite, dark haired lady whose name began with the initial 'C' was to be avoided at all costs. That would do it; no more details. I knew I was wrong to interfere in this way, but if it gave Cynthia time to step back and see Lover Boy for the rat he is – when he dumps her without a word – then, hopefully, she might become aware of what a wonderful loyal husband she has.

Chapter 34

Elvaennia's Journal Entry, a week later

Today, I met another time traveller. It is an amazing story.

Doreen told me that she had visited a place known as 'The Black Country Museum' at Dudley in the West Midlands. It's what's known as a 'living museum' on a large site of more than 40 buildings. It recreates the history of the Black Country from the 19th to the early 20th century. People wearing costumes demonstrate a way of life long past. She went on to tell me that she and her partner were having a lovely day out, trying out the various modes of transport, meeting William – the Shire horse – who, she said, was a real sweetie. After a ride on a trolley-bus, they then got on a tram. It was while she was travelling on this, that she suddenly found herself leaving the tram and stepping off it into Birmingham city centre. She said:

It was so unbelievably strange, Elvaennia. One minute, I was on this tram in Dudley, and the next thing I know I'm in Birmingham and all around me there are people dressed in clothes of the 1960s. I must confess that I had forgotten just how different the fashion was back then. I knew it was the '60s as I had lived through that era. I wandered around, lost and confused for a while. I thought I would make my way back to Dudley, but it seemed pointless as the museum wasn't even built then – I know it was started in 1976.

I felt helpless. Fortunately, I didn't feel too out-of-place as I had a full length coat on – it being quite a chilly day. It was so strange, as I realised immediately that I had time-travelled. I wasn't scared or worried, despite anything like this having ever happening to me before. I began to feel excited about this experience.

I headed off towards St. Martins, having a good look around. The city was very busy, bustling with people, old and young. I got the strong impression it was a Saturday. Suddenly, I saw someone in front of me collapse, and I flew forward to help. It was a grey-haired elderly lady. She was wearing one of those long, old fashioned black coats. I crouched down beside her. Her face had gone grey, her eyes were shut, and she had no pulse. 'My goodness,' I thought, 'She is dying,' I immediately began to put my St. John Ambulance training into action and, as I worked on her, everything faded away. All that was important was bringing this lady back to consciousness. Suddenly, I was aware of ambulance men and police crowding round me. One of the ambulance men said, 'Well done, luv.' He had a strong 'Brummy' accent. 'You've saved this lady's life.' As he uttered the words, I knew at once why I had been brought back to this time and place. With that thought, I found myself back with my husband at the Black Country Museum; back in the here and now.

The audience clapped heartily at this story, and Elvaennia was impressed – knowing that there is always a reason for time travel. Thank goodness that Doreen had been chosen for that particular day's work.

Chapter 35

Elvaennia had many requests to visit haunted homes, and businesses, more so since starting the show, unfortunately her busy schedule prevented her taking on these offers, but she felt drawn to one invitation she had received, and seeing that it was not too far away had decided to pop along and investigate.

The house was in Stafford and the owner had said it was many hundreds of years old.

She had asked the W.M.G.C. if they wanted to investigate the house with her, but regrettably they had a prior booking. Armed with thermometers, video camera and cassette recorder, she arrived at around 9 p.m. on a dark, wet, windy night.

Greeted by Adele, one of the owners, she immediately set her equipment up in the enormous lounge with its huge oak beams. How she loved the furnishings: squishy, dark maroon leather corner sofas, glass-topped coffee tables nonchalantly scattered around the room, along with magazine racks containing every type of publication you could ask for – they were certainly not the normal country house periodicals you would expect. There were even the tabloids and weekly magazines. She was surprised.

Dark-haired Adele had smiling currant-brown eyes, was very down to earth and had a broad Brummie accent. Elvaennia immediately felt at home with her as she stroked their family dog. He was a real mixture, she noticed delightedly. 'We call him Rags, Adele chuckled with a mischievous smile, quirking her generous mouth.

Suddenly Rags ears lifted. The fur on the back of his neck and spine almost seemed to stand on end and he growled deep in his throat. He ran to the door, yapping and scratching at the oak panel door, trying to get out.

Nervously, Adele glanced at Elvaennia.

'Do I let him out?'

'Yes, he's scared.'

Adele quickly ran to the door and took the dog off, returning in a few minutes.

'I've let him into the kitchen gardens. Poor boy looked so happy once he was outside.'

Twisting her trembling hands together, she asked in a shaky voice, 'Any ideas of what frightened him, Elvaennia?'

Chewing her lip, Elvaennia decided not to tell Adele her immediate thoughts. She wanted to be certain first.

'I have some ideas Adele, but let's go and check a few more rooms first and then come back here.' Double-checking that her equipment was set up correctly, the women then left the room. The shadows began to merge as soon as the door closed.

Adele cheered up once they had left the lounge.

'Don't know why, but the lounge has always spooked me, and lately it's got worse.'

'No wonder,' thought Elvaennia, but she planted a smile on her face as she entered the dining room. A very nice room it was too, she observed, placing her other cassette player gently on the highly-polished oak table. She lightly stroked the wood, feeling the life force still held within its centre. Admiring the oak panelled walls, sensing the history that had walked through this house, she sat down on one of the tapestry backed chairs and began absorbing the knowledge that was being given to her.

Adele, realising that something of magnitude was taking place, stood with her back to the door, not knowing whether to be awed or to take her leave. She jumped when Elvaennia's voice broke the silence.

'Sorry,' Elvaennia exclaimed, 'didn't mean to startle you. I'm sure everything will be fine. Please try not to worry.'

Adele backed out of the room, followed by Elvaennia.

'One more room,' Elvaennia remarked cheerily, 'then we'll return to the lounge.'

Tripping up the wide, centrally-carpeted staircase, she glanced idly at the huge portraits lining the walls. Suddenly, she stopped in front of one. Looking closely into the face of the young boy depicted in the artwork, she was more-than-convinced that this was one of the boys causing the disturbances, what a great pity she thought sadly to herself, continuing up the stairs.

'That was my Neil, my son, he died not long after that picture was taken.'

Adele gazed sadly at the picture a look of longing in her eyes.

Elvaennia turned and placed a comforting arm around the woman before continuing her quest.

'Okay, here we are. Last room,' Elvaennia remarked, placing thermometers at various points around the old nursery.

'Your son slept here?' she asked Adele.

'Yes.'

She was still twisting her hands nervously.

'I must admit he never settled very well and we eventually moved him to another room. Let's go and make a coffee.'

Adele briskly led the way down the staircase, along a gloomy passage, and through a double swing door into a surprisingly modern kitchen. 'Anything rather than go back into the lounge,' she shuddered.

Sipping her coffee, Elvaennia thought she would check the rooms and then tell Adele what was causing the disturbances. In fact, she had no need to place thermometers and such like in various rooms, but she realised some people felt more reassured if they saw you using equipment around their homes. It seemed to add a certain nuance to the proceedings, so on certain occasions she used the instruments.

Checking and collecting the equipment, she busily made notes. Adele hung back, fidgeting with her rings and her watch. Back in the kitchen, where Adele seemed most relaxed, Elvaennia told her the findings.

'Adele, your house has been haunted for many years by the ghost of a young boy, who was unfortunately killed in a serious accident while riding his pony in the grounds, the horse also kicked out and unfortunately killed the family dog as well. The thing is, the young boy who caused the accident also haunts the nursery. This is the reason your son was so disturbed, as a child, when he slept in the old nursery.'

Adele's eyes opened wide in shock.

'Two ghosts. The house is haunted by two boys?'

She frantically stirred her coffee, spilling some into the saucer.

'And the dog.'

I smiled across at her and patted her arm.

'Don't worry; they won't be troubling you again after tonight.'

'But the lounge, Elvaennia. I know there is something very unsettling in that room.'

'Do not worry any more, Adele. Your house will be peaceful after tonight.'

Elvaennia was determined not to tell the woman about the man she had seen hanging from one of the oak beams in the room. He had committed suicide after discovering his wife was having an affair with a much younger man. He had felt cheated and dishonoured and had decided to end his life, but not before he had changed his will, disinheriting his wife because of her adultery.

After finally clearing the house of all the ghosts, past and present, Elvaennia took her leave – glad that Adele looked so relieved.

Neither woman saw the smiling faces of the three young boys looking out of the old nursery window: two were dressed in night attire of the Tudor age, and Neil, Adele's son, dressed in his 'Dr. Who' pyjamas was hugging the dog. To spare Adele's feelings Elvaennia had decided not to mention Neil haunted the house.

Chapter 36

The last, live, Saturday morning show of the second series is drawing to an end when through her earpiece, Elvaennia's producer says there is a gentleman who insists that he knows her. He needs to talk to her immediately. Puzzled, she agrees to him being brought on stage. Her eyes open wide with shock, her mouth dries up, and she goes into complete shock as she sees Deimuiss striding towards her. The colour drains from her face and she feels herself begin to shake. Through her earpiece, her producer, who is, of course, watching like a hawk on the monitor, says, 'be professional, Elvaennia. No matter what he means to you, keep your cool. The show ends in a couple of minutes.'

Gathering her wits together and taking a huge breath, she jumps up and rushes to meet him.

'Well, this is a wonderful surprise. Ladies and gentlemen, meet one of my oldest friends.'

'They don't know how old either,' she thought to herself, 'Like a few thousand years.'

'Deimuiss.'

This was the end-of-show surprise her producers had been promising her. 'You would be surprised at how far he has travelled to be with me,' she exclaimed, turning to the applauding audience. She was so overjoyed to be reunited with her lost love in this time that really, she hadn't a clue what she was saying and she prayed for the lights to dim so she could be with Deimuiss. Dim they did, on the biggest round of applause of the series, leaving the couple gazing rapturously into each other's eyes.

Back in her dressing room, she clung to him, frightened that he would be snatched away from her as on previous occasions.

'My love, my life, I don't want to let you go again, ever.'

'Neither do I,' he murmured, overwhelmed by this new, professional looking, 21st century Elvaennia. She still possessed his soul, his love, his life. He knew that he would never love another woman, no matter how many lifetimes he lived. Despite how she had changed, he loved her even more. She was, if it were possible, even more beautiful, and still unaware of it.

Pressing her to him, he never wanted to let her go. Their time apart had been agony. Now, all he wanted was to be alone with her and discover everything that had happened to her.

'Deimuiss, I have to attend the end-of-show meeting. Please come with me,' she begged him, her liquid silver eyes shining with love for him.

'She is irresistible,' he thought, following her into the producer's office.

Despite sitting beside her amongst the show staff, he never really heard a word of the meeting. His heart was racing at her closeness, and he wondered anew at her sheer professionalism as she conducted herself with a natural grace. There was an authority in her voice that had not been there when they had lived back at the settlement. He worried about whether she would be able to adapt to the old ways when they returned to their own time. Had she matured beyond her years in this new century? He was relieved when they were on their way 'home', as she explained that 'home' was now a suite of rooms in a castle.

'There will be time for us to be together later,' she promised him. 'We will have a meal sent up to us, and then we can relax. I can't believe that we are together after all this time.' Stopping the car in a lay-by, she reached over and kissed him passionately. Deimuiss was astonished again at this new woman who seemed so in charge of every area of her life.

Curling up in his arms later that evening, Elvaennia asked him to tell her exactly what had happened to him from his time of riding away from her that fateful day.

Chapter 37

The day he had gone hunting for food in the forest had started just like any other. He passed the six Standing Stones and was making his way across the heath land when a bright light momentarily blinded him. Blinking his eyes, he happened to see what he thought was movement at the bivouac on the hill.

Dismounting from his horse, he went inside the cave. Walking around, he saw no sign of any recent disturbance and he made his way to the rear of the cave. Leaning against the rear wall, he thought how strange the cave felt that morning, as if it was waiting for someone or something. Suddenly, the wall felt as if it was drawing him into it and he tried to leap away from it but, too late, he found he was being drawn upwards by a strange force. Higher and higher he was pulled. The more he struggled, the tighter, harder, and faster he was pulled. Shouting out at whatever invisible being was dragging him with such brute force, he called, 'Leave me alone and take me back.' He knew he was moving through time and space, but to where, he had no idea.

'What will Elvaennia think?'

His first thoughts were of the young woman he loved as much as life itself. 'My family and Elvaennia's family will believe me to be dead,' he thought wildly, trying desperately to release himself from the force. He swirled upwards, spiralling around and around like one of the tops that the children of the settlement played with. He could not understand what was happening to him. His head began to ache and he felt nauseous. 'I can't take much more of this,' he thought. 'I can't breathe.'

As this thought went through his mind, he hit the ground so hard – as if he had been flung from a great height. He lay there thoroughly winded, head aching and spinning, his stomach churning. He felt so sick, and a tremor of fear shot through his body, adding to his pain.

Proceeding with his story, he related what happened next as he clasped Elvaennia tightly to his chest, fearing she might disappear.

'Fearfully opening my eyes, I was shocked. I was back in the cave. What's going on, I thought. I had been whisked, spun around, and pulled by an unimaginable force; only to return to the cave. It just didn't make sense.'

He removed his arm for a moment and kissed Elvaennia on the tip of her nose. 'I wasn't feeling particularly brave at that point, my luv,' he murmured, raining butterfly kisses over her face. 'It was the strangest thing that had ever happened to me. I have always been so in control of my life, that to be pulled and pulled without being able to stop whatever it was, was scary.'

Elvaennia resisted butting-in to tell him that the way he had been brought here was almost identical to the way she had travelled through time.

'I lay down, curling into the foetal position, drawing comfort from the warmth and familiarity of my cloak, sinking into its fur lined folds. The sounds of the herds of wild animals running filled my ears. Instead of the roaring, I could hear in the distance the sound of their feet pounding the earth as they ran through the ancient forests of the Chase.'

Deimuiss looked down at the face of the woman he loved and thought he had lost forever. Now that they were reunited, he resolved he would never lose her again, knowing he somehow had to convince her that he had not murdered her Grandmamma and sister.

Turning to gaze at her, he looked deep into her silvery eyes.

'Elvaennia, please believe me, I had no hand in the murder of your relatives. How could I? From the time I arrived here, I had never been able to return to the settlement until that day when the horror happened to you.

I was working on the details of my healing tour when I sensed you were in danger. I tried hard to tune in to you, to discover where you were. I heard you cry out in despair, and I thought of you as hard as I could – willing myself to find you. Suddenly, I found myself lying in a heap on the cave floor. I could hear you shouting in anger. I got to my feet when suddenly, you saw me and kicked out where it hurts most. Believe me: that was painful.'

Looking down at her, he explained, 'I was trying to help pull The Delphs off you, not to help them attack you. As you backed away, I was struggling to get to you when you suddenly disappeared from the back of the cave. I tried to follow you, wanting to be with you. I kept calling you but, to my utter dismay, I found myself back in my office. Many times, I thought you were lost to me forever my little one, particularly when we met briefly in other centuries.'

Stroking her fall of silver hair. His heart felt as if it would burst with the love he held for her. Kissing the top of her hair, he continued with his story:

'Lying on the cave floor, I groaned out loud in pain and despair. I turned on to my side, squinting through the gloom. Looking around me, I could see a glimmer of light through the entrance of the cave. It slowly dawned on me that this was a different cave. It was a lot smaller. There was no way you could stand up in this small cave. The air was bad and I could hear strange noises coming through the cave entrance. I was concerned, to say the least. I did not recognise this place. It was odd really, as I thought I knew all the caves on our tribe's lands; but I was more-than-certain I had never been to this one. I sat for a few seconds, doodling with a stick on the ground. I scribbled my name in the soil. I then wrote our initials intertwined. For good measure, I then wrote of the Calegi tribe. My head had stopped spinning so I decided to investigate my surroundings.

I crawled slowly towards the cave entrance. 'Ouch,' I shouted out loud. Hell, something had cut my hand. Blood dripped onto the sandy soil. Turning to a sitting position, I looked at my injury. There was a weird-looking clear object piercing my skin.

Agh, it hurt.

This was the strangest thing I had ever seen. Looking around, I noticed other odd objects lying around. Before investigating them, I had to remove this shard from my hand. Whispering a prayer to the gods, I pulled it out as fast as I could. Blood spurted from the cut and I had nothing to hand to stem the flow. My tunic and cloak were in no state to bind this cut. Only one thing for it: I decided to cut some of my hair. Taking my flint knife, I quickly cut a thick strand of hair and tied it tightly round my hand. It eased the pain considerably and stemmed the blood flow. Very carefully, I again made my way towards the cave entrance. I knew I had some serious investigating to do, but I really wanted to get my bearings.

There was a strange roaring noise emanating through the cave entrance. I wondered what it was; it did not sound like any animal I had ever heard. There was also a strong smell hanging in the air. I longed to be back at home with you Vinny, and my family. This cave was unlike any cave I had ever been in, and I wondered which tribe used it. Would they come and kill me? Having escaped The Delph tribe many times, and also been in numerous fights and dangerous situations with the boar and bears, was I now going to be captured or killed by warriors out hunting? The strange sounds were not coming any nearer, so, cautiously, I reached the cave entrance. There were tall grasses growing and I gently parted them. Taking a deep breath I looked at the landscape and with a shout, dropped the grasses.

Where the devil was I? The air was tainted outside; it reeked of unusual smells and there was a background noise like a loud hum. I wondered if I could hear a distant battle. My heart thumped crazily in my chest. Where was I? I kept repeating this to myself like a mantra. My world had disappeared, and now it seemed the gods were punishing me by bringing me to this strange place of tainted air and terrible noise. Telling myself to be strong – after all, I am a warrior of some repute – I cautiously parted the grasses again. The noise was a continuous sound, and I coughed as I inhaled the air that was so different from anything I had ever known. The hillside I had known all my life was no longer in sight; the cave I was in was situated on the side of a hill, and there were wooded hills in the distance. There was a clump of trees not far away. My head began to spin with the confusion of it all and I leant on the cave wall. Yoicks! I quickly jumped away. There were some strange yellow flowers attached to green prickly branches, and they stung. What was I to do? The most important thing was to find the way back to the settlement, away from this place of strange air and noise.

I worried about my horse. He is a fine stallion and I hoped against hope he had found his way back to the settlement.

Head in hands, I sat on the cave floor, trying to understand my changed circumstances. I had never felt so alone and desperate in all my life. I wanted to be out of this situation. I knew instinctively that this was not my time; everywhere was alien to me. I needed to be back at the heart of my tribe. What would they think of my disappearance? Would they worry that I had been captured? Or worse, would they think I was dead, lying alone in a bleak desolate place, my bones being picked over by some marauding animals?

Suddenly, I heard a scrambling at the cave entrance. My heart skipped a beat. Was this some wild creature coming to attack me? Grabbing the flint knife, I held my breath, ready to defend myself to the death.

The creature was suddenly inside the cave with me. Through the gloom, it looked like a young, woolly, black bear – a complete fur ball. It ran straight toward me and started squeaking, sniffing and licking me as if it had known me all my life. My bear quickly changed into a dog. My scent had obviously attracted him to me. Dropping my knife, I fussed the dog, and then I heard a voice shouting,' 'Merlin, Merlin, come out here you scamp.'

The dog pricked-up his ears and ran, barking towards the voice.

'Good boy, well done. Oh no, Merlin come back here.'

Merlin had run barking back to me! 'Go boy, go,' I whispered, pointing towards the entrance and giving him a friendly push. He was torn between me and his mistress, and decided this was a great game – rushing to and fro between us.

'Okay, you win,' I heard the woman say. Then the grasses parted and

247

she was there, the owner of the voice, looking straight at me.

'Who on earth are you?' she asked, holding Merlin by the scruff of his neck, pushing her thick, golden blonde hair from amber eyes.

Glasses magnified her beautiful eyes – now how did I know those strange things were called glasses? In fact, despite the fact that she was wearing different clothing to any I had ever seen, I knew the name of each and every item. Something significant had happened to me, and I could not comprehend what it was.

'May I ask the same of you?'

At the sound of my voice, Merlin broke free of her grip, chased back into the cave, and resumed licking my face and sniffing me.

Raising an eyebrow, giving me a quizzical look, the woman called the dog to heel in a no-nonsense voice:

'MERLIN, HEEL.'

The dog took off, exiting the cave in a couple of leaps. He knew who was in charge; that much was obvious.

Deciding there was nothing for it, I made my way out of the cave. The woman's face registered amazement when I stood up. In fact, it probably mirrored my face as I had never seen a woman clothed as she was.

We stood for a few moments, taking stock of each other. Then, she asked my name.

'Deimuiss, of the Calegi Tribe,' I told her.

'Oh. My name is Caroline. I live not too far from here,' she said, pointing south.

I was totally confused by her appearance and seeming acceptance of me. Shaking my head, trying to clear the fuzzy feeling, the woman took a step nearer saying, 'You are injured and the hair you have bound your wound with could lead to infection. You need treatment.'

I shrugged, 'I'll be fine, but thank you,' turning to return to the comparative safety of the cave.

'Where are you going? Don't be so stupid – you cannot spend the night in that damp cave. For goodness sake, man, follow me.'

'My goodness Elvaennia, she was a strict woman. There was no one like her at the settlement. Talk about bossy.'

Deimuiss gurgled with laughter and kissed Elvaennia on the brow, stroking the straight fall of silver hair that he knew sparked silver lights in the sunlight.

Elvaennia gazed into his deep, dark eyes. She felt as if she was spinning deeper and deeper into their depths. Never had she felt so close to Deimuiss, and she knew she never would again. Her heart froze at the thought. This was her man, her love, her life. What was going to happen? Surely she wasn't going to lose him again, not after they had just found each other again.

'It's my imagination,' she thought. 'I will never let him go again.' Some instinct told her that Deimuiss was attracted to Caroline. She also knew he would not admit to her as he was in denial himself. Her spirits plummeted at this realisation. I will think about it later she thought, when I go to bed.

I had no choice but to follow her. Deimuiss continued. We walked along the track to the edge of the field (I had to match my strides to her shorter ones). As I tried to take in my surroundings, we reached the top of the field. We climbed over a stile and headed towards a distant gate along a hedge-lined pathway. I could hear horses on the other side of the hedge. Their scent lingered on the air, reminding me of my time. Oh yes, I was aware by now that I had time travelled and was in 2007. My only current concern was that I did not want anyone to see me dressed in my cloak and other clothing from our time. This was the beginning of my new life as the time traveller that the Mystics had predicted. Different smells assailed my senses the nearer we got to the houses, and I wasn't impressed. Each step was drawing me deeper into this time and I was uncertain about what part I had to play in it – apart from the obvious one, and that was to use my healing skills wherever they were needed. I also knew I would be travelling to other centuries. My new life had begun.

We reached the field gate when, suddenly, I nearly jumped out of my skin. There was a tremendous noise and an animal went roaring past with smoke coming out of its back end! I had never seen such an animal in all my life and people were riding on its back. Elvaennia, I had never been so confused.

Caroline smiled, telling me not to worry as things would slowly become clearer to me.

'Get in, please.'

She was holding open the door to what looked like another of the strange animals. I felt nervous, but she was motioning me inside. I shook my head, wanting to return to the safety of the cave. Maybe if I stayed there, I would return to our time. Suddenly, more knowledge came to me. I knew that the strange animal I had seen was a motorbike and that I was getting into a vehicle called a car. Information was pouring into my brain at a tremendous pace. I quickly jumped into the car, and you know, Elvaennia, it did not feel strange in any way. Everything I saw made sense, if you understand me. I knew the buildings were houses; the cans lying about were 'Coca Cola' cans. Yes, if I am honest, there was a certain strangeness − of course there was − but I was more than confident in myself that I could accept this new world for a time but not forever.

Nuzzling up to him, Elvaennia told him that what had happened to her, once she had left the cave, was almost identical to his story, saying:

'Everything became clearer once I had shaken the fuzzy feeling out of my head. The same as you, I knew the name and use of everything I saw. It was most peculiar and once I was wearing the clothing of 2007, outwardly, I became the person they thought I should be. I know it sounds a little convoluted, but I'm sure you will understand what I mean.'

Elvaennia thought it strange that he should have met Caroline, and that she had never mentioned it to her. What was so sad was that something had obviously happened to Merlin, and she now had Connie. She was glad she had not mentioned seeing the dog in the garden; it would have upset Caroline, she was sure.

'Indeed I do little one.'

Kissing her eyelids, he whispered loving words in Calegian speech, much to her delight.

He continued his story:

I sat silently alongside her. Merlin was in the tailgate. I wondered where we were heading and I felt nervous, and then ashamed, that I, a fully fledged warrior, felt afraid. Indicating left and proceeding slowly over a hump-backed bridge, Caroline drove past a deserted building on the right, then stopped across the road from a group of eight semi-detached houses. I saw other houses along the lane. I gulped, seeing the ghostly face of an elderly man peering through the upstairs window of the first house, it was empty.'

'Who's he?'

I jerked my thumb in the direction of the house. Caroline glanced upwards but said there was no one there.

I told her that there was the ghost of an elderly man staring at us. She gave me a quizzical look and again glanced at the window.

'Deimuiss, there is no one there and the house has been empty for a couple of years. The was an old gent, who lived there – he died but I have never seen his ghost.'

'Hmmm, well he's watching us now.'

'Come on now, you need a shower and some decent clothes to wear.'

Following her into a cosy hall, she turned saying,

'Welcome to my home. There are no ghosts here to trouble you.'

With a smile, she pushed the facing door open and we entered a beautifully warm, comfortable room. This place spoke to me in the strangest manner, and despite what Caroline had said about there being no ghosts, I knew that there were; and what's more, I knew that Caroline knew they were here. Looking around, everything came sharply into focus and I became even more aware of this new world opening up around me. I looked into her amber eyes and saw that she was a good, kind person. Her no-nonsense attitude was simply a cover up to keep people at a distance. In fact, I was looking forward to discovering exactly what made this lady tick.

'Come Deimuiss, let me clean that injury up,' she said.

Watching Caroline tend my injured hand, I realised how attractive she was. Her hair was a wonderful golden blonde, not from a packet, either. The kitchen light brought out the beautiful golden highligh.'

'Deimuiss, were you attracted to her?'

'Not at all, my little one. I am just setting the scene for you. You have no need to be jealous whatsoever. The whole time we were apart, you were constantly in my thoughts. And, you are forgetting that Caroline is a few years older than I am.'

For a second she thought she saw a fleeting look of longing flit across his face, as he spoke of Caroline; almost she thought, as if he is really attracted to her. She was certain her earlier suspicions were right.

As if he sensed her thoughts, Deimuiss gave her a hug and Elvaennia settled back into the warmth of his arms, listening to his story of his time here before she arrived.

After dressing my wound, I followed Caroline as she showed me to the bathroom, telling me this was where I could bath or shower, and that, when I had, she would find suitable clothing for me. I was to leave my cloak and other items, and she would see that they were cleaned. Without question, she was helping me to settle into this different world; and what's more, I accepted that this was the way it was to be for the time being, just as when I would travel to other centuries to do my healing work.

'Elvaennia, do you not think that it is almost beyond belief that the two of us should come through time and meet for a third time? Isn't it also amazing that we gained all the knowledge we needed to live in this time together?'

'It is startling, Deimuiss. And I could never explain it, so perhaps we would be wrong to question how it happened. We should thank the gods that we met with good decent people, who had our well-being at heart. Oh, dear Deimuiss, what if other people have made the journey and met with the wrong type of people? I had never thought of that. Obviously, there must have been others that have not only arrived in this time, but also journeyed to other centuries. And there are others trapped in the shadows of this time.'

,Suddenly, she remembered the hall at the farmhouse where the shadows were trapped.

'Oh, my goodness, how could I have forgotten?'

'What? Who?'

'When I arrived, I passed through a small hallway at the farmhouse and there were shadows trapped in this time. I meant to return to speak to them, and help to release them. How could I possibly have forgotten?'

'It's understandable after everything that has happened. When we return, we will rescue them. It is part of the work we were meant to do,' he said in a very solemn voice. 'We will also travel to other worlds beyond time. But first, we have to release those you mention who are trapped in the shadows.'

Elvaennia sat up, her silver grey eyes beneath the sweep of her long, grey eyelashes, were almost opaque with fear. She shivered.

'What do you mean, beyond time? Like the television, program Dr. Who? Will we be meeting aliens and awful creatures?'

He resisted a smile at her imagination.

'Wesh not, little one.'

He hoped the childhood words would comfort her.

'Nothing like Dr. Who, I promise.'

But, for the first time ever, her Grandmamma's words did not soothe her.

'I don't understand Deimuiss. We were returning to the settlement to marry, not to travel beyond space and time.'

Elvaennia's eyes suddenly flooded with tears as his words had turned her world upside down. She seemed to revert to the young girl he had left behind. In a way, he was pleased to see that underneath the sophisticated veneer, his old Vinny was still there.

Cuddling her, Deimuiss was at a loss as to how much information he could tell her.

'Remember the Mystics' words, Elvaennia? We have work to do.'

Nodding and rubbing her eyes, she breathed deeply, listening to him.

'Yes, we have work to do here, but, in the information I received, there were other messages that were not given to you.'

She stiffened at his words.

'Why not?'

'I do not know, but I was told that we would travel beyond time itself. I do not know exactly when, where, or how, but I can assure you that we will return to our time very soon.'

Relieved at his last words, Elvaennia drank some of her coffee. 'Gosh this coffee is foul. I'm sure it is the water they use,' she groaned, taking a sip.

'You know I long for the sweet water of the springs back at the settlement.'

'I too, my love, just be patient a little longer.'

Nodding his head, Deimuiss decided that now was not the time to discuss 'the others' and definitely not the time to discuss the 'Time Beyond'.

He continued his story:

'I was worried about what had happened to my flint knife, as I could not find it. Thinking I must have left it in the cave, I wondered whether I could ask Caroline to take me back to see if I could find it – but decided against this, thinking it might be pushing my luck a bit. After all, she had been so good to me, opening her home without question to a complete stranger who had been dressed in very strange clothing. She knew I meant her no harm, and that was all that mattered to her. I could go or stay as I pleased. She lived on her own apart from her dog, Merlin, but she sensed I would move on quickly as I had work to do. I jumped at her words, remembering the Mystics telling me exactly the same a few years ago. How did she know that? Looking down at my clothes, I wondered what you would say if you could see me in a shirt, jeans, socks and trainers; not a spear, axe-head or arrow in sight.'

'Now then young man,' Caroline said one morning, 'I know you have a plan, so tell me.'

'I have to work Caroline.'

'Yes, every man has to work, and I will help you if you need me to.'

Caroline was, as usual, very precise and straightforward. She could come across as curt at times, but I knew that beneath the hard exterior she presented to the World, she was an extremely caring person who had been very badly hurt.

At the moment she was on leave from her job as a nursing sister at Stafford Hospital.

'I have time to help you Deimuiss.'

I thought it strange that we both worked in the healing profession. No wonder I had warmed to her from the start. I reached out and touched her hand saying, 'thank you.'

Just for a second, she let my hand rest on hers before snatching it away.

After I explained how I helped the sick through spiritual healing, she used the computer to find the nearest spiritualist church: 'Lichfield, Cruck House'.

She pointed the mouse at the address online, also the email address and left me to it.

Chapter 38

'And that was how it started, my little one. After attending a few meetings in Lichfield, holding workshops and healing sessions, the invitations began to arrive thick and fast. And quite honestly, I have rarely stopped working in all the time I have been here. Keeping busy was, of course, a way to fill the empty hours until you joined me.'

'But the cave, Deimuiss. What were you doing in the cave with The Delphs when Grandmamma and Trieainia were murdered? At first, I really thought you had a hand in their killings, but admitted to myself you would never hurt another soul.'

'Elvaennia!'

He nuzzled her neck through her wonderful hair.

'I told you. I heard you from this time. You were so very much on my mind and your voice broke through time and space. It was an agony to me, knowing you were in so much distress and danger. Suddenly, I found myself hurtling through the centuries and landing on the floor of the cave. I was devastated to see what had happened; and then you disappeared too. Afterwards, I thought The Delphs were going to kill me, as they approached, looking at me with evil intent in their eyes. Then, without warning, I was torn out of the cave and I re-entered this century with an enormous thump!'

Elvaennia wrinkled her nose.

'What I don't understand, is how I met you in different centuries.'

'Ah, at times, I am drawn back into the past to help others in distress. This is the work that the Mystics have always predicted I would do. My life is to heal the sick, not just in our own time, my love, but *through* time. But, never despair Elvaennia, we will always be brought back together through time...and beyond time. We are as one, and never forget that my love. No more explanations. We have a lot to catch up on.'

Enfolding her slim body to him, he kissed her and she felt a sensation that she had never felt before. She felt as if she was being drawn into his body, as if they were indeed becoming as one. She was enraptured and felt a gold light surrounding them. Her eyes closed. She was in ecstasy and knew nobody would ever replace him in her life.

'Oh my little love,' he said softly, stroking her silver hair that glowed like crystals on a starry night, 'we will marry soon, and then our real lives will start.'

'Yes, we will, but what of our families Deimuiss? I so want them to be with us.'

'Of course, they will be with us.'

'But how?'

'We will be returning to our time, of course.'

'We will?' she exclaimed in delight. Leaping from the sofa, she danced around the room. 'You mean we can return? How? Tell me quickly.'

Again, he caught a glimpse of the young girl who he had left at the settlement, and a smile wreathed his lips.

'Ah, she is still here, my impetuous young love.'

'Deimuiss!' she suddenly cried out, rushing across the room.

She picked up her pouch and taking a well-wrapped, small packet from it, she handed it to him. His eyes widened in astonishment when he saw, within the layers of wrapping, his flint knife.

'You found it, how truly amazing. I never thought I would see this knife again, and you kept it despite thinking I had committed a heinous act. That proves to me, more than anything, that underneath it all, you knew I really would never kill anyone – unless, of course, it was to save my own or someone else's life.'

He hugged her to him, loving her more as time passed.

'Obviously, we both have loose ends to tie up. We cannot walk away from our responsibilities, I'm sure you will agree.'

Nodding in acquiesce, her hair falling charmingly around her face, he took her in his arms and kissed her, longing to make love to her. However, he knew that first he had to marry her. If their child was to be born in this time, awful consequences could be the result. In addition, he wanted his daughter to be born of their time, to have her roots at the settlement. It would be the best beginning he could give his child and the others who would follow.

He smiled contentedly at the thought.

Chapter 39

A few days later, Mary phoned to ask if I would like to accompany her on a walk with Pip. I readily agreed. Deimuiss had left early to attend a pre-arranged meeting, and I knew that a break from work would do me good. Grabbing my jacket, I drove to the farmhouse.

Parking the car at a place called Brindley Heath we opened the tailgate. Out jumped Pip and we were off.

'This place is known as Birches Valley,' Mary informed me. 'A couple of years ago, it was beautiful. Watch out!' she yelled, pushing me out of the way as a couple of men raced past on bikes.

'Phew, that was a lucky escape. You okay, Elvaennia?'

I nodded.

'I'm astounded that they are allowed to ride on a path where people walk, Mary.'

'Terrible place for walkers now; particularly if you have children. These mountain bikers rip past you at great speed and woe-betide the small children and dogs. I brought you up here to show you just how different the Chase is from your day.'

'I cannot describe to you how beautiful this area was in my time, Mary.'

I felt sad to see the desecration that had been wrought on the picturesque landscape.

'I always thought the countryside should be a natural environment.'

Shaking my head despondently, I gazed at some strange objects that Mary called sculptures. They were hanging up in trees and standing in the forest. I must admit, some of them were really scary and I jumped once or twice when the sculptures loomed threateningly. But, on reflection, no doubt people would think the sculptures and artwork of my time were very strange.

I was pleased when we had finished our walk. I felt incredibly sad, remembering how beautiful it had once been. The settlement had not been far away and, despite it now being totally different, it pained me to see how awful a once-attractive area now looked. How I longed to step back into my time, to be amongst my own people once more; to see Mamma and my siblings; to be with Deimuiss; to visit the Cave of Spirits with Deimuiss and to see the wondrous drawings and paintings; to visit the Cave of Crystals and to breathe the sweet air of our time, and listen to the silence broken only by the sound of the song birds. I longed for the peace of our world. I ached to be able to look up at the sweep of the heavens and see the stars and planets. When we sat high up on the Chase, we felt we could touch the stars in the night-time skies. It was a magical sight. I missed my world, and wondered, looking around me, how people in this time could so disrespect their heritage.

'Elvaennia, do stop day dreaming!'

Mary's voice cut across my thoughts.

'We're nearly back at the car. Is there anywhere else you would like to visit?'

'Oh, yes please Mary. Could you take me to where the settlement used to be?'

'I have a good idea where it might be, so jump in the passenger seat while I put Pip in the back.'

Driving down Stafford Brook Road, Mary pointed out various landmarks and farms. She knew every one in the area. I never ceased to be amazed at her knowledge.

'Now,' she chattered on, 'There is Park House where the Wolseley family once lived, and if I have my bearings right, the settlement was definitely in this vicinity. It covered a large area of land. I haven't a clue where the boundaries were. We will come back one day and have a walk around. It isn't far, but you will see how you were able to see the lights as they appeared at The Standing Stones. You can also see the Hill of the Spirits clearly, and the Hill of Souls is in that direction.'

She pointed East.

Nodding my head in agreement, I knew Mary had the correct location. Instead of seeing fences and hedging, I could actually see the settlement spread out around us. Wood smoke curled its way from the houses, a steady stream of thin smoke widening as it entered the upper atmosphere. Sniffing, I could have sworn I smelled the sweetness of the apple trees in the smoke. The thatch was tinged purple from the heather that had been used in the making of the roofs. I could hear the children running and laughing, their voices filled with happiness at the joy of being young and free. I wanted to reach out and touch them. Their eyes dancing with the pleasure of each other's company, they ran and chased the dogs. I could hear the piglets grunting as they foraged into the red soil in their pens. The voices travelled through the centuries. I could swear I heard Mamma's voice calling me back. Could swear I had a whiff of the pigs on the breeze, not one of my favourite smells then or now for that matter.

Jumping out of the car, I called to Mary, 'Just give me a minute. I want to check on something.'

I walked past the tall pine trees that stood like sentinels along the dusty track. I followed it as it veered right, and I walked slowly across a field.

'Yes,' I thought, 'this is the right area.'

Passing a prickly gorse bush, I suddenly spotted something. Bending down, I picked up a piece of old pottery. Turning it over in my hands, I suddenly recognised it. Excitedly, I clutched it to me for a moment. This had come from one of Grandmamma's old pots. I was over-the-moon and I carefully placed it in my pouch. I was so happy at my find. I retraced my steps back to the car, thinking of the settlement and my family. I couldn't wait to show it to Deimuiss.

'Elvaennia, you are day-dreaming again.'

I jumped back into this time sharply on hearing Mary's voice. She was laughing at me.

'Come child, we have to go back and cook dinner for David.'

Taking a last look around, I determined to walk this way tomorrow if possible. I needed to be near my roots, albeit maybe only for a few hours, but I was more than persuaded it would help me to answer some of the questions that were constantly on my mind. Soon, I knew I would be hearing from the archaeological society.

Travelling home, Mary piped up:

'By the way, Elvaennia, remember John and Pat who we met at Lichfield Spiritualist Church with their daughter Maria? She had her fiancé with her.'

I nodded, shuddering as I remembered the Delphs.

'Well, you are not going to believe this. He, Afreionnia, got run over by a bus and died of his injuries not so long ago. Maria was upset, Pat said, but not quite as much as she would have imagined she would be.'

'Not surprised,' I thought, hugging the good news to myself.

Knowing that Maria was safe now filled me with delight, and the awful Delph and his shadow spirit would now be where they belonged, at the Winter of Despair. Some days were so good.

'Thanks for taking me out Mary.'

I gave her a hug as we entered the kitchen at the farmhouse.

'I will just wash my hands and then help you with the cooking.'

'That's fine, deary, but don't worry. You go and have some time to yourself. I seem to remember you wanted to check your email.'

'Yes, you're right. Thanks Mary.'

I logged onto my laptop and discovered I had a message from the Archaeology Group that I had contacted. They wanted to arrange a site meeting. I was excited and told Mary straightaway.

She gave a small smile, but looked, I thought, a tad uneasy.

Chapter 40

'Hope the archaeologists find something definite, Mary,' Elvaennia chirruped, eating her morning slice of toast as fast as she could. Having arrived at the farmhouse earlier with great excitement, Elvaennia was longing to leave for the dig.

'Slow down, you'll get indigestion. We have lots of time.'

'I know, but I am so excited that they have agreed to excavate where the settlement was.'

Nodding her head, Mary swiftly cleared the breakfast remnants away. Turning to Elvaennia, she said:

'I'll be ready in 20 minutes or so, okay?'

'Fine I'll be waiting.'

Eyes dancing with excitement, Elvaennia did a quick skip around the kitchen, much to Mary's amusement.

'But why are you so excited, Elvaennia? You already know that the site is there!'

'I want everyone to know that what I have been saying is true. So much of the media call me a fraud and a liar. This will prove I am who I say I am. That's the only reason. I do know there are many who will never believe me, but then in life, there will always be disbelievers.'

Nodding her understanding, Mary continued with her seemingly endless tidying up, cooking, and preparation of her herbal balms. Elvaennia got the impression she was using delaying tactics, and could not understand her reluctance to go to the site.

Eventually, Mary was ready. And now, sitting beside her in the car, they headed for the dig.

Enthusiasm shone around her. Mary smiled at the way Elvaennia was sitting as far forward in her seat as she could.

'Good thing she has a seatbelt holding her back,' she thought.

In fact, the air around Elvaennia seemed to pulsate with joy. Her beautiful hair was actually sparking lights as she twisted and turned in her seat. Her eyes glowed with happiness.

'This is it Mary. It's really going to happen and I will prove to everyone that I am who I say I am.'

'My dearest Elvaennia, isn't it enough that we know who you are?'

'Yes, but it just has to be done.' she sighed. 'If only Deimuiss could have been here for the dig; but he has work to finish. He did say he will be here as soon as he can.'

Nodding her white curls, Mary looked dispirited and troubled, as if sensing things were finally coming to a head. She continued the short journey to the site.

Chapter 41

Getting out of the car, she saw the archaeologists were marking out the first area for digging. Elvaennia knew they were in the wrong place. Running across the field to them, she breathlessly said:

'No, no, if you're looking for the actual settlement, you have to dig over there.'

She ran further across the field and waved to them, calling, 'Over here, I can show you exactly where each house stood.'

The archaeologists looked at each other saying, 'But geophysics showed that there was a lot of activity in this area.'

The younger of the two men – who incidentally, was much taken with the startlingly beautiful, young woman – shrugged and made his way towards her.

'What makes you think this is the settlement?'

Looking into her silvery eyes, he was almost hypnotised by their beauty.

'I know it sounds strange, but trust me. The settlement was here.'

Taking the marker from him, she proceeded to outline the whole area where she had lived. A brilliant smile, a flash of her silvery eyes, and the young archaeologist, Mark, was lost.

'Okay, we will go with you. We have the time as this is only the first day of the dig.'

'Over here, all of you. This is where we will start.'

Waving his arms and shouting directions, the diggers and the other members of the team gathered to watch the first trench being dug.

Standing to one side, Elvaennia watched the JCB. A mixture of sorrow and happiness washed across her. She did not want her home dug and exposed to the cameras, but she knew she had to be strong and go through with it if she was to prove herself to a doubting world.

Mark came to stand beside her and introduced himself. Elvaennia, in turn, told him her name.

'Interesting, huh?'

Nodding, Elvaennia described exactly where each home had stood; and she daringly went as far as to name the occupiers, much to his astonishment.

Mark was not as startled as he would have been if someone else had revealed this information to him. At first sight, he had known that this woman was different from any he had ever met. He had thought nothing she could tell him would surprise him. He knew she had an inner knowledge of this place. He thought this would be one of the most interesting digs he had ever been on.

Silently, Elvaennia observed as the digger's shovel went deeper and deeper to where the settlement now slept its longest sleep. Each turn of the soil made her feel as if part of her soul was being torn away. How she wished Deimuiss was here beside her instead of Mark. 'Hopefully,' she thought, 'He won't be long. I need his strength to help me through this ordeal.'

Watching the expressions flit across her face, Mark felt sorrow fill him, and went so far as to place a comforting arm around her slim shoulders. Raising her face to look at him, he saw tears glazing her unusual silver-grey eyes. They glittered on the sweep of her long eyelashes. Giving her a squeeze, for some reason, unknown to him, he whispered:

'Wesh not my little one.'

Elvaennia leapt away from him.

'Why did you say those words?' She queried him, almost angrily.

'What?' he stuttered, 'I don't know; they just came into my head.'

'Hmm, I wonder;' she looked at him, trying to read his thoughts. Unusually for her, she couldn't. She found herself clawing at an impenetrable wall. He lowered his gaze under the piercing silver of her eyes, smiling a secret smile at her failure.

A shout from the site made them head towards the diggers. Elvaennia was slower to follow Mark, as she had begun to dread the coming day. Far from her earlier excitement, she now felt reluctant to participate in the dig.

'What is it?' Mark called to Dennis, the other archaeologist working in the trench.

'Look what we've found.'

Proudly, he showed Mark a beautiful pot that, on seeing it, made Elvaennia draw in a heavy gasp. She acknowledged it as having belonged to her Mamma who in turn had received it from her Grandmamma. It was a family heirloom – and seeing it exposed after so many centuries, sent a shiver down her spine.

She hated having to follow this through. 'It's a bit like watching 'Big Brother',' she muttered under her breath – 'having to expose your whole life to the world.' But she knew that if she allowed it to continue, her aim would be achieved. She wondered, 'How could I have been so excited?' Her thoughts were chasing around her head.

'Am I letting them unearth a monster that will be too big for me to cope with? Will I be able to escape the media in time, before the cauldron boils over?'

Her book was being published shortly, and this would be further evidence of her words. Depression was grabbing at her, but she knew there was no going back.

'And anyway, very soon it won't matter at all. I will have proved my point.'

Looking across at the trench, she could see all the team admiring their latest find. Their body language told her they were 'made up'. She knew she had to play her part, or all this would be for nothing. Painting a smile on her face, she approached the team members to admire the finds, telling them to whom they had belonged, and where the owners had lived.

Chapter 42

The last day of the dig dawned, and Elvaennia was so glad. The archaeologists were overwhelmed with their discoveries, stunned by Elvaennia's knowledge of the area, and grateful of her help in identifying the finds and demonstrating their uses.

Mark, by now, realised that Elvaennia's information had not been gained in this world. If anyone had asked him to explain his thinking, he knew he would not be able to, but he was more than positive that he was right. There was something 'other worldly' about her, which he would have had difficulty putting into words if asked. At times, he saw a golden light shimmering around her. He knew it was her aura. He had seen the light of auras that shone around people before, but never one that shone such a pure gold as the one around Elvaennia. Also: where else would she have gained her inner knowledge of the site, if she had not once lived there? His report, he knew, would be electric and would stun the world of archaeology. In fact, it would stun the whole World, he thought.

Some auras he had seen around people in the past had made him shudder. (He had always had the ability to read an aura). They told him the character of a person instantly. Whether the person was selfish, malicious, obnoxious, greedy, cruel, or told lies, he could read most people's life story – past, present and future – within minutes. Elvaennia's aura had, and still did, puzzle him greatly. And no wonder, he thought.

At times, this ability disturbed him greatly. Knowing almost all there is to know about a person could, at times, make life very difficult indeed.

On the other hand, it was also very beneficial. When he had to interview someone, it was an added bonus. Girlfriends could never deceive him. This made him smile, recalling the time when a partner had cheated on him, and his 'gift' had enabled him to tell her almost to the second when she had 'played away'. The look of astonishment on her face had been almost comical and Mark was more than relieved to have 'seen' her deceit.

On the other hand, he recalled almost literally bumping into a man as he was leaving a shop one day not so long ago. The man had been almost running down the High Street and narrowly missed Mark in his haste. Mark grabbed the man's arm as he looked as if was going to fall. The distaste he felt as he grasped him was almost palpable. On glancing up, he saw the man's aura was black. Mark shuddered in horror, knowing that he had unwittingly stopped a murderer.

Recovering very fast, the man had tried to free himself by attempting to throw Mark off. Mark restrained him by calmly saying, 'Be careful, and take a deep breath. You've had a bit of a shock.'

He was really at a loss as to what else he could say, and was relieved when a strong hand clapped the man on the shoulder and asked him to, 'come in for questioning.'

Mark nodded gratefully at the police officer, thinking that it was a close shave. He didn't want to be the next victim.

Meeting Elvaennia was certainly different. The golden light that hovered around her was unlike any aura he had ever seen. He longed to know more about this special person. But now, the dig was almost over and Mark had not managed to talk or get any closer to her. Whenever he approached, he sensed her trying to read his thoughts and he immediately erected a wall around himself; but so did she and he could not see her emotions or gain access to her inner psyche.

'Fair play to her, she's an astute little thing who knows far more than I do.'

But he really did want to get to know her and to find out as much as he could before he missed out on this golden opportunity.

He sensed that she would not be in this time for long, and the thought of never seeing her again filled him with despair. 'She is so unaware of the effect she has on other people,' he thought. 'She is truly amazing. She has no knowledge of how beautiful she is.'

The situation he was caught up in surprised him, as he had never felt so tied emotionally to a virtual stranger. He felt that Elvaennia was now living in what, to her, was a virtual world. He longed to become part of the time that she had once lived in. With her beside him, he knew his life would be complete. She was the missing link that he had been searching for all his life.

Shaking his head ruefully, he walked to the last trench that was being dug. Somehow, he sensed that this would be the one that clinched the dig, and he knew that Elvaennia had deliberately kept this place as the last to be dug. He knew that, to her, it was the most important and he wondered what secrets it would reveal.

Elvaennia had insisted that Mark dig this last trench. She watched with trepidation as he took up his spade and gently began to dig the soil that would reveal the final secret the world had not known.

She was aware that Mark thought she was different from anyone he had ever met. She also knew that he longed to get closer to her. But Elvaennia had distanced herself emotionally from him. There was only one man for her, and that was her first love, Deimuiss. If she was truthful, she was attracted to Mark. She knew he understood every twist and turn of her complex make-up, but she had restrained herself from getting involved with him. They were never meant to be together. Hers was a separate world, one that he could not enter; and she did not want to be involved with any man apart from Deimuiss.

Yes, she had seen this time in her dreams when she was younger, as she had the other times. Why she had been chosen to travel through time and space, she would never know. The Mystics' words haunted her, their voices still clear in her mind.

'You will have many journeys backwards and forwards Elvaennia before your work is concluded.'

'How true,' she mused. 'I hope my travelling through time will soon come to an end and I can then return to the settlement.'

'Not yet,' the voice whispered. 'You still have work to do.'

Wearily, Elvaennia sat on a rock and closed her eyes, thinking how exhausted she was.

Her thoughts turned to Mark. She knew he wanted more than she could ever offer. 'I love Deimuiss,' she reasoned. 'Hopefully, he will be with me soon and will never have to leave me again.'

Secretly, she could not deny that she was attracted to this darkly handsome archaeologist, but knew it was merely a passing attraction – unlike anything she felt for Deimuiss.

She walked across to Mark watching as he dug the last trench. She could feel the animal magnetism of him as his muscles rippled beneath his skin each time he lifted and turned the red, sandy soil from the trench.

Mark turned, looking up into her silvery eyes. The contact made Elvaennia step closer to him. Their eyes locked together for that moment in time; secrets were exchanged; a message of longing and deep attraction held their glance, neither wanting to break contact. But sadly, it was not to be, and Elvaennia asked:

'How's it going Mark?'

'Fine,' he muttered darkly, shoving his spade back into the soil. Then, in an instant, he threw the spade to the ground and said, 'I cannot go on,' grabbing Elvaennia's hand, he practically dragged her away from the trench.

Puzzled by his words, the team gathered in a group, watching as he strode away with the young woman. Reaching his caravan, Mark almost lifted Elvaennia up the steps, pointing to the small bench seat. She sat and looked at him across the small table.

'Now Elvaennia, do you really want me to dig up your final secrets? Do you honestly know what will happen if I do?'

As she nodded her head, Mark thought he had never seen a more beautiful woman with her ash blonde silvery hair floating around her beautiful face and shoulders. He longed to take her in his arms. Restraining himself, he moved to sit beside her on the small bench. He knew she wanted to be with him as much as he wanted her. Stroking her beautiful hair and face was almost painful, as he knew this would be the only time he would ever spend alone with her. They both sensed the magic that was allowing them to experience this special moment between two worlds. She moved away from him quickly.

'No,' she whispered. 'It cannot be. I must leave now. Please do not follow me.'

Mark knew his life was changed forever, and his soul belonged to Elvaennia.

Knowing that at some point she had to return to her own time, he did not attempt to stop her. He reached out, and touching her hand, said, 'I am sorry. I cannot complete the dig. It is impossible for me to return to the trench.'

'Do not fesh yourself dearest Mark.'

Standing on tip toe, she kissed his cheek, knowing it was her final goodbye. He was incredibly sad. He knew he would never love any woman as much as he loved Elvaennia.

Elvaennia slowly began to walk back to the dig alone, wondering who would complete the final stages. She felt so alone. She scanned the area in the hope of seeing Deimuiss, but there was no sign of him. A rapport had grown between her and Mark – but that was now shattered and scattered to the four winds. She knew he would be watching her departure if she looked back but she chose not to, she knew she had to resist the temptation Mark offered. Heart heavy, she walked towards the last trench, trying to prepare herself for the final uncovering of what lay beneath the red, sandy soil that covered the settlement.

Thinking she heard a voice in the distance, she glanced to her side and was amazed to see a familiar figure running towards her. Her heart almost stopped beating as she gasped, 'Deimuiss, Deimuiss.'

'Vinny! Vinny!'

He was shouting her name at the top of his voice.

'Quickly, my love.'

She ran towards him, arms outstretched, tears of happiness falling unchecked down her cheeks.

Reaching him, she threw her arms around him as he smothered her tear sodden face with kisses.

'Elvaennia, we must reach the cave before sunset or we will not be able to return to our time.'

Grabbing her hand, they ran from the site.

'Damn! The car won't start. We will have to make a dash for it across the fields.'

Terrified now that they would be trapped in this time, they ran at great speed through the woods and fields of Rugeley.

Nearing the farmhouse, Deimuiss was worried that they were going to be too late to reach the cave. But a sudden thought stopped him in his tracks.

'Your clothes Elvaennia, you must get them from the farmhouse.'

'Yes,' she gasped, holding her sides. 'You're right; quickly, my love – not a minute to spare.'

Despite her anxiety, she was almost beside herself with excitement at the thought that they were going home to the settlement. She was going to see her family and rescue them from their enemies.

Entering the house, she was surprised how quiet everywhere was. The kitchen had lost its bustling air. Even the flowers in their vases were dead. Strange: no sign of Pip or the cat. Rushing upstairs, she was amazed to see her cloak and tunic spread out in readiness on her bed. They smelled fresh and clean and she could smell the heather in the cloak's fur. For a second, she buried her nose in the silky folds. Changing quickly, she glanced down and was amazed to see her animal skin shoes looked as good as new.

'My, these were nearly wrecked when I arrived.'

She stroked the soft surface as she changed into them.

'It feels so good and right to be wearing my own clothes again.'

Gazing at her reflection one last time in the mirror, she quickly tied her pouch around her slim waist, and then fastened her jewelled clasp. She hastily made her way down the stairs, hearing Deimuiss urging her to hurry.

'Still no sign of the others,' she thought. 'Not even the animals are making a noise out on the farm.'

An eerie silence had descended over all.

Reaching the hall, Deimuiss shouted, 'Oh my goodness, hurry Elvaennia. We must release the shadows now and make haste or our journey is doomed to failure.'

'Have we time?' she queried worriedly.

'If we don't, then we will not be allowed to return.'

Walking up the hallway together, they felt the shadows pressing into them.

'Release us, please,' they cried, agitated beyond measure.

'How Deimuiss? How do we do this?'

Elvaennia was almost crying now, longing to help, but desperate to reach the cave before the sun set.

Deimuiss raised his arms high in the air.

'David did this to these poor people. He trapped them in his time for his own selfish reasons. Now, if I release them, he will never be allowed to return to our time.'

'Pardon?'

Elvaennia looked at him in astonishment.

'He came from the settlement?'

Deimuiss bobbed his head grimly.

'Yes, my love, he and his mother Mary were entrusted with the time travellers over the years, to guard and nurture them, as was Caroline. The trouble was, any that did not follow the pathway that David chose for them became trapped here by him and they could not move on.'

The young woman's eyes were like saucers. So much began to fall into place. Then, she let out a sharp cry, 'But Mary, dear Mary. She will be able to return surely? She would not have allowed this to happen. And Caroline: what of her?'

Sadly, Deimuiss shook his head.

'I'm afraid not, my love. Mary had an idea of what was happening, but refused to believe her beloved son could become involved in such a terrible thing. She has lost the trust of the Mystics, and now they will both be trapped in time once the shadows are released. It is only fitting that they should suffer the same fate as the people they trapped. Caroline is safe and has chosen to live in this time for now.'

Elvaennia's eyes swam with tears. She so loved Mary, but what David had done was indeed a despicable thing and he deserved his punishment. But, Mary did not deserve the same fate, surely? She was relieved that Caroline was safe. But Mary? Elvaennia had no time to ponder this question as Deimuiss began to chant the incantation that the Mystics had taught him to release lost souls, who, one by one, took on a shape and form, laughing with relief after years of imprisonment.

Deimuiss ensured they were all free, and asked them to follow quickly if they wanted to make the journey to their time.

Chapter 43

Running down the hillside towards the bivouac, hand in hand, the man and girl began to disappear into the mist and lights surrounding the cave. The lights above began to strobe down. Glancing behind her as she entered the cave, Elvaennia noticed she had dropped her pouch just outside the entrance. It was too late to pick it up. The shadows began crowding in behind them; no one noticed the dark haired man who slipped in behind them. Despite it appearing small, there was sufficient room for all the travellers. The more people that entered the cave the larger it grew until all were inside. The young dark haired man hid himself far back in the deepest recesses of the cave.

Outside the farmhouse, the figure of the Druid faded as the shadow transfigured into a man.

The man freed from the Druids presence looked around angrily shouting out, 'Elvaennia, Elvaennia, where are you?'

He paced around outside the farmhouse but his strides got shorter and slower. He began to breathe heavily.

'No, no. I need the strength to find her. I cannot lose her now after all this time.'

Looking up, he saw David's face high up in the farmhouse. With the last of his vanishing strength, he entered the farmhouse. Slowly, he climbed the stairs to the loft.

David, looking thin and afraid, gazed across the loft as Carnaan entered. Heatedly, he spat out, 'You trapped me for all this time with the other shadows. Even the Druid refused to release me to find Elvaennia.

Now David where is she?'

Nodding towards the window, Carnaan followed his gaze and looked across the field towards the cave. He saw that the lights and mist were now almost as one. Realising what had happened, Carnaan moved furiously towards David, trying to feed from his energy field.

Watching this battle of wills between the two men, Mary was afraid of the outcome.

'Stop it,' she cried. 'There are no winners here. Elvaennia has gone with Deimuiss, and she is lost to both of you.'

Knowing he needed David's strength and power to get back to the settlement, Carnaan stayed within his energy field, watching as the strength left the other man's body.

Mary was lost. There was nothing she could do to fight Carnaan. She watched helplessly as David collapsed exhausted at the table.

With shaking hands, David, sadly held the final piece of the jigsaw he had been working on. He looked gaunt; frail; unhappy. He had lost the love of his life. Knowing that he had lost Elvaennia forever, he was devastated – downcast at the awful future that now awaited him and his mother. Mary had gone to fetch herbs and food to try to replenish his energy after Carnaan's attack. She knew that once the others had left on their journey, she and David would be locked in time, as the others had been because of David's selfishness. The thought of what was to happen to them upset her deeply. Her only consolation was in knowing that David would still be with her. She also carried the hope that at some point in the future another time traveller would release them.

David, too, carried the vain hope that at some time, they would be released, and he made a silent vow that when that happened he would search again for Elvaennia.

'Even if it takes to the end of time, I will find her,' he declared. 'There will never be another woman for me.'

Already, the farmhouse had lost its energy. All around them was silence. There seemed to be no life force apart from theirs.

'We are outcasts now mother,' he commented morosely.

Mary glanced at him apprehensively.

'Whatever are you thinking about son?'

'Nothing. Nothing for you to worry about, mother.'

He gave a sardonic smile, but before she could stop him, he had placed the remaining piece of the jigsaw into the puzzle. Knowing what was going to happen, Mary ran to her son. Flinging her arms around him, she cried out:

'We will always be together son. I will never leave you.'

Her voice faded into the room, as slowly the pair vanished from view, going to the place where they became shadows of themselves.

With a shout of triumph, Carnaan ran from the farmhouse towards the cave, knowing that he now only had a few minutes left. He ran as fast as he possibly could, watching the lights and mist slowly mingling into a huge cloud of energy over the bivouac. His energy levels were dropping as he neared the cave, but he knew that, once inside, he would have the energy of the others gathered inside to draw off. Moreover, once home, there was always Pranny, his wife, to use as his energy source.

'Then,' he gloated smugly to himself, 'I can continue my pursuit of Elvaennia.'

'She will always be mine,' he affirmed. 'Until the end of time we will be as one. Deimuiss will never possess her. I will make certain of that.'

With a giant stride, he flung himself into the cave quickly running into the darkness he hid himself away.

Chapter 44

Brian, the archaeologist who had taken Mark's place in the team, asked, 'Wonder where Elvaennia is.'

'Haven't seen her for some time. Only a few hours left here now. She will probably be back before the dig is finished.'

His companion, Roy, replied as he dug another layer of sandy soil out of the trench.

Bending down, Brian began to sift through the latest mound of earth they had dug. His face suddenly lit up as he yelled to all and sundry:

'A find, over here, a find.'

He repeated himself in his excitement.

The team scurried across to Brian's trench, smiles plastered all over their faces. More finds. They couldn't believe their luck.

Picking up the find, Brian's face took on a look of complete surprise.

'Well, this is quite extraordinary.'

His voice and hands trembled with emotion. 'There are some photographs,' he glanced through them, 'one of them is of Elvaennia taken at the settlement when she was younger. This is simply impossible and look there is a map on an old slate: the diagram is of how the Chase looks today, but the markings are very old.' He and the others were astonished on seeing the photographs and the map. Shaking their heads in disbelief but they could see without a shadow of doubt the 'finds' were genuine.

'This cave is not too far from here,' he said, tracing the route on the old slate. 'Follow me. We will go and look.'

Nosing his car through the tree-lined Chase roads, Brian's mind was trying to solve the mystery of the slate – but he could reach no solid conclusion. Parking his car, the others followed him as he walked up a narrow track. Leaving the track, he scrambled nimbly up the side of a steep slope. The others were amazed at how accurately he had followed the map. 'How did he know the route from such a small diagram?' they wondered between themselves. Suddenly, Brian dropped to his knees and, pushing branches and foliage to one side, revealed a tunnelled entrance. He scrambled through as the others followed hearts in mouths. In the light, airy cave, their mouths dropped open in sheer astonishment as they viewed the ancient paintings on the walls. They looked as perfect as on the days they had been painted all those centuries ago. The first paintings depicted events in Elvaennia's lifetime at the settlement before she visited this time. As the archaeologists moved around the cave, they had to rub their eyes. It was all so unbelievable, so many paintings of Elvaennia seemingly in other lifetimes. When they came towards the end of the artwork, they gasped anew at a painting of themselves, it showed them digging for the settlement. Dennis asked Brian if he knew, 'what the broken lines within the paintings depicted?' Shrugging, Brian remarked he had no idea and made his way to the final painting. It was of a map. Brian studied it, nodded and told the men to follow him.

On reaching the farmhouse, the men parked their vehicles at the now silent farm. An eerie silence seemed to hang heavily in the air around them. Looking towards the fields, they were astonished to see them empty of animals. They realised something serious had happened and hurried towards the house, no words were exchanged, the silence was all-encompassing as Brian led the way up to the attic. Opening the door, they stood back in amazement. Each of the cave paintings were reproduced in jigsaws hung on boards around the walls of the room.

'The jagged lines in the cave paintings,' one of them cried out in astonishment.

They examined each one, silently wondering how David had managed to replicate each work of art so perfectly. On reaching the final jigsaw, they stood back in wonder as it showed Elvaennia and Deimuiss entering the Mesolithic cave surrounded by the eerie mists and strange lights. How could David have known any of this was going to happen?

What's more, where were mother and son?

Chapter *45*

In the cave, Elvaennia and Deimuiss unaware of anything else around them were clasped in each other's arms. Their worlds as one, they travelled back to the settlement.

Looking Ahead

In the summer of 2009, the cave stands waiting. Outside the entrance, the spelt and emmer wheat seeds that Elvaennia dropped as she entered the bivouac took seed and now sway effortlessly with the common wheat in the summer breezes – they will link the two Worlds forever at the Summer Solstice when the time travellers return.

C. Arnall 2009

A glimpse of the first chapter of the sequel to Dancing with Spirits

SPIRITS OF THE LIGHTS

PROLOGUE

The dark haired man was bitterly cold, curled up in the back of the bivouac; he could hear the wind raging outside and the ice storm beating on the rocky outcrop. He shuddered with the biting cold, curling into himself seeking warmth from his body. His very bones ached from the frozen ground. He knew that in order to survive, he would have to leave the cave soon. Never before had he experienced cold such as this and he longed for warmth and comfort. Oh, for a cup of hot coffee, he mused or a whisky would be even better, he thought grinning despite himself. Somehow, he thought I am not going to be getting either for a very long time.

Unfurling his lean body, he staggered to his feet, shaking his head trying to relieve the headache and fuzziness that had overtaken him since his journey through time, the man gazed around the sandstone cave. There was no sign of the other travellers having been here. The shadows had simply disappeared at some point on the journey, leaving Elvaennia and Deimuiss and he had kept himself well hidden from them. He had heard them leave some time ago, their voices carrying on the wind, telling of their excitement to be home in *their* time.

Elvaennias voice had carried sweetly back to the cave,

'Deimuiss, we're really home, I can hardly wait to see Mamma and Papa again.'

'Yes, my love it is good to be back, best hurry my sweet it's not far to the settlement.'

A bolt of pure jealously shot through Mark, how he wished it were he accompanying Elvaennia to the settlement. Despite his impulse at following Deimuiss and Elvaennia to the ancient cave, he had no regrets. Once he had regained his balance and his head cleared, he planned to find the settlement and throw himself on Elvaennia's mercy. He smiled thinking of her reception, she would be so shocked to see him, he knew but he had no doubts at all she would make him welcome. The young man had deliberately kept himself hidden from the others on the journey, knowing if he presented himself to Elvaennia when she was alone, she would be far more open to offering him a place to stay. The trouble was he had not envisaged the weather being so bad and he wished he had something warm to wrap himself in until the storm abated. Pacing backwards and forwards to keep his circulation moving Mark thought of the beautiful woman he had followed through time, remembering her beautiful silver grey eyes and slim young body he longed to hold her. If only she was mine, he thought but now I am here Deimuiss had better be prepared to lose her.

From their first meeting at the archaeological dig back in the 21st century he had known that Elvaennia was the woman for him. Sensing she was not of this time, he had followed her when she had left the dig with her young lover knowing instinctively she was returning to her home at the settlement. He did not want to lose the beautiful young woman he had fallen in love with; on seeing her enter the cave with her lover his every instinct had urged him to follow knowing they were journeying back through time.

Swinging his arms back and forth, he walked up and down up and down the icy cold cave gradually gentle warmth suffused his body and he suddenly became aware that the storm had abated. He stopped his pacing and was amazed at the total silence broken only occasionally by the sound of a bird screeching overhead. Purposefully he made his way to the cave entrance and peered outside, 'my goodness,' he breathed excitedly, 'this *is* another world,' stepping outside he let his gaze sweep the area. 'I really *am* in another time,' he muttered awestruck, 'there is not a house or anything to be seen.'

Do Elvaennia and Deimuiss finally marry or does Mark get his wish and marry Elvaennia?

Do they return to the safety of the 21st century?

End Notes

There is a Mesolithic cave not far from Rugeley, Staffordshire.

I read about the history of the cave many years ago. Two skulls were found outside the cave: one of an old lady, and one of a much younger woman. I wondered for many years about the women, and then, one day I began to write 'Dancing with Spirits'.

Originally, the story of the massacre on the hillside was purely fictional, but I received information from Hanley Museum, Stoke-on-Trent, Staffordshire, of further investigations being carried out on findings from the cave. These indicated that many people had, at one time, been inside the cave and died there – a case of fiction reflecting history.

The cave is very small now, having been back filled, and oh, how I would love to visit it.

The bivouac is, in fact, on private land; and unfortunately, no one is allowed to view it.

For further information visit **www.carolarnall.com**